STARS OF FORTUNE

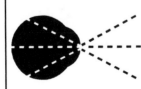

This Large Print Book carries the
Seal of Approval of N.A.V.H.

STARS OF FORTUNE

NORA ROBERTS

LARGE PRINT PRESS
A part of Gale, Cengage Learning

GALE
CENGAGE Learning·

Farmington Hills, Mich • San Francisco • New York • Waterville, Maine
Meriden, Conn • Mason, Ohio • Chicago

LIBRARY OF CONGRESS CATALOGING-IN-PUBLICATION DATA

Roberts, Nora.
    Stars of fortune / by Nora Roberts. — Large print edition.
        pages cm. — (Thorndike Press large print core) (The guardians trilogy ; #1)
        ISBN 978-1-4104-8133-7 (hardcover) — ISBN 1-4104-8133-6 (hardcover)
    1. Large type books. I. Title.
    PS3568.O243S73 2015b
    813'.54—dc23   2015032232

ISBN 13: 978-1-59413-881-2 (pbk.)
ISBN 10: 1-59413-881-8 (pbk.)

Published in 2015 by arrangement with The Berkley Publishing Group, an imprint of Penguin Publishing Group, a division of Penguin Random House LLC

Printed in the United States of America
1 2 3 4 5 6 7 19 18 17 16 15

For Sarah, daughter of my heart

As flies to wanton boys, are we to the gods;
They kill us for their sport.

Was it a vision, or a waking dream?
Fled is that music: — do I wake
or sleep?

JOHN KEATS

PROLOGUE

Once, in a time long ago, in a world beyond our own, three goddesses gathered to celebrate the dawn of a new queen. Many who'd traveled across the land and skies, through time and through space, had brought gifts of gold and jewels, of rich silks and precious crystals.

But the goddesses three wished for more unique gifts.

They considered a winged horse, but news came that a traveler had flown in on one, making it a gift for the new queen.

They debated gifting her with beauty beyond compare, with wisdom or uncommon grace.

They couldn't make her immortal, and knew from those who were that this was both blessing and curse.

But they could give her an immortal gift.

"A gift that will shine for her, for all time." Celene stood with her friends, her sisters, on the sand, white as diamonds, on the verge of the ink-blue sea, lifted her face to the night sky, to the swimming moon.

"The moon is ours," Luna reminded her. "We cannot give what we are pledged to honor."

"Stars." Arianrhod lifted her hand, palm up. She closed her eyes, her fingers. And smiling, opened them again. Now in her palm a jewel of ice glowed. "Stars for Aegle, the radiant."

"Stars." Now Celene held out her hand, opened it. She held a jewel of fire. "Stars for Aegle, who will shine like her name."

Luna joined them, produced a jewel of water. "Stars for Aegle, the brilliant."

"There should be more." Celene turned the burning star in her hand.

"A wish." Luna stepped closer to the sea, let the water lay cool kisses on her feet. "A wish from each for the queen, and into the star. For mine, a strong and hopeful heart."

"A strong and questing mind." Celene held the fiery star aloft.

"And a strong and adventurous spirit." Arianrhod raised both hands, one holding the star, the other lifted toward the moon. "These stars to shine while worlds turn."

"They shed their light in the queen's name for all to see." The Fire Star began to lift into the sky, and the star of ice, the star of water with it.

They spun as they rose, showering light, over land and sea, pulled toward the moon and its cool white power.

A shadow passed under them, a silent snake.

Nerezza glided across the beach toward the water — a shadow smearing the light. "You meet without me, my sisters."

"You are not of us." Arianrhod turned toward her, with Luna and Celene flanking her. "We are the light, and you the dark."

"There is no light without dark." Nerezza's lips curved, but fury lived in her eyes, and with it the early blooms of a madness yet to fully flower. "When the moon wanes, the darkness eats it. Bite by bite."

"The light prevails." Luna gestured as the stars flew now, trails of color in their wake. "And now there are more."

"You, like supplicants, bring gifts for the queen. She is no more than a weak, simpering girl when it is we who could rule. Who should rule."

"We are guardians," Celene reminded her. "We are the watchers, not rulers."

"We are *gods*! This world and others are ours. Only think of it, and what we can make from our powers combined. All will

13

bow to us, and we would live in youth and beauty forever."

"We have no desire for power over the mortals, the immortals, the demimortals. Such matters bring blood and war and death." Arianrhod dismissed the notion. "To crave forever is to dismiss the beauty and wonder of the cycle." She lifted her face again as the stars they'd made spilled their light.

"Death comes. We will watch this new queen live and die as we did the last."

"She will live a hundred years times seven. This I have seen. And while she lives," Celene continued, "there will be peace."

"Peace." The word hissed out between Nerezza's sneering lips. "Peace is nothing but a tedious lull between the stretch of the dark."

"Go back to your shadows, Nerezza." Luna dismissed her with a careless wave of her hand. "Tonight is for joy, for light, for celebrations — not your ambitions and thirsts."

"The night is mine." She slashed out a hand, and lightning, black as her eyes, sliced the white sand, the dark sea, and arrowed up toward the flying stars. It cut through the streams of light moments before the stars found their home in a gentle curve at the base of the moon.

For an instant the stars trembled there, and the worlds beneath them trembled.

"What have you done?" Celene whirled on her.

"Only added to your gift, *sisters*. They will fall one day, the stars of fire, ice, and water, tumble from the sky with all their power, their wishes, the light and the dark combined."

Laughing now, Nerezza lifted her arms high as if to pluck the stars from the sky. "And when they fall into my hands, the moon dies for all and ever, and the dark wins."

"They are not for you." Arianrhod stepped forward, but Nerezza carved black lightning through the sand, left a smoldering chasm between them. Smoke streamed up from it to foul the air.

"When I have them, this world dies with the moon, as you will. And as I eat your powers, I will open others long sealed. The pale peace you worship will become all raging torment, all agony and fear and death."

Through the smoke, she lifted her hands, glowing in her own desire. "Your own stars have sealed your fortunes, and given me mine."

"You are banished." Arianrhod lashed out,

and hot blue lightning that cut like a whip wrapped its tongue around Nerezza's ankle.

The scream ripped the air, shuddered into the ground. Before Arianrhod could drag the dark into the chasm of her own creation, Nerezza spread thin black wings, snapped the whip of light as she flew up. Blood from her ankle burned and smoked in the white sand.

"I make my fate," she shouted. "I will come back, take the stars and the worlds I wish. And you will know death and pain and the end of all you love."

The wings folded around her, and she was gone.

"She can do nothing to us or ours," Luna insisted.

"Do not doubt her power or her thirst." Celene stared into the dark gulf, felt a terrible sorrow. "There will be death here now, and blood, and pain and sorrow. She has left it behind her like a stain."

"She must never have the stars. We'll bring them back now," Arianrhod said. "Destroy them."

"Too much to risk while her power still stings the air," Celene replied.

"So we only wait, and guard and risk all?" Arianrhod argued. "We allow her to twist a bright gift into something dark and deadly?"

"We cannot. We will not. They will fall?" Luna asked Celene.

"I can see they will, in a bright flash, but I cannot see when."

"Then we will make the when, and the where. This we can do." Luna took her sisters' hands.

"In another place, another time, but not together." Nodding, Arianrhod looked up at the stars, so bright and beautiful over the land she'd loved and guarded since her time began.

"If even one falls into her hands, or one like her . . ." Celene closed her eyes, opened herself. "Many will seek the stars, the power, the fortune, which is the same. And the fate. It is all one. And we, reflected light, must send of us on the quest."

"Of us?" Luna repeated. "We do not go to retrieve them?"

"No, that is not for us. I know we must bide here and it will be done as it is done."

"We choose the time, the place. In silence," Arianrhod added. "Even in our minds. She is not to know when and where they will fall."

They joined minds as well as hands, and each took her journey, followed her star where it willed as it tumbled from the sky. Each hid her gift, each laid the power of protection over it.

And with minds joined, with no words spoken, each understood what must now rest in the hands and hearts of others.

"Now we must believe." Luna tightened her grip on Arianrhod's hand when her sister said nothing. "We must. If we do not, how will those who come of us?"

"I believe we have done what we must. That is enough to believe."

Celene sighed. "Even gods must bow to Fate."

"Or fight what tries to destroy them."

"You will fight," Celene said, smiling now. "Luna will trust. And I will do all I can to see. Now, we wait."

Together they looked up to the moon that lived in sky and soul, and the three bright stars that curved to it.

CHAPTER ONE

Dreams plagued her, waking and sleeping. She understood dreams, visions, the *knowing*. They had been part of her all of her life, and for most of her life she'd learned to block it out, push it all away.

But these wouldn't relent, no matter how she pitted her will against them. Dreams of blood and battle; of strange, moonstruck lands. In them, the faces and voices of people unknown but somehow vitally familiar lived with her. The woman with the fierce and canny eyes of a wolf, the man with the silver sword. They roamed her dreams with a woman who rose from the sea laughing, the man with the golden compass.

And through all of them, strongly, the dark-haired man who held lightning in his hands.

Who were they? How did she — or would she — know them? Why did she feel such a strong need for them, all of them?

With them walked death and pain — she *knew* — and yet with them came the chance for true joy, true self. True love.

She believed in true love — for others. She'd never sought it for herself, as love demanded so much, brought such chaos into a life. So much *feeling.*

She wanted, had always wanted, the quiet and settled, and believed she'd found it in her little house in the mountains of North Carolina.

There she had the solitude she'd sought. There she could spend her days painting, or in her garden without interference or interruption. Her needs were few; her work provided enough income to meet them.

Now her dreams were haunted by five people who called her by name. Why couldn't she find theirs?

She sketched her dreams — the faces, the seas and hills and ruins. Caves and gardens, storms and sunsets. Over the long winter she filled her workboard with the sketches, and began to pin them to her walls.

She painted the man with lightning in his hands, spending days perfecting every detail, the exact shade and shape of his eyes — deep and dark and hooded — the thin white scar, like a lightning bolt, scoring his left eyebrow.

He stood on a cliff, high above a boiling sea. Wind streamed through his dark hair. She could all but feel it, like hot breath. And he was fearless in the face of the storm as death flew toward him.

Somehow she stood with him, just as fearless.

She couldn't sleep until she'd finished it, wept when she did. She feared she'd lost her mind, and visions were all she had left. For days she left the painting on the easel while he watched her work or clean or sleep.

Or dream.

She told herself she'd pack it for shipping, send it to her agent for sale. And dipping her brush, she signed it at last.

Sasha Riggs — her name on the verge of the storm-wrecked sea.

But she didn't pack it for shipping. She packed others instead, the work of the long winter, arranged for transport.

Exhausted, she gave in, curled on the couch in the attic she'd converted to her studio, and let the dreams take her.

The storm raged. Wind whipping, the sea crashing, jagged spears of lightning hurled from the sky like flaming bolts from a bow. The rain swept in from the sea toward the cliff in a thick curtain.

But he stood, watching it. And held out his hand for hers.

"I'm waiting for you."

"I don't understand this, any of this."

"Of course you do, you more than most." When he brought her hand to his lips, she felt love simply saturate her. "Who hides from themselves, Sasha, as you do?"

"I only want peace. I want the quiet. I don't want storms, and battles. I don't want you."

"Lies." His lips curved as he brought her hand to them again. "You know you're lying to me, to yourself. How much longer will you refuse to live as you were meant to? To love as you were born to?"

He cupped her face in his hands, and the ground shook under her.

"I'm afraid."

"Face it."

"I don't want to know."

"See it. We can't begin without you. We can't end it until we begin. Find me, Sasha. Come find me."

He pulled her in, took her lips with his. As he did, the storm broke over them with mad fury.

This time, she embraced it.

She woke, tired still, pushed herself up, pressed her fingers to her shadowed eyes.

"Find me," she muttered. "*Where?* I wouldn't know where to start looking if I wanted to." Her fingers trailed down to her lips, and she swore she still felt the pressure of his.

"Enough. It's all enough now."

She rose quickly, began to pull the sketches from the walls, the board, letting them fall to the floor. She'd take them out, throw them out. Burn them. Get them out of her house, out of her head.

She'd get out herself, take a trip somewhere, anywhere. It had been years since she'd gone anywhere. Somewhere warm, she told herself as she frantically yanked down her dreams. A beach somewhere.

She could hear her own breath heaving, see her own fingers trembling. Near to breaking, she lowered to the floor amid the sketches, a woman too thin with the weight the dreams had stolen, her long blond hair bundled up into its habitual messy bun. Shadows plagued her eyes of a clear and crystal blue.

She looked down at her hands. There was talent there. She always had been, always would be, grateful for that gift. But she carried other gifts, not so gratefully.

In the dream, he'd asked her to see. Nearly all her life she'd done all she could to block the sight she'd been born with.

Yes, to hide from herself, just as he'd said.

If she opened to it, accepted it, there would be pain and sorrow. And the knowledge of what might be.

She closed her eyes.

She'd clean up — give herself time. She'd pick up all the sketches and file them away. She wouldn't burn them, of course she wouldn't burn them. That had been fear talking.

She'd file them, and take a trip. Get away from home for a week or two, let herself think and decide.

On her hands and knees, she began to gather the sketches, organizing them in her way. The woman with the fierce eyes, the man with the sword, sketches of her dream people together.

Seascapes and landscapes, a palace shining on a hill, a circle of stones.

She laid one of the dozens of the man she'd just dreamed of on a pile, reached for another.

And knew.

She'd drawn the sickle-shaped island from various viewpoints, and this one showed its high cliffs, its undulating hills thick with trees. Showed it floating in the sea, washed with sunlight. Buildings jumbled together to form a city in the foreground, and the stretch of land, speared with mountains spread in the distance.

The pencil sketch took on color and life as she studied it. So much green, a thousand shades of it from dusky to emerald. So much blue, deep and rich or frothing with waves surrounding it. She saw boats sailing, figures diving off seawalls to swim and splash.

And she saw the promontory where she'd stood with him as the storm flew in.

"All right then, I'll go." Was she giving in, she wondered, or standing up? But she'd go, she'd look.

It would either end the dreams, or bring them to life as the sketch came to life in her hands.

She went over to her little desk, opened her laptop. And booked a flight to Corfu.

Giving herself only two days to pack, arrange details, close up the house meant she couldn't change her mind. She slept on the plane, dreamlessly, grateful for the respite. And still the cab ride from the airport to the hotel she'd chosen near Old Town was a blur. Disoriented, she checked in, struggling to remember to smile, to exchange the expected small talk with the front desk, with the cheerful bellman with the cheerful eyes and thick accent as they rode the narrow elevator to her room.

She hadn't asked for a particular floor or a view. It was enough she'd taken this step, wherever it would lead her. But she wasn't surprised, not at all surprised, when steps into the room she barely noticed, she faced the windows, the blue sea, and the spread of the sand she knew so well.

She smiled away the bellman's offer to fetch her ice, or anything she might wish. She only wanted solitude again. The airports, the plane, so many people. They crowded her still.

Alone, she walked to the window, opened it to cool spring air that smelled of the sea and flowers, and studied the scene she'd sketched weeks before, and carried with others in a portfolio in her suitcase.

She felt nothing, not now, but the fogginess of jet lag and travel fatigue. And some wonder that she'd actually traveled so far on impulse.

Turning away, she unpacked to give herself some sense of place and order. Then just lay down on the bed and dropped into sleep again.

Lightning and storms, the beat of the sun, the beat of the sea. Three stars so bright and brilliant her eyes stung. When they shot away from the curve of the moon, fell in streams of light, the world trembled from the strikes of power.

Blood and battle, fear and flight. Climbing high, diving deep.

Her dream lover taking her mouth, taking her body, making her ache with feelings. So much. Too much. Never enough. Her own laughter, barely recognized, sprung from joy. Tears shed, flooding from grief.

And in the darkness, a light burned through. In the darkness she held fire in her hand. As she held it up, for all to see, the earth quaked, rocks tumbled. What was fury flew at her with claws and teeth.

For God's sake, Sasha, wake up! Get your ass moving.

"What?" She woke with a start, the voice still echoing inside her head, her heart still thumping with fear.

Just another dream, she told herself, just one more to add to her collection.

The light had softened, and lay now like silk over the water. She had no idea how long she'd slept, but the dream voice had something right. It was time to wake up.

She showered off the travel, changed into fresh clothes. Since she wasn't working, she left her hair down. She ordered herself out of the room. She'd go down, sit on the terrace, have a drink. She'd come, given up her quiet and alone, and come.

Now something or someone needed to come to her.

She found her way out, strolled under a pergola thickly twined with wisteria already starting to bloom. Its scent followed her as she turned away from the pool, the canvas sling chairs lined up around its skirt, toward a stone terrace. Clay pots gloriously crowded with flowers of hot reds and purples glowed as the sun wheeled west. The fronds of palm trees hung still.

Tables under shading umbrellas — all in bright white — scattered over the stone. She noted only a few were occupied, and was grateful. Not solitude perhaps, but quiet. She thought to take one a bit apart from the others, started to angle away.

The woman also sat a bit apart. Her short, sun-streaked brown hair had long bangs that swept down to the amber lenses of her sunglasses. She sat back, her bright orange Chucks propped on the other chair of her table for two as she sipped something frothy out of a champagne flute.

The light shimmered for a moment, and Sasha's heart stuttered with it. She knew she stared, and couldn't stop. And understood why when the woman tipped down her sunglasses, and stared back over them.

The eyes of a wolf, tawny and fierce.

Sasha fought back the urge to simply turn around, go back to her room where it was safe. Instead she mentally shoved herself forward and walked over while those golden eyes appraised her.

"I'm sorry," she began.

"For what?"

"I . . . Do you know me?"

The woman raised her eyebrows under the long bangs. "Are you somebody I should know?"

I know your face, Sasha thought. I've seen it countless times.

"Could I sit down?"

The woman angled her head, continued her cool, unblinking study. Carelessly she slid her feet off the chair. "Sure, but if you're thinking about hitting on me, except for a one-nighter in college, I stick with men."

"No, it's not that." Sasha sat, tried to find her bearings. Before she could, a waiter in a white jacket stopped by the table.

"*Kalispera.* Could I bring you a drink, miss?"

"Yes, actually, yes. Ah, what are you drinking?"

The woman lifted her glass. "Peach Bellini."

"That sounds just right. Would you like another? I'll buy you a drink."

Under her thick sweep of bangs, the woman's eyebrows lifted. "Sure."

"Two then, thanks. I'm Sasha," she said when he left to fill the order. "Sasha Riggs."

"Riley Gwin."

"Riley." A name, she thought, to go with the face. "I know how this is going to sound, but . . . I've dreamed about you."

Riley took another sip, smiled. "It sounds like you're hitting on me. And you're really pretty, Sasha, but —"

"No, no, I mean literally. I recognized you because I've dreamed about you, for months now."

"Okay. What was I doing?"

"I can't expect you to believe me. But the dreams are why I'm here, in Corfu. I don't — Wait." The sketches, she thought, and pushed to her feet.

A picture was worth a thousand, after all.

"I want to show you something. Will you wait until I come back?"

Riley only shrugged, lifted her glass. "I've got another drink coming, so I'll be here for a while yet."

"Five minutes," Sasha promised, and hurried away.

Sipping her drink, Riley considered. She knew all about dreams, and wouldn't discount them out of hand. She'd seen and experienced far too much in her life to discount anything out of hand.

And this Sasha Riggs struck her as sincere. Nervy, wound tight, but sincere. Still, she had her own reasons for being in Corfu, and they didn't include starring in someone else's dreams.

The waiter came back with a tray, set the drinks, a bowl of fat olives, another of fancy nuts on the table. "The other lady?" he asked.

"She forgot something. She'll be right back." Riley handed him her empty glass. *"Efkharisto."*

She tried an almond, went back to contemplating the sea, glanced back again when she heard the hurried footsteps — wedged sandals on stone.

Sasha sat again, holding a leather portfolio. "I'm an artist," she began.

"Congratulations."

"I've had these dreams all winter. They started right after the first of the year. Every night." Waking dreams, too, but she wasn't ready to share that much. "I sketched the people, the places in them, the ones that

31

kept reoccurring."

She opened the portfolio, chose the sketch that had brought her to where she sat. "I drew this weeks ago."

Riley took the sketch, lips pursing as she studied it. "You're good, and yeah, this is Corfu."

"And this is you."

Sasha laid down a sketch, full body, of Riley. She wore cargo pants, hiking boots, a battered leather jacket, a wide-brimmed hat. Her hand rested on the butt of the knife sheathed at her belt.

As Riley lifted the sketch, Sasha set down another. "So is this." A head-and-shoulders sketch this time, of Riley looking straight ahead with a curled-lip smile.

"What is this?" Riley muttered.

"I don't know, and need to find out. I thought I was losing my mind. But you're real, and you're here. Like me. I don't know about the others."

"What others?"

"There are six of us, including me." Sasha dug into the portfolio again. "Working together, traveling together."

"I work alone."

"So do I." She felt giddy now, both vindicated and a little crazed. "I don't know any of them." She held out another sketch. "I have individual sketches of all of them, and others with some of us together, more with all of us, like this one. I don't know them."

The sketch showed Riley, dressed much as she'd been in the other, and Sasha, in boots, pants, a snap-brimmed hat rather than the sandals and flowy dress she wore now. Another woman with hair tumbling to her waist, and three men. Three hot men, Riley thought, all standing together on a trail, forested hills around them, grouped together as if posing for a photograph.

"You — Sasha, right?"

"Yes. Yes, I'm Sasha."

"Well, Sasha, you sure know how to dream men. They're all smoking."

"I've never seen any of them before, outside of the dreams. But I feel . . . I *know* them, know everyone here. And this one."

Unable to resist, Sasha touched a finger to the figure standing beside her, standing hipshot, his thumb hooked in the front pocket of worn jeans. Sharp cheekbones, dark hair — she knew it to be a deep, rich brown — carelessly curling past the neckline of his T-shirt. His smile spoke of confidence, and of charm — and a little mystery.

"What about this one?" Riley prompted.

"He holds lightning. I don't know if that's a symbol or what it means. And I dream we

— that we . . ."

"Sex dreams?" Amused, Riley took a closer look at him. "You could do a hell of a lot worse."

"If I'm going to have sex dreams with a man, I'd like to have dinner first."

Riley let out a bark of laughter. "Hell, a girl can eat anytime. Are you a dream-walker, Sasha?"

"Dream-walker?"

"Some cultures use that term. Do you have prophetic dreams? Why hold back now?" Riley said when Sasha hesitated. "You're already telling me you have sex with strange men, and you haven't even had your drink yet."

"I don't have to be asleep to dream." Yes, Sasha thought, why hold back now? "And yes, they're usually prophetic. I knew my father would leave before he walked out the door when I was twelve. He couldn't handle what I am. I don't control it, can't demand to see, can't demand not to."

Sasha picked up her glass and drank, and waited for the wariness or the derision.

"Have you ever worked with anyone on that?"

"What?"

"Have you ever worked with another dream-walker, explored learning how to block it or open it?"

"No."

"You look smarter than that." Riley shrugged. "Is it just visions, or do you read minds?"

She might have asked if she painted in oil or acrylics. Emotion clogged Sasha's throat so thickly she could barely speak. "You believe me."

"Why wouldn't I? The proof's all over the table. Can you read minds, and can you control that?"

"I don't read minds. I read feelings, and they speak just as loud. I can control it, unless the feelings are so intense they push through."

"What am I feeling? Go ahead." Riley spread her arms when Sasha hesitated. "I'm an open book, so read it."

Sasha took a moment, focused in. "You feel some sympathy for and curiosity about me. You're relaxed, but on guard. You tend to stay on guard. You feel a need for something that's always been out of your reach. It's frustrating, especially because you like to win. You feel a little sexually deprived just now because you haven't taken the time . . . felt you had the time to fill that need. The work fulfills you, the risks, the adventure, the demands of it. You've earned

35

your self-reliance, and you're not afraid of much. If there's fear, it's more for the emotional than the physical.

"You have a secret," Sasha murmured. "Closed up tight." Sasha jerked back, frowned. "You asked me to look, all but insisted, so don't get angry when I do."

"Fair enough. And that's enough."

"I believe in privacy." She'd never read anyone that openly, that purposefully. It left her flushed, and mildly embarrassed. "I don't dig into people's secrets."

"I believe in privacy." Riley raised her glass again. "But I freaking love to dig."

"Your work brings you a lot of pride and satisfaction. What is it?"

"That depends. At the base? I'm an archaeologist. I like looking for things no one else can find."

"And when you find it? What do you do with it?"

"That depends, too."

"You find things." Sasha nodded, nearly relaxed. "That must be one of the reasons."

"For what?"

"For our being here."

"I've got a reason to be here."

"But at this time, in this place?" Sasha gestured to the sketches again. "I know we need to look, we need to find . . ."

"If you want my attention you have to spit things out."

Rather than speak, Sasha pulled out another sketch. A beach, a calm sea, a palace on a hill, all under a full white moon.

And curved under the moon shone three stars.

"I don't know where this is, but I do know these three stars, the ones near the moon, they don't exist. I'm not an astronomer, but I know they're not there. I only know they were, somehow they were. And I know they fell. See this one." She laid out another sketch. "All three falling at the same time, leaving those cometlike trails. We're supposed to find them."

Sasha looked up, saw Riley's eyes stare into hers, feral and cold.

"What do you know about the stars?" Riley demanded.

"I'm telling you what I know."

In a fast move, Riley reached out, gripped Sasha's arm at the wrist. "What do you know about the Stars of Fortune? Who the hell are you?"

Though her stomach trembled, Sasha made herself keep her eyes level with the fierce ones, ordered her voice not to shake.

"I've told you who I am. I'm telling you what I know. You know more about them.

You know what they are. You're already looking for them — that's why you're here. And you're hurting my arm."

"If I find out you're bullshitting me, I'll hurt more than your arm." But she let it go.

"Don't threaten me." Temper, hot and surprised, leaped up and out. "I've had enough. I didn't ask for this, I don't want this. All I wanted was to live in peace, to paint, to be left alone to work. Then you and these others are crowding my dreams, you and these damn stars I don't understand. One of them's here, I know it, just as I know finding it won't be peaceful. I don't know how to fight, and I'll have to. Blood and battle, dreams full of blood and battle and pain."

"Now it's getting interesting."

"It's terrifying, and I want to walk away from all of it. I don't think I can. I held one in my hand."

Riley leaned forward. "You held one of the stars?"

"In a dream." Sasha turned her palm up, stared at it. "I held it, held the fire. And it was so beautiful it blinded. Then it came."

"What came?"

"The dark, the hungry, the brutal."

Suddenly she felt queasy, light-headed. Though she struggled, what moved through her won.

"She who is darkness covets. To have what she desires consumes her. What the three moons created out of love, loyalty, and hope, she would corrupt. She has burned her gifts and all bright edges of her power away, and what remains is a madness. She will kill to possess them, fire, ice, water. Possessing them, she will destroy worlds, destroy all so she lives."

Sasha lifted both hands to her head. "Headache."

"Does that happen often?"

"I do everything I can to stop it."

"And that's probably why you have a headache. You can't fight your own nature, trust me. You have to learn to control it, and to adapt." Riley caught the waiter's eyes, circled a finger in the air. "I'm getting us another round."

"I don't think I should —"

"Eat some nuts." Brisk now, Riley shoved the bowl closer. "No way you're faking this — nobody's that good. And I've got a sense about people — not empathic, but a reliable sense. So we'll have another drink, talk this through some more, then figure out where we go from there."

"You're going to help me."

"The way I look at it, we're going to help

each other. My research indicates the Fire Star is in or around Corfu — and your dreams corroborate that. You could come in handy. Now —"

She broke off, flicked a hand at her bangs as she looked over Sasha's head. "Well, well, it just keeps getting more and more interesting."

"What is it?"

"Dream date." Riley aimed a deliberately flirty smile, crooked a finger in the air.

Swiveling in her chair, Sasha saw him. The man who held the lightning. The one who'd taken her body.

His eyes, so dark, flicked away from Riley, met hers. Held them.

And holding them, crossed to their table.

"Ladies. Spectacular view, isn't it?"

His voice, Irish and easy, brought a shiver to Sasha's skin. She felt trapped, as if a shining silver cage had dropped around her.

And when he smiled, she yearned.

"Where you from, Irish?" Riley asked.

"Sligo, a little village you wouldn't have heard of."

"You'd be surprised."

"Cloonacool."

"I know it. Sits at the foot of the Ox Mountains."

"So it does, yes. Well then." He waved his

hand, and offered Riley the little clutch of shamrocks that appeared in it. "A token from home, faraway."

"Nice."

"Americans?" He looked back at Sasha. "Both of you?"

"Looks that way." Riley watched his gaze shift, land on the sketches. She said nothing when he reached down, lifted the one of six people.

Not shocked, she thought. Intrigued.

"Isn't this a fascination. You'd be the artist?" he said to Sasha. "You've a clever hand, and eye. I've been told I have the same." He smiled. "Mind if I join you?"

Without waiting for assent, he got a chair from a neighboring table, pulled it up. Sat.

"I'd say we've a lot to talk about. I'd be Bran. Bran Killian. Why don't I buy you ladies a drink, and we'll talk about the moon and the stars?"

CHAPTER TWO

Sasha struggled to find her balance as he made himself comfortable, ordered a glass of the local red.

He'd walked out of her dreams, as if she'd wished him into being. She knew his face, his body, his voice, his scent. She'd been intimate with him.

But he didn't know her.

He didn't know her heart beat fast fists at the base of her throat, or that she had her hands clutched together under the table to keep them from shaking.

She needed a moment alone to gather herself, thought to scoop up the sketches and get away, but he turned those dark eyes on her.

"Do you mind?" he asked, and before she understood, without waiting for an answer, he picked up one of the sketches of Riley.

"She's captured you very well."

"Seems like."

"Have you known each other long?"

"About a half hour."

His only reaction was a single quirked eyebrow — the one with the lightning bolt scar. "Fascinating."

He picked up, studied sketch after sketch, ordering them as he went. "And the other three people?"

"She doesn't know. You don't seem too weirded out about it."

"The world's full of mysteries, isn't it?"

"What are you doing in Corfu?" Riley asked him.

He sat back with his wine, smiled. "I'm on holiday."

"Come on, Bran." Riley gestured with her own drink. "After all we've been through together."

"I felt this was the place I needed to be," he said simply, and picked up the sketch of the moon with its three bright stars. "And apparently it is."

"You know what they are."

Bran shifted his gaze to Sasha. "She speaks. I know what they are, yes. *Where* is altogether another matter. I have one of your paintings."

"What?"

"The one you called *Silence*. A forest in soft morning light, with a narrow path winding through trees green with summer, some coated with moss that shimmers in light quiet as a whisper. Beyond the path, that light glows, brighter, bolder, in a kind of beckoning. It would make the observer wonder what lies at the end of the path."

He picked up another sketch, one of himself, feet planted, head back, with bold blue lightning flashing from the tips of his upstretched fingers. "It's all very interesting, isn't it?"

"I don't know what any of this means. I don't understand any of it."

"But you came nonetheless. From America?"

"Yes."

"And you're from America, Riley."

"Originally. I move around a lot. And you came from Ireland."

"Originally. But to here, from New York. I have a place there."

"Doing what?" Sasha demanded.

If he noticed her sharp tone, he didn't show it. "Magic," he said, and offered her a passionflower, richly purple. "The hand's quicker than the eye," he said easily, "especially since the eye's so easily misdirected."

"You're a magician."

"I am. Stage magic — street magic when the mood strikes."

A magician, Sasha considered. The lightning could symbolize his line of work. But it didn't explain all the rest. Nothing did.

She looked down at the flower in her hand, then up at him.

The sun was setting in the west behind him in an explosion of fiery red and hot licks of brilliant gold.

"There's more," she said, but she thought: You're more.

"There always is. Considering that, and this." He set the sketch of the stars on the top of the stack. "I think the three of us need to have a discussion. Why don't we have that over a meal?"

"I could eat. You buying, Irish?" Riley asked him.

"For the privilege of sharing dinner with two beautiful women, I am, of course. What do you say to a bit of a walk, till we find a place that suits our needs?"

"I'm in."

When Sasha said nothing, Bran took the flower from her, tucked it over her ear. "You're no coward, Sasha Riggs, or you wouldn't be here."

She only nodded, put the sketches back in her portfolio, and rose. "I'll tell you what I know, in exchange for what you know."

"Fair enough."

■ ■ ■ ■

They walked the narrow, cobbled streets of Old Town with its colorful shops and stalls and pavement cafes. Dusk gave the air a quietly lavender hue, one Sasha stored away knowing she'd have to paint it. Old, sun-baked buildings, madly blooming pots of flowers, a bold red cloth hanging on a line overhead among other linens, waiting to be brought in and put away.

If she thought about perspective, tone, texture, she wouldn't have to think about what she was doing. Walking around in a strange place with people she didn't know.

She marveled at how easily Riley and Bran exchanged small talk, envied their ability to be in the moment. They gave every appearance of enjoying a pretty evening in an ancient place with the scents of grilled lamb and spices in the air.

"What appeals?" Bran asked. "Indoors or out?"

"Why waste a good clear night inside?" Riley said.

"Agreed."

He found a place, as if by magic, near the green of the park, where the tables sat under the trees and fairy lights. Happy music played somewhere nearby — close enough to add some fun, far enough not to intrude.

"This local red's good. The Petrokoritho. Up for a bottle?" Bran asked.

"I never say no to a drink."

Taking Riley's answer as assent all around, Bran ordered a bottle. Sasha thought of the Bellinis as she looked at the menu. She'd take a couple sips of wine to be polite, and stick with water. And food — God knew she needed some food in her system.

She felt empty and quivery and out of place.

She'd go with fish, she decided. They were on an island after all. She studied her choices while Riley and Bran talked starters, with Riley making suggestions.

Reading Sasha's questioning glance, Riley shrugged.

"First time on Corfu, but not my first time in Greece. And when it comes to food, my stomach has a endemic memory."

"Then I'll leave it to you." Bran turned to Sasha. "Take a risk?"

"I was leaning toward fish," she began.

"Got you covered. How about you?" Riley asked Bran.

"I've a mind for meat."

"Done."

Once the wine was tasted and served, Riley rattled off several dishes in Greek. Sasha's own stomach shuddered at the prospect of strange dishes.

"Have you traveled much?" Bran asked her.

"No, not really. I spent a few days in Florence and in Paris a few years ago."

"Maybe not much, but you chose well. I thought you'd been to Ireland."

"No, I haven't. Why did you think that?"

"The painting I bought. I know the place, or one very like it, not far from home. So, where is your forest?"

She'd dreamed it. She often dreamed her paintings. "It's not real. I imagined it."

"The same way you imagined me, and Riley, and the others we've yet to meet?"

"Lay it out, Sasha," Riley advised. "The guy's an Irish magician. He's not going to bolt over a little strange."

"I dreamed it." She blurted it out like a confession. "All of it. All of you. I dreamed of Corfu — or I finally figured out it was Corfu, so I came. And I walked out onto the terrace of the hotel, and saw Riley. Then you."

"In dreams." He drank some wine, watched her with those dark, hooded eyes. "You're a seer. Are your visions only when you sleep?"

48

"No." It struck her that he didn't react — nor had Riley — as others usually did. With skepticism, smirks, or with giddy questions about their own futures. "They come when they want to."

"Bloody inconvenient."

She let out a quick laugh. "Yeah. Bloody inconvenient. They'll come here, the other three. I know that now. Or maybe they're already here. But they'll find us, or we'll find them. Once that happens, I don't know if there's any going back."

"To what?" Bran wondered.

"To our lives, to the way they were before."

"If that's what's put the worry in your eyes, it's always better going forward than back."

She said nothing while the waiter served the starters. "You both want to find these stars, and your reasons probably matter, but all I know is something wants us to find them or we wouldn't be here. But something else doesn't want us to have them. That something is dark and dangerous and powerful. It may not be a matter of going forward or back, but of not existing at all."

"Nobody lives forever." So saying, Riley dug into her eggplant starter.

Bran brushed a hand over Sasha's, lightly. "No one can make you do what you don't want to do. It's your choice, *fáidh,* to go forward or back."

"What does that mean — what you called me?"

"What you are. Vision-seer, prophet."

"Seems to me a prophet should see things more clearly."

"I'll wager others with your gift have thought the same."

"If I go back, I don't think I'll ever find peace again." While that was true enough, she knew a deeper truth. She couldn't walk away from him. "So it looks like forward. I've never had dinner with two people who just accept what I am. It's good."

She sampled the dish Riley had called *tzatziki,* found the smooth yogurt, the bite of garlic, the cool tang of cucumber went down easily after all.

"And so's this."

The food settled her. Maybe it was the wine, or the fragrant night, or the fact that she'd finally fully accepted her decision, but the raw edges of her nerves quieted.

When Bran cut some of the meat, put it on her plate, she stared at it.

"You should try it," he told her.

To be polite, she told herself, she did — but the act felt ridiculously intimate. To distract herself from the heat that had nothing to do with a bite of grilled lamb, she picked up her wine.

"How do you know about the three stars?" she asked Bran. "They're why you're here. Why we're all here. How do you know about them? What do you know?"

"I'll tell you a legend I've heard of three stars created by three gods — moon goddesses, they were. Or are, depending on where you're standing. They made these stars as gifts for a new queen. Just a baby, say some legends, while others . . ." He glanced at Riley.

"Others say young girl. Kind of an Arthurian riff — a true queen chosen at the end of another's reign through a test of sorts."

"There you have it. These sister goddesses wanted a unique and lasting gift for the queen they knew would rule for the good, who would hold peace softly in her hand as she did. So each made a star, one of fire, one of ice, one of water, all brilliant and filled with strength and magic and hope, which can be the same."

"On a beach — white sand," Sasha added.

He continued to eat, but watched her carefully. "Some say."

"There's a palace, silver and shining, on a high hill, and the moon's white and full, beaming over the water."

51

"You've seen this?"

"I dreamed it."

"Which can be the same," Bran repeated.

"They weren't alone on the beach."

"They weren't, no, not alone. Another like them, but as unlike as white to black, wanted what they'd made, and what the queen had, which was power over worlds. The three knew her for what she was, knew as they tossed the stars toward the moon, and the other struck out at them with her dark, they would need to protect what they'd created, and all that lived.

"The stars would fall," he continued, "the other had seen to that, and she could wait. So the three used what they had to see that when the stars fell, they would fall away from one another, as their full power is only reached when together. They would fall in secret places, hidden and safe until the time came for them to be lifted out, brought together, and taken to the next new queen."

"It's a pretty story, but —"

"Not all of it," Riley interrupted. "Give her the other side."

"If the other takes possession of the stars, all the doors on all the worlds will unlock. The dark, the damned, the destructive will spring free and devour all they can. Human worlds, and others as vulnerable, would not survive it."

"Worlds."

Smiling, he topped off her wine. "Do you ever wonder at the arrogance of men who think they alone exist in the universe?"

"Most native cultures and elemental faiths know better," Riley commented.

"You're a scientist."

"I'm a digger," she told Sasha. "And I've dug up enough to know we've never been alone. There's a little more to the legend."

"A bit," Bran allowed.

"Those who seek it risk death — natch — but if they prevail, they save the worlds, which is pretty important. And each will find their own fortune."

"Both of you believe this."

"I believe it enough. I've been looking for them, off and on, for about seven years."

"Twelve," Brad told her. "On and off as well."

"It's been kind of a hobby for me, until now. Now?" Riley polished off the last of her wine. "I think it's become my freaking mission." She set the glass down, leaned toward Sasha. "Are we in this — the three of us?"

"Six. It has to be the six. I don't think we'll get far until it is."

"Okay, but that doesn't mean we can't

start looking."

"Where?"

"The mountains to the north, a lot of caves there. That might be a good place to start."

"How do we get there?"

"I've got a jeep. That'll get us somewhere. Got hiking boots?"

"Yes. I do a lot of hiking at home."

"How about you, Irish?"

"Not to worry."

"Great. So we'll meet up in the morning, head out, what, about eight?"

Bran winced. "A morning person, are you?"

"I'm what I need to be."

Sasha walked back with them to the hotel in a half daze. Too much wine, too much travel, too much stimulation. She'd sleep, just sleep, and sort the rest out in the morning, she told herself.

"What floor?" Bran asked when they stepped into the elevator.

"Third."

"So am I."

"And I make three on three," Riley said.

"Naturally." With a sigh, Sasha leaned against the wall, dug out her key.

When they got out, turned in the same direction, Sasha all but felt Fate's sticky fingers pinching the back of her neck. She stopped at her door. "My room."

"I'm across the hall from you," Bran said, smiling now.

"Of course you are."

"And right next door." Riley strolled down to the door beside Sasha's.

"Where else would you be?" she mumbled, and unlocked her door.

"Night, kids!" Riley sang out.

"Good night. Thanks for dinner," she said to Bran, and closed the door.

Bran walked into his own room, switched on the lights. The evening, he thought, had certainly been more entertaining than he'd anticipated. He'd intended to wander out, maybe have a drink, take a solitary walk around to let himself absorb where he'd been driven to go.

Then the women.

He could admit here, alone, that seeing himself in that sketch as one of six had given him a jolt. But such an *interesting* jolt. As interesting as realizing the artist happened to be the same Sasha Riggs whose work hung in his New York home.

She'd claimed the scene had come from her imagination, and perhaps it had. But he knew that forest and knew it well. And he knew what waited at the end of the path in the shimmering light.

He got a bottle of water, and the tablet he traveled with, plopped down on the bed. And began to research the two women Fate had apparently dropped at his feet.

There were other ways to learn more about them, of course, but this seemed the most fair and aboveboard. He believed in being fair, at least initially.

He had no doubt they hadn't shared everything with him — the adventurer and the seer — but he hadn't shared all with them. So that seemed fair as well.

He took the adventurer first, because in truth he felt far too hard a pull toward the seer.

Not simply Riley Gwin, he noted, but *Doctor* Riley Gwin, who'd earned the title in archaeology and folklore and myths. Born thirty years ago — and two doctorates by thirty meant she was no one's fool — to Doctors Carter Gwin and Iris MacFee, archaeology and anthropology, respectively, she'd spent a good portion of her childhood traveling.

She'd written two books and an assortment of papers and articles — publish or perish, after all. But devoted most of her time, from what he could glean, on digs or traveling on her own in pursuit of lost treasures and myths.

Searching for the stars certainly fit.

He switched to Sasha.

She was twenty-eight, he noted, only child of Matthew and Georgina Riggs, née Corrigan — divorced. She'd studied art at Columbia. Articles on her were few and far between, which told him she shied away from the media. But she was represented by one of the top artist agencies in New York. According to her official bio, she'd had her first major showing at the Windward Gallery, New York, at the tender age of twenty-two, and lived quietly in the mountains of North Carolina.

Unmarried, which was handy.

There was, he thought, a great deal more to Sasha Riggs than that.

So he'd have to find out the great deal more, one way or the other. But not tonight, he decided. For tonight, he'd let it all rest, and see what came.

He set the tablet aside, stripped down. He might have preferred the night to the morning, but since he had morning to face, he'd get a decent night's sleep.

He left the curtains and windows open and, listening to the night, thinking of stars, of fortune, of women with secrets, began to drift off.

The knock on the door brought him out of the half sleep and into mild annoyance. Rolling out of bed, he snatched up his jeans, tugged them on.

It didn't surprise him overmuch to find Sasha at the door, but it did to see her in the hallway wearing a thin white sleep-slip that barely hit the middle of her very pretty thighs.

"Well now, this is interesting."

"She's at the window."

"Who would that be?" He'd started to smile, but when his gaze finally managed to travel from those thighs up the white silk, beyond breasts and throat to meet her eyes, the smile faded off.

Dream-walking, he thought. The trance glazed her eyes like glass.

"Where are you, Sasha?"

"With you. She's at the window. She said if I let her in, she'd give me my heart's desire. But she's made of lies. We should make her leave."

"Let's have a look."

He took her hand, led her back across the hall, into her room. Shut the door behind him.

She had it dark as a cave, he noted, curtains drawn tight across the windows. He added some light, and Sasha lifted a hand, gestured toward the curtains.

"There she is. I told her to go away, but there she is."

"Stay here." He walked to the window, yanked the curtains open. He saw a shadow pass — a bare flicker — thought he heard a rustle, like the dry wings of a bat. Then there was nothing but the sea under a three-quarter moon.

"There, she's gone." Sasha smiled at him. "I knew she'd leave if you were here. You worry her."

"Do I?" he queried.

"I can feel some of what she feels. Not all. I don't want to feel all." Hugging herself, she rubbed her arms. "She left it cold. It's fire she wants here, but she left the cold behind."

"Come, back to bed with you, where it's warm."

To settle it, he moved to her, picked her up, carried her over.

"You smell of the forest I painted."

"Well now, I've spent considerable time there." He tucked the covers around her. "Warmer now, are you?"

"She'll come back."

"Not tonight."

"Are you sure?"

"I am. You can sleep now."

"All right." And with a trust that baffled him, she closed her eyes.

Studying her, Bran considered his options. He could go back to his room, assume she'd come for him if she needed to. He could spend a very uncomfortable night on the floor. Or . . .

He stretched out beside her, watched night press against the window. She smelled of orange blossoms, he realized. And breathing her in, slept.

CHAPTER THREE

Warm, blissfully content, Sasha rose out of sleep slowly, like drifting up to the surface of a quiet pool to float. Wanting to cling to that sensation of feeling safe, happy, she kept her eyes closed, gave herself permission to snuggle in for just five minutes more.

On a sigh, she glided her hand up the sheet.

And froze.

Not the sheet, but skin. Warm, firm skin. With a heart beating under her palm.

Her eyes popped open. The first shock was seeing Bran, sleeping still, his face inches from hers. The next was realizing her head was nestled on his shoulder as if it belonged there. They were curled up together like contented lovers, his arm cradled under her, her hand resting on his heart.

And it wasn't a dream.

On a strangled gasp, she scrambled back, rolled, nearly tumbled off the bed before she gained her feet.

He sat up with a jerk, all tousled hair, stubble-shadowed cheeks, and hard, naked chest. "What?" he demanded, as those dark eyes cleared of sleep instantly. "What?"

"What?" she tossed back, pointing at him. "What?" And jabbed her finger in the air. *"What!"*

"Christ." He scrubbed both hands over his face. "Bad enough, isn't it, to wake when it's barely past the middle of the bloody night, but then to have a woman shrieking on top of it."

"I'm not shrieking." Those crystal-blue eyes fired like flames. "You want to hear shrieking? You will if you don't tell me what the hell you're doing in my bed."

"Relax, *fáidh,* for it was nothing but sleeping on both parts." A pity, he thought, as she was fairly glorious when wound up.

"Don't tell me to relax. Why are you in my room, in my bed, instead of in your own?"

"Well, I'll tell you if you stop shouting. By all the gods, is there no tea or coffee in the world at this moment?"

"I'm two seconds away from calling hotel security." After a frantic glance around, she grabbed one of her sandals, brandished it like a weapon. "Explain."

He angled his head, apparently uncon-
cerned, lifted that scarred eyebrow. "If you
throw that at me, darling, I'll be very annoyed, I can promise you." He shoved out
of bed, spotted her minibar, strode to it.

He plucked out a Coke and, rolling his
shoulders, had the lightning-bolt tattoo on
his left shoulder blade rippling. "Ah well,
you take what there is and be grateful."
Opening the bottle, he guzzled it down.
"That's something anyway."

"Get out."

He turned around again, tall, leanly mus-
cled, in nothing but the jeans he'd hastily
pulled on and hadn't bothered to button.
Through her fury, lust clanged like iron
bells.

"Are you wanting me to get out or to
explain?"

"I want you to explain, then get out. How
did you get in here?"

"I walked in, with you."

She cocked the shoe back another inch as
if prepared to pitch. "You absolutely did
not."

"I may dance around the truth here and
there, but I don't make a habit of stomping
on it. You were dream-walking. You came
knocking on my door."

"I — I don't walk in my sleep." But she

heard the doubt in her own voice.

"It's not altogether sleep, is it?" He sat on the side of the bed, drank more of the Coke, then held it out. "Want a bit?"

"No. Yes. I'll get my own." Halfway to the minibar, she realized she wore nothing but her chemise and detoured quickly to grab the hotel robe.

"A bit late for that now, don't you think, as I've already taken in the view. And it's a fine and appealing one." At her sharp look, he laughed. "And if I were going to do something about that, I had plenty of opportunity in the night." He held up his free hand, palm out. "Hands off, I swear to you."

She shoved her arms in the robe. "I don't remember."

"I can see that, and in your place I'd hate it as much as you. It was an hour or so after we'd parted ways for the night, you came knocking on my door. Not quite awake, not quite asleep — you understand what I mean. You said she was at the window."

"Who?"

"I asked the same. She wanted to be let in, and you knew better. She promised you your heart's desire, and you knew better. You came for me."

Fear crawled on sharp hands and knees up her spine. "Did you . . . Did you see

64

anything?"

"A shadow, nothing more than a shadow, and what sounded like the rustle of wings. I don't doubt there was something." He gave her a long, direct look. "I don't doubt you."

His last words brought tears to her eyes, so she turned away quickly, went to the minibar. Fighting the tears back, she found a small bottle of orange juice.

"You stayed with me."

"You were worried she'd come back, and you were cold. She'd left you cold. So I tucked you up as I might a . . . sister, and as I didn't fancy sleeping on the floor, I shared the bed. And here we are now."

"I'm sorry. I should've known. I would have known if I hadn't jumped so fast."

"You jumped to logical enough conclusions."

"Maybe." Now she sat on the side of the bed. He took the bottle from her, opened it, handed it back. But she only stared down at it. "Thank you for staying with me."

"You're welcome." But he took the shoe she still held, set it on the floor. Just in case.

And wished those sizzling sparks of outrage hadn't died away into weariness.

"It's just the beginning, isn't it? Shadows at the window. They're only the beginning."

"It began long ago. This is another step

along the way. You'll do fine."

"You think so?"

"I do, as I'm the one who nearly got bashed in the head with a shoe. You're not alone in this." He gave her a friendly pat on the leg before he pushed to his feet. "What do you say we meet down for breakfast in an hour?"

"All right. An hour."

He reached down, tipped her face up. "Remember. You didn't let her in."

When she nodded, he walked to the door and out.

And nearly into Riley.

Her eyebrows rose, her lips curved as she tugged earbuds out of her ears. "Quick work, Irish."

"Not of the matter you're thinking. You're up and about early."

"Got a workout in."

"If you can slap yourself together in a half hour, I'll go down to breakfast with you, tell you what happened with Sasha. She'll be an hour, and that would save her from having to go over it all again."

"Now you've got me curious. Make it twenty minutes." Riley jogged to her door, stopped to look back. "She okay?"

"She is. Tougher than I thought, and certainly than she thinks of herself. Twenty

66

minutes," he repeated. "If you're not ready I'll meet you downstairs, as if I don't have coffee by then I may murder someone."

"I'll be ready."

She was as good as her word and rapped on his door closer to fifteen minutes than twenty. They went down, agreed to grab coffee, take it out by the pool so he could fill her in.

"First, just to get it out of the way, I've gotta respect you didn't dive into the pool — and I don't mean this one."

"Sex?" He shook his head. "A man who'd take advantage of a dream-walker doesn't have much respect for himself or the woman. Add in, if we're in this together, we need some level of trust."

"You're right there. And I trust you're not telling us everything about Bran Killian."

"I'm not, Dr. Gwin."

On a laugh, she toasted him with her coffee. "Googled me?"

"I did."

"Only fair. I did the same with you. That club of yours — or clubs, because you've got another in Dublin — looks pretty kick-ass."

"I like to think so."

"I'll have to check it out, next time I'm in

New York or Dublin. But right now, we should probably get a table. Sasha strikes me as the timely type. Plus I'm starving."

Rising, they strolled toward the open-air buffet with its billowing white curtains. "You got any ideas on who was at her window last night?"

"A few."

"Funny, I have a few, too."

After telling the waiter they'd be three, they got a table, waited for the coffee refill. Riley took a notebook out of one of the pockets of her cargo pants, tore off a sheet.

"You write down your first choice, I'll do the same. And we'll compare."

"I don't have a pen on me."

"You can use my pencil in a minute." Riley scrawled a name on her sheet, tossed him the pencil.

"Is this to make certain I'm not winding you up?"

"Let's say it'll show if either of us is full of shit." She held her sheet out to him between two fingers, and he did the same.

"Nerezza," he murmured.

Riley set his sheet down beside her, nodding to Sasha as she walked to the table. "Nerezza."

"She's the mother of darkness." Sasha stared at the billowing white curtains. "She is made of lies."

Bran rose, took her arm, felt her shudder. "Sasha."

"Yes."

"Sit down now. Will you have coffee?"

She slid into the chair, nodded. "Yes." She picked up the two sheets of paper. "I know this name. I've heard it in my head. This was who came to the window. She was outside the window, a third-floor window. It wasn't a dream, not really a dream. How can that be? Who is she?"

"It's more what," Bran said, shifted his gaze back to Riley. "Have you ever taken on a god before?"

"Can't say I have. This should be fun." She stood up. "I'm hitting the buffet."

Sasha watched Riley stride off to one of the loaded buffet tables, lift the lid on a chafing dish, and begin to pile on food.

"If I had a million dollars, I'd give every cent of it to have her confidence."

"You've got your own," Bran told her. "You've just tucked it away here and there. We'd best get some breakfast before Riley eats all there is."

Riley's jeep, a rough, rusted-out red, was battered and battle-scarred and roofless. After a long study, Bran climbed in the back.

69

"Where did you get this thing?"

"I have contacts, worked a deal. Figured I'd need transportation." She got behind the wheel, tossed a folded map at Sasha. "Shotgun navigates."

"All right, but it's helpful to know where we're going."

"North along the coast to start. It's a big island, but my research leads me toward a coastal location."

"Why?" Even as the question formed, Riley hit the gas.

It might have looked like it hovered one step out of the nearest junkyard, but the jeep had enough kick to leap forward like a panther.

"Why?" Riley shouted over the engine's roar as she punched down a narrow road, the shops a blur at the edges, toward the coast. "What makes an island an island?"

Sasha wondered if a crash hurt less if the eyes stayed closed. "It's surrounded by water."

"So why choose an island to hide treasure if you're just going inland? The coast — bays, inlets, caves. Most translations of the legend talk about the Fire Star waiting to light again, that it sleeps in the cradle of land beneath the sea. Some mythologists figure Atlantis."

"That follows, as Atlantis is a myth."

Riley flicked Sasha a look. "You're here looking for a fallen star created by a moon goddess, but dissing Atlantis?"

"And hoping I don't die in a car crash."

"That's what the roll bar's for. I have a colleague who's been searching for Atlantis for nearly twenty years now. I'm leaving that one to him."

The road was like a speedway where every driver seemed determined to cross his personal finish line before the rest. Riley drove like a maniacal demon, barely slowing when they zipped through a village.

"Kontokali, if you're checking the map," she said. "It's got one of the oldest churches on the island, and a castle ruin I'll check out if I have spare time. How you doing back there, Irish?"

He'd angled sideways, propped his feet up on the second seat. "You drive like a hellhound, Riley."

"I always get where I'm going. Seeing as there are three of us now, I had a thought. We can each keep shelling out separately for a hotel room, or we could pool it, rent a place. It'd be cheaper all around."

"And more private," Bran added, as he'd had the thought himself. "It gets a bit awkward trying to discuss hunting for stars and evading dark gods in hotel restaurants. What do you think, Sasha?"

She stared out at the sea, and the skier flying along the blue behind a bright white boat. "I guess it's more practical."

"Done," Riley announced. "I'll make some calls."

"To your contacts," Bran finished.

"Pays to have them. Gouvia," she added as they came to another village. "Old Venetian shipyards. Multiple beaches and coves. May bear looking into."

Sasha had time to consider the sun-washed color of buildings, pedestrians in holiday gear, a stream of coastline before the village lay behind them.

"You don't appear to need a navigator."

"Not yet."

Sasha got used to the speed, at least used enough for her heart to stop knocking at every turn of the road. She soothed herself with the sea, the movement of it, the scent of it in the blowing air. The fragrance of flowers mixed with it as they bloomed wild and free on the roadsides, their colors more vivid and intense than any she'd seen. Madly red poppies springing out of a field, greedy morning glory smothering hedges in violent blue, the curving branches of a Judas tree bursting with searing magenta.

She was here, Sasha thought, to find answers to questions that dogged her. But she was here in such bright, hot beauty, and that alone was a personal miracle.

She gave over to it, lifted her face to the sky, let the warm, perfumed air wash over her.

Riley had some tidbit about every village they passed through. Sasha wondered what it was like to be a kind of human guidebook, to have traveled so widely, to actually and actively seek out adventure.

For now, she let herself be in the moment, one of sun, speed, scenery.

She could paint for years here.

Maybe her heart knocked again when they sped along a stretch with sharp turns, with the sea a breathless drop tucked close to the road.

Gradually they turned west, bypassed a large and busy town Sasha identified on the map as Kassiopi.

The road snaked again, skimmed by a lake she longed to sketch.

"Coming in to Acharavi. Originally called Hebe — probably after Zeus's daughter — in ancient times. Then Octavian sacked it in like 32 BC, so the current name, which basically means 'ungracious life,' since being sacked and burned is pretty ungracious.

"We'll take a pit stop there," Riley continued as they flew by a water park. "And I'll make those calls. Albania." She gestured to the land mass across the water.

"Albania," Sasha repeated, both giddy and astonished. "Imagine that." A family water park where she could hear squeals as kids came down the slides on one side, and the coast of Albania on the other.

Was that really any more amazing than a star of fire?

Acharavi bustled with its wide array of shops lining the main street. April had barely begun but holiday-goers thronged the resort town, wandering the shops or enjoying lunch at one of the pavement cafes.

"Spring break," Riley commented, and turned off the main road. "A lot of Brits and Americans, I'd say, because I see a lot of pale skin that's going to burn. Hope you stocked up on the sunscreen, Irish."

"I'm covered there, thanks." The minute she stopped, he boosted himself out, rolled his shoulders. "You picked a good spot to stretch things out."

"Aim to please." She pulled out her phone. "If you two want to walk down to the beach, I'll catch up."

Golden sand, sea oats, blue water, and the boats on it, some trailed by skiers. And

Albania shadowing the horizon.

Sasha grabbed her pack. She wanted ten minutes — maybe twenty — just to sketch.

"You're going to want to get yourself a hat," Bran told her. He took his own, dark gray with a wide, flat brim, and dropped it on her head.

"If I'd been wearing one, it would've blown off in the first five minutes."

"She can drive." He hoisted his own pack on his shoulder as they walked. "So, did anything strike you along the way? I'm thinking she's doing this coastal tour to see if something does."

Of course, Sasha thought. Not just a wild ride along the coast — but another kind of search.

"I should've thought of that. No. It's all beautiful, even at the speed of sound, but I didn't feel anything. I don't even know if it works like that. I've never tried."

"Why not?"

"Having something unusual, it separates you, makes you feel like the odd man out, I guess. I used to want to fit in, so much, then I finally realized, well, that's not going to happen. I've just focused on my work, at least until all this started. And now . . ."

"Now?"

"I'm in Greece and I'm looking out at

Albania — so close it looks as if you could swim to it. It's more than anything I could imagine." She closed her eyes, breathed deep. "Even the air's exotic. But if she drove here, stopped here hoping I'd have some sort of vision, it's not happening."

"I think it won't be so easy."

She thought of the visions she'd had. Blood and fear and pain and the dark. "No, it won't be."

"We need to find a place, Riley had the right of that. A place the three of us can spread out, study up, plan. A kind of HQ."

The idea made her smile. HQs seemed as far removed from her world as swimming to Albania. "HQ."

"Exactly. And as I don't know that the other three you've drawn will just walk up to us, as we did to each other, we'll need to ramble about like we are today."

"We have to come together. Until we do, we can look but we won't see; seek, but not find. Not a vision," she said quickly. "Just a kind of knowing."

"Which strikes me as the same."

"Maybe. I want to sketch while we're here."

"We'll need to get you a chair. We can rent one, I expect, or . . . There's a taverna right over there. How's that view?"

"That would be fine."

Once they had a table, and she'd angled her chair, he studied the view as she did. "Want a beer?"

"Oh, no, thanks. Maybe something cold." Pulling out her pad, she began to draw the flowing sea oats and long slice of beach.

He ordered a Mythos for himself, and the Greek juice that was a combination of orange, apple, and apricot for Sasha. As she sketched, he took out his phone to check his emails.

Even as he dealt with work he watched her, those slim, pretty hands conjuring a scene with paper and pencil.

She left out things that were there, he noted. The people. Her beach was deserted but for birds winging over the sea.

She flipped to another page, began another. He supposed she'd term them rough sketches, but he found them both wonderfully lean and fluid. It was a kind of magic, he thought, that she could with quick, sure strokes of a pencil create her vision.

She started a third — a different perspective, he saw. Not quite the beach spread in front of them, and hers with a moon, not quite full, floating through a drift of clouds over a sea where waves tossed.

A woman stood at the edge of the sea, facing it, her dark hair a tumble to her waist. Her skirts billowed around her knees. To her right, high, sheer cliffs rose, and on them stood the shadow of a house where a light glowed in a single window.

When Sasha stopped, turned back to finally pick up her drink, he set his phone down.

"Will she go into the sea or back to the house on the cliff?"

"I don't know." Sasha blew out a breath, sipped again. "I don't think she knows either. It's not here. I don't know why I looked out there and saw this so clearly."

"Maybe we're close. She's the only person you drew. In the other sketches of this beach, you left out the people."

"Oh." She shrugged. "It's more peaceful without them. I don't usually draw people. Or I didn't. When I was studying and we used models, I'd end up reading them. It's the focus, and it always felt so intrusive. I learned how to block it out, but it didn't seem worth the effort. I like the mystery of a scene empty of people."

She propped her chin on her fist, smiled at him. "You like scenes full of people."

Conversations — something she'd avoided tucked away in the mountains — took a different tone, had a new appeal, when she had them with someone who knew what she was, and accepted.

"And how would you know?"

"Clubs," she explained. "You own clubs, and perform, so you must like people. And audiences who marvel at your magic tricks."

"I can appreciate an empty beach as well. But . . ." He held up a hand, empty palm toward her, closed it into a fist, flashed out his other hand. Then offered her a curved white shell from his once-empty palm. "I like the marvel."

She laughed, shook her head. "How do you do that?"

"Nothing up my sleeve."

"And no smoke and mirrors around either." She traced the edges of the shell. "How did you learn to do magic?"

"You could say it's a family tradition. My mother actually taught me my first . . . bit."

"Your mother. Does she perform, too?"

"In her way." Because he liked her laugh, he took a deck of cards from his pack, fanned them out. "Pick a card, any card."

She drew one out, glanced at it. "Now what?"

"Back in it goes, and you take the deck. Shuffle it up. We should reward ourselves with a swim at the end of the day. Which would you pick, sea or pool?"

"The sea." If no one else was on the beach, she added to herself. "How often will I have the chance to swim in the Ionian? Is that enough?"

"It is, sure, if it feels enough for you. Set the deck down again, and fan it out yourself."

She did as he instructed, leaned forward, eyes sharp.

"Now where do you suppose your card might be. Here?" he tapped a card. "No, no, maybe here. Ah, here comes our Riley."

"Playing cards and drinking beer, while I've been sweating over a hot cell phone." She dropped down, picked up what was left of Bran's beer, and drained it.

"He's doing a card trick, but I don't think it's working out for him."

"Such lack of faith and wonder." Bran sighed. He ran a fingertip along the fanned cards. "Not here or there at all, it seems, because . . . Do you mind?" he said to Riley and took the hat from her head, turned it over. "Your Queen of Hearts is in Riley's hat."

Sasha's eyes widened. "That's not possible."

"And yet it is." He held up the queen between two fingers, turned his hand at the wrist, and held nothing.

"I've gotta say," Riley commented as Sasha gaped. "That's some of the best close-up magic I've seen. I also have to say I've done some magic of my own. We've got a place if we want it."

"How did the card get in Riley's hat when she wasn't here?" Sasha demanded.

"But she is here, and she's polished off my beer."

"But . . ." Then with a laugh, Sasha held up her hands in surrender. "I want to see you do it again when — Did you say you found a place?"

"Yeah, and that earns me a beer of my own. But I'll wait until we get there, take a look at it. It's not far. Just outside of Sidari."

"I saw Sidari on the map — west of here."

"You got it. I had some luck." Now Riley reached out, took a long sip of Sasha's juice. "Friend of a friend of an uncle. It's his villa, and he's in the States on business for the next few weeks. His lucky day, too, as the couple who was caretaking the place had to leave just yesterday. Guy took a bad fall, broke his leg. So the friend of a friend of an uncle says we can use the place if we do the caretaking thing."

"What does that mean, exactly?" Bran asked.

81

"Yard work, gardening, maintaining the pool — did I mention there's a pool? There's also a dog — so feed and water — and chickens."

"Chickens?" Sasha repeated.

"Feed and water again, and help ourselves to the eggs. We take care, we stay for free until he gets back in about four weeks. Sounds like a hell of a deal to me."

"We should certainly have a look." Bran put his cards back in their case. "Ready for it?"

Nodding, Sasha got to her feet. "I think I could live with staying at a villa on the Ionian Sea. It's just when things sound too good to be true . . ."

"There's usually a catch." Bran stood, took her hand. "Why don't we go find the catch, see if we can live with whatever it might be."

The road west was nearly straight, until it wasn't. Then it was a quick series of curves and loops Riley drove with the same careless speed.

Sasha saw clearly why Sidari was billed as the top resort area in the north. Its situation right on the bay, its spectacular views. Too many people was her first thought, far too many filling the streets, the beaches, the shops.

The noise of them made her head ache, stretched her nerves wire thin. But the jittery feeling didn't pass, even when they'd left the town behind, turned onto a narrow road. She shifted her gaze to the sea again, trying to recapture that sensation of being in the moment.

She saw it, knew it, understood the feeling now. The promontory rose up from the sea, high and proud. She'd stood there with him, in the night wind of an oncoming storm. He had lightning in his hand, and she a terrible burning in her heart.

Her painting.

She hadn't shown them, either of them, and yet the road had brought them here.

Dimly she heard Riley's voice talking about coves and inlets, caves, both above and under water.

"It's going to get bumpy," Riley added. "House is up, on the cliff. Views ought to be killer."

She didn't look, not yet. She already knew what she'd see. Instead she concentrated on the wildflowers, blooming heroically along the side of what was now no more than a track, even blooming in the track itself.

The jeep banged and bumped, forced Riley to at last slow down, then stop when they came to a set of iron gates.

"I've got the passcode." She leaned out, punched the code into a keypad. "He said he had a neighbor come by this morning to feed the dog, do the chicken deal, check on things. And claims the dog's friendly."

The road smoothed out a bit, then made a sweeping turn.

"Just let me say score!" With a little war whoop, Riley arrowed toward the villa. "Not the kind of digs I usually bunk in."

In rich cream against blue sky, the villa rose on its high perch. It angled toward the sea, offering that sweep of view from front and back. The impressive front boasted enough room for a swath of flowering bushes, a few fruit trees, and a verdant lawn before the stone wall. And there the land dropped off as if cleaved by axes. Even the rough steps leading down to the beach made Sasha think of muscular gnomes or trolls with primitive tools hacking at the stone. It owned a majestic set of doors, jutting terraces, wide expanses of glass.

More flowers, more trees graced the side of the house where a stone pathway wandered. Even as Riley turned off the car, a big white dog, a fuzzy polar bear with a long, feathered tail, came strolling out of the shady trees toward the car.

"He's *huge.*" Sasha forgot her nerves long

enough for new ones to shove in. "You said friendly."

"He's just a big boy. Hey, Apollo — his name's Apollo." Fearlessly, Riley got out of the car, crouched, held out a hand.

The dog stopped, stared into her eyes. The moment stretched so long Sasha considered jumping out, pulling Riley back in. Though she wondered if a dog that big could simply eat the jeep, with them in it.

Then he walked over to Riley, tail wagging, and nuzzled her outstretched hand.

"You're a good boy." She straightened, set a hand on Apollo's head when he sat. "What are you guys waiting for?"

"Just waiting to see how big a chunk he might take out of you." Bran launched himself out of the jeep and, just as casually as Riley, stroked a hand down the dog's back.

"Come on, Sasha, read him if you're worried. You should be able to read a dog," Riley pointed out. "They have feelings. What's he feeling?"

"Happy." Sasha sighed and got out of the jeep. "He's feeling really happy."

"Pack animals." Riley bent down, kissed the dog's head. "Need a pack, and that's going to be us for a bit. I've got the alarm code, too, and it seems the caretakers left the keys in the potted palm by the cliff wall, so . . ."

Riley, striding confidently in worn boots, the dog at her heels, walked over to the wall. "Wowzer view. Have a gander."

Sasha made herself walk over to the stone wall, and there, far below, was the beach she'd drawn at the table at the tavern, when the image of it had overlaid the other.

"It's only missing the moon and the woman," Bran said quietly.

"Say what?"

"I drew this while we were waiting for you at Acharavi," Sasha told Riley. "I didn't know where it was. Now I do. She was there, down there at the edge of the water. The woman we haven't met yet. And the villa was a silhouette on the cliff."

Pleased, Riley fisted her hands on her hips. "Excellent. So this is where we're supposed to be."

"I guess it is." The dog bumped his head under Sasha's hand, looked up at her with appealing dark eyes, radiating the happiness she'd just felt from him. It made her smile again. "This is where."

"Then let's go check it out. I call first pick on bedrooms." Riley set off at a run, and with a joyful bark, Apollo raced behind her.

"We can flip a coin for second pick," Bran

offered, and Sasha felt her balance return.

"As if I'd flip a coin with a magician. I call it," she announced, and ran after the dog.

CHAPTER FOUR

Sasha believed herself to be a creature of order, of practical routine. When she elected to do something outside that routine, it was after careful thought and deliberation.

Or it had been until she'd flown to Corfu.

Now, roughly twenty-four hours after she'd checked in, unpacked her bags, she was packing them again, preparing to check out, to move into a villa with two people she'd known less than a day.

And no matter how many times she questioned the sanity of it, she knew it was the right thing to do. The only thing to do if she wanted real answers.

The villa was beautiful, spacious, and even a woman who considered herself practical couldn't deny the thrill of walking through it, considering she'd live there for . . .

However long she did.

Tumbled tile floors, she thought as she carefully packed, wide, wide stretches of sparkling glass, the soaring entranceway and double curves of stairs leading to the second floor. Where, Sasha recalled, Riley had arrowed toward.

Her new friend chose the master with its massive bed, one Riley had bounced on gleefully before bulleting into the en suite and crowing in triumph over the freestanding stone tub — big enough for a party — and the equally generous shower.

For herself, Sasha had studied several options, all lovely, but had fallen for the four-poster with its domed and pleated canopy of sea-blue linen. Like the other bedrooms, it opened to a terrace, and she imagined herself painting there.

Even when she realized her view would include the promontory, she couldn't persuade herself to select a room facing away.

She closed her suitcases, checked the room twice to be sure she'd left nothing behind, and was about to call for a bellman when someone knocked at the door.

She opened it to Bran.

"Are you set then?" he asked.

"Yes, just now. I was going to call for a bellman."

He glanced in at her suitcases, pack, tote.

"We should be able to handle it." He hooked her tote around the handle of one suitcase, slung her pack over his shoulder. "Can you manage the other?"

"Sure, but can we handle your bags, too?"

"I've already taken them down, loaded them. Of course, I've about half of what you've got here."

"Of course you do. You're a man." Sasha walked out behind him without giving her room a backward glance.

"I am that. I'll just check on Riley, and we'll — Well, no need," he added as Riley stepped out, rolling a single wheeled duffle behind her.

"That's it? Your backpack and a duffle?" Sasha demanded.

"Got everything I need and room for more."

Sasha looked at her own luggage, actually *felt* Riley's smirk. "I have my art supplies," she began.

"Uh-huh." With the smirk still in place, Riley headed for the elevator.

"I do! And my travel easel, several small canvases, a spare sketchbook, not to mention paints, brushes."

"Your brushes aren't going to make it in this elevator on this trip."

"You two go," Bran suggested. "I'll take the stairs."

"That case is heavy," Sasha began.

"It's the spare sketch pad."

Sasha gave Riley a scowl, then laughed. "Oh, shut up."

She maneuvered her case into the elevator, turned to thank Bran. But he was already gone.

By the time she'd checked out, they had her luggage loaded, and everything strapped in with bungee cords out of Riley's duffle.

Sasha eyed them doubtfully, thought of her painting supplies. "Will those really hold?"

"Haven't let me down yet. Kick-ass villa, here we come."

Riley roared off just as she had that morning. This time, Bran shared the backseat with luggage.

"You should have the front." Sasha swiveled around. "I didn't think of it. I'm smaller than you, and wouldn't be as crowded."

"Oh, we're fine here, me and your paintbrushes. And the way Riley drives, we'll be there long before my legs have time to cramp."

The speed — outrageous — seemed slightly more exhilarating than frightening this time. Sasha took in the blur of sea and flowers, cars, sun-washed buildings while she half listened to Riley and Bran debate whether to stop somewhere for lunch or just get where they were going.

She didn't care either way. It was all so surreal, and reckless. Prior, the most reckless thing she could remember doing had been hacking off her hair when she'd been twelve. An act of anger and defiance she'd regretted before the last snip of the scissors.

Clearly, this reckless act carried more risk and weight — and yet, just at the moment, it felt absolutely right.

She'd unpack first, she decided. She wouldn't feel settled until she did. And then she'd set up her easel . . . maybe outside, try a chalk study of the gardens. Or try a watercolor. She rarely used that medium, but —

"What's your vote?" Riley demanded.

"Sorry, what?"

"Food or destination? You're the tie breaker."

"Oh, it doesn't matter."

"Tie breaker," Riley insisted. "It has to matter. Bran's for getting there. I'm for food."

"I don't want to be the tie breaker."

"You're stuck with it. He's all 'there's food in the villa' — the caretakers had it stocked and we've got the green light to use what we want, but we have to get there, then throw something together. Can anybody cook?"

"Of course I can cook," Sasha began, and immediately saw her mistake. "I'm absolutely not going to be in charge of the kitchen."

A big, beautiful kitchen, she remembered, and she wouldn't mind making a meal or two, but —

"Somebody has to be. If you want something fried up on a Coleman stove, I'm your girl, otherwise, I'm sandwiches and stirring. I can stir. And chop," she added. "I'm hell on chopping."

"I don't know how to cook for people."

"What do you cook for?" Bran wondered. "Bears?"

"Myself. But —"

"I'm not bad at breakfast." Bran rolled right over her objections. "But I doubt anyone's up for a full fry every meal. Sidari's not far, for going out to eat, but if we're wanting more privacy to discuss our business, a home-cooked seems the thing."

"Sasha's definitely elected. Popular vote."

"I abstain." Honestly, she felt a tickle of panic in her throat at being voted in charge of anything. "Or abdicate."

Miles flew by as they argued about it, and

as Sasha began to see herself in a losing battle.

"We're definitely stopping for lunch — tie broken — and if anyone's hungry tonight, they can eat one of Riley's famous sandwiches."

"My specialty."

"I'll cook something tomorrow night after I've had time to think about it, but after that . . ."

She trailed off, struck by the sight of a hitchhiker, brim of his ball cap tipped down, his thumb cocked out.

"We still have to eat after that," Riley said. "I get cranky when I'm hungry, and you don't want me —"

"Stop!" She'd only glimpsed his face as they'd passed, but it was enough. "Stop the car!"

Riley reacted quickly, hit the brakes. "What's the deal?" she demanded as she swerved to the side of the road.

"Back up. The hitchhiker. Turn around or back up. The hitchhiker."

"Oh, yeah." Riley tipped down her sunglasses, aimed a look as sarcastic as her tone. "We've got plenty of room for one more."

Sasha pushed out of the jeep. "He *is* one more. Of us."

"No shit?"

Bran boosted out of the jeep as Sasha took a step down the shoulder. "Just let's hold here a minute then, darling. He's coming to us. Let's gauge our ground first."

He jogged up the road and still seemed to saunter, a pack hitched to his back, hiking boots worn and dusty. He wore the black ball cap over shaggy, dark blond hair.

His eyes, though she couldn't see them behind the dark glasses, she knew to be gray.

He sent them a quick, sunny smile. *"Kalimera,"* he began. *"Efkharisto,* ah —"

"Don't strain yourself," Bran advised. "English works."

"Good thing. Thanks for stopping."

"American, are you? I'm surrounded."

"Yeah. Sawyer, Sawyer King." He added a fresh smile and a nod when Riley walked up.

"Where are you heading, Sawyer King?" she asked.

"Oh, around for now. A ride however far you're going would work, but you look pretty packed in."

"That we are," Bran agreed. "We're going a bit past Sidari. Bran Killian."

"Irish, huh?" Sawyer accepted the offered hand. "Y'all vacating?"

"Not exactly." Riley turned, looked mean-

95

ingfully at Sasha. "Well?"

"Yes, I'm sure."

Sawyer hooked a thumb in his belt loop — an easy stance — but clearly went on alert. "Sure of what?"

A picture could be worth any number of words, Sasha decided. "Can you wait a minute?"

"Yeah." He flashed a grin — quick lightning — but stayed on alert. "I've always got time."

She went to the jeep, leaned in to pull out her tote from where it was wedged on the floor of the backseat. She dug out her portfolio, then the sketch of the six.

She took it back to him, offered it. "I drew that about three weeks ago, in North Carolina — where I live."

He studied it, took his sunglasses off, studied it a bit more. Yes, gray eyes, like evening mist over a shadowy lake.

He said, "Huh."

"I know how strange it sounds — is — but I've got other drawings in here. Of us, of you — of this," she said, waving her arms.

"Who are you?"

"Sasha Riggs, and this is Riley Gwin."

"Who are the other two in the drawing?"

"I don't know."

"The way things are moving," Bran said,

"I don't think it'll be long before we find out. As I don't think this strikes you as strange as it might, you'll know what I mean by the Stars of Fortune."

Sawyer swung his sunglasses by the earpiece. "Yeah, I know what you mean."

"So we can discuss all this here, on the side of the road, and risk being mowed down by a passing car whose driver enjoys great rates of speed, as does our Riley, or we can go discuss it over a pint."

"Wouldn't say no to a beer." Sawyer handed the sketch back to Sasha.

"I change my vote. We should go straight to the villa."

Sawyer lifted his eyebrows. "You've got a villa?"

"Friend of a friend of an uncle." Hands on hips, Riley studied the jeep, the luggage. "I'm good at making things fit, but this is it. Sasha's going to have to sit on your lap, Sawyer."

"He'll have the back," Bran corrected. "She can sit on mine, as she's known me longer."

"That can't be legal. To drive like that."

Riley snorted, headed to the driver's door. "You kill me, Sash."

"It's only about twenty more kilometers." Bran nudged her toward the jeep. "We'll all

97

be fine." He got in, patted a hand on his legs. "Come on then."

"Don't be so delicate, Sasha. Jesus, you've already slept with the guy."

"I did not. Well, technically, but —"

To solve it, Bran took her hand, pulled her in.

"This should be fun." Sawyer swung long legs over the back, slid down.

"Yeah, we're a merry band." Riley bulleted back on the road, and had Sasha's knuckles whitening on the dashboard she gripped like the last thread of life.

"Relax." Amused, Bran wrapped his arms around her waist, eased her back. "It's clear enough we're not meant to die in a car crash in a borrowed jeep on the way to a borrowed villa."

"Speaking of villas." Riley flicked a glance in the rearview. "You cook, Sawyer?"

And Sasha, crushed on Bran's lap, flying down the road like a reckless and carefree teenager, laughed until her sides ached.

By the time they bumped up the track toward the gate, it had been established that Sawyer could cook, which, according to Riley, made him cocaptain of the kitchen with Sasha.

"Three bedrooms are spoken for," Riley continued. "But there are four more, so you've got next pick."

"Just like that?"

"We'll have that drink, and maybe Riley will create some of her world-renowned sandwiches. Then," Bran added, "we can all decide."

"He's one of us," Riley said simply as she took the turn that brought the villa into full view.

From the backseat, Sawyer let out a whistle. *"Yobanny v rot."*

Riley angled back to study him. "How'd a nice Virginia boy — that's a coastal Virginia accent you got there."

"Good ear. Little place called Willow Cove, on the Chesapeake."

"Yeah, so how'd a nice Virginia boy learn to swear in Russian?"

"Russian grandfather. You speak Russian?"

"I'm multilingual in obscenities. And yeah, the place earns a *yobanny v rot.*"

"What does it mean?" Sasha asked.

"Cleanest translation? Holy shit." Riley pushed out of the jeep to greet the dog. "Hey, Apollo. We're back."

"Look at that." With a young boy's delight in his voice, Sawyer swung out and, without preamble or introductions, scrubbed his hands all over the dog. "You're one big, handsome bastard. This your house? You're a lucky dog."

Apollo sat, offered a paw.

Watching them, Sasha forgot her situation until she turned her head, smiled at Bran. And found their faces intimately close.

"Oh, sorry. I need to get off — out."

"I suppose you do. Though it's cozy here." He opened the door, then slid an arm under her legs. "Let me give you a hand," he said, and swiveled her around. Just held there.

"Ah. Thanks."

"You're welcome."

He let her go, took his time getting out behind her.

"Everybody grab something," Riley ordered. "Let's haul it in. Bran, maybe you can give the newest member of our club the tour while I make those sandwiches. If I don't eat soon, I'm going to take a bite out of somebody."

When they carted luggage in, and Sawyer's head turned side to side and up, Bran gave Sasha's ponytail a tug. "We'll haul this up, Sawyer and I. Why don't you see about those pints?"

"Okay."

So she wouldn't unpack first — she'd have a sandwich, help Riley and Bran explain things to Sawyer. And hopefully have Sawyer explain things to them.

And she wanted a couple minutes to really look at the place, so crossed the entrance with its warm golden tiles into the airy living area. The wide windows could be shuttered against the beat of the sun, but she loved the light pouring in.

Twin sofas in bold peacock blue formed a conversation area centered by a large leather ottoman of chocolate brown. Cream-colored built-ins flanked a fireplace of glossy tiles in that same blue and held a colorful collection of glassware and pottery.

A vivid pattern of exotic birds that seemed poised to take flight covered deeply cushioned chairs. A tall chest boasted doors carved in a similar pattern and looked old and exquisite.

But the pull of the room lay outside the glass, in the sweep of flowers and trees that led to the cliff edge and out to the rich blue sea.

"Hey."

She turned to Riley. "It's just beautiful."

"Yeah. Bask later. Food now."

"You're in charge of sandwiches."

"It's a big kitchen. Plus I just got a text letting me know we can hit any of the wine up here. If we go through it, there's a wine cellar — but anything we take from there, we replace. I'm going for wine instead of the brew. How about you?"

"I usually don't this early in the day."

Obviously amused, Riley cocked a hip. "Are you usually in a villa in Greece about to talk about god-stars this early in the day?"

"No." Good point. "I'll have the wine."

Sasha followed, past an archway that opened into a room with a piano and another smaller fireplace, another room filled with books, a formal dining room, a masculine den or study, and on to the kitchen.

Riley had thrown open the triple doors of glass to the shaded terrace beyond so the scent of lemons and roses danced in on the breeze.

"This is the most incredible place. I can't believe anyone would just let us stay here."

"Pays to have contacts. The guy has vineyards." Riley tapped a bottle of white she'd taken from the wine cooler. "I figured it's only polite we start with one of his. Why don't you deal with that?"

"Okay." She ran a hand over one of the counters, the granite swirled with gold and cream and brown. "A kitchen this big should be intimidating, but it's homey. Everything's really up-to-date, but you contrast that with the dishes in the breakfront there, the butcher block table and island, the cottagey-style chairs, and it's relaxed."

"I'll be more relaxed with food and wine."

Sasha hunted up a corkscrew while Riley poked through an enormous refrigerator. "Big pantry over there — you could live in it. And a vegetable garden outside we're to harvest from. We'll work out some sort of divvying for the yard work. And the chickens. The coop's out behind the garden."

Riley sliced from a big round of brown bread. "That's a commercial stove," she added, "which means I'm not going near it."

Though she couldn't wait to try it out, Sasha decided to keep that to herself before Riley decided she was full captain of the kitchen again.

"The men wanted beer. Is there beer?"

Riley jerked a thumb at the refrigerator, and switched from slicing bread to slicing tomatoes.

"We should eat outside. I'll set that up."

She found bamboo place mats, opted for the colorful plates, cherry-red napkins, and entertained herself setting a festive table under the wooden slats of a pergola. She transferred the bowl of fruit from the butcher block to the outside table, turned

103

back when she heard male voices.

"Let's test it out then."

She came back in as Bran poured a small amount of the wine into a glass. After a sip, he nodded.

"I'll go with it."

"Make it unanimous. You scored a hell of a place here."

"My thoughts exactly. Sasha says we eat outside, and I'm all for it." Riley set the last of four enormous sandwiches on a platter, dumped half the contents of a bag of chips into a bowl. "Let's eat."

Sasha eyed the size of the sandwiches, and when they sat down, cut one in half, put the second half back on the platter.

Bran took a hefty bite of his own. "You're definitely the queen of sandwiches."

Busy with her own, Riley nodded. "It's a gift. So, Sawyer King, we'll start with the lightning round for the fabulous prize of a stay in a fabulous villa by the sea. What's your version of the Stars of Fortune?"

He held up a finger until he swallowed, then picked up his wine. "The way I heard it, a long time ago, in a galaxy far, far away —"

"Points for the *Star Wars* reference."

"A favorite. Three goddesses of the moon, to celebrate the rise of their new queen, created three stars, one of fire, one of ice, one of water."

He told it well, seemed to have no problem being the focus of attention.

"Okay, that jibes." Riley crunched into a chip. "For the second part of the round —"

"A two-parter."

"Yeah. How do you know about them?"

"My Russian grandfather."

"Is that so?" Bran poured more wine all around.

"Yeah, that's so. It was one of his favorite stories, which is what I thought it was when I was a kid. Just a story. But he got sick a while back — we didn't think he was going to make it, and neither did he. That's when he sat me down, told me it was truth, and more than truth, a kind of destiny. Mine."

"And you believed him?" Sasha asked.

"He'd never lied to me in my life," Sawyer said simply. "*Dedulya* told me the story, and the responsibility, had been passed down in the family for generations. Over . . . time, many had searched, but no luck. But, well, into each generation a seeker is born."

"Oh." Riley pointed at him. "Serious bonus points for the paraphrase of *Buffy*."

"I like to rack them up. He said I was it, and I'd know I was on the right path when I met five other seekers." He plucked a couple of grapes from the bowl. "Looks like three out of five so far. *Dedulya* — and it shouldn't sound any more weird than the rest of this — he's sort of psychic."

"And was that passed down, too?" Bran wondered.

"Not to me."

"Why here?" Sasha asked. "Why Corfu?"

Since they were there, Sawyer dumped more chips on his plate. "I've been at this awhile, hitting dead ends, but gathering some information. Separating the obvious bullshit from what might not be is the key. I was on Sardinia — hell of a place — and traced a lead. This story about Poseidon — not Neptune, so Greek not Roman, and I'm in Italy. Anyway, Poseidon and Korkyra."

Pleased, Riley, took a handful of grapes for herself. "The beautiful nymph he loved, and who he brought to an unnamed island. He named it Korkyra, for her."

"Right, and that became Kerkyra. Corfu. The story talked about a Fire Star, gone cold, hidden between land and sea, and waiting to flame again. So, I followed the lead."

"Same lead I picked up." Riley popped a grape in her mouth.

"You?" Sawyer gestured to Bran.

"Mine spoke of the land of Phaiax."

"Poseidon's and Korkyra's son, so the island inhabitants were once Phaeacians, and Corfu the island thereof."

"You know a lot about it," Sawyer commented.

"She has a doctorate," Bran told him.

"No shit? Well, Dr. Gwin, did I pass the audition?"

"You've got my vote."

"Sasha dreamed of you, with us," Bran pointed out. "So there's no question, really."

"I have one. I just wonder," Sasha began, "what you do? How you support yourself while you search?"

"I'm a traveler, and I fix things." He held up his hands, wiggled his fingers. "When you're handy, you can always pick up work."

"And one more? You spoke of your grandfather in the present tense, so he recovered."

Now Sawyer grinned. "Yeah. He's tough."

"I'm glad."

"What about you guys?"

"Seer, magician, digger," Riley said, pointing to each in turn.

Sawyer studied Sasha. "I figured that, with the dreams and the drawing."

"I'm an artist." If she could have, Sasha would have shrugged the term *seer* off like an itchy sweater. "The other is just what it is."

"Okay. So what's a digger?"

"Archaeologist, mythology a specialty."

"Huh. Indiana Jones. Fits. And magician." The grin came back. "Like: Watch me pull a rabbit out of my hat?"

"Oh, if that's *Rocky and Bullwinkle,* this could be love."

Sawyer laughed over at Riley. "Alumnus of Wossamotta U. Tricks and illusions, escapes?" he asked Bran.

"That's right." Bran held up a coin, turned his hand, vanished it. "It pays the bills."

"Very cool. So, what now?"

"It could be we ended up here so we'd hook with you," Riley speculated. "But you were heading in the same direction."

"Felt right."

"Yeah, it feels right."

"The drawing you made of the beach, the moon," Bran said to Sasha. "It wasn't of Sawyer, but a woman. From the back, yes, but the body type, the hair, it's clear she's the one in your other drawings."

"I'd like to see it again," Sawyer said. "And you've got more?"

Sasha rose. "Yes. I'll get them."

"You're not going to eat that?" Riley gestured to the half sandwich.

"No, I couldn't."

"I can."

"Where do you put it?" Bran wondered. "You eat like a bird — as in triple your own weight."

"Fast metabolism."

"I'll do my share, clear this up, while Sasha gets the drawings." Sawyer pushed away from the table, turned to the view of the sea. "Beats the hell out of pitching a tent."

"I hear that," Riley agreed, and bit into the sandwich.

They spent more than an hour going over the sketches, discussing theories, locations they'd tried — except for Sasha — stories they'd heard.

Then Riley announced she was giving her brain a rest, and trying out the pool.

"Resting the brain's a good idea," Bran decided. "It's been an illuminating couple of days."

"I wouldn't mind getting my bearings." Still Sawyer picked up a sketch of the woman they'd yet to meet. "Do you think she's really this hot?"

"That's how I see her."

"Can't wait to meet her. I'm going to wander around." Sawyer got to his feet again. "I like to have a better sense of where

I am while I'm there. The pool looks good. Might end up there."

"Plenty of room. Regroup later?" Without waiting for an answer, Riley strolled back into the house.

"It's the first time I've had a team on this. It's been interesting so far." With that, Sawyer wandered off.

"Your sense about him?" Bran asked Sasha.

"Oh, Sawyer? Adores his grandfather — that's a tight bond. Optimism. I get a strong sense of optimism, and a strong sense of purpose. I don't like to pry," she added, "but it seemed we should know. There's something more to him — I don't know what — but I didn't get any . . . evil. I guess it's not too strong a word, considering. I don't get anything dark or evil. In fact, so much the opposite."

"You trust him."

"Don't you?"

"I'm a bit slower with that than you might be, but he strikes me as true enough. And there he is, after all." He tapped the sketch. "Well, I'm after a walk on the beach. Come with me."

"I haven't even unpacked."

"What's the hurry?" Smiling, Bran rose, offered a hand. "It's just a walk down the cliff steps."

She should unpack, organize her tools, but she found herself putting her hand in his. "All right. I want to find some good perspectives to sketch or paint anyway."

"There, you've found your sensible reason for a walk."

"I think for the rest of you, adventure and risk come naturally."

"And you think you're the quiet and settled sort."

"I am the quiet and settled sort."

"Not from where I'm standing. You're the most courageous among us."

Stunned, she gaped at him as they circled toward the stone wall. "Courageous? Me? Where do you get that?"

"The rest of us? We knew what we were after, and why, and why we came here. But you?" He walked to the pillars and gate, opened it. "You left your home, came all this way, not knowing. And when you saw Riley, you walked right up to her, you risked telling a stranger a story you didn't understand yourself. That's courage."

She looked at him, the dark, compelling eyes, the way the wind blew his hair around his face. And the yearning came back into her, so strong she had to look away.

"I don't feel brave."

"You don't recognize your own bravery. That's all it is."

He took her hand again, started down the rough steps.

"They're really steep." And high.

"But look where they'll take us. I like a fine beach, though I often find myself more drawn to the forests and mountains. What are your mountains?"

"The Blue Ridge."

"Lovely, are they?"

"Yes. Lovely, and peaceful. I can't think the last time I was at the beach. Anywhere."

"It can be lovely and peaceful as well. See there, that high point?"

Her stomach jittered as he gestured toward the promontory. "Yes."

"And the bit of land there, the channel of water between? It's called Canal d'Amour, that channel, and it's said if you swim there, from one end to the other, you'll meet the love of your life. That's a pretty thought, isn't it?"

"Do you believe in that? Not the swimming part, but the love of your life part? That someone — anyone — loves for a lifetime?"

"Absolutely."

"So you're a romantic."

"I wouldn't have thought. My own parents

have been married over thirty years, and not just because they have four children and are used to each other. They love and enjoy each other."

"You have siblings."

"I do. A brother and two sisters, so my mother's fond of saying, she balanced it all out well with two of each sort. And that was enough of that."

"It's nice, a big family."

A deaf man could have heard the wistfulness, Bran thought. "It is, yes."

"Do you get back to see them?"

"I do, of course, and they travel to me from time to time. We're a noisy bunch — not quiet and peaceful at all — when we're all together. And here we are, at the bottom."

She'd barely noticed the rough climb down. "You kept me talking so I wouldn't panic."

"You don't panic so easy." The last step was a drop. Bran jumped down easily, turned to take Sasha by the waist and lift her down. Then stood, testing both of them, with his hands on her. "Do you, *fáidh*?"

She knew the taste and feel of his mouth on hers, the way his hands moved on her skin, the angles of his body under her own.

And the need to know all that outside of

dreams was far too strong.

"Maybe," she said, and stepped away.

"There's something you're not telling me. I can see it." He tapped a finger between her eyes. "Why is that?"

"We all have secrets, and when we find the other two, they'll have them. I guess trust doesn't run deep enough yet."

"Hardly a wonder in this short a time. Well then, we'll take what we have."

What they had was golden sand and blue water. People, yes, but only a few sunning under the warm spring rays or sitting under the shade of an umbrella. Some children digging with plastic shovels, others wading in the surf.

"I expect the beaches closer to Sidari are more crowded than this, though," Bran continued. "From what I've read, there'll be plenty who'll jump from the seawall into the canal, hoping to find their true love. That would make a fine painting, I'd think. The rock, the water, the hopeful who take the leap."

Intrigued by the idea, Sasha stopped, looked back. The colors, the textures, the angle of light. A figure, she imagined, poised to leap, another caught on the jump between wall and water. Perhaps one more with speared fingers just meeting the surface. She should have grabbed her sketch pad, then she could —

She saw a flash, something shimmering like jewels in the sunlight sliced out of the water. An instant, an instant only of sparkle and foam, of swirling blue, then gone.

"Did you see that?"

"See what?"

"In the canal. Something . . . It came out of the water, then in again."

"I didn't see, but I was looking up."

"It was beautiful, like a sweep of jewels, just glittering in the sunlight."

He laid a hand on her shoulder. "The stars?"

"No, no, it was sinuous, and alive. The movement. Some sort of fish?"

"A dolphin maybe." He took his hand, fisted it lightly around the hair she'd tied back, skimmed it down. "Looking for true love."

"A dolphin." And the idea of a dolphin swimming the canal hoping for love made her smile. "It must've been. It was only a second, but it was gorgeous." With a sigh, she walked again, with the sea air flowing around her.

CHAPTER FIVE

She finally unpacked, and felt she'd restored some order to her world. Then she walked out on the terrace to marvel at the view that would be hers for . . . as long as it was. She hoped to see the dolphin again — it must've been a dolphin, and the sunlight and water that had given it the illusion of shimmering blues and greens.

While she'd thought she'd sit out with her sketch pad on the terrace, she realized she didn't want solitude. Instead, she took her pad and pencils and went out to look for . . . her team.

Sawyer had called them that — a team. And she'd never been a part of one before. It felt good, even oddly comforting. Remembering, as part of that team, she was likely in charge of dinner, she went to the kitchen first to consider her options.

She wished she knew how to make some traditional Greek meal, but failing that, she could do a pasta dish she often made herself at home, as it was quick and easy, and it appeared she had everything she needed at hand.

Logically she'd quadruple what she normally did, but that didn't take into account two of the four were men, and Riley ate like a starving wolf.

"So just make a lot," Sasha told herself. And it if didn't work, well, someone else could be in charge of the kitchen.

She stepped outside, just breathed in, wondered if she'd be allowed to cut some flowers for her room, for the house. She recognized lemon trees as the yellow fruit basked in the sun, and the dusky leaves of the olive, the orange trees. But others were beyond her, including the cactus with large flat leaves and gorgeous blooms.

She took a moment to sketch one, then wandered on, past the vegetable garden, the coop where chickens clucked and pecked in their little fenced yard. Past shrubs of rosemary, toward the pool where she saw Riley and Sawyer in what appeared to be an animated conversation as they sat facing each other on white padded chaise lounges.

The big white dog sprawled under the shade of Riley's chair and slept.

Sawyer wore cutoffs and a golden tan, and

Riley a red tank-style bathing suit. Still talking, Riley waved at her, gestured to come on out.

"We're debating Khan."

"Genghis Khan?"

"No. Khan Noonien Singh."

"I don't know who that was — is."

Star Trek.

"Oh. I saw the movie."

"The, as in singular? Which one?" Riley demanded.

"I'm not sure. It was on cable."

On a sigh, Riley patted the space beside her. "Girl needs an education."

"Want a beer?" Sawyer gestured toward a wide stone table Sasha saw held a barbecue pit. "There's a fridge back there. We stocked it from the kitchen."

"No, I'm fine. It's wonderful out here, but it feels too cool yet for swimming."

"Not for hardy souls, right, Sawyer? Plus it's solar heated." She angled her head to look at the sketch. "Prickly pear."

"Is that what it is?"

"Yeah. It should fruit in a couple months."

"What do they taste like?"

"Mmm. Watermelon, sort of."

Sasha let out a quick laugh. "Watermelon on a cactus. As strange as mythical stars. I saw a dolphin — I think — in the water. In

118

what Bran said they call Canal d'Amour."

"Going for a swim to look for your one true love?" With a quick smirk, Riley lifted her beer.

"I don't think so, but I may paint it."

"Might be fun to try it — the swim," Sawyer explained. "We mate for life in my family, so maybe I'd run into her."

"Huh. Same with mine. They mate for life. Which is why," Riley said definitely, "I wouldn't risk the swim. I find my mate, that's it. No more playing around."

She rose, stretched. "What about you, Sash? The field or the goalposts?"

"What?"

"Playing the field or the touchdown with love?" Sawyer interpreted.

"I . . ." She saw Bran, in black trunks and white unbuttoned shirt, crossing the lawn. Hearts did skip beats, she thought. It wasn't just a cliché. "I don't really think about it."

"Everybody thinks about it," Riley claimed. "I'm going back in." She dove off the side, surfaced sleek as a seal, then rolled to float. "Hey, Irish, water's good. Take advantage. We'll be hunting and scouting and digging before much longer."

"You're right about that."

"And not much time for a beer by the pool." Sawyer set his down. "I'm on pool

119

maintenance, unless you want it."

"It's all yours." As Sawyer jumped in with Riley, Bran shrugged out of his shirt. "Can't swim?"

"Of course I can swim."

"Good."

He plucked her right up.

Her utterly shocked "Don't!" had Apollo bellying out to dance and bark.

"Do!" Riley shouted as Sasha tried to wiggle free. "Dare you."

"Oh, well then, she dared me."

"This isn't funny. Just —"

Whatever she'd started to say ended on a scream as he got a running start and jumped in with her.

She surfaced, sputtered.

"It's pretty funny," Sawyer said.

With no choice, Sasha tread water. "It's *cold*!"

"You're just not used to it yet." To help her along with that, Bran went under, and pulled her with him.

"Better?" he asked when she came up again.

"What are you, twelve?"

"The man who loses the boy is a sad and serious man."

"Irish philosophy?" Sasha responded to it by shoving the heel of her hand through the water, and sending it into his face.

Then she just sank down because it was pretty nice after all.

Her pasta dish turned out well, if she did say so herself. She might not want to be responsible for planning and cooking meals routinely, but there was some satisfaction in seeing the enormous amount she'd made vanish down to a small container of leftovers.

They didn't talk of the stars until Riley broke out a bottle of limoncello.

"I did lunch, Sasha did dinner — and kudos on that — so I'd say you boys are on cleanup."

"Seems fair, and we'll deal with that," Bran said. "But I'd say it's time we knuckled down a bit and got serious about why we're all here."

"But we're not all here," Sasha pointed out. "Until we are, I don't think we stand much of a chance of finding anything."

"Doesn't mean we can't scout the area," Riley pointed out. "I've got some maps, and some ideas on that."

"Standing still's doing nothing," Bran pointed out. "If we hadn't been moving forward, we might not have met Sawyer. And now we're four."

"Like I said, this is the first time I've looked with a team, and the first time I've really felt close." Sawyer studied the liquid in his shot glass, then knocked it back. "Nice kick. A couple of good meals, a few hours by the pool, and a kick-ass roof over my head, that's all pretty great. But you don't find without looking."

"You got it." Riley tossed back her shot as well, poured herself and Sawyer a second. "So I say we break out the maps first thing in the morning, make a plan, and pull on our hiking boots." She toasted with her drink. "Time for some spelunking."

Noting Sasha's expression, Bran gave her hand a pat. "Are you claustrophobic then?"

"Not so far, but then I've never spent any time in caves. But I know caves make me think of bats."

"Bats are enormously cool," Riley told her. "And contrary to popular belief, aren't blind. And don't go for your hair."

"She uses the form, twisting it to her needs. And the dark is hers. The dank and shadowy places, and what lives there she rules. Banished from the light, she craves it, and covets the flame. The light to extinguish, and the flame to burn until there's nothing but the dark, and ashes."

Her eyes cleared, and her breath came

back with a force that burned her throat.

"Okay, wow. Are you all right?" Sawyer asked her.

"She'll be fine." Bran spoke sharply as he gripped Sasha's hand. "Look at me. Look at me now, and listen. You're still trying to block it, and so when it comes it gives you pain. You have to stop mistrusting yourself and your gift."

"I don't want it."

"Well, you have it, don't you, so steady up."

"Hey," Sawyer began, as Bran's tone was harsh, and Sasha pale. But Riley shook her head, warned him off.

"You don't know what it's like to have something in you that takes you over."

"And you don't know what it's like to embrace it, to learn to use it instead of trying to deny it so it uses you."

"My own father walked away because he couldn't live with it, with me. Every time I've tried to get close to anyone, this *gift* has pushed through and ruined it, so I have no one."

"You have us. And we won't be walking away." He spoke briskly, without a hint of sympathy. "But it's you who does the walking, from what I can see. Away from yourself."

"We wouldn't be here if I hadn't come."

"Now that's exactly right. You should think about that, deal with that instead of weeping over what brought you."

Too shocked and angry for words, Sasha shoved away from the table and walked away.

"You might go after her," Bran said to Riley. "See that she takes something for the headache she's brought on herself."

"Yeah." She rose. "Take a swipe at me like that? I hit back."

"You might be the one to teach her to do the same."

"Maybe I am."

When she walked off, Sawyer shook his head. "That was harsh, man."

"I know it." And left him with a hint of a headache himself. "It's harsher yet, to my mind, for her to make herself ill. We are what we are, don't you think, mate?"

Sawyer considered his second shot. "For some, maybe most of some, being different from everybody else is tough."

"Is it?" Bran smiled, lifted his own glass. "I find being unique is something to celebrate and respect. Until she does, what she has only hurts her." He turned the little glass of limoncello in his fingers, drank it. "We'd best clean this up, and do it right, or we'll be unlikely to get another meal out of her."

"She matters to you, beyond what she is, and what we're after."

With considerable care, Bran set the little glass down again. "She's a beautiful woman with a damaged heart and a bright courage she doesn't recognize. Yes, she matters, beyond, or I wouldn't have spoken to her as I did."

"Okay then."

Once they'd dealt with the dishes, set the kitchen to rights, Bran went outside, did a couple of circuits around the house. A kind of border patrol, he thought. But he saw nothing but moon and stars and sea, heard no whispering of bat wings, only the rush of water against land and rock.

Pausing, he looked up at Sasha's room, saw it was dark, her terrace doors closed. He hoped she slept, and peacefully. And hoped to Christ she didn't come knocking on his door in the night looking beautiful and dreamy. It had been one thing to share her bed, in sleep, the night before. But he accepted doing so again would severely test his will.

She was far too appealing, in all manner of ways.

He considered options, discarded them.

And knowing sleep wouldn't come calling soon, he went back in. There was work he could do while the others slept.

Sawyer sent long, detailed emails home as he did whenever he was able. He tried reading, gave it up, and tried to work. But he was far too restless.

A walk on the beach, he decided. Alone.

For a man who enjoyed companionship, he was often alone and knew how to occupy himself and his mind. He pulled on a jacket, as the night was cool, went out through the terrace doors and down. He could appreciate the fragrance in the air, the way the clouds sailed over stars and moon, the steady heartbeat of the sea.

And could be grateful those clouds were thin, and the moon bright enough to light the cliff steps.

He considered his companions, as he'd written about them.

Riley, sharp, solid, and smart. A traveler, somewhat like him, and a woman who could handle herself. A scholar, but far from fusty. They shared a passionate attachment to science fiction, fantasy, and graphic novels.

Bran? Clever, charming when he wanted to be, and plenty mysterious. Protective. He might've been hard on Sasha after dinner, but he'd been truthful when he'd said she mattered. Sawyer sensed Bran would do whatever needed to be done to protect someone who mattered.

And Sasha. Talented — gifted — and conflicted. Unsure of her footing, but she still walked the walk. So he'd give Bran points for insight. She had courage she didn't recognize. And, Sawyer thought, was certainly the magnet that had drawn them all together.

He wasn't entirely sure where he fit. After ten years of traveling, he could tell them where the stars weren't. But the world was a very big place.

He had theories, and he'd come to them through trial, error, and experience. Having someone like Sasha should give them better direction. Maybe.

The other two? They had secrets. But then again, so did he.

A few hours, some drinks, and a couple of meals together didn't build the sort of trust it took to share secrets. He wasn't sure, yet, what would.

So, it was wait and see.

He liked the deserted beach, the moonlight floating on the water, the whoosh and whisper of waves. Those waves tempted him to take a quick swim. He'd freeze his ass off, but it might finish clearing his head so he could sleep.

He decided to walk back, and if the urge was still there, strip down and dive in — closer to the cliff steps, the house, and the warmth.

And he saw her, standing on the edge of sea and shore. She looked out at the water, the thin white dress she wore swirling around her knees in the night wind. What seemed like miles of dark hair tumbled down her back.

The sketch, he thought. Sasha's sketch, alive and in person.

He shouldn't have wondered, but he did. Shouldn't have been surprised, but he was. He started up the beach toward her, kept his eyes on her in case she vanished like a dream.

Instead, she turned toward him, and he saw her face in the splashing moonlight. One of the six in the sketches, one who had stood beside him in the first sketch they'd shown him on the side of the road.

A face made out of dreams, he thought as she smiled and walked toward him. Stunning. Beyond beautiful. Wide eyes tipped just a bit at the corners, a wide, full mouth curved now in what seemed to be both delight and welcome. Skin that looked soft, smooth, and pale gold in the moonlight. Tall and willowy in a thin white dress that flowed in the breeze.

He stopped a foot away from her because with all he'd seen, all he'd experienced, he'd never looked on anything like her.

She said, "Hello," with a hint of a laugh on the word.

"Yeah, hi. Where did you come from?"

"I've been here, for a little while. And you came." Reaching out, she took his hand. "I hoped you would."

"Do you know me?"

She only smiled. "I don't know your name."

"Sawyer."

"Sawyer." She repeated it, carefully. "My name is Annika. I come — I came," she corrected, "to help you find the stars. Will you take me with you?"

Just like that, he thought.

"Yeah, I think I'd better. We're up there." He pointed up to the villa, where — as in the sketch — a single light glowed.

"I have some things."

"Where?"

"I'll get them."

She ran up the beach, the movements almost like a dance, then with a swirl of white dress and long dark hair, she disappeared behind the rocks.

"Wait. Shit." He ran after her, cursing himself for being so dumbfounded he'd frozen.

But she came out again, carrying two large bags.

Not luggage, exactly, he noted, but two sacks, he supposed, both brightly patterned with trees, flowers, birds, and secured with the sort of clasps you might see on treasure chests.

"Let me get those."

"You take one, I take one, and the weight is half. The steps are wonderful!" With her one bag, she raced for them. "They go so high. We'll be closer to the sky."

"Be careful, they're steep."

"Someone always says be careful." She beamed at him as they started up. "Annika, you are too reckless. But I don't think so. I only want to try everything."

Not reckless, he thought, going off with some strange guy in the middle of the night? If not reckless, then way too trusting.

"Oh." At the top of the steps she paused, laid a hand on her heart. "This is home for you? It's very beautiful."

"It's borrowed. I mean we're just staying here for a while."

"I can smell the flowers." She trailed her

hand along flowering shrubs. "And the trees, and the grass. Look at this."

She stopped to trail her fingers over a low-hanging lemon. "It's so cool and smooth."

"A lot of lemon trees around here."

"Lemon," she repeated, as she had his name.

"I didn't bring a key, so we'll go around and up the back."

She looked at everything as they walked, went up the terrace steps with him without protest.

Since the light remained on in Bran's room, Sawyer gave a rap on the terrace doors.

Still in his jeans and T-shirt, Bran opened one of the doors.

"Look who I found."

"Hello." Annika smiled at him.

"Annika, this is Bran Killian."

"Brankillian, hello."

"Happy to meet you, Annika."

"I like happy."

"Sure and who doesn't? Best take her down — the kitchen, I guess, as this may call for either wine or coffee. I'll get the others."

"I like wine," she said as Sawyer led her down the terrace toward his open doors. "Will I have some?"

"Yeah, we're loaded."

"Oh, this is very pretty. All the pictures and the little things. And the bed. Is the bed soft?"

She dropped her bag and sat on the side of it, bounced, then flopped back, arms spread. "It is!"

She flung her arms back over her head, wiggled down. The gesture went straight to his loins. Down boy, he ordered.

"We should go on down."

"Down?" She sat up, and for the first time looked distressed.

"Downstairs," he explained. "So you can meet the others."

"The others, yes." She bounced off the bed, offered her hand.

He led her out, started down the stairs while she tried to look at everything at once.

"I had the same reaction when I first got here. It's a hell of a place."

"Hell of a place," she repeated, her tone awed.

When they got to the kitchen, she released his hand, ran hers over the refrigerator. "It shines." After tugging on the handle, she let out a long *ahh.*

"Are you hungry?"

"Yes! It's very cold inside."

"Professional grade. We've got some pasta

left over from dinner. It's good stuff." He pulled out the container. "Go ahead and sit down. I'll heat it up."

"Thank you very much." She sat at the table, running her fingers over the top. "This is very pretty, too. Everything is."

She watched him dump the pasta onto a plate, stick the plate in a microwave, punch buttons.

Before she could speak, the others came in, so she said, "Hello."

"And then there were five," Riley said. "Annika?"

"Yes! Hello."

Riley reached in the wine fridge. "I guess this calls for a bottle. Riley. Riley Gwin. What's the rest of yours?"

"The rest of mine?"

"Name. Your full name?" After a long beat of silence, Riley dug out the corkscrew. "As in first and last. Riley, first name, Gwin, last name. And we have Sasha."

"Riggs." Studying the newcomer, Sasha selected wineglasses. "And you met Bran."

"And Sawyer." Annika beamed at him. "King."

Her eyes went huge, her voice dropped to a reverent whisper. "You're a king?"

As Riley snorted, Sawyer looked into those wide eyes, sea green, flecked with gold. "My last name's King."

"I'm Annika, first name . . . Waters, last name. Annika Waters," she said more definitely. "Hello."

"I think she's a little high," Riley said to Bran in an undertone.

"We climbed the steps to the house. It's very high."

"Good ears. You been doing some drugs, Annika?"

"No. Am I supposed to?"

"No." Sasha sat across from her, set the portfolio on the table. "Where are you from?"

"My — family — we go many places."

"Originally? Where were you born?"

"I don't know. I was only a baby."

Laughing now, Sawyer set the plate in front of Annika. "Got you there, Sasha."

Annika picked up the fork, turned it to study, and very carefully stabbed a piece of penne. She slipped it into her mouth, then pressed her hands to her lips as she laughed. "Warm." She speared a piece of cherry tomato, then a black olive. Closed her eyes a moment as she ate, then opened them, and ate more.

"It's good stuff," she said. She lifted the glass Riley had given her, sipped. "It's good stuff," she repeated. "I like wine, and this food. Thank you."

"You're welcome." Sasha opened the portfolio, took out the sketch of all six, then slid it across the table.

Annika let out a delighted gasp, traced her finger over her own face, then Sawyer's. "It's a picture. This is I, and this is Sawyer. Riley, Sasha, Brankillian. Bran," she corrected. "Everyone is so pretty! But this one isn't here?"

"No."

"Where is he?"

"We don't know. Do you know him?"

She shook her head. "I like my hat. Where did I get it?"

Rolling her eyes, Riley sat. "Why are you here?"

"Sawyer brought me."

"No, Annika, why are you here, on Corfu. Why did you come with Sawyer?"

"Because Sawyer is . . . the one who came. I'm here to help find the stars."

"You know about the Stars of Fortune?" Bran asked.

"Yes, everyone does."

"Everyone?" Riley demanded.

"In my . . . family. And the one who reads fates told me I would help find them. If I was —" She broke off, ate more pasta. "Willing. It's a search. That's not the word,

135

but like it. It's a . . ." She circled a finger in the air. "Qu-qu-"

"Quest?" Bran suggested.

"Yes! Thank you. It's a quest of danger, so I must be willing. I am. I came. They must be found, and taken back."

"Taken back?" Riley repeated. "Where?"

Annika blinked in surprise. "Why, to the Island of Glass."

"That's a myth."

"I'm apology. A mist?"

"Myth. A fable," Riley added. "Usually a traditional story regarding the history of a people, and often containing supernatural beings."

"I like stories. May I have more wine?"

"I've never heard of this." Sasha looked around. "I can see everyone else has. What is the Island of Glass?"

"A mythical island that appears when and where it wills," Bran told her. "A place out of time. A world to itself."

"Like Brigadoon?"

"No." Riley shook her head. "Brigadoon appeared every one hundred years like clockwork, same place. While in Brigadoon only a day would pass. I like a good myth — obviously — and there are a lot of great stories built around the Island of Glass. But it doesn't exist."

"It is real. And it is always there, but only a few have seen it, only a few have been allowed. The one who reads the fates does not lie. When we find the three stars, we must take them back to the place they were born."

"You're saying the stars were created on the Island of Glass." Riley narrowed her eyes.

"Yes. By the goddesses three. Celene, Luna, Arianrhod, as gifts for the new queen, who is Aegle, the radiant."

Riley leaned back, drummed her fingers. "Where did you study?"

"I studied very hard." Annika's face lit like the sun. "Many places. I like to learn new things, and old things, and all things."

"Who's Nerezza?"

"You should not speak her name in the night." Annika looked toward the windows. "Or risk summoning her."

"Bunk. Who is she?"

"She is the dark one, the mother of lies. She must never have the stars. I don't like to fight, but I would fight with you to keep them from her. We are together." She pointed to the sketch. "And you are Sawyer's friends, so you are mine."

"Just like that?"

"You are very curious." Annika leaned

137

toward Riley. "I am very curious, too. So we will be friends. And I will help. This has been foretold."

Riley glanced at Sasha. "I can't piss on foretelling. But we'll see what we see. How —"

"Riley," Sawyer interrupted. "Give it a rest. Do you have any questions, Annika?"

"I have so many. My mother says I'm made of questions. But it's enough to be here for now. I'm very tired. Can I sleep in the soft bed?"

"Still a couple to pick from. I'll take you up, and you can decide which room you want."

"I won't sleep in your bed?"

"What? No." Sawyer caught Bran's amused look, rubbed the back of his neck. "Everybody gets their own room."

"I'll take her up." Riley rose. "Since we're going to be friends."

"Thank you. And thank you for the good stuff and the wine."

After Riley took her out, Sawyer lifted his arms. "She was just there, standing on the beach. Like in the sketch. Just there."

"And now she's here." Bran looked at Sasha. "What did you read?"

"Joy. So much joy I nearly burst with it myself. And an incredible sweetness. Is she holding something back? Yes, I'm sure she is. But everything she said about the stars, about this island, she believes is truth."

"Clearly English isn't her first language," Bran speculated. "But if she needs to keep where she's from to herself for now, it's a small thing."

He picked up the sketch. "She's meant to be here, with us, and so she is."

"Five down," Sawyer said, "one to go."

"Let's hope the one to go waits at least until morning. I want some sleep." Bran turned to Sasha. "You're tired yourself."

"I'm not used to introductions and pow-wows at nearly two in the morning."

"I'll wash this up." Sawyer picked up the plate. "Go ahead. I'm right behind you."

Bran took Sasha's hand as they walked out and, testing, brought it to his lips. "Not angry anymore?"

"Oh, I'm still angry. I can put it aside for the big picture."

"I get angry myself when I see you making yourself sick."

"It's my problem, my business."

He flicked a nosegay of lavender out of the air, handed it to her at her door.

"Magic flower tricks don't charm me."

"They do. But more important, you're my problem and my business now as well."

Cupping a hand behind her head, he pulled her in, took her mouth in a quick, warm warning of a kiss. "You'll have to deal with that as well. Good night, *fáidh.*"

She stepped quickly into her room, shut the door before she did something insane like pull him inside with her.

It hadn't been a lover's kiss, she told herself, as she traced a finger over her own lips. Not brotherly either. It was more . . . making a point.

That's what she needed to remember.

He wasn't attracted to her. They were teammates, and he was trying to keep her in line.

Well, she'd keep herself in line.

But she slept with the lavender on her pillow, and slept without dreams.

CHAPTER SIX

Sasha awakened to sun diamonds sparkling on blue water, and wondered at the turn her life had taken. Whatever came after, moments like this offered wild beauty. The idea of setting up her easel, trying to interpret that beauty on canvas had her pushing up in bed. Until she remembered she was part of a team, and the team had an agenda.

A team of five now, she thought, with the addition of the gorgeous and quirky Annika Waters.

She lifted the little nosegay from her pillow, held it to her nose. Immediately she was thrown back into that brief kiss, felt the warmth, the light pressure on her lips.

A team, she reminded herself. Not a romance, but a mission.

Though she'd do her duty, she gave herself the pleasure of throwing open her terrace doors, stepping out into that wild beauty. She smelled fruit and flowers and sea, gave herself the assignment of finding a watering can so she could tend the terrace pots, all filled with spearing and tumbling flowers in breathlessly hot colors.

She leaned on the iron railing, scanned the empty beach, then saw Annika topping the cliff steps. She wore a pink dress today, pale and pretty with a skirt that floated around her thighs as she started across the grass in bare feet.

She paused every few feet to sniff flowers, stroke leaves. When she looked up, saw Sasha, she beamed a smile, waved.

"Hello!"

"Good morning. You're up and around early."

"I don't want to miss things, and I needed to swim."

In what? Sasha nearly asked, then decided it wasn't her business.

"Everyone was sleeping, but you're awake now."

"Yes, I am. I'm just going to get a shower and dress. I'll be down soon."

Sasha basked in the shower, wondered what it would take to have body jets installed in her shower at home — and thought whatever it took, it would be worth it.

Considering the agenda, she put on jeans, a tank, and a camp shirt, then laced up her hiking boots. She reordered her pack, lightening her load. And though it embarrassed her, even with no one to see, she took a sprig of lavender from the clutch and pressed it between the pages of the journal she'd bought for the journey.

Muttering at herself, she banded her hair back in a tail, and went downstairs.

She heard voices as she approached the kitchen, and caught the morning scents of coffee and bacon. Bran said he'd take breakfast, she remembered, and put on the casual smile she'd practiced in the mirror.

She walked in to see Annika frowning down at a mug of coffee. "Why doesn't it taste the way it smells?"

"Too strong, is it? I don't see the use of coffee unless it's strong enough to stand up and dance, so I've a habit of brewing it that way."

Bran stood at the stove, scooping bacon from the frying pan with a fork, tossing it onto a plate covered with paper towels. Casual, Sasha thought, and strolled in. "The stronger the better."

Annika turned, held out the mug. "You would like it?"

"Thanks. There's juice in the fridge if you'd rather." At Annika's blank smile, Sasha walked over, got out the pitcher.

Then, as the woman seemed so pleasantly helpless, a glass.

Annika took a testing sip. "Oh! This is very nice. I like it much more than the coffee. I'm apology, Bran."

"Sorry. You're sorry," he corrected. "And no need to be."

"When did you learn English?" Keeping it casual, Sasha leaned back against the counter.

"English?"

"The language."

"Oh. I know this one and some others. But sometimes the words are wrong. You can tell me when they are, and I can learn. Can you cook, like Bran?"

"I can cook."

"You can teach me. It looks fun and smells nice."

"Sure, I guess. But for now, maybe you could set the table."

Annika pointed. "The table."

"The one outside. We could have breakfast outside, on the patio. So you could set that table."

"Where should I set it?"

With a laugh, Sasha put her coffee aside. "You could put the plates, the flatware, the napkins out. We're five," she said and chose five plates from the cabinet. "So five plates, five sets of flatware." She opened a drawer. "And the napkins are in the top drawer of that breakfront."

"I can set the table." Annika rattled around in the silverware drawer, counting under her breath. When she had her supplies, carried them out, Sasha turned to Bran.

"She never answered the question."

"Evaded it, charmingly." He scooped potatoes he'd chipped and boiled out of the pot with a slotted spoon, dumped them in the frying pan. Grease snapped and sizzled. "She's clever."

"Part of me wants to pin her down, and the other part wants to watch it all evolve. I know there's no harm in her."

"Then the evolution might be more interesting. How did you sleep?"

"Fine. In fact, great. You?"

"The same."

To keep busy, Sasha unwrapped the second — and last — round of bread, began to slice some for toast. "It looks like it'll be a good day for hiking, though if we're going to be exploring caves I guess it doesn't matter much. I didn't pack a flashlight — never thought of it, but —"

The knife clattered on the table as Bran spun her around.

"What —"

"Last night wasn't enough."

His mouth took hers. Then came the whirlwind.

Not the almost brotherly brush of lips, but a long, deep possession that spun everything she was into greed and need. For an instant, the storm blew in, all whipping wind, roaring thunder, and that bold, bright flash of lightning.

She wanted to leap into it, ride it, no matter where it took her.

But the risk, and the pain. She already knew the pain, knew it could shatter her beyond repair.

She pressed a hand to his chest, and he gave her a breath. His eyes — and she swore she saw worlds, wild worlds, swirling behind them — locked on hers.

"We're a team," she managed, and the hot, dangerous glint shifted into what might have been humor.

"That we are, *fáidh,* but you're the only one I want for this."

He lifted her to her toes and took her again.

He hadn't been able to pry her out of his mind, to drain this singular desire out of his blood. There were countless reasons he should resist, to keep her as friend and teammate only. And only one reason to ignore all the rest.

That simple touch of lips the night before had lit something in him. He wanted to see how hot it might burn.

And she called to him, her wounded and courageous heart. Surely there was purpose there.

But beyond purpose, beyond reason, the fire burned.

"Oh, hell."

He eased back at Riley's voice, but kept his eyes on Sasha's as Riley wandered in, Apollo happily at her heels.

"I figured you'd circle around that for at least another day or two." She went straight to the coffee, grabbed a mug. "If you want privacy, try one of the bedrooms." She poured her coffee, all but inhaled the first sip. "I'll take the dog — the care and feeding thereof. And I nominate the new girl for chicken duty. Beginning after coffee. When's breakfast?"

"Shortly." Bran ran his hands down from Sasha's shoulders, along her arms, then stepped back to the stove to put the pan he'd had the wit to take off the flame back again.

"Good. Starved."

"I . . . need a watering can."

Sasha turned quickly, aimed for the doors.

Riley shook her head at Bran, then a long glance at the dog sent Apollo trotting outside. "Office romances, Irish, sticky business and usually get somebody fired."

"Lucky then, isn't it, we're not being paid." He gave the potatoes a turn.

Sasha doubted the morning air would cool her skin, her blood, but she needed a moment just to stand in it, try to settle.

What should she do now? How did she behave now? He'd changed everything. Or no, she admitted, he'd pushed it along the path.

She looked over at the promontory, thought of the storm.

Apollo brushed up to her, nuzzled his great head under her hand. After her absent stroke, he raced off.

She needed to focus, Sasha warned herself. To concentrate on what needed to be done, not what she wished could be. Others depended on her keeping her balance, so —

She glanced over at the sound of laughter, watched Annika run in circles with the dog. She twirled, executing three very impressive cartwheels that had the dog letting out deep, joyful barks.

Sasha couldn't stop the smile, and couldn't stop the wish she could be just that free, just that carelessly happy she'd turn cartwheels on soft spring grass.

With a sigh, she turned toward the table. Stopped dead.

The plates fashioned a tower — four balanced on their rims holding the fifth, with a glass filled with wildflowers atop it.

She'd balanced the flatware as well, crossing pieces like swords to form a kind of arbor, and under it grass, clover, buttercups twined together. A shrubbery, Sasha realized, fascinated and charmed.

She'd draped napkins around the tall salt and pepper mills, like capes, and formed more grass into crowns to top them. Other napkins flowed out — bright blue. The sea, Sasha thought.

Glowing from her game with Apollo, Annika ran back.

"I set the table."

"I see. It's wonderful. A castle by the sea."

"The rulers are giants," Annika began. "Sawyer!" There was a joy — like cartwheels — in the single word.

"Yeah, morning." He came out barefoot, gulping coffee, then studied the table presentation. "Wow."

"Do you like it?"

"Very cool."

"Breakfast's up," Riley announced, carry-

149

ing out a platter loaded with bacon, eggs, potatoes, toast. She set it down, studied Annika's work.

"Nice."

Bran followed her out with the pitcher of juice, a pot of coffee. They all stood, studying the castle.

"Is it wrong?" Annika asked.

"Not at all," Bran told her. "In fact it's lovely and fun. We're all wishing we didn't have to take it down so we can eat."

"Oh, I can make another. The food smells good."

"Okay." Riley rubbed her hands together. "Let's sack the castle."

Once they'd set the table in a more mundane fashion and passed around the platter, Riley turned to the dog, who sat, watching hopefully.

"That's yours," she told him, pointing to the bowl of kibble she'd set out. He heaved a sigh filled with disappointment, but moved off to eat. "So, we'll look over the maps, but my best sense is to head south, follow the river into the hills. My intel says there's a cave up there, multichambered, largely unexplored. The locals call it Anasa tou Diavolou. The Devil's Breath. Sounds promising," she added, forking up some eggs.

"What about underwater caves?" Sasha

began, and Riley nodded as she ate.

"Got some on my list. But we're going to need a boat, some gear. I'm working on that. Anybody know how to handle a boat? I'm okay with it, but I'm better with a canoe or a kayak."

"Depends on the boat," Sawyer put in.

"What sort of gear?" Sasha wanted to know.

"Snorkeling for certain, scuba most likely."

"I've never done any scuba diving."

"We've got a pool to practice in if we need to. I'm certified — or was. Probably still am." Riley shrugged. "Maybe we'll get lucky on land. In any case, we'll eliminate areas, and get some scuba practice in." She gestured at Annika with her fork. "That dress isn't going to work for the sort of hiking we'll do today."

"You don't like it?"

"Looks good on you, but you need pants. Jeans or cargoes to protect your legs. A jacket, a hat, a backpack. And hiking boots."

"I don't have those things."

"I was afraid of that." Riley looked under the table at Annika's bare feet. "I've got spare boots, but your feet are longer than mine."

"Looks like a trip into the village to outfit her," Sawyer said. "It shouldn't take long."

"Been on many shopping trips with women, mate?" Bran asked him.

"Shopping." Annika bounced in her chair. "You buy things. I have coins."

"No trouble understanding how shopping works," Bran added. "Coins?"

"I have many coins. I'll get them."

When she raced off, Riley turned, jabbed her fork toward Bran. "You'll eat that insult to my species, Irish. I can get her outfitted inside twenty minutes."

"Bet you a fiver you can't."

"Done. So into the village, deal with that. We can drive south from there for the first ten, twelve kilometers, but we're off-road after that."

"I'd like a look at your maps, if it's all the same to you, before we head out."

Sawyer nodded at Bran, then Riley. "I'm going to second that."

"No problem. Nothing to say on this, Sasha?"

"I'm still stuck on Devil's Breath. Anyway, I can read a map well enough, but I'm pretty sure one cave will strike me the same as any other."

Annika came back, hauling a royal-blue drawstring bag with gold braiding. She set it on the table with a little *oof,* where it thudded heavily.

"My coins."

"She meant it literally." On a laugh, Sawyer got up to walk to the end of the table, look into the bag. *"Yobanny v rot!"*

"What are those words?" Annika demanded.

"It's Russian." Riley got up herself to circle around, looked into the bag. "And to borrow a phrase. *Yobanny v rot.* Mind?" she said to Annika, and without waiting for an answer, tipped the bag onto the table so part of the contents poured out.

Gold coins and silver, copper and bronze. Many, even with her untrained eye, Sasha recognized as old. Possibly ancient.

"We have here a lot of euros," Riley began, "your pounds, punts, lire, drachma, yen, ducats, francs — Swiss and French — U.S. and Canadian coins, halfpennies, and yo-ho-ho, me hearties, your pieces of eight."

"Pirate coins?" The notion had Sasha getting up for a closer look. "Like this?"

"Yeah, a reasonable shitload of them, from what I see. They'd be worth about a hundred bucks each."

"Each." Sasha turned the oddly shaped coin in her hand.

"Each, if they're in decent condition and the inscription's legible, like the one you're holding. And this?"

Riley did a butt wiggle. "This is a Carlos and Johanna. Gold doubloon, stamped 1521. A collector would pay a grand easy for this."

She poked through more as Annika stood back smiling in delight.

"Hell of a collection here," Riley muttered. "And you shouldn't keep it in a sack like this. Christ, this is a silver tetradrachm, circa 420 BC, probably worth a few thousand easy. And . . . *Gamoto.* Greek for holy shit." She held up a gold coin. "Do you have a clue what this is?" she demanded of Annika.

"A coin."

"See this guy on here, the one wearing the laurel? See this name? This is Augustus Caesar, founder of the Roman Empire. And this cow on the back — it's a heifer. This coin? It was made somewhere between 27 and 18 B fucking C. It's worth millions."

"Of dollars?" Sawyer managed.

"There are only a handful of these known to exist. One went up for auction a couple years back. Went for, I think it was about fifteen, and yeah, brother, that's freaking million."

"It will buy hiking boots."

Riley stared at Annika as if she'd grown gossamer wings. "You could buy a small third-world country with what's in this sack, and I've only skimmed over a part of it. Where the hell did you get this?" She shook the gold coin.

"I found it."

"You . . . found it."

"Yes. It's fun to find things, and I like pretty things. Do you like it?"

"I freaking love it."

"You can have it."

"Say what?"

"You can keep it. A gift."

Seeing Sawyer about to speak, Riley held up a finger. "You're going to just give it to me."

"You like it, so a gift. For a friend."

"Riley, you can't —"

She cut Sawyer off with a look. "What do you take me for? Can I have another one instead?"

"One you like better? Yes, you pick. Everyone should pick one, the one they like better."

"I'd like this." Riley picked an old drachma. "Ten, maybe fifteen bucks," she told Sawyer. "I'm going to keep it with me, for good luck. Thanks."

"You're welcome. Sawyer, you pick! You came for me. Pick something pretty."

He kept it simple, picked out a U.S.

quarter. "For good luck."

"Sasha is next. Pick one!"

"Take one of the pieces of eight," Riley told her. "You know you want to."

"It's too —"

"Believe me, she can spare it. Go ahead."

"For luck then. Thank you, Annika."

"Now, Bran. Breakfast was very, very good. Pick one."

For sentiment, he took an Irish punt, then kissed her cheek. "You're a fine, good friend, darling. Now, will you trust me with your coins, as I'd like to put them somewhere safe."

"I trust my friends. You're my friend."

"And you're a rare flower. Let's get these back in the bag here."

"The Augustus," Riley began.

"It's handled it so far. I'll put these away, Annika, and today we'll buy you your hiking boots and whatever else there is. A gift from us."

"Oh, thank you."

He hefted the bag, looked at Sawyer, Riley, Sasha. "Trust me with it?"

"You wouldn't break her trust," Sasha said.

"Make it right and tight, Irish." Riley blew out a breath when he nodded and walked back into the house. "Hey, Sawyer, how about you and Annika handle the KP. Sash and I will deal with the chickens today."

"Sure. Let's clear the table, get the dishes done."

"Then we'll go shopping?"

"Looks like."

Riley gestured to Sasha, walked out of earshot. "Is she, you know, challenged?"

"Oh, no, it's not that. She's . . . I don't know how else to describe what I get from her. She's pure."

"It's more than that. I'm not saying she's not pure, but she's evading. People just don't find priceless coins on the floor, on the ground, in the back of a drawer. And she had hundreds of coins. Hundreds, and the couple dozen I saw? Even taking out the heifer, she had a tidy little treasure there. Where'd she get it?"

"If you think she stole it, I have to say I don't think she's capable of that sort of dishonesty."

"I don't think she stole them, but, Sash, I make my living finding things, and I'm damn good at it. Nobody's good enough or lucky enough to just find coins like that."

Riley paused at a little shed, pulled out two buckets, scooped feed into one of them.

"She would've given it to me. She'd have been happy to give me that priceless coin, so money doesn't mean a thing to her. There are secrets in there, and likely major ones."

"I know. I know it, but I just don't want to push her to tell us. I'd rather she told us when she's ready to."

Riley angled over a look as they walked past the garden to the clucking chickens. "A lot of people, probably most, get pissed when someone holds something back, then lets it spill."

"I think we're all entitled to judge for ourselves when and if we're ready to tell our secrets. Everyone has them."

"Let's all remember that. Okay, do me a favor?"

"If I can."

"I've got that five riding with Bran that I can get our new girl in, outfitted, and out inside twenty minutes. Help me keep it moving, will you?"

"Sure. What are friends for?" Frowning now, she watched the chickens strut around — and stare at the humans, she thought, with tiny eyes. "I don't know how to feed chickens. Or get eggs from them."

"We'll figure it out."

CHAPTER SEVEN

Riley lost the bet. Despite the team effort, it took twice the time she'd calculated to outfit Annika in practical hiking-wear. She figured she could've gotten herself in and out in a fraction of that time, but then again, she didn't insist on touching every freaking thing first.

Bran simply held out his hand, and she slapped five euros into it. And found it hard to bitch too much as he took out a credit card to pay for Annika's boots and shoes, and the hat he'd snagged for Sasha, as it matched the one she'd drawn on herself in her dream sketch.

"You rich, Irish?"

"I've enough to cover this. And with what we've locked away, she's more than good for it." He glanced over to see Annika holding up a bright pink rash guard, turning this way and that in the mirror while Sawyer just grinned at her.

"Better get her out of here before she decides she needs to try on another two dozen things."

"God, you'd think we were trolling at Saks instead of a sporting goods store. Hey, princess! Let's move out."

"Can we get more? Do they have earrings? I like earrings."

"Some other time. Some help here, Sawyer."

They flanked her, maneuvered her — now clad in boots, cargoes, T-shirt, vest, and hat — to the door.

"I can pitch in with this." Sasha moved up behind Bran.

"Quicker this way, and we can sort it all out later." He picked up the hat, settled it on her head. "Suits you. Why don't you go make sure Annika doesn't drag them into another shop?"

Maybe he was the *fáidh,* Sasha thought as Annika was indeed trying to negotiate her way into a gift shop with a display window full of trinkets.

"We'll come back." Going the direct route, Sasha grabbed Annika's hand and tugged.

"I like shopping. There are so many pretty things." She frowned down at her boots as

160

they walked to the car. "The boots are not pretty."

"Neither is twisting an ankle on a rough trail," Riley declared, and let out a whoosh of relief when they piled in the jeep with Sasha and Sawyer sandwiching Annika between them in the back.

Bran came out, stowed the bags, dropped into the passenger seat.

"Thank you for all my things, even the boots."

Riley punched it, headed out of the village.

"We may have to look into a bigger ride," Sawyer called out over the wind.

"I've got plenty of room." Riley flicked a glance in the rearview mirror, smirked.

"If we do find the guy in Sasha's sketch, no way he's going to fit in here."

"We haven't found him yet. Any feel on that, Sash?"

"I just know we will." She watched the world rush by, and thought how quickly she'd grown used to Riley's speedy driving. "He rides a dragon."

"A what now?"

Sasha shook her head. "I don't know where that came from or what it means. We'll find him, or he'll find us."

Riley turned, headed inland. The land rose

into hills and forests with bright splashes of wildflowers, a blinking flash of a small settlement. Lambs, fluffballs of white, played in olive groves. She could no longer smell the sea, but instead the warm, sun-struck green of cypress and olive.

Riley turned again, onto a spit of a road that slithered and snaked up. And though she hadn't tried to, she felt Annika's heart thunder.

"Are you all right?"

"It's beautiful. The trees are so many."

Yes, they were so many, Sasha thought, and made her think of her little house in the woods. It would be the same when she returned to it. But she wondered if she would be.

Riley pulled off into what was essentially a ditch.

"On foot from here."

Armed with their packs, with Riley, her roughly drawn map and compass on point, they left the road, started west. Sasha found it amazing to cross a field where donkeys cropped at grass and wildflowers. So amazed she didn't have time to worry when one walked over to her, stared.

"Hoping you have something edible to share, I wager." Bran stopped with her, gave the donkey a scratch between his long ears.

"He has such sweet eyes. I wish I had an apple."

"Well, let's see." Bran turned her around, tapped at her pack. When he turned her around again, he held out a small, glossy green apple.

"You really have to show me how to do that."

He smiled as he took out his pocketknife, cut the apple in half. "I might be persuaded. Here, give it to him."

"And the firsts continue. I'm feeding a donkey."

"Then we'd best get moving before his friends come round looking for theirs."

"I feel like Annika. It's all so beautiful."

They walked on, leaving the field for a rough track where brushwood of myrtle and bay tangled, and tall, slim towers of cypress speared among the olives. They passed a jumble of rocks decorated with the sturdy wildflowers that pushed their way through cracks toward the sun.

She felt that way, as if she'd pushed through barriers toward the light.

"You're happy," Bran commented.

"I'm hiking the hills of Greece on a gorgeous spring day. There's so much to see. To smell," she added, dragging her hand over a bush of wild rosemary to send its fragrance rising. "I'm not going to think about where we're going. It's enough just to be here.

"Why did you kiss me?"

She hadn't meant to ask, and hadn't been able to stop the thought from forming into words.

"Well, the usual reasons apply."

She told herself to leave it there, leave it alone. Then thought the hell with it. "You could have kissed Riley or Annika, for the usual reasons."

"That's true enough, isn't it? They're both appealing, attractive, interesting women in their own ways. But I wasn't inclined to kiss them. And now that you've got me thinking about it, I can tell you there's no doubt I'll be inclined again where you're concerned."

He said it so matter-of-factly, she wasn't sure whether to be amused, insulted, or a little afraid.

"Don't you have someone back in Ireland, or New York?"

"I do, of course. But not the way you mean. I've friends on both sides of the ocean, and family as well. But no woman waiting for me to sail home again. If there were, I'd never have put my hands on you, and certainly wouldn't take you to bed."

"I never said I —"

"When you do," he said easily. "There's more here than a hike in the hills, than a quest. Don't you wonder, *fáidh,* what it is?"

She didn't know how to do this, Sasha decided, didn't know how to hold up her end of flirty, sexy conversation. And she quit while she was behind.

"I wonder why Riley's taking the left fork when the cave's to the right."

"Is it then?" Bran asked.

"Riley! It's that way."

Up ahead, Riley stopped and turned. "Map says left."

"But it's right. You can see —" She broke off, stared ahead where she'd clearly seen the dark mouth of the cave under a stone ledge. It simply wasn't there.

"I thought I saw . . ."

"Maybe you did. The seer or the map?" Bran asked the others.

After a moment's hesitation, Riley nodded. "We'll take the right fork."

It offered a harder climb, and didn't that just figure. The grade went steep, and the track rutted and rocky. Yet flowers bloomed, sturdy and stubborn, and a narrow stream, barely a handspan wide, cut its way down through springing green and dusty rock.

A Judas tree bloomed gloriously where the rutted track forked yet again.

"Which way?" Riley asked her.

"I don't —"

"Don't think." Bran laid a hand on her shoulder, featherlight. "Know."

"The left this time. They missed the first fork when they told you. It's to the left, but they didn't see . . ."

What lived inside her spread — arms lifted to pull away a veil.

Sasha's own arms dropped to her sides; her eyes went to cobalt.

"The devil's breath comes through its dripping jaws. In its belly lie the bones of murdered men who scream in the dark, of women who weep for lost children. Only light from fire, from water, from ice, will free them.

"Sorry." She braced against the trunk of the tree while her head spun with visions, with the echo of her own words. "I'm a little dizzy. It came on so fast, like a shove off a cliff."

"Here." Annika offered a bottle. "It's water. It's good."

"Thanks."

"My boots aren't pretty."

"Oh, for Christ's sake —" Riley began.

"But Riley was right. You were right," she said to Riley. "They aren't pretty, but they are strong. And strong is important."

"Yes." Sasha took a steadying breath. "Yes, it is." She handed Annika the bottle. "Thank you." To the left, fear pricked at her skin, tiny little thorns, but she couldn't turn away.

"We're close now."

She followed the track, and her instincts. Her legs ached from the hike, but she ignored the pain. Her lungs labored, but she pushed up the track toward what she feared.

When the sun flashed in her eyes, she blinked the glare away.

Then stood staring at the dark mouth under its wide stone ledge.

"Does everyone see it?" she asked.

"Straight ahead. Good work, Sash." Riley gave her a light punch on the arm. "We'd have gone the wrong way."

"Maybe someone wanted us to," Sawyer suggested. "Bran and I should go in first, get the lay of it."

"You get one really stupid man remark," Riley commented, and made a check mark in the air. "Make another, and I punch your pretty face."

"Then I'll take mine as well, and say he has a point. All five of us go in straightaway," Bran continued, "there's no one out here to get help should something go wrong."

"You've got two minutes." Riley held up

her arm, tapped her watch. "On my mark."

"Into the belly then." Bran moved forward with Sawyer.

Not the belly, Sasha thought. The mouth. The belly lay deeper.

They stepped under the ledge and in. Dark spread ahead, light shone behind, as if they walked out of day into night.

Each pulled out a flashlight, swept the beam.

"Got your dripping jaws right here."

Sawyer shined his light over the thick stalactites dripping with moisture. Over time the wet had formed a small pool behind the tooth curve of stalagmites.

The rhythmic *plop* of water against water echoed like a quiet heartbeat.

"Tight quarters here," Bran noted, "but —"

"Yeah, it opens up. No way of knowing how far back it goes."

"Not from here."

Sawyer scanned the area, shifted his weight. "What are the chances of talking them into staying out while we go back?"

"None. And more, I think however it goes against the instincts, it must be all of us, whatever the risks. Whether the star is here or not, I think it must be all of us."

"Yeah, I know it. I'll give them the come-ahead." But he'd only started back when Riley ducked under the ledge, came in with the others behind her.

"Time's up. There's your jaws, Sasha, as advertised. Devil's Breath. I'm betting that pool throws off a mist, and when it carries outside the mouth of the cave, you've got your breath." Leading with her flashlight, she circled the mouth. "Little low in here for you tall people. More headroom as you go back, at least initially."

She moved through the bars of stone, crouched by the pool. "Not deep, fairly clear. Nothing in there I can see." She glanced over at Sasha.

"All right." Though she dreaded it, Sasha moved to the pool. "I don't see anything, in it or from it."

"Okay. Is everybody up for heading in?" She shook her head as Annika waved her flashlight in a circle, watched the beam.

"It's —"

"Yeah, pretty." She pushed up, and as Bran had already started back, the others followed.

The walls stood no more than six feet apart, but the roof of the cave rose until the men could walk comfortably upright. Noting Sawyer kept Annika close, Sasha decided she didn't have to worry about their playful teammate.

"It's bigger than I imagined," Sasha said, and nearly jumped as her voice echoed.

Bigger, she thought, and darker.

The walls widened, offered two chambers.

"Which way?" Bran asked her. "What does your instinct tell you?" he added when she hesitated.

"To the right. But —"

"To the right it is."

"Hold on." Riley dug chalk out of her pack, marked the wall of the chamber. "Always good to know where you've been."

The chamber opened, higher and wider yet. Stalactites, stalagmites, and the columns they formed when they met glimmered in the light in golds and reds and umbers.

"Like jewels," Annika said.

"Different minerals in the stone." Riley studied the area. "But I'll give you pretty here."

Sasha played her light over a column, moved to it. "You need to see this. It looks like a woman. Look, her head, shoulders, body, all beautifully proportioned. Her face — eyes, nose, mouth. It's not painted or carved. How could the stone have formed this way?"

She stood, long, dark hair, lithe form in flowing robes. Her eyes looked down, as if watching them. One hand, lifted, gestured to the back of the cave. The other held a globe.

"No way that's a natural formation," Riley said. "It had to be made."

"It's not painted," Sasha repeated.

"There are other ways." Bran aimed his light where the figure pointed. "There's a ledge there, and an opening above it."

"I'll go in, scout it out," Sawyer began, then caught the movement. "Riley."

"It's what I do," she reminded him, and boosted herself onto the ledge and through.

"Hell. All of us then. Stay close," he ordered Sasha.

Annika went in behind them, glanced back at the stone figure. "I don't like her," she murmured as Sawyer pulled up the flank.

They crawled for about ten feet, where it suddenly occurred to Sasha she might be a little claustrophobic after all. Then Riley called out.

"Another chamber, and a big one. There's a drop, about three feet."

Sasha heard the scrape of boots on rock, then the thud of a landing.

"I'll have you," Bran said before he dropped lightly into the dark. With his flashlight showing her the way, he held up a hand for hers. "Relax your knees," he warned her.

She took the leap, caught her breath.

Before Bran could turn to offer Annika a hand, she'd jumped down gracefully.

Not dark, Sasha realized, or not completely. A light came from somewhere, pale and slightly . . . off. But it showed her the size of the cave, the smoothed teeth of rock stretching toward the floor, the others that soared up from it. All red, she thought, all red as blood.

A weight dropped on her chest, and her head swam.

"Don't." She reached out as Riley approached a formation that resembled a raised table. "Don't touch it. Dark deeds done."

"Riley," Bran said sharply. "Touch nothing."

In silent assent, Riley lifted her free hand, playing the light over the table stone. "There's writing carved here. Ancient Greek."

"Bones. Human bones piled over here." Sawyer turned from them.

"Can you hear them screaming?" Sasha fisted her hands over her ears. "The children. She craved the children. The youth. The innocence."

"I'm getting her out of here."

172

"Wait, just wait," Riley snapped at Bran. "I can read this. 'In blood taken. In blood given. So she may live, so she may rise. In the name of Nerezza.' "

As she spoke the name, came a stirring, the dry rustling overhead.

"Just bats. Don't panic."

Riley's warning came seconds before the screams, and the dark flood of wings.

Instinctively Sasha covered her head and face, curled up to make herself smaller. She felt the spidery wings brush her hair, shuddered.

Just bats, she told herself. Just bats.

She gasped at the quick pain as something sliced her arm. Grabbing it, she felt the warm, wet flow of her own blood.

"They bite!"

"They're not just bats." Riley pulled a gun from the holster snugged at the small of her back. "Run." She shot one flying toward her face, and the sound crashed through the chamber.

Echoed by another as Sawyer fired another gun.

Blood fell on the ground, splattered on the altar.

And the ground shook.

Bats circled, looking down with hungry, somehow human eyes.

She formed out of the dark. The black robe swirled around her, and her hair, dense as midnight, curled in sleek coils around her face.

The face formed in the stone, and she smiled with terrible beauty.

"I have waited." While the bats swooped and squealed, she lifted her hands. In one she held the glass ball. "I have watched."

Her voice rang over the chaos, over the ring of bullets, of shouts and screams. Armed with only her flashlight, Sasha swung out to defend herself, saw Sawyer pivot to take aim at a bat diving toward Annika.

In a liquid blur of movement, Annika flipped back, pushed off with her hands and sent the bat smashing into the cave wall with a powerful thrust of her legs.

"Your blood." She stepped off a pedestal, bent gracefully to run her finger through the blood that had dripped from Sasha's arm to the cave floor. "It is warm," she said as she licked it delicately from her finger as she might a dab of rich chocolate or cream.

"Your power is strong and . . . tasty. Through your blood I will drink that power. Through that power the path to the stars."

Trapped, fighting to avoid fangs, claws, wings, Sasha stumbled back only to find herself pressed against the wall.

Across the chamber, Riley shouted, fired. But the bullets passed through the figure walking toward Sasha.

Something gripped her mind, something cold and fierce. She fought to pry it loose, felt it give, just a little.

"Very strong."

Now that same force, the cold and fierce, gripped her throat, cutting off her air. All she felt was her own fear, and pushing against it dark hate, bottomless greed.

"Come with me, and live."

Lies. The mother of lies. Nerezza.

Something — someone — leaped out of the shadows. A sword flashing silver in the dim red light. It cleaved through the swarming bats, severing them. As if through water, Sasha heard someone shouting.

"Get out! Go."

"Give me what I want." Nerezza loomed closer. "Or I will crush you, and all you love."

"Not today." Bran shoved Sasha behind him. While she gasped in breath, choked it out again, he threw up both his hands. Lightning bolted from them, blinding white.

Nerezza threw up an arm to shield her eyes, and from her came a roar more beast than human.

"Get her out!" Bran shouted. "Get her

175

out of here. This won't hold long."

The bats swirled up, reformed, and like a great winged arrow came at him. The swordsman thrust, hacked, sent severed bodies tumbling to the ground while bullets pierced more.

"Get her out." Bran's voice, ice cold, snapped out. "Get them all out."

The swordsman grabbed Riley, all but tossed her into the tunnel. He caught Annika as she finished a series of flips that sent bats tumbling. "Go!"

"Get Sasha," Sawyer ordered, and ranged himself beside Bran. "I'm not leaving you, man."

"Then get ready to move." Out of the corner of his eye he saw the swordsman lift Sasha under one arm, glance back with a kind of fierce regret, then boost her with him into the tunnel.

"Go when I say," Bran said. "There won't be time to hesitate. I'm right behind you. My word on it."

"If you're not, I'm coming back."

Bran felt Nerezza pushing back against his power, knew he didn't have enough. Not here, not yet.

"Now. Go now!" he shouted at Sawyer, then heaved both bolts to the ground. The explosion rocked the chamber, filled it with wild light, thick smoke.

Understanding that fierce regret, he dived into the tunnel behind Sawyer.

"Don't stop," he ordered. "I don't know how long a reach she has."

The rock shook under them. Contrary to orders, Sawyer paused after he jumped out of the tunnel until Bran came out behind him. White smoke curled out of the opening.

"I'd say you've got a pretty damn long one. Nice work," he added as they ran for the mouth of the cave.

Just outside the mouth, the man and his sword stood guard with Riley, arguing bitterly.

"That's a sword, this is a gun. Guess who wins." She swiped at the blood on her face, smeared more from the cuts on her hand. "I don't want to shoot you, but you can bet your ass I will if you don't get out of my way. I'm going back for my friends."

"If you shoot me, you're going to piss me off." Then he turned when he heard running footsteps. "They're coming," he said, and stepped aside.

The minute they stepped clear, Riley punched Bran in the chest — though she pulled it. Then she threw her arms around both of them. "Son of a bitch. Son of a bitch. Don't ever push me out like that again." She dragged Sawyer's head down, kissed him soundly on the mouth, then took Bran's head in turn. "You've got some 'splaining to do."

"This isn't the time or place." He patted her cheek, nudged her aside to go to where Annika sat on the ground beside Sasha, gently tending her wounds with Riley's first-aid kit.

He crouched down, stroked a finger down her cheek, then over the raw, red bruising around her throat. "I'm sorry I couldn't get to you more quickly. I'm sorry she hurt you."

"Who *are* you?"

"What I've told you. Perhaps a bit more."

"Her nice shirt is ruined, but the cuts aren't very bad." Annika wound a bandage around the long gash in Sasha's arm. "But she is shocked."

"In shock," Riley corrected. "She got the worst of it. It was going way south before you stepped in with the light show. We just couldn't hold our own." She glanced back at Sawyer. "But nice shooting, Tex."

"Back at you."

"Who the hell are you people?"

They looked back at the newcomer. He'd housed his sword in the sheath he wore on his back and stood, legs spread, face scowling.

Just as Sasha had depicted him, in detail, in one of her sketches. The breeze caught at his black, disordered sweep of hair, tossing it around a face that might have been carved with razors. The high slash of cheekbones, the sharply sculpted, unsmiling mouth, the long, patrician blade of nose. His eyes were fierce and burning green.

Riley ran a measuring gaze over him, from the scarred boots that laced up to midcalf, the long legs in well-worn jeans, the blood-splattered shirt over a broad torso.

She pushed to her feet. "Riley Gwin, archaeologist; Sawyer King, dead-eye; Annika Waters, adorable ass-kicker."

"Aww," Annika said, delighted.

"Sasha Riggs, seer. And Bran Killian, magician. To say the fucking least. And who the hell are you?"

"McCleary. Doyle McCleary. And if you lot hadn't been in the way, I might have had the bitch at last."

"Fat chance," Riley tossed back.

"We can have a fine argument about all of it, away from here. Do you mind?" Bran asked as he tapped Sasha's backpack. When she shook her head, he reached in and found, as he'd thought he would, the sketch of the six of them.

Rising, he walked over to Doyle. "First, I'll thank you for the assist. Sasha was hurt, and I don't know if I could have held the bitch and gotten everyone out safe without it. As to who we are, well, there's this." He offered the sketch. "We're a team, and you'd be the last of us."

"Who drew this?"

"I did." Sasha's voice came hoarsely through her abused throat. "Weeks ago."

"How did —"

"Not now," Bran interrupted. "We're all of us bloody and battered. We have a place where we can talk. Private."

"How the hell are we going to fit him in the jeep?" Riley wondered.

"I have my own way of getting around." Doyle looked at all of them, back at the cave. Shook his head. "I'll go with you, and talk about this." He handed the sketch back to Bran. "Then we'll see."

"Fair enough."

Bran went back to Sasha, started to lift her. She pushed his hands away. "I can walk." She got to her feet. She might have been chilled and queasy, but she could damn well walk.

To prove it, she started back toward the track.

"Yeah, some 'splaining." Riley patted Bran's arm, then went after Sasha.

"She didn't know you're a wizard?" Doyle commented.

"No. I hadn't found the right time to tell her, or the others."

Doyle gave what might have been a sympathetic grunt, then walked away.

"She'll come around." Sawyer reached out a hand to help Annika to her feet. "You've got some wild moves, Anni. I really liked the one where you ran halfway up the wall, flipped backward, then did a handspring."

"It's fun. I don't like to fight."

"Maybe not, but you're good at it."

When they followed the others, Bran looked after them, then back at the cave. His white smoke blocked the mouth, for now, but was already beginning to thin. It told him he had a great deal of work yet to do.

He hefted his pack back into place as he watched Sasha walk — limping a bit, he noted — down the rough track.

A great deal of work yet, he thought, in several areas.

Chapter Eight

Doyle's way of getting around turned out to be pulled off into the brushwood well down the trail. As he brought it out, Riley fisted her hands on her hips.

"Classic. Harley Chopper. Twin Vs?"

"That's right."

"Bet she moves."

Like his boots, the bike showed some battle scars — and like its owner, looked muscular and tough.

"The dragon!" Annika pointed to the red dragon, wings out, talons curled, painted on the side of the engine. "You ride the dragon. Sasha said."

"Yeah. Where am I riding it?"

"Just west of Sidari," Bran told him. "It would be easier if you followed us in."

"All right. That yours?" he asked, gesturing to the jeep farther down.

"It is."

"Can I ride the dragon, too?"

Doyle hesitated, then shrugged. "I hate saying no to a beautiful woman, so I won't." He swung a leg over, nodded to Annika. "Hop on."

Sawyer hesitated. "You have to hold on to him," he told Annika. "And lean into the turns — not against. Just lean into them a little. Okay?"

"Okay." She got on behind Doyle, and laughed when he turned on the engine. "It roars!"

"Hold on to him," Sawyer repeated, then quickened his steps to catch up to the others. "She'll be all right."

"I don't think we just came through that little experience for her to take a header off a bike." Riley got behind the wheel. "Relax."

"Take the front." Bran got into the back. "You're pissed, and I won't argue about it," he said to Sasha as Riley navigated down the excuse for a road. "I'll explain once we're back at the villa and settled down some."

"I just want to sleep." And turning away from him, closing her eyes, Sasha surprised herself by doing just that.

She woke, headachy, her throat burning, her arm throbbing, when Riley bumped up the road to the villa.

When she got out, found her legs shaky, she wanted to crawl back into sleep.

"I need to clean up. You can start without me."

Bran took her arm. "Sasha."

She yanked free. "I can *feel* her on me. I need a shower." Shaky or not, she got her legs moving, rushed straight into the house.

"Give her a little space," Riley advised, giving the welcoming Apollo a quick rub. She glanced over toward Doyle as Annika jumped off the bike. "Look, we'll get some food first, give her time to settle." She looked down at her hands. "I want to clean up some myself."

"Fine. We'll all have a nice wash."

"I'll take mine down at the beach," Sawyer decided.

"Oh, yes, a swim! I'll go with you."

"Great. Grab your suit."

She looked blank. "My suit?"

"Bathing suit."

"Oh, yes. I have one." She dashed into the house, and Sawyer went up the terrace steps.

"What's her story?" Doyle asked Bran.

"We've a lot of stories among us. If you'd wait a half hour. We're a bloody mess, so we'll do better cleaned up, and getting some food. There are two rooms left, and you can

184

have your pick."

"I'm a long way from staying."

"That may be, but you've bat blood and guts and Christ only knows on you same as the rest of us. You can use the shower, do what you do after we talk. I'll show you which rooms are left, and you use whichever you like."

"I wouldn't mind a shower."

"Come inside, and you can have the two-penny tour along the way."

"Hell of a house in a hell of a spot. Whose is it?"

"Friend of a friend of an uncle — of Riley's. She's connections."

"Handy."

"It has been. McCleary, is it? So your people are from Ireland?"

"Back a ways," Doyle said as they started upstairs.

"Mine are still there — or most of them. Sligo."

"Clare. I'm told."

"Well, McCleary. Either of these two rooms are open to you."

"This one's fine."

"Then it's yours. Be at home, and if you'll come down when you're ready, we'll put some food together and talk this through."

He went into his own room, stripped

down, and took a good look at his side. The cuts and slices on his arms didn't bother him overmuch, but his side showed a maze of punctures and gashes from when a group of the bastards had swarmed him when he'd tried to get to Sasha.

Gone now, he thought. He'd burned them to cinders, but they'd gotten some pieces of him along the way. He moved to the dresser, brushed a hand over the drawer to release the locking spell he'd put on. He lifted out a case where he kept some potions and brews, took what he needed, locked up the rest again.

In the shower, he hissed as the water hit the wounds, then just braced his hands on the tile wall, and let those wounds run clean.

Once he'd washed, let the water beat most of the aches away, he got out of the shower, examined the wounds again, and laid the salve on thick. Immediately the raw edge of pain eased. He bandaged it as best he could, dressed, then went to face the music.

Sasha wept in the shower. The jag increased the headache, but she felt steadier purged of tears. She ran the water as hot as she could bear until it no longer felt as if spiders crawled over her skin. She scrubbed that skin, ignoring the pain when she hit cuts and scrapes, washed her hair. Scrubbed again, washed again.

And finally felt clean.

After wrapping herself in a towel, she wiped the mirror clear of fog, studied her face, traced the bruising at her neck.

She'd been weak, she thought, and couldn't, wouldn't be weak again. If she continued this — and she knew she would — she had to be smarter, stronger, more prepared. She wouldn't cower back a second time while some demon goddess from hell tried to take her over.

She wouldn't be used again or deceived again.

"People underestimate you because you underestimate yourself," she told her reflection. "That stops now."

She walked out of the bath, then stopped when she saw Bran at her open terrace doors, looking out.

"I need you to leave."

He turned back, studied her as she stood, hair sleek and wet, her hand clutching the towel between her breasts. And insult and anger in her eyes.

"I have a salve." He held up the small jar. "I can help with the wounds, and with the pain."

"I don't want —"

"Stop being a git. You're not a stupid woman. You want to be pissed, be pissed," he invited as his own temper clawed at him. "Stay pissed after I explain, that's your choice to make, but now you'll sit down and let me help."

"You're not in charge of me."

"And thank the gods for that. But we're all in this together, and I'll do what I can to help the others in turn. But you took the brunt of it. Now sit down, and be pissed *and* smart."

Refusing, she realized, was weak, was letting her hurt and disappointment cloud judgment. She needed to be strong and well to fight.

So she sat on the side of the bed.

He came over, set the salve down. And laid his hands gently on her head.

"That's not —"

"Your head aches, that's clear to see. She tried getting into your mind, didn't she? And you've been crying. So your head hurts." He brushed his thumbs over her temples, her forehead. "I'm not as good at this as others, but with you being an empath—"

"I'm not."

"For Christ's sake, woman, don't argue with what I know." Impatience snapped, a whiplash. "You block most out, but it's there. Use it now, in a kind of reverse, and that will help me help you. Let me feel it, open up and let me feel. We'll start with the headache, as you'll think clearer then."

Because he was right, because there'd been impatience rather than pity, she closed her eyes, offered her pain.

"There now," he murmured, and his fingers stroked her brow, her skull, her temples. "It's a dark gray cloud." He ran his hands down, pressed thumbs into the base of her neck. "It's whisking away as a breeze comes up. Cool and fresh. Feel it."

She did, and the horrible, gripping pressure eased. "Yes, that's better. That's better," she repeated, and nudged his hands aside. "Thank you."

"You've cuts and scrapes and bruises, and a puncture or two. The salve alone will do for that, but this gash needs more. Annika did a fine — what do they call it? — field dressing. She's an array of disparate talents. Let me feel it.

"Yes, it's hot, and it throbs." And would scar if he couldn't fix it. It surprised him how the thought of that upset him. "But it's clean. Nothing to fester here."

"How do you know?"

"You know, and I can see what you know

here. Help me cool it now, help me close it."

She lost herself in his eyes. It occurred to her later he must have taken her into some light trance, but her feelings seemed to touch his, like fingertips, and the heat of her arm cooled.

"That's good now, that's fine. And the salve will do the rest right enough."

A little dazed, she looked down to see the gash closed, and no more than a long scrape remaining.

"But, that's —"

"Magick?" he suggested. "It's healing, and you're doing most of the work. What about your leg? You're favoring the right one."

"I don't know. I must have twisted or turned my ankle in the cave. When the bats . . ."

"We won't think of them now." He crouched, skimmed his hands over her ankle, eased back when she flinched. "Tender, is it? We'll fix it."

She understood now, let him in. Imagined the swelling, the tendons and muscles while his fingers circled and stroked.

Then he rose. "Your throat, that's the worst of it, and the hardest. She touched you."

"She didn't. Not physically."

"And that's the deepest wound, you see? Her power against ours. I think it will hurt to heal this, at first. You have to trust me."

"Then I will. For this."

"Keep your eyes on mine. I don't have what you have, but what I have will help you lift this away."

He closed his hands lightly, gently, around her throat, covering the raw bruises.

It did hurt. A sudden shock of pain stole her breath, had her gripping the side of the bed to hold herself in place. She fought not to cry out — weak, weak — but a moan escaped.

"I'm sorry. A little more."

He murmured in Irish now, words that meant nothing to her, but the tone, both comfort and distress, helped her bear it. Then, as the rest, it eased. The relief made her head spin.

"It's better."

"It needs to be gone. I won't leave her mark on you. I should have stopped it."

"You did. With blinding bolts of lightning. That's enough. It doesn't hurt."

She shifted away, stood. "You should take the salve for the others."

"That's for you. I have more."

"I'll be down as soon as I get dressed. We all have a lot to talk about."

"We do." But he stood where he was, waited.

"You lied to me."

"I never did."

"The absence of truth —"

"Isn't always a lie. Sometimes it's just personal business."

"I told you everything about me, everything I knew, and you . . . What *are* you? A warlock?"

He winced, had to struggle not to be insulted. "Some will insist on turning that word away from its origin — which is one who does evil, even the devil — and making into a man with powers. I'll take witch, even sorcerer, but I prefer magician, which is what I told you when we met."

Accusations, and worse, much worse, disappointed hurt lived in her eyes.

"You know what I thought you meant."

"I do, and there's an absence there. Still, I do stage magic to make a living and to entertain myself. And my blood, my craft, my gift, and my honor is in white magicks. But it's considerable to share with someone who doesn't trust her own gifts, *fáidh*. What would your reaction have been, I wonder, if I'd shown you more than a bit of sleight of hand at first?"

"I don't know."

"My family keeps our bloodline to ourselves, not out of shame, but caution. I can wish now I'd been able to show you what I am, who I am, in its entirety, in a less dramatic way, but Nerezza took the choice out of my hands."

"She meant to drain me."

"I never anticipated, and for that . . . I'm sorry. I'm sorry I didn't plan it better, or find a better way. But I can't be sorry for what I am, or for waiting until I felt there was real trust before I told you, or the others."

"Did you kiss me to help create trust?"

He cursed, surprising her with the quick flare of anger as he strode around the room. "That's an insult to both of us. Bloody hell."

He grabbed her, yanked her to him without any of the care or gentleness he'd shown in the healing. The flare of anger remained hot and ready in the kiss.

"You know it all now, so what was that about, do you suppose?"

"I have to think about it."

"Fine then, you do that."

"I'll be down when I'm dressed."

"That's grand." He strode out, gave the door a quick, bad-tempered slam.

She turned, walked to the mirror. No marks remained on her throat, and color had come back into her face. She didn't feel weak now, Sasha realized.

And that was a damn good start.

Sawyer put his spin on sandwiches with grilled ham and cheese. Annika once again created a tablescape with napkins folded into flowers arranged along a winding river of plates. Once again wearing one of her flowy dresses, she stopped her work to turn and give Sasha a hard and heartfelt hug.

"You look pretty, and you feel better."

"Thanks, and I do. Were you hurt?"

"Only a little, and Bran gave us a salve that smells very nice. Don't have mad at him."

"I'm working on it. Where's . . . I can't remember his name."

"You mean Doyle. Doyle McCleary. Riding his dragon is fun. He came down, and he wanted to walk around the villa, to see the lay of the land."

"Can't blame him. Annika, thank you for helping me when I was hurt."

"We're here to help each other."

As simple as that, Sasha thought. "You're exactly right. Let's have some wine."

"I like wine."

"I'll get it."

She went into the kitchen, where Sawyer

flipped the last of the sandwiches onto a platter, and Riley pulled beer from the fridge.

"Dead-Eye here has hidden depths," Riley said. "He made salsa."

"Everything was here." Sawyer turned. "Ready to eat?"

Sasha hadn't thought she could face food, and now found the opposite true. "More than, and those look great. We're missing Doyle and Bran."

"They're doing a walkabout. Snooze you lose," Riley announced. "How're you doing?"

"Fine now. How about both of you?"

"Bumps and cuts, and nothing a hot shower and Bran's magic salve didn't deal with. Probably shouldn't have said magic," Riley realized.

"It is what it is. Annika and I are having wine." She chose a bottle, got glasses, and took them out with her.

"She came around quick," Sawyer observed.

"Men." Pitying him, Riley screwed a half dozen beers into a bucket she'd filled with ice. "She's pissed, cutie. Down to a smolder maybe, but pissed — and trying to figure out how she feels about the fact that she was locking lips a few hours ago with a guy who turns out to be a sorcerer."

"Oh, yeah? Lip-lock?"

"Talk about smoldering." She winked at him, hefted the bucket. And noticed when she carried it out, Bran and Doyle rounding the side of the villa. They struck her as pretty easy with each other already.

"Order up!" she called to Sawyer, then plucked out a beer, dropped down into a chair. She waited until Sawyer brought the food, until others had taken wine or beer. Then lifted her own bottle.

"Here's to a damn good fight."

When Sasha just stared, Riley gestured with the bottle. "Any fight you walk away from and polish off with a cold beer is a good fight."

"Can't argue with that." Doyle took a sandwich. "Got beer, got food — and appreciate it. But I still don't have answers. Mr. Wizard's being vague. Let's get specific."

"Mr. Wizard." Riley snorted out a laugh. "That's a good one," she insisted as the others kept silent. "Sash, you should start rolling the ball, seeing as you got things going."

"I don't think I got anything going, but all right." She took a sip of wine first. "I'm an artist."

"I could see that from the sketch."

"I live in North Carolina, now. I've always had . . ."

"A gift," Bran finished, as if daring her to contradict him.

She just ignored him. "Right after the first of the year, I began having dreams, about us — all of us here — and about the stars."

She took him up to her arrival at the hotel in Corfu.

"So you just hopped on a plane and . . . followed your dreams?"

"I couldn't ignore them, couldn't make them stop, so yes, that's what I did. Riley, you should take it from there."

"Sure. Most excellent salsa," she added, and dipped a chip in the hill she'd put on her plate. "Tracking legends, myths, finding antiquities and artifacts — that's what I do. The stars have been on my radar for a long time, and I'd dug up some information that arrowed here. I'd just finished a job, had some time, and decided to see what I could find out on the spot."

She waved the bottle, took another hit.

"The thing is — and I didn't mention this before — I didn't plan to stay in that hotel. I'd planned to come to this area all along, but I had this impulse, is the best I can say. Treat yourself to a good hotel for a day or two, Riley, take a break. So there I was, taking a break with a very nice Bellini on the hotel terrace, and up walks the blonde."

When she'd finished her side of it, she reached for another beer. "Over to you, Bran."

He'd wrangled with himself over how much to tell them, what he should hold back. And decided, considering all, on full disclosure.

"Someone in my family, generation by generation, has been tasked to look for the stars, to hold them safe, and to one day return them to where they began, to where they can never be used for ill. So it came to me. We descend from Celene."

"The goddess?" Riley set her beer down. "You're a god?"

"I'm not." Impatience sharpened his voice. "I'm what I told you. I'm a magician, and descended from her. She mated with a sorcerer — a mortal — and bore his son."

"The demigod Movar," Riley prompted, "conceived with the sorcerer called Asalri."

"As you say."

"And Movar had five sons and three daughters. I know the legend. Or," Riley corrected, "your family tree."

"The gift of magicks has come through the blood, and so has the quest for the stars. I came here because, as with you, Riley, I

198

came upon some information. While once again scouring books until my eyes bled, I came on a passage that spoke of a fallen star, one of fire, waiting in a land of green. You might think Greenland, and I did, or Ireland, but there was more that convinced me it was here. It was written the maidens of Korkyra had hidden it, away from the mother of lies."

"Not much different from what I found," Riley said. "And the timing? You, me, Sasha? It cements it."

"I'd barely arrived, and like you, booked the hotel on impulse as I thought to rent a villa. For the quiet, the privacy, as I'd need to work, and hotel rooms aren't always . . . convenient for certain work."

"When you make magick," Annika said, and made him smile.

"When I do. And so I walked out on the hotel terrace, annoyed with myself for changing my plans and direction. Imagine my surprise when I found myself lured over to two beautiful women, with fascinating stories to tell."

"So you teamed up," Doyle said.

"I'd be the last to ignore power or turn away from the fates. And beyond the stories there were the sketches, Sasha's brilliant sketches, which made it clear this was meant. Still, I felt it best to keep what I'm telling you now to myself."

He frowned at his beer, then shrugged. "Others have been deceived by lovely faces, by fascinating stories, by the whiff of power and the promise of trust. So I bided some time — and it can't be said I bided long, can it?"

Temper flared around the edges of his tone as he looked over at Sasha. "A bit of time to be more certain what I felt, what I knew was truth, and that meeting, that joining of forces was for the right of it."

He paused, considered having another beer. "So we piled ourselves into Riley's borrowed jeep and headed north and west, where I had always planned to go. And Riley, being enterprising and well-connected, arranged this place for us. On the way back, after we'd gone to get our things from the hotel, there was Sawyer, walking toward this place, on the side of the road."

He opted for the beer. "And there," he said to Sawyer, "you come into it."

"It's a family thing for me, too. The story of the stars came down through my family. I'm not much of a scholar, not like Riley here, so most of what I know is through those stories. And . . ." He scratched the back of his neck, frowned into the distance.

"Didn't tell us the whole of it either, did you?" Bran asked.

"Not exactly. It's the sort of thing people don't buy into, and like you said, it hasn't been long since we teamed up. A psychic's one thing — I mean a lot of people buy into that. Hell, it's an industry. No offense."

"None taken," Sasha assured him.

"But after today. Mutant bats from hell, evil gods, and, well, Bran, it might not seem so weird. Family deal again. An ancestor, back in maybe — nobody's exactly sure — the fourteenth century. He was a sailor, and his ship went down in a storm. So he's drowning and, the story goes, he was rescued, pulled to shore by a mermaid."

Doyle let out a short laugh, and Annika a gasp.

"Yeah, yeah, I know, but that's the story. He woke up, the only one of the crew to survive, on the rocky shore of some island in the North Sea. And the, uh, mermaid, she'd gotten hurt saving him, cut up on the rocks, and too weak to swim. Dying."

"No," Annika breathed.

"He was pretty banged up himself, but he got some dry wood, some dry leaves, started a fire. He didn't know if he should try to get her all the way into the water, or if she'd just drown, so he scouted up some plants, made a poultice for her cuts. Some of the supplies and pieces of the ship washed up, so he used what he could, built a kind of shelter, fed her what he could, took care of her."

"Did she get better?"

"Yeah, happy ending."

"Happy endings are good."

"One night he woke up, and saw her swimming away. And he was alone."

"But this isn't happy," Annika objected.

"Wait for it. Days later, she came back, and he went out into the shallows to meet her. For the first time, she spoke. She'd taken him from the sea because it was his fate, and those who came after him, to look for the three stars. He would tell the story to his sons, and they to their sons until they were found and taken home. She gave him a gift, a compass, and said it would guide him. This, too, he would pass to his son, and his son to his, and down the line."

"You've got the compass?" Riley demanded.

"Yeah." He dug in his pocket, held it out on his palm, lifted off the protective cover.

"Nice piece. Mind?" Riley took it, examined it. "Bronze case, nice-looking rose — you've kept it in good shape. It's old, but I'd gauge it more seventeenth century."

"Yeah, but that's how the story came down."

"That doesn't explain why you came to Corfu," Doyle pointed out.

"Well, it will."

He hitched up, took a plastic sleeve from his pocket, and carefully drew out the map folded inside. After pushing dishes aside, he unfolded the map on the table. Held out his hand, wiggled his fingers at Riley for the compass.

"One way or the other, it's always accurate."

He set the compass on the map. Within seconds the old brass casing glowed, and the rose began to shine. Then the compass slid over the map.

"Like a Ouija board," Riley said.

"No." Watching the movement, Bran shook his head. "This doesn't open a door. It shows the way to one."

"Pretty much, and see?" Sawyer tapped his finger on the map. "It stops right here, on Corfu. So, I followed the map."

"It's done that before?" Sasha asked.

"Oh, yeah, plenty. Nobody's found any of the stars, but for me? It's always taken me somewhere I pick up something fresh on them, or confirm something, or just get an experience. This time? See how it's shining?"

"It's beautiful," Annika murmured.

"Yeah, but that shining? That's new. It would glow some, but not like this. I had to figure coming here was pretty damn important. Turns out it was. I was hitching my way here, and y'all came along. That made four of the six. That night, I went for a walk on the beach, and found Annika."

He shifted to her. "Your turn."

"I was sent to help. To be one of you." She bowed her head. "I can't explain. I don't have a magick compass, or the powers like Sasha and Bran. I don't have such a smart mind like Riley, but I can help. I don't like fighting, but I will fight with you. Don't send me away."

"Hey." Sawyer put an arm around her shoulders. "Nobody's sending you anywhere."

"I came to you." She turned into him. "You found me."

"That's right. We can leave it at that for now." He looked over at Bran as if daring him to disagree.

"You're one of us, Annika, and that's more than enough. Not all stories need telling at once."

"How about you, McCleary?" Riley sat

back, studied him. "What's your story?"

"A family thing, and the duty that comes with it. And here? An urge I couldn't shake led me to Corfu, then to the cave. It's the closest I've come. It's the closest I've ever come."

"Where are you from? What do you do?"

"Nowhere in particular, and whatever needs doing. You haven't had much time together, but more than a couple hours, so that's all I'm going to tell you until I decide to tell you more."

"You don't trust us. Why should he?" Sasha glanced at Riley. "It's true we haven't had much time, but it's been intense, even intimate. And today, in the cave, it was life and death. Both you and Sawyer brought guns, but you didn't tell the rest of us."

Sawyer shifted. "Shit. Combat knife, too."

Riley pulled a wicked blade out of her boot. "Throwing knife."

"Which only proves we've yet to reach the point where we're fully honest. We know about Bran only because he . . . used what he has to get us all out of the cave alive. And we know about the compass because Sawyer felt guilty not telling us after we found out about Bran. Annika's not ready, and Doyle? You're still annoyed we got in your way."

"You're right on that."

"You're not, because we didn't get in your way, and you know that, under the annoyance. We were all where we were supposed to be today. We all made the choice to go into the cave."

"What? Wait." Riley's gilded eyes narrowed. "Do you think it was a kind of test?"

"I don't know. I'm really new at this. But I think gods are pretty demanding. We all went into the cave. We fought. Well, all of you did."

"Sasha." Bran reached for her hand, but she drew it away.

"I didn't fight. I froze. But it won't happen again. Still, we got out, and we — six now — are sitting right here. I haven't heard anyone say they want out. We faced down a god, and not one of us is walking away from doing it again. So I think we passed the test."

"Smart brain there, too," Riley said to Annika. "You've got a point. Throughout lore and legend, gods are notoriously demanding. And fickle, and often bloodthirsty. No quest is ever completed without tests and sacrifice and battle."

"Sasha's blood woke the dark." The moment she spoke, Annika looked distressed. "I'm apology —"

206

"No, don't be sorry. You're right. I felt it myself, and maybe it's part of the reason I froze. I don't know. I know she wanted to drain me."

"Because she's not running on full power," Riley pointed out.

"If she was, you'd be dust." Doyle took another beer. "Mortal against god? Who do you lay your money on?"

"I'd bet on myself," Riley tossed back, "and my four friends here. I don't know about you yet, big guy."

"We're more than mortals," Bran pointed out. "So I'd say, however fickle, the gods gave us some edge. We'll use it."

"The star isn't in the cave. I spent considerable time looking," Doyle continued, "before things got interesting."

"There are other caves." Riley frowned into her beer. "I'll make some calls, get us a boat, some gear. We talked about trying some of the underwater caves. Maybe that's the next step."

"I have some things I can put together, in case she goes at us again. We weren't prepared enough." Bran pushed to his feet. "That's the bottom of it. We weren't prepared, and we need to be."

"Then we will be. I'll take care of the

dishes." Sasha got up to clear.

She had some ideas of her own.

CHAPTER NINE

Once she'd set the kitchen to rights, Sasha went upstairs for her easel and paints. She'd take an hour for herself, smooth out any remaining jagged edges.

She set up on the terrace, commandeering one of the tables and covering it with a drop cloth from her kit.

After filling several jars with water, she set out brushes, palette knives, a palette.

And began to prep a canvas. She chose a golden, fluid acrylic — it would give the painting she saw in her head an underglow. She covered the edges first, then began to scrub the paint into the canvas so it would soak in. She kept the mix thin and lean, brushing it out, wiping it down until it satisfied her.

Then she set the canvas on her easel, began a line drawing. Clouds and sea, the curve of sand, the rise of cliff, the shape of the channel that cut through.

A sweeping view, she thought, not the more dramatic and focused study she'd been compelled to paint, not the storm-tossed night, but sparkling day. No figures caught in that storm and one another on the cliff, but the hint of people on shore and sea, bright drops of color and life.

She mixed colors — greens first — the deep, dark green of cypress, the duskier hue of olive, the richer of citrus trees. All this against the sun-bleached brown of the cliffs.

It gave her peace, the process of it, and the ability to translate not only what she saw but what she felt with paint and brush and canvas.

The blues, dreamy, bold, soft, sharp — the hints of green and aquamarine around the rocks. The pale gold of sand flowing into deeper tones where the sea rolled over it, retreated, rolled again.

The clouds she painted cotton white against the pulse of blue sky, then changed brushes to add their shadows, like an echo on the sea.

She lost track of time in the work, in the pleasure. With the sparkle in front of her, and on her canvas, the cold, dark shadows of the cave in the hills didn't exist.

She stepped back to study what she'd done, reached for a detail brush. Stopped when she heard Riley's voice, heard her coming up the terrace steps.

"I'm all over that. Yeah, yeah, probably by nine. Really appreciate it, and tell Ari I owe him." She laughed as she came to the top of the steps. "I don't owe him *that* much. Later."

She swiped off her phone, stuck it in her pocket as she saw Sasha and the easel.

"Hey, sorry. Didn't know you were playing up here. I just got us . . . Wow." She stopped in front of the canvas. "And let me repeat. Wow. That's amazing."

"It's not quite finished."

"You're the boss, but it looks perfect to me. I Googled you, you know."

"You did?"

"Oh, yeah, the first night. Wanted a sense of who was what. I brought up some of your paintings, and they were pretty great. But this? Alive and in person, it's freaking awesome."

"Thanks. I wanted to do something sunny, something clear and beautiful. Like cleansing the palate, I guess." A thought struck her. "I'll trade you."

"Huh?"

"I'll make you a trade for the painting if you want it."

"I did enough digging to have an idea

211

what an original Sasha Riggs goes for. But . . . I figure my firstborn's a ways off, so that's safe."

Interested, she shoved her hands in her pockets, studied the painting again. Wanted it. "What did you have in mind?"

"Teach me to fight."

"You want me to teach you to fight?"

"Today, in the cave, I froze. Now that I've calmed down, and finished my pity party, I accept that wasn't altogether my fault."

"A god had you by the throat, Sash. It's give-yourself-a-break time."

"Yeah, there was that. But my instinct right along was duck and cover, or run and hide. It wasn't stand and fight. You had the gun, but now that I can look back on it, see it all more clearly than when it was exploding around me, you weren't just shooting. You used your fists, your feet. Kicks and spins. And Annika . . ."

"Yeah, she had that whole Cirque du Soleil thing going."

"And I just stood there because I don't know how to fight, not physically fight. You could teach me."

"You don't have to give me the painting for me to teach you some basics." Thumbs hooked in her pockets now, Riley studied the painting again. "But since I'm not an idiot, I'll take it."

"Can we start now? I just need to clean my brushes."

"I don't see why not."

"But somewhere more private."

"You should change into a T-shirt or a tank, something that gives you more room. Meet me in the olive grove around back."

"All right. Thanks, Riley."

"Hey, fun for me — plus the painting. I need a couple of things."

She cleaned her brushes, knives, jars, exchanged her shirt for a black tank. By the time she got out to the grove, Riley was there, and pulling on leather gloves.

"Private enough?"

Sasha looked back at the villa. You could see if you looked, she thought, but she wouldn't feel nearly as exposed as she would have on one of the terraces or on the lawn in front of the house.

"Yes. Just enough."

"Okay, first things first. Make a fist." When Sasha did, Riley shook her head. "Just as I figured. You keep your thumb up like that, you're going to —"

"Ow!" Sasha snatched her hand away after Riley bent her thumb back.

"Exactly. Remember that, and keep your thumb folded down. See?" She demonstrated; Sasha mimicked her.

"Thumb down."

"Always outside, never inside the fist. Okay, punch me."

"I'm not going to punch you!"

The smirk came quickly. "I can guarantee that. But try. Come on." She tapped her nose. "Straight in the face or this lesson's over."

Irritated, intimidated, Sasha struck out. Riley tipped to the side, and let the half-hearted punch meet air.

"Like you mean it this time. It's my face, Sash. I can promise you're not going to hurt me. A little faith here."

That's what it came down to, didn't it? All across the board. A little faith. She punched out again, putting enough into it that when Riley sidestepped, she stumbled forward.

"Okay, see, you're punching like a girl."

"I am a girl."

"Nobody's a girl in a fight. You're a fighter. You need to distribute your weight, your balance, and for right now, you're going to plant your feet. Knees a little soft, but you need to feel solid on the ground."

Riley circled her. "That's better. When you punch, don't throw your body at it, bring the punch out from your shoulder. *Lift* your shoulder as you extend your arm. No, don't straighten your legs. The power comes up from your legs, and when you straighten them or lean forward like that, you lose power and balance. Keep your body centered. And exhale on the punch."

Riley nodded or frowned as she circled, as she ordered Sasha to try it with her left. Left again. Left then right.

"Don't flap your elbows like chicken wings. The jab's not sexy maybe like a cross, but it's your most powerful punch. Defense, offense. It punches, it pushes, and best of all it can distract while —"

She jabbed out at Sasha with her left, followed it with a right cross. Both fists stopped less than an inch from Sasha's face, and came so fast and hard she lost her breath.

"Didn't see the right coming, did you?"

"I hardly saw either of them. How many fights have you been in?"

"I don't keep count. Here." She held up her gloved hands, palms toward Sasha. "Fist in the palm, like the ball in the glove. Left. Come on, rookie, left! Left. Right. Left. Better. Lead with your knuckles, *exhale,* lift your shoulder. Concentrate. I want you to rotate your arm. You lift, and as you jab, you rotate. All one motion now. Left!"

Sasha threw jabs until her arms ached.

215

When she lowered them, Riley poked her. "Come on, you haven't even broken a sweat yet." But she reached in the small duffle she'd brought out, handed Sasha a bottle of water. "Hydrate anyway."

"I thought you'd show me some martial arts, not just have me punch your hands."

"Baby steps, Sash."

She opened the water, drank. "I've never actually hit anyone before."

Riley widened her eyes. "I'd never have guessed."

"Oh, shut up." But rolling her aching shoulders, Sasha laughed.

Bran thought yanking some bloody weeds from the bloody vegetable garden might purge him of the considerable resentment still stuck in his gut. And he'd take some of the herbs and roots while he was about it. He could use them.

Armed with a hoe and work gloves from the garden shed, his own boline for harvesting, he made his way to the garden gate. Over the odd and homey hum the chickens made, he heard Sasha laugh.

The woman plagued him, he thought with no little bitterness. Those big blue eyes filled with her hurt feelings. And worse. *Disappointment.*

As if telling everybody and their brother you were a hereditary witch was part and parcel of everyday conversation over a bloody pint in the bloody pub.

He hadn't known her a week, for Christ's sake. And let's not be forgetting that being what he was, using what he had, saved her from an ugly fate.

But not before she'd been hurt, he thought. It fucking killed him she'd been hurt.

And he didn't have time for that. They were, all of them, going into a situation that risked more than cuts and bruises, so he couldn't afford to find himself worrying about her the way he found himself worrying about her. Each of them had to hold their own, use whatever skill or power at their disposal.

There was a lot more at stake than one woman.

He could want her, he thought, glancing toward the grove again. That was allowed. Sex never hurt anyone if done right and both were willing. And did a lot more to ease the mood and clear the mind than hoeing rows or pulling weeds.

He caught movement and, curious, propped the hoe against the fence, walked to the far corner of the garden.

He could see now, through the trees, Sasha in a skinny sleeveless black shirt punching into Riley's open hands. She'd twisted her hair up somehow or other, he noted, leaving the back of her neck exposed.

Entertained, and considerably charmed, he leaned on the fence, watched the show.

Teaching her a right cross, he realized.

Doyle wandered down, stood on the other side of the fence. "What's the deal?"

"Looks like a boxing lesson."

Doyle watched a moment. "Brunette's got form. The blonde hits like a girl."

"She does, but I've got twenty says she won't when Riley's done teaching her."

Doyle watched another moment, the way Riley demonstrated technique, or came around to take Sasha's shoulders, move her body with the punch.

"Sucker bet, but I'm going to take it anyway. What's life without a gamble?"

"Done. She won't give up, you see. And Riley, she won't give up on her. She may not turn her into a brawler, but Sasha will learn to hold her own. And that's needed for all of this."

"You could walk away from it."

"We all could. None of us will, if that's what you're wondering. We all got our arses handed to us today, yet here we are."

With a tug of pride, Bran lifted his chin toward the olive grove. "And there's the two of them, getting and giving boxing lessons under the olive trees. The gods, I think they don't understand the mortal's stubborn resilience. So they underestimate us."

Doyle hooked his thumbs in his pockets, watched Sasha throw a combination of jabs and crosses into Riley's hands. "Boxing lesson, such as it is, makes sense. More than a sorcerer with a hoe digging up weeds. You could . . ." He wiggled his fingers. "And get rid of them."

"The physical helps the brain, and I've been taught not to use magick to be lazy. Still." As a kind of test, Bran held his hands out, spread them. After no more than a quiet shimmer, not a single weed remained.

"Quicker that way," Doyle commented.

"It is. You don't have much of a reaction to the magickal."

"Dated a witch."

Intrigued, Bran lifted his scarred eyebrow, leaned companionably on the fence. "Did you now?"

"Redhead, built in a way made you sure God's a man."

"It didn't work out between you?"

"For a while it did. She wasn't shy about using what she had. She wasn't shy about anything," Doyle added with a grin.

"She couldn't help you with this venture?"

"Not for lack of trying. But she told me there would be five others, each with a separate power. Once united, we might forge the sword that would pierce the heart of a vengeful god. Then again, she also told me love would pierce *my* heart with fang and claw and lead me to the path of death."

He let out a half laugh. "She had a way, that redhead. So . . . you got dibs on the blonde?"

"No." It seemed childish, and he — Bloody hell. "Yes."

"Just getting with the program. Hey, that was a decent combination." Frowning, Doyle watched Sasha repeat it. "Decent," he repeated. "Fuck me, I'm going to owe you twenty. I can already see it."

As it struck him as foolish to put the weeds *back,* then hoe and yank at them again, Bran harvested the herbs he wanted, then walked up the hillside, through another olive grove for the roots and plants he found useful.

He'd continue to work in his room, he decided, as he didn't see the point in pushing what he did and was in everyone's face. Clearly they'd need more salve if their first encounter with Nerezza was any indication. Plus, the way his side had begun to pull, he needed another application himself. He considered making salves and basic potions housewifery — with no offense to the housewife — in that it was both tedious and necessary.

Since it was, the work on the more interesting potion and spell he'd only begun would have to wait.

As he wasn't in the mood for more conversation, he took the terrace steps, intending to slip into his room, deal with what needed doing.

He saw the easel, the painting and, struck, stopped.

It was . . . glorious, he decided. He could all but smell the sea breeze wafting out of the canvas. Everything glowed, as if lit not only by the sun, but some secret, inner light.

There were all manner of magicks, he thought, and she had her own.

He heard her coming — her laugh, or more a laughing groan, and her voice mixed with Riley's as they came up the steps. Rather than slip into his room, he turned.

She glowed, he thought, like the painting. From the sun, the exercise, and he decided, the accomplishment.

"I was just admiring your work."

"It isn't finished."

"Isn't it?"

"And it's mine," Riley said, definitely, "so don't get any ideas. If you want anything from the village, speak now. I'm heading in to get the makings for my world-famous margaritas."

"Actually, there are a couple things."

"Make a list or come with." Riley nodded at the herbs and plants in his hands. "You making dinner?"

"No, I have other uses for this, and since I do, I'll just give you the list I've already made up, as I was going to ask for the loan of the jeep and go in for them myself."

She took the list, glanced at it, shifted her eyes up to his. "I'll see what I can do."

"Thanks for that." He took some money out of his pocket. "Let me know if it runs more."

"Count on that. I'll see you back here at cocktail time."

"When would that be?"

"When I get back. I'll dig out those bands for you," she told Sasha and strode off.

"And how's your arm?"

"It's fine," Sasha said, just a little primly. "Thank you for what you did."

He cupped her elbow, examined it himself. If she'd asked him — which she hadn't —

he would have advised waiting at least a day before a damn boxing lesson. As it was, the graze showed pinker than he liked.

"Use the salve again, then once more tonight. By morning it should be well healed."

"All right."

"And the ankle?"

"It's fine, Bran."

He lifted those hooded eyes, pinned her. "And you'd tell me, would you, if it was otherwise?"

"We all have to be strong and healthy if we're going to face off with Nerezza again. So yes, I would. What are those for?"

"These? For what you'd call medicines for the most part. It's best to be prepared."

He felt a burning in his side, and for a moment, his vision blurred.

"What is it? What's wrong? Oh! You're bleeding."

He glanced down toward the burn, cursed when he saw the spread of blood on his shirt. "Fuck me."

"How bad is it? Let me see." Before he could stop her — proving he was more than a little off his game — she'd tugged his shirt up. "Oh, God! Did this happen today? Why didn't you *tell* anyone? Why are you an idiot?"

"It's better than it was. I just ran out of salve. And aren't I about to make more? I'll see to it."

"And you continue to be an idiot. I still have plenty. Go in. Sit down. Take off your shirt." She touched her fingers to the rawness around the scatter of open wounds. "It's hot to the touch."

"You think I can't feel it, seeing as it's myself?"

As fed up as she was afraid, she grabbed the plants from him, tossed them on her makeshift worktable. "Inside, and sit down. Damn it, you're fussing over a cut on my arm when you've got this?"

"I know what to do for it," he snapped, as she shoved him toward the doors.

"Good. You'll tell me what that is, and I'll do it. It's no wonder it wasn't done right when you insisted on doing it yourself. You can't possibly reach it all well enough to do it right, and you wouldn't have run out of salve if you'd kept enough for yourself."

"I thought I had." Heat rolled up through him until he feared he might drop from it. "I told you this isn't my strength — the healing."

But he sat on the side of her bed as the room wanted to spin on him. "I thought I'd let it run clean, but I missed something."

"Get this off." She dragged the shirt over his head, then used it to staunch some of the blood. "Some look like they're healing fine — like my arm — and others are raw, a little swollen. But this one around toward your back, it's the worst. A puncture — a pair of them."

Fangs, she thought.

"I don't have to be a doctor to know infection when I see it."

He twisted, winced, then bore down until he could see. And didn't care for the red streaks on his skin.

"That's what I missed, though I got some of the salve on it, so now . . . I need a couple of things from my room."

"You're white as a sheet," she said, easily pushing him back. "And you're burning up, clammy. Tell me what you need and I'll get it. I won't touch anything else," she said between her teeth when he hesitated.

"It'd be best if you didn't. I need a knife — should be on the table I set up for work. And there's a leather case — I can unlock it from here. Inside are vials and jars. I need the vial with the diamond-shaped stopper. There's a blue liquid inside. Like your eyes. Clear and crystalline blue. And . . . Why didn't I think of this before? A small copper bowl. Three white candles wouldn't hurt.

That's another case, much like the first. There's a triquetra on the top."

"All right. I'll be right back."

Careless, he told himself. But his whole side had been a misery, and he couldn't see the damn punctures on his back. Now, as she'd said, there was infection, and that was running through him hot and fast, inflaming the other wounds along the way.

He knew what to do, and some good could come out of it.

Provided he didn't pass out first, and die while unconscious.

And he'd be damned if he would.

She came rushing back with the bowl, the candles, the vial — and three knives.

"I didn't know which one."

"My fault." Focusing against the pain made his heart hammer. He couldn't slow it. "The silver handle would be best. If you'd get a glass of water? Whiskey's better — but that's a matter of taste. The water will do fine. Three drops from the vial — no, make it five, considering."

She got a glass of water from the bathroom, carefully added five drops from the vial, re-stoppered it.

"What does this do?"

"Think of it as a kind of antibiotic." He gave the glass a scowl, then downed the

226

contents. "Ah, God. Whiskey masks the taste of it, but beggars can't be choosers. You should get Sawyer or Doyle for the next."

"Why?"

"Because I can't reach the fecking wound with the knife myself. It needs to be opened a certain way, and we'd catch the blood — and the poison in it — in the bowl. It'll be useful."

"Poisoned blood, useful?"

"Don't ask if you don't want to know. It'll be messy, but it should do the job. So if you'll get either Sawyer or —"

"Do you think I'm so weak?"

"I don't think that at all." He swayed, had to catch himself, grip the bed to sit upright. "It's only that —"

Because she worried she was weak, she picked up the silver-handled knife. "How do I open it?"

"All right then, all right. I need to stand." He gripped one of the bedposts, pulled himself up. Fresh sweat popped out on his skin. "The candles on the floor, they're three points of a triangle."

She set them out. "Do they need to be lighted? Should I get matches?"

"Yes, and no." He stretched out a hand, and the wicks flickered to life. "Stand behind me, and hold the bowl under the wound in your left hand, the knife in your right. When I tell you, you're to draw a circle around the two punctures."

"With the knife?"

"Not deep, just enough to break the skin. And when I tell you, you'll open each puncture by carving them with an X. Sharp and quick now, and if you feel you'd hesitate, get one of the men."

"All right."

He gripped the bedpost with both hands, and stared at the candles.

"Whatever you see or feel, do just as I've said."

He took a moment to steady himself, center himself.

"Airmed, Brigid, Dian Cecht, hear your son and servant. This pure light I offer you, one by three." As he spoke the flames speared up, shone white as the wax. "Banish the dark within my blood. Within this circle, draw it clear. Now, Sasha, the circle."

His fingers whitened on the bedpost as the knife point scored over his inflamed flesh. "I call upon you, power to power and blood to blood, till the black runs clear, runs true.

"As you will, so mote it be."

He braced himself. "Open them, catch all

that comes in the bowl. Quick and sharp."

It felt as if she scored him with a flaming blade, both burn and cut sliced deep, and hot.

Then the fire was in him, a burning-hot wire through his blood. His skin quivered; his knees shook and wanted to buckle.

Her voice came through the throbbing in his head.

"Just hold on. Hold on. It's nearly done."

He focused on her voice — it quivered as well, but she continued to talk him through.

"The redness is fading. How much more?"

"Not done. It's better, not finished, but better." He could breathe now, and as the dizziness passed, loosened his vise grip on the bedpost.

"It looks clear now."

"Nearly," he told her. "Very nearly."

"How will I know when —" The three candle flames flashed, a quick, hard burst of light, then glowed quiet. "Oh."

"That should do it."

"Let me get a towel to — You've stopped bleeding. Just stopped."

"Well, three healing deities should be able to staunch blood if they've a mind to. Especially with some fine assistance." He turned, took the bowl from her.

"It's black. It came out black until . . ." It

made her stomach roil to look at the blood. "What should I do now?"

"If you can manage it, you could coat the punctures with the salve. I can reach the rest. And that should take care of things."

She took it from the top of her dresser, coated her fingers, spread it as gently as she could on the punctures. Then moved on to the scoring along his ribs.

"You should take this," she told him.

"I'll make more."

"How long does it take to make?"

"A bit of time." She'd helped him, he reminded himself, so he owed her honesty. "And a day to cure."

Nodding, she took more salve, coated her injured arm with it, closed the jar, and then to his amused surprise, dropped it in one of the pockets of his cargoes.

"If I need more, I'll ask for it."

"All right."

She looked at the bowl, the way his healthy red blood lay over the sick and black. "What will you do with it?"

"I've some ideas to work out. For now, seal it up. You've a steady hand, Sasha. And I'm grateful."

"Then don't be careless again." She bent down for the candles, handed them to him. "I'm going to finish Riley's painting, then

230

I'm really going to be ready for one of her famous margaritas."

"I could do with one myself." He set the candles down, slid the knife in his belt, then picked them up again. "I'll see you downstairs."

He started to the door, stopped to turn back to her. "I've never thought you weak, not for a moment. I hope you've stopped thinking of yourself that way."

"I have."

"I'm glad of it."

He took his knife, his candles, and the copper bowl with poisoned blood and clean mixed to his room, then went back for the herbs and plants.

A day to cure, he reminded himself when he considered putting off making the salve.

So he cleansed his knife, sealed the blood. And got to work on the housewifery.

CHAPTER TEN

Riley mixed margaritas on the terrace, and considered playing bartender her kitchen contribution for the day.

Along with the full pitcher and glasses, she brought out her maps.

She poured the first glass, held up a finger while she sampled, then smiled. "Definitely. More where this came from," she said, and sat. "I got us an RIB," she began.

"What is that?" Sasha asked.

"Rigid-hulled inflatable boat," Doyle told her. "How big?" he demanded as Sasha murmured, "Inflatable?"

"Twenty-eight feet, with a wheelhouse. My contact says she'll do seventy knots."

Bran considered the pitcher, decided why the hell not, and poured out glasses. "The friend of a friend of an uncle?"

"Not this time. Cousin of a friend's husband."

"Outboard?" Doyle asked.

"Yeah. Can you handle an RIB?"

"I can, and have."

"Good, that makes two of us."

"When you say inflatable . . ." Sasha began.

"Fast, open — stable. It's a good dive boat," Riley assured her. "I can score us diving equipment, but we're going to have to shell out some."

"I can get shells, all you need," Annika said.

"Pay," Riley explained. "I've worked us a deal, but it's not free."

"I don't know how to dive."

"You'll stick with me when the time comes. I figure we start with the easier-accessed caves, work our way up — or down. Can you snorkel?"

"I haven't in years."

"It'll come back to you."

As they spoke Sawyer studied Riley's maps. "I've done some research on some of these caves. The easier accessed won't be a problem, which strikes me as the problem. I don't think we're going to find what we're after somewhere anybody can get into."

"That's a good point. But we should eliminate in any case." Bran glanced around the table for agreement. "And practice as well."

"What about your compass?" Sasha tried a sip of the margarita and thought Riley was right. Definitely. "Would it help with location or direction?"

Obligingly, Sawyer took it out, laid it on the map. Where it sat, still and quiet.

"Battery low?" Riley suggested.

"Ha. Usually it means I can't expect miracles until I put some work into it."

"It's fair." Annika nodded. "To deserve miracles, you must work, and believe. This is very nice," she said to Riley as she drank.

"World famous for a reason. Okay, I can outfit us, get us going for the cost of fuel, oxygen, and a hundred euro a day. If that works, we can pick up the boat in the morning."

"More than a fair price." Bran deliberated over the maps. "I'd say we could explore and/or eliminate several of these caves in a day or two. Then move on to the less accessible."

"Works for me."

"Will you be able to dive?" Sasha caught the flare of annoyance in Bran's eyes, simply pushed forward. "He was hurt more seriously than he told us. And there's no point being angry with me. We're a team," she reminded him. "So the health of one is of concern to all."

"What the hell, Irish."

"Sasha's not being fully accurate. It was more serious than I realized, and since it's been dealt with now, there was no reason to bring it up."

"Let's see." Riley circled her finger in the air. "Come on, show and tell. Nobody dives if they're not fit for it. That's just common sense."

"Bugger it." He shoved up, tugged up his shirt.

Annika made a sound of sympathy, but Riley rose, gave the healing wounds a careful look. "Okay, bitch got you good, but you're healing. Next time, ditch the stoic."

"It's true what he said. He missed treating the one on his back — and it got infected, badly. And fast," Sasha added. "We should use a buddy system if . . . if and when this happens again. Any of us might not see how bad we're hurt until it festers."

"Good thinking. We can pick up the boat at nine tomorrow morning. Is everyone in?" Riley got nods or shrugs. "Done," she declared, and poured herself another drink.

Sasha opted to make it an early night. Battling gods in the morning, boxing lessons in the afternoon, margaritas in the evening, followed by putting together a reasonable meal for six could wear a person out.

And she didn't want to think about the idea of strapping on an oxygen tank and jumping off a damn inflatable boat.

She got into bed with her sketch pad, leaving the terrace doors open so she could hear the sea. And unwound her crowded thoughts by drawing the olive grove, then amused herself by adding Riley and herself in boxing shorts and gloves.

She did a study of the blooming prickly pear from memory, and considered the idea of doing a series — small, square canvases — of local flora.

She drifted off, lights on, before she'd finished her study of a mandarin tree.

In her own room, Riley worked on her laptop. She toggled between research and journal entries. Knowledge was a weapon to her mind, and the more you knew, the better armed.

She had maps tacked to the mirror for easy reference. Some books she'd downloaded to her tablet, but there were many, a great many, not available by that system. So she had a pile of old books nearby, and had already made arrangements to send for others from her library.

The experience in the cave told her they

didn't know nearly enough. Yet.

Like Sasha, she'd left her terrace doors open, and enjoyed the sound of the sea mixed with the quiet snores of Apollo, who sprawled sleeping by her chair.

She had her gun, loaded and unholstered, within easy reach. And she laid her hand on it when a new sound — feet padding quietly on stone — joined the others.

Her hand relaxed again when Sasha stepped up to the open doors.

"Hey. Thought you were conked."

"Bran's room is empty."

"He's probably still downstairs. I had some work I wanted to . . ." She trailed off when she got a good look at Sasha's eyes in the wash of moonlight. "Oh, okay. Dreamwalking." She got to her feet, and Apollo stirred himself with a heroic and noisy yawn.

"Do you need Bran?"

"He should know. You should all know."

"Absolutely. Let's go find him." She walked up to Sasha, laid a hand on Apollo's head to stop him from rubbing up against her dreaming friend. "We can go down this way."

"Yes, we'll go together." She looked at Riley, then walking with her, up at the sky. "The moon will soon be full."

"Yeah, it will. Did you dream about the moon?"

"Not yet."

By its light they went down the terrace steps, and together turned toward the sound of voices.

The three men sat at the long table, each nursing a beer.

No Annika, Riley noted. A men-only deal, which stoked suspicion.

"You boys talking sports and the stock market?"

Doyle gave her a long look out of hooded eyes. "You girls having a slumber party?"

"Maybe we'll braid Sasha's hair — when she actually wakes up. Where's Annika — Okay, here she comes."

"She's dream-walking." Bran pushed away from the table. "Be careful with her."

"She came to me, when she couldn't find you. You're wet," Riley said to Annika.

"I had a swim. Is something wrong?"

"Not wrong." Very gently, Bran touched Sasha's shoulder. "Did you want me?"

"I do. I have. I will. There are secrets here, each holds them. I will keep them, even from myself, until . . . She can't see them. Though she wonders, and she watches. She watches even now, in the Globe of All."

"The Globe of All?" Bran repeated, glancing at the cupped hand Sasha held out.

"It is precious to her, but is not hers. What is taken in lies and through bloodshed cannot belong. But it serves her. And we are there." She cupped one hand above the other. "Caught in the globe for her to see."

"Then she should see this." Doyle shot up a middle finger.

"She will come. Your sword is needed. It will take weapons and warriors, but it will take wile and will, faith and fortitude. Unity that only comes through trust and truth. She watches." She laid a hand on Bran's heart. "Will you draw the curtain?"

"I can try."

"There is no try, only do. Sorry," Sawyer said immediately.

"Yoda's never wrong." Riley patted his shoulder. "Where should we look, Sasha?"

"Where no one has. She watches, but it waits. Its fire cold under the blue light, it waits, the first of three in the willing heart. She cannot see, and would drain me to sharpen her sight."

"She won't." Bran clasped her hand in his. "I swear it."

"She destroys what loves because she does not. And when she comes, death marches with her."

"When and where?" Doyle demanded.

"Can you see that?"

"I . . ." On a choked gasp, Sasha clamped her head in her hands. "She claws at me. Inside my head. She tears and bites. Draw the curtain. Oh, God, draw the curtain."

"Wake up." Bran gripped her arms, shook her. "Sasha, wake up."

"Locked in. She locks me in."

"No, you have the key." He pulled her to her toes so her eyes were level with his. "You are the key." He kissed her, not gently. "Use what you are." He kissed her again, and light snapped around them. "Wake up!"

She sucked in air like a swimmer surfacing from deep water. When her bones melted, Bran scooped her up, then sat cradling her.

"You're all right."

"My head."

"You came out too fast, and you will fight it. Just breathe through it. Annika, would you get her some water?"

"What happened? Why —" She broke off when she realized she sat on Bran's lap, outside, and in nothing but a night slip. "Oh, God. Again?"

When she tugged the slip down her thighs, Riley let out a bark of laughter that sounded like relief. "Relax, you're covered. If I'd been the one wandering around dream-walking, I'd be standing here naked. I've got plenty of aspirin, and a couple Percocet I hold back for emergencies."

"I can see to it. Breathe," Bran repeated. "And relax." He laid his hands on her head, stroked, ran his fingers through her hair, took them over her forehead, back, over her scalp to the back of her neck.

"Put it in my hands," he murmured as Annika rushed back with a glass of water. "It's only pain. I can ease it if you put it into my hands."

"I remember."

"Good. Remembering means you're not fighting it. The less you fight it, the less of an opening you give her."

"The Globe of All." She sipped the water. "What is it?"

"I don't know. But," Riley vowed, "I'll find out."

"She had it, in the cave. In her hand. Did you see it?"

"A glass ball," Sawyer said. "I didn't get a good look — a little busy — but there was movement in it. You said it wasn't hers."

"I don't know whose it was, I'm sorry."

"I'll find out," Riley assured her. "It's what I do. Now what's this about a curtain?"

"What happens when you draw a curtain?" Bran continued to rub Sasha's head. "You

241

block or hide things. I'll work on that. Draw curtains, you could say, around us, so we're not as exposed to her."

"It's better now. Thanks." When she tried to get up, Bran simply held her in place.

"You're fine where you are."

"I can't add more to any of this, at least not right now. I don't understand half of what I said, and I'm too tired to think. I need to sleep."

"I'll take you up."

"You don't need to —"

"I need a few things from my room."

He walked her up, held her for a moment in the doorway. "I can protect you, at least to a point."

"What?"

"Charms and spells," he said, and drew her back. "I'd want your permission for that."

"To block her out."

"As much as I can. The rest is for you. You are the key, Sasha. You are the master of your own gift."

"It doesn't feel like it. Yes. Blocking her out doesn't just help me, it helps all of us."

"Go on to bed then, and I'll start drawing the curtain."

He went to his room, gathered what he needed, got out his book. He made up two charms specific to Sasha. By the time he went back to her room, she slept.

He slipped a charm under her pillow, then lifted her head to fasten the stones he'd fashioned into a necklace on a thin leather cord around her neck.

It would serve, for now, he thought.

"The rest is up to you," he whispered, and laid his fingers on her temple, murmured the spell that would give her quiet, dreamless sleep until morning.

Then he left her to do the real work of the night.

He found the others still on the terrace.

"Is she okay?" Riley asked him.

"Sleeping."

"What's in the bag?"

"A bit of this, some of that." He stepped back to scan the house. "Big, bloody house, and we'll need to cloak every door and window."

"We can help. We want to help," Annika said.

"For more usual protection, there are basic spells, chants, charms. But when dealing with a god . . . Still, you could help. We'll cast a circle, but first we could use a broom."

"Seriously?" Sawyer grinned. "You're not going to like —"

He made a whooshing motion with his hand.

"I'm absolutely not, no. Two brooms would save time if we have them, and as I doubt we've a cauldron handy — I'll be rectifying that soon — a large pot of water, three bowls. Glass or metal."

While the others went to get what he needed, Bran went down to the lawn, set out white candles in a large ring on the grass.

He set the pot Sawyer hauled out to him in the center, crossed the two brooms in front of it, set out the bowls. Carrying his bag, he walked inside the ring.

"We'll form a circle in the circle," he said, and set the bag down. "You'll need to clear and open your minds as best you can. And don't break the circle."

He glanced up to Sasha's doors. "She asked for trust, so I'm trusting it's the right thing to share what's mine."

He flung out his arms, and the white candles flamed.

Annika applauded, then hunched, crossing her arms over her chest. "I'm apol— sorry."

"Not at all."

"It's serious."

"It is, but there should always be joy."

Now he held his palms up, elbows bent at his waist. "On this night, in this hour, I call upon the ancient powers. We cast the circle within this light, and here we make magicks white. I am your servant, your soldier, your son. All you bid I have done. These hearts and minds the fates entwined join here with me and cast together our destiny. As you will, so mote it be.

"Fire bright, candlelight." Under the pot, flames sparked and lit. And the candles shot up white spears of light.

"Earth lift, air drift." The ground under the bowls rose into smooth mounds. The crossed brooms floated a foot above the ground.

"Water clear, simmer here."

As the water in the pot bubbled and steamed, Bran took crystals from his bag, closed them in his fists. When he opened them, he flicked the powder they'd become into the simmering water.

Vapor and blue smoke rose.

"Here I brew, here I make the veil of white, and all within are blocked from sight. Safe in body, mind, and heart." As he spoke he circled the pot, circled a hand in the air that stirred the wind. "No power can this curtain part. And so all within remain concealed, my blood forms the seal."

He took the knife from his belt, scored it across his palm. Flicked his blood into the vapor.

For an instant it washed red, seemed to pulse. Then it rose thick and white.

"So it is done," he stated. He frowned down at his palm, closed his fist over the shallow wound.

"I feel like applauding myself." Riley studied the floating brooms, barely resisted tapping one just to see what happened. "You put on a hell of a show, Irish."

"In the immortal words? You ain't seen nothing yet." He smiled at her. "Take a broom."

She did, ran her fingers over the handle. "Feels like a broom."

"Because it is. If you'd take the other, Annika, and you'll sweep over every door and window."

"Every one?"

Laughing, he patted Riley's shoulder. "As I said, big, bloody house. Doyle and Sawyer, you'll take a bowl each, fill it from the pot. And you'll sprinkle a bit of water along windowsills and thresholds. Think of it as the base layer."

As Sawyer did, Doyle took a bowl, dipped it into the pot.

"What's your second act?" he asked.

Bran took the last bowl, dipped it. Then, holding it in two hands, smiled again. "I'll be bringing the curtain down from above."

So saying, he levitated, rising up over the lawn, then the house.

"I hate to repeat myself, but holy shit. In any language," Sawyer added.

"He's got more than he let on." Considering that, Riley propped the broom on her shoulder. "Okay, Anni, let's get sweeping."

Though it was barely dawn, Sasha made her way down to the kitchen. She thought she'd make breakfast, as she wanted to keep her hands busy — and hopefully keep everyone else's mind off the fact that she'd paraded around half naked the night before.

Very first chance, she'd invest in some pajamas.

She found Riley already in the kitchen inhaling coffee.

"I thought I was the first up."

Riley kept inhaling, shook her head. "Ended up researching late, conked a couple hours. Woke up restless and itchy. So coffee. Figured I'd break some eggs or whatever for breakfast, but now that you're here . . ."

"I'll do it."

"Even better. Nice necklace."

Sasha lifted her hand to it as she walked

to the refrigerator. "I was wearing it when I woke up. I assume it means something."

"Closer look." Riley slipped a finger under it, studied the stones and crystals. "Research mode tells me these are protective stones. To, like, ward off negative thoughts and intentions — against you. Since it's easy money Bran put it on you, I'd say it's potent and aimed at Nerezza. How's your head this morning?"

"It's fine. I need pajamas."

On a hooting laugh, Riley walked back for more coffee. "I don't think the little number you were almost wearing had the biggest impact. Not that you weren't fetching."

"Up yours, Riley."

"That's the way. Plus, as it turned out, you were only the warm-up act."

"What?" Sasha nearly bobbled the eggs she'd pulled out. "What happened?"

"Bran happened." She leaned against the counter, crossed her ankles. "You know, I've seen all sorts of rituals, ceremonies, and seen some wild stuff in my line, but he topped all of it. We got bacon?"

"Yes. For God's sake, Riley."

"I'm hungry. No reason you can't do the breakfast thing while I talk."

"Can you work a juicer?"

"I can figure it out."

"Oranges." She pointed to the bowl. "Juicer. Talk."

While bacon sizzled and the juicer whirled, Riley filled in the details.

"He . . . flew?"

"More floated. Annika and I are on broom detail — I confess I straddled mine once, just to see if it would take off. No luck. But every once in a while, one of us would hit, like, this little pocket of . . . dark. Just something like a shadow, but more tangible, then we'd hit it with the broom, and poof. All gone. And the other guys are sprinkling water, and this white vapor would puff up for a second. Wild stuff. All the while Bran floating up there with his bowl, and the vapor's drifting down over the house. Like the curtain you said we needed."

Riley poured herself a short glass of juice to test. "Good stuff. You really missed it, Sash. And my take? He's got a lot more than he's shown us."

Sasha hesitated, glanced toward the doorway. "I've dreamed about him."

"Yeah, you said."

"I didn't . . . not everything." She'd spoken — or prophesized — about the need for trust, then didn't give her own. "Out there, on the cliff, Bran and I. Standing there, in a storm. Lightning, thunder, the wind, the sea crashing. He called the storm. He holds the lightning like reins. And we're together. I don't just mean on the cliff together."

"I get what you mean. Why does that worry you? Being with him?"

"Because I've never been with anyone."

"I admit it'll give you a minute thinking about sex with a sorcerer but . . . Whoa." Riley stopped herself, turned fully around. "Anyone? Ever? At all?"

"Every time I came close — had feelings, thought I was close to someone — I'd do or say something that ruined it, and they'd step back."

"First lesson — like the jab. Why are you to blame? Some of the time, sure. We all screw up. But every time it's you? That's bullshit and it's annoying."

"I'd be the one saying or doing it. I'd forget to be careful, and something would slip. Then I'd be an oddity instead of a person. Or at least an oddity as well as a person. And I'd feel their feelings shift away."

"That's on them. I'd say picking the wrong guy's on you, but you've got to try a few on to see what fits. So, maybe you should try him on. You're no oddity to any of us, and certainly not to Bran."

"This doesn't seem like the time to . . . try anyone on."

"More bullshit. We could lose. I don't intend to, but you've got to factor it in. Do you want to go out not knowing? Think about it," she said as she heard bootsteps approach. "And cut yourself — and from where I'm standing him — a break."

She could think about it, Sasha decided. She wasn't sure which brought more stress. Thinking about being with Bran or thinking about riding in an inflatable boat, then diving under the water. They both gave her the jitters.

After breakfast, eaten in shifts, she packed sunscreen, an extra shirt, her sketch pad. Then stopped stalling and went to Bran's terrace doors.

He glanced up from studying the contents of one of his cases.

"Ready, are you? I'm nearly."

"I wanted to — to thank you. I found the little bag, the charm, under my pillow. And this." She touched the necklace.

"They helped?"

"They helped."

"This." He stepped over, tapped one of the stones on the necklace. "Cobbled together a bit hastily."

"I like it. I wanted to give you this." Taking the leap, she opened her bag, and the sketchbook, to take out the sketch she'd laid inside.

His easy smile faded; his eyes sharpened as he took it. "When did you draw this?"

"Before I met you. It was one of the strongest dreams, recurring. I even painted it, felt I had to. I know things can be changed. A different choice, a different outcome. At least some of the time. And I realized by not showing you, I wasn't giving you that choice."

"And what of your choice?"

"I made mine. I guess I made mine by giving that to you." Gathering her courage, she framed his face with her hands, touched her lips to his. "They'll be waiting for us," she said, and turned for the doors.

He closed them with a thought before she reached them.

"Do you think I need a sketch to decide if I want you?"

"I thought you should know that, just like the six of us being here . . . It's all part of it. And you shouldn't be bound by that, not for something so personal."

Nerves frayed, she reached behind her, twisted the knob. "Would you open the doors?"

"No."

"They'll be waiting for us."

"They can bloody well wait." He crossed to her, laid his hands on the glass on either side of her head. "Nervous, are you?"

"You're deliberately making me nervous."

"You should be nervous. Be a little afraid as well, of what the man you drew is able to do."

"You won't hurt me that way, and I'm not helpless. Not anymore."

"You've never been. My choice? That's what you're asking?"

He took her mouth, hard and fast, trapping her against the door with his body, letting his hands mold hers. "That's my choice. That's been my choice since you came knocking on my door, eyes dream-struck. It's not your dreams binding me. It's you."

His lips came back to hers, but this time she held on, this time she poured herself into the kiss. "I've wanted you since before I met you. I want —"

She broke off at the pounding on the door. "We're rolling!" Doyle called.

"All right." But he kissed her again. "We'll be finishing what we've started here, *fáidh.*"

"Yes." The laugh fluttered up from her heart. "We will. But now you have to open the doors."

CHAPTER ELEVEN

It didn't look like an inflatable boat. As Sasha's imagination had formed a big yellow life raft with paddles, seeing an actual boat with motor, covered cabin, benches — and one that remained reasonably steady when she stepped on board — flooded her with relief.

Until she saw the diving equipment.

"Buck up." Riley slapped her shoulder. "You'll do fine. What about you, Irish, and the bit about sorcerers not being able to cross water?"

"It's not can't so much as would rather not." He took a small vial from his pocket, downed the contents. "I'll do fine as well. Who'll be piloting this thing?"

Riley hesitated, then glanced over at Doyle as he checked over the equipment in the wheelhouse. "Can you handle it?"

He shrugged. "Sure."

"I'll give you the bearings. That way I can

go over the equipment and basics with the novices."

"Meaning me," Sasha said. "Shouldn't someone stay with the boat? I could stay with the boat."

"That's what anchors and buoys are for. You've dived?" Riley asked Bran.

"A few times, yes."

"And you?"

Sawyer nodded. "More than a few."

"I know this," Annika put in before Riley asked.

"Okay, grab wetsuits, and I'll get us going." She walked to the wheelhouse.

Sasha might have been full of doubts, but she reassured herself. She was a good swimmer, a strong swimmer, so if worse came to worst . . .

She stripped down to her bathing suit — a simple black tank, and a far cry from Annika's microscopic bikini — and busied herself slithering and tugging herself into a wetsuit while Doyle eased the boat out of its slip.

"It's fun," Sawyer told her as he zipped up his own. "A whole new experience."

"It feels like I've been having whole new experiences daily since I got to Corfu."

He grinned, turned to the tanks to check them. "That's what makes it fun."

When she saw him lift a harpoon, examine it, she thought he — all of them — had to prepare for more than fun.

"Okay." Riley walked back on deck, opened the top of a long, low bench. "First dive site's only a few minutes away. Masks, regulators, belts. We'll go over all of it," she promised Sasha. "Captain Bligh up there's not too happy about it, but we're going to start with a nice, easy dive. We're not likely to find a flaming star waiting for us, but it'll give everybody a chance to — har-har — get their feet wet. Visibility should be good, so let's everybody stay together-ish — stay in sight. Standard buddy system."

"I've got her, Riley." Bran took his own dive knife out of his bag. "She'll stop being nervous once she's in the water."

"Will I?"

"Trust me."

"Let's go over the gear." Riley picked up a thick vest. "Your buoyancy control device — BCD. This will hold your tank, and help you maintain neutral buoyancy. That's the goal. On the surface, you tend to float, so this, being weighted, will help your descent. The deeper you go, the less buoyancy, so it will regulate. You want the science?"

"I think no."

"You've got clips here for accessories and

necessities. Regulator gauge, depth gauge, knife. You want to keep everything clipped off and tucked."

Riley started talking about drag, swimming "trim," breathing techniques. All of it spun around in Sasha's head as she stood and the various equipment being explained was attached to or loaded on her.

Doyle cut the engine far too soon.

"Let's keep it at about thirty minutes, see how it goes."

"A half hour? Down there?"

"It'll go quicker than you imagine," Bran told her as he competently saw to his own gear.

Doyle weighed anchor; Riley tossed out the marker buoy.

"The cave's due east." She pointed toward the cliff face. "Sawyer, why don't you and Annika go in, then Sasha can follow with Bran. Doyle and I should be right behind you. Just take a couple minutes to get used to it," she told Sasha, and strapped on a BCD.

Sawyer put on his mask, his mouthpiece, and sitting on the side, gave a thumbs-up before rolling backward into the water.

Sasha had time to think — Oh, my God — before Annika laughed, then mimicked Sawyer.

"You can go in feetfirst if you'd rather," Bran began.

"Ladder on the port side," Doyle said as he zipped his wetsuit.

"Why don't I help you down that way?"

Help her, Sasha thought. Watch her, look out for her.

The hell with it.

She clomped over to the side in her fins, boosted herself up.

"Hold your mask in place with one hand. Just roll out." Bran gave her leg an easy pat. "I'm two seconds after you."

Before she could talk herself out of it, Sasha shut her eyes and let herself roll back.

It was a longer drop than she'd anticipated. When she hit the water, she let out a short scream, sucked in too much air. She started to kick back to the surface, but Bran was there, taking her hand.

He made a slow, downward movement with his free hand, clearly signaling her to slow down, relax. Though she wanted to go up, go up into light and air, he pointed down, and drew her with him.

Panic tickled at her throat, brought on an odd dizziness. She knew she was breathing too fast — exactly what Riley warned not to do — but couldn't seem to control it.

Then she saw Annika through the impossibly clear water, doing fluid somersaults with the sunlight cutting through the surface to spotlight her.

Oh, to be that free, she thought, then realized she was — or could be. Nothing held her back but her own fears. Maybe she wasn't ready for somersaults, but that didn't mean she had to give up.

She struggled with her breathing — still too fast, but better — and gave Bran's hand a light squeeze to let him know she was all right.

And finally let herself see the world around her.

The colors, so deep and rich in the coral, the waving plants, the boldly darting fish. So much more than what she'd experienced in the very rudimentary snorkeling she'd done when she'd talked herself into a winter vacation in Aruba some years before.

This time, she wasn't just looking down at the world — like peering through a glass window. She was part of it.

With Bran she swam along the reef, gestured with wonder when she spotted a pumpkin-colored starfish clinging to a rock. She saw another, and a deep red sponge, and watched a lobster scramble across the sandy bottom as if late for an appointment.

When she saw the mouth of the cave, the

panic wanted to rise again. Then Riley streaked by her, glanced back with a quick wave before spearing straight toward the dark, shallow mouth ahead.

Doyle speared through the water after her, might have cut straight into the cave but Riley blocked him.

Waiting for her, she realized, the four of them, with Annika swimming a circle around the other three. She kicked her feet, sent herself forward with Bran beside her.

The six went into the cave, two by two, where the light hung murky. Here, the world was a shadowy green and what lived in it came as shadowed blurs. The blurs became a long, sinuous eel, a pair of octopi with undulating tentacles. The wavering plants hid things, she imagined, that could sting and bite.

She heard the beat of her heart in her own head as she swam through the eerie green light of the tunnel.

It opened, reminding her of the land cave she thought of as Nerezza's. She looked up, almost expecting to see bats swimming and swooping. Instead she saw light, trees, and stared in wonder at the open ceiling between worlds.

Another octopus, uninterested in them, flowed across the bottom of the cave while a school of silvery fish speared away as one as she reached out a hand to touch. She forgot fear as she explored the madly artistic shapes of coral, the living sponges, the oddly fluid movement of a starfish that left its perch when disturbed.

She thought of the painting she could do if she kept all this in her head long enough to sketch it. She forgot her fears, and for a time the true purpose, in the thrill of exploration.

It surprised her when Riley tapped her shoulder, pointed at her watch, then the tunnel. With a reluctance she hadn't anticipated, she swam out again with the others.

When she surfaced, the bright flash of sun, the taste of air, the feel of it on her skin disoriented her. She pulled herself up, then stood, mask in her hand, staring at the water. Knowing what lived in it.

"You're a natural." Riley gave her a light punch on the shoulder before sitting to take off her flippers. "Up for another?"

"Yes."

"I think we stick with one or two more, easy ones, today. You didn't get any sense when we were down there?"

"Sense? Oh. No. No, but I wasn't thinking about the stars, not once we got going. I should have —"

"I think the pull might come more naturally if you're relaxed." Bran handed her a bottle of water. "If all of us are. You enjoyed it."

"You were right. Thirty minutes went by so fast, and wasn't nearly enough."

"You kept trim." Sawyer grabbed a can of Coke from the cooler and, at Riley's nod, tossed it to her, got another for himself. "Not everybody who knows how to swim translates it for diving — not right away. This one?" He pulled another Coke out, handed it to Annika. "She's a freaking fish."

"It's fun to swim with friends."

"The chances of finding what we're after in the other two caves you've got down here are zilch." Doyle broke out a water for himself.

"That's how we cross them off the list, and give Sasha some practice."

"I wish you wouldn't hold back on my account. I'll do okay."

"Yeah, most likely. But what you have to consider is that's not your environment down there, and you're only alive down there because you have equipment that makes it possible. If we run into trouble while we're under, the way we did in the cave up here? Getting out of it's going to take some experience."

She turned to Doyle then, shoved a hand over her water-slick hair. "Am I wrong?"

"No." He drank deep from the bottle. "No, you're not wrong. And it's not like we don't have time," he said to Sasha.

"But you're ready to get it done."

"I'm long past ready." He shook his head, drank again before he turned toward the wheelhouse. "But there's time."

They dived twice more, and Sasha felt more comfortable each time. But she had to admit, to herself at least, the idea of coming up against a dark god while twenty or thirty feet underwater caused considerable anxiety.

Pain, she remembered. Her dreams had been painted with pain and blood and battle. But she could recall none about drowning.

Maybe that was a good sign.

They headed back in to have the tanks refilled, and by popular vote grabbed lunch in the village. They ate on the sidewalk, keeping the conversation about the dives, rather than their underlying purpose.

The combination of the food, the sun, the voices, the bustle all around shifted Sasha's exhilaration into a comfortable, cat-lazy fatigue.

Too used to Riley's driving to worry about

it, she half dozed on the short drive back to the villa, imagining curling up on her bed in her quiet room and napping.

"Got some things I want to check into." Riley got out as the dog trotted over. "Told you we'd be back." She gave him a good rub. "Same deal tomorrow, so I guess we should work out a strategy, try at least one of the more challenging dives."

"Can I take the jeep? I want to pick up a few things," Sawyer explained.

"We were just in the village."

"Didn't want to hold everybody up."

With a shrug, Riley tossed him the keys.

"Can I go with you? Can I shop?"

"Oh, well . . ." But Sawyer made the mistake of looking into Annika's sparkling eyes. "Sure."

"Man down," Doyle commented.

"Later, you can get the coins out, Bran. I've got a contact who'll give Annika a fair price on a few of them. I can sort those out, and we can make that stop before we get on the boat in the morning. You'll have some actual spending money," Riley told Annika.

"Shopping money."

"Yeah, that, too. I'll touch base with him. Bring that back in one piece," she added, and walked toward the villa with Apollo.

"Got work of my own." Doyle trailed off

behind her.

"You should pick up some fresh supplies."

Sawyer shot Sasha a look as he got behind the wheel. "Hell. Yeah, I figured. I'll work it out."

"I want new earrings." Annika jumped into the passenger seat.

"What is it with women and earrings?" Sawyer wondered.

"They're pretty. Bye." She waved to Sasha and Bran. "We're going shopping!"

"May the gods take pity on him," Bran stated, then took her hand to lead her toward the terrace steps.

"I feel like I should do something productive. It's not even three in the afternoon."

"Productive."

"I should sketch out what's in my head, what I saw today. The light in the cave. I want to capture that. And I know I shouldn't try when I feel this lazy."

"Then you'll capture it when you're not. Meanwhile . . ."

He turned into her room with her, booted the doors closed, then whipped her around to press her back against them.

"I think this is where we left off."

He took her mouth, and took her under.

"Now?"

"Oh, absolutely now." He took his lips on

a lazy journey along the column of her throat. "Do you have a problem with that?"

Everything inside her sparked. "No. No, now would be fine. Now would be good."

His hands skimmed up to brush over her breasts. "Now would be wonderful."

Wanting, willing, she wrapped around him, thrilled by the rush of her own pulse, the flood of her own needs. Needs she'd locked away for so long spun free — and there was such joy in them.

She laughed, only a hint of nerves, when he turned her again, walked her backward toward the bed with his mouth still hungry on hers.

Then she was tumbling back, and he with her. And oh, what a sensation, the weight and shape of his body pressed to hers, to feel her own yielding to it. His hands, so strong and sure, molding her like clay until her blood ran hot under her skin.

She wanted to touch him, feared she'd fumble something as she fought to pull off his shirt. She wanted her hands on flesh, on muscle.

"I need to tell you —"

His teeth scraped lightly down her throat; her fingers dug into his shoulder blades.

"In case I do something wrong . . ."

"Nothing could be wrong."

He flipped open the buttons of her shirt, his lips following his fingers.

"It's just — I might. Oh, God, this feels amazing. I've never done this before so I might make a mistake."

She realized she'd just made one when everything stilled. She closed her eyes, asked herself why, *why,* couldn't she have just let it go, just said nothing until it was done.

"Not done what before, exactly?"

She opened her eyes, found his, so dark, so intense, on hers. "Sex. I shouldn't have said anything. Why does it have to matter?"

He shifted, sitting up, drawing her with him. And she felt all the joy and delight leak away into mortification.

"Of course you should have told me, and of course it matters."

"You either want me or you don't." She dug for anger, for anything that would cover the humiliation of tears that wanted to spill.

"That's not the issue. It matters," he repeated, taking her arms when she tried to turn away. "In approach, in tone. The first shouldn't be rushed and greedy, and I was feeling both."

"Since I was feeling the same, why can't we just —"

"Because you don't know. But you will." He lifted her hand, turned it over to lay a kiss lightly in her palm. "If you're sure. It's a gift that can't be taken back."

"I'm sure. I want to feel what you make me feel. I want to be with you. Now."

"Then trust me."

"I couldn't be here if I didn't."

"We want moonlight and stars." As he spoke the room went dusky blue. Lights — candles? stars? — glimmered through it. "The song of the sea, the scent of flowers."

She heard the waves, like a whisper as he laid her back on what had become a bower.

"You're so much more than you've shown us."

Illusions, he thought, but the moment called for them. And for romance, and tenderness. He found he had them for her, and could call on them as easily as he could whistle up the wind.

He cupped her face with one hand, took her lips slow, slow, deep, deeper, until he felt her melt into his bed of feathers and flowers.

He could seduce, degree by degree, give them both the sumptuous. She smelled of the sea, tasted of honey. And under his hands her skin was soft as satin.

On impulse he ran his hands through her hair, scattered tiny rosebuds through it. Looked down to enjoy the way it spread and tumbled over his bower.

"You look like a faerie queen. If I had your gift, I would paint you just like this. Or . . ." He waved a finger through the air, and she was naked but for a scatter of flower petals.

"Oh!" Instinctively, she lifted a hand to cover her breasts, but he caught it, brought it to his lips as he skimmed his gaze over her.

"Yes, just like this. I'm commissioning you to do this self-portrait. Name your price," he murmured and took her mouth again.

How could she have known she could float and fly, could soar and dive all at the same time? That she could burn and shudder. And want, want, want.

His mouth took hers with soul-deep kisses and whispered words she didn't understand. And his hands glided over her, awakening fresh thrills.

His thumbs brushed her nipples, then his tongue, stirring something deep in her belly. Then his mouth closed over her, and that stirring, that pulling flashed into a fast, shocking leap of pleasure.

She cried out from it, arched up as it struck like an arrow.

"You're quick," he murmured.

"What? What?"

"Just the start. Just a sample." He pressed

his lips to her thundering heart. "This time you'll take, and taking, you give."

He gripped her hands with his, as her touch, her explorations tempted him to rush. So he used only his mouth on her, roaming down her torso, pleasing himself when her belly quivered under his tongue.

She moaned for him, moved for him, and the mix of her need and surrender sparked like a wire in his blood. Another time he would give in to that, another time he would let that hunger loose. But now he would seduce her, now he would torment them both.

He brushed his lips over her thigh, and then his tongue along the vulnerable line beside her center. And his teeth, lightly, lightly, until her breath became long, sighing moans, until her body undulated.

He found her warm and wet, so ready to fly up again.

It was like being showered with warm liquid gold, showered with melted jewels. Every inch of her sparkled, shone, glimmered, gleamed. The world was warm and soft, and smothered in flowers, drenched in moonlight.

And the world was only him.

As his mouth came back to hers again, as her hands were free to touch and stroke, she thought nothing could ever be more beautiful.

"Will you look at me now? Look at me, Sasha."

She opened eyes dark and heavy with the glorious weight of pleasure. "Bran."

"This is ours, only."

He banished even the thought of pain as he slipped into her. And she learned there was more beauty. She opened for it, welcomed it. Keeping her eyes on his, she moved with him, let that beauty, the glory of it saturate her.

It took her higher to where the air thinned, the world spun. As even the air shattered around her, she laid her hand on his cheek. "Yes," she said. "Yes," she sighed, and let herself slide down.

She imagined her body pulsing off light. Pale pink and gold light. Warm and soft and lovely. He lay full on her so she imagined the light pulsed right through him as well, and filled the room with color.

She wondered, if this is how sex made you feel, how people managed to do anything else.

"Well, we can be a bit preoccupied with it."

"What? Did I say that out loud?"

"You did." He raised his head, gave her

face a study out of dark, sleepy eyes. "And it's a fine compliment to me."

"You gave me a bed of flowers and moonlight. I'm full of compliments."

He shifted, rolled so he could draw her up against his side. "I want that painting."

She laughed, happy to rest her head on his shoulder. "I don't know how I looked."

"I'll see that you do. Is it bad timing to ask why you haven't been with someone before this?"

"No. I felt I had to be honest about things before I slept with someone. And whenever things got to that point, the man was either put off or too interested in that part of me. It wasn't about me anymore, about wanting *me* anymore. You already knew. And you have something . . . it balances things. That sounds calculated."

"No, it sounds human."

Now she shifted, propped up so she could see his face. "This?" She gestured to the flowers, the moonlight. "What you have, are? It's fascinating. It's compelling. But it's not why I'm here with you now."

"This?" He laid a hand on her temple. "What you have and are is fascinating and compelling. But it's not why I want you here."

Content, she settled down again. "We have

so many things to deal with, to figure out. Gods and stars and caves and vanishing islands. Right now none of it seems real. But it is."

"And we'll do what needs doing. We'll find the star that's here for us. You've seen it."

"Not everything comes through exactly as I see it."

"We'll trust this does, and more, keep looking until we find it."

"You've had more time than I have to believe. I'm still working on it. I guess we should go down, start planning tomorrow's search."

"Be good soldiers," he agreed and stroked a hand down her arm.

"Can I ask you a question first?"

"I think you could ask most anything under the circumstances."

"Is it always like that? Sex? Well, it's not — not from what I've read, or heard. But do you think it was amazing because it was the first time, or it might be amazing for us?"

"I couldn't say, but I can be sure of one thing. We're going to find out."

When he rolled over onto her, she laughed. "I guess they can get started downstairs without us."

CHAPTER TWELVE

The second time proved amazing — and as for the third, sex in the shower was an experience she definitely wanted to repeat. Often.

Sasha wondered if going without sex for her entire adult life had given her a voracious appetite for it. Regardless, she considered herself well and truly sated, and made her way down to the kitchen to attend to another appetite.

She was starving.

She grabbed an apple out of the bowl, poured a glass of wine before perusing the contents of the fridge.

Someone, she noted, had done some shopping. And since she'd contributed nothing there, unless anyone objected, she knew what to do with the lamb chops.

Humming, she put together an easy marinade, hunted out a bowl deep enough to hold the dozen chops, poured it on, set it aside.

And turning, let out a squeak when she saw Riley leaning against the doorjamb.

"God! You scared me. I didn't hear you."

"You were too busy singing to bluebirds and butterflies and making rainbows."

"I'm marinating lamb chops."

"Uh-huh." Riley eyed the wine bottle, got herself a glass. "Well, I have to cross off any idea of using you if we need to sacrifice a virgin."

"What? Oh. Ha."

"No need to ask if you're okay, as you've got those rainbows coming out of your ears."

"It was amazing. I keep using that word. There has to be a better word."

"It works." Riley toasted her. "Congratulations."

"Does everybody know what we — That we . . ."

"Anybody who's not brain-dead. Where's your studly sorcerer?"

Sasha winced, glanced at both doorways. "He had some things to do, and I was starving."

"Good sex burns a lot of calories."

Sasha held up three fingers.

"Three times? Now you're making me jealous."

"Is that usual? It's probably a stupid question, but I don't have anyone to ask."

"Let me just say congratulations again." Riley boosted herself up to sit on the table. "Three's a lot for your first rodeo, but you look pretty fresh yet. And let me also repeat: stud."

"He made it magic. Literally. I probably shouldn't talk about it. Tell you."

"Oh, *au contraire.* You really should, and step-by-step is best. How long does that sit?" Riley gestured toward the bowl with her glass.

"An hour would be good."

"Great. Let's take a walk, and you can give me the play-by-play." Riley pushed off the table. "Look, Annika may be more of a girl, but I'm girl enough to know when it comes to sex — especially the intro to — you're allowed to share. Plus, I haven't had any myself in a while, so I need my perks where I can get them."

"Where is everybody else?"

Riley topped off both glasses. "Sawyer — and we can thank him for the provisions — went down to the beach for a swim. He looked a little shell-shocked, as Annika dragged him around the village for earrings. She's either upstairs admiring them or she went down for a swim, too. The Seventh Samurai —"

276

"Who?"

As they walked outside, Riley mimed pulling a sword out of a sheath, wielding it.

"Oh, Doyle."

"Yeah, since everybody else was, we'll say occupied, he and I sat down with the maps. And butted heads over where to look tomorrow. He's got a really hard head."

"Where are we going?"

"My pick. And his," Riley added. "We decided on both before blood was spilled. So we're heading out at seven thirty. Now, you can describe magical sex, in finite detail, while you practice your combinations."

"My combinations?" Puzzled, Sasha punched her fist. "But I've been drinking."

"Sash." With a headshake, Riley set her glass on the stone wall. "The best fights happen when you've been drinking." Riley danced on her toes, bounced her shoulders. "Show me some stuff."

"Well, all right. But I don't know how I'm supposed to punch and talk about having sex at the same time."

"Multitask."

As he worked, Bran caught the movement outside. He paused to step closer to his open doors, and saw Sasha practicing her boxing with Riley.

Not in the cover of the olive grove this

time, he noted. But in the open. So much about her had opened.

It seemed miraculous that less than a week had passed since he'd stepped out onto that hotel terrace and seen her. Fated, he didn't question that. Fated for the six of them, all so different, all from other places, to come together here. To join together here for the search that had been part of his family's legacy, part of their duty, for countless generations.

But had he been fated to have such strong feelings for the reluctant seer from America? The attraction, the desire? Basic, normal, simple. But the rest . . . He needed time to explore and evaluate the rest. And time was so crowded.

He'd taken more than he should to be with her that day. Was taking more now just to watch her. But it was a bright thing, wasn't it, to see her laugh when Riley snapped her head back, flung out her arms and dropped to the ground as if suffering a knockout punch.

That was friendship, he thought. An oddly tight one for so short a time. The tough little scientist and the insular artist.

As he considered it, Annika came up the cliff steps, a flowered sarong blowing around the very tiny bikini she wore.

Another oddity, he thought as Annika went toward the other women while Sasha executed what he thought was meant to be a side kick and Riley shook her head — her amused pity all but visible.

The three of them stood in the softening sunlight, all beauties in their own unique way. Annika flung her arms around Sasha in one of her joyful hugs, then did a trio of cartwheels that sent her sarong flying — and the dog chasing it.

Not to be undone, he supposed, Riley did a handspring. Annika a backflip.

Then the two women began to coach Sasha — who clearly needed it. He watched a moment more, struck by the way the setting sun gleamed over them, the way their laughter carried to him on the evening breeze.

Then he went back in to finish the work. The laughter was a tonic, he thought, but the lessons were honing weapons.

And he would do the same.

Sasha found Sawyer sniffing at her marinating chops when she came back in. He glanced up at her.

"Got plans for them?"

"Oh, did you?"

He shrugged. "I was just going to toss them on the grill. This looks fancier."

"It's really not. I thought Greece, lamb, and looked up some recipes last night. It's pretty basic and quick. Some browning in olive oil and garlic. A little seasoning, some lemon juice."

"Have at it."

"I haven't thought about sides, and it's later than I meant it to be."

"I'll handle that part." He got out a beer. "Teamwork." He popped the beer, took a hit. "You look . . . healthy."

"Healthy?"

"Yeah." He grinned. "Healthy. I'm going to go grab some herbs."

"I could use some thyme for the lamb."

"You got it." He tapped her cheek as he walked by. "Healthy."

Great, she thought, and moved to the sink to wash up. There was nothing wrong with a grown woman looking healthy. She just wasn't sure how she felt about advertising it, as she apparently was.

She got out an enormous skillet, the oil, picked up a bulb of garlic. Annika breezed in to get dishes. She heard Riley's voice from outside, and Doyle's as she bundled her hair up and out of the way to cook.

As she prepped the garlic, Sawyer came back with the herbs. He put a pot of water on the stove before dumping some new red potatoes in the sink.

"Boil 'em till they're tender," he said, scrubbing, "then sort of sauté them or whatever in butter and herbs, heavy on the rosemary. Looks fancy, like your chops, but isn't."

"Teamwork."

"Completely."

She grinned at him, then saw Bran come in. And felt very, very healthy.

"This looks domestic and under control. Need a hand with anything?"

"Know how to prep asparagus?" Sawyer asked him.

"Haven't a clue," Bran said as he helped himself to Sasha's wine.

"You're about to get one."

She heated her oil as the potatoes boiled. Got Bran his own glass of wine as Sawyer instructed him how to prep the asparagus. Riley came in to feed the dog; Doyle got a beer and asked when the hell they were going to eat. Annika came in for more candles.

Like family, Sasha thought. It felt like family.

Whatever happened tomorrow, tonight she had family.

She found out what it was like to share a bed with a man. They took up considerable room, but it made waking up an entirely new experience.

With Bran on breakfast detail, she took time to send her mother an email, with pictures of her view attached. What it lacked in detail — eliminating sex, vengeful gods, and learning how to box — it made up for in bright chatter.

And she thought how pleased her mother would be that she was enjoying her . . . holiday. And making friends.

Once sent, Sasha grabbed the exercise bands Riley lent her, used them as instructed for biceps curls, triceps kickbacks, lateral raises, shoulder raises.

She thought there was more, but couldn't quite remember — and since her arms felt like rubber, called it a session.

She grabbed her bag, her hat, and took the terrace doors out.

The sun, brutally bright, had her lifting a hand to shield her eyes as she dug with the other for her sunglasses. When she reached the base of the steps, pushed them on, the world went night-dark.

"There," she said, and lifted an arm to point out toward the sea. "Her black dogs come, malformed curs riding the night on bat wings. Formed for death, no more, no less. Steel to slice, to tear. But fire, red as bloodshed, hot as the hell her hounds spring from, must burn and burn and burn. Red is the star, fire is its heart. Fire will shield it. The time of transformation is here. The bright, white moon, and the bright, white magick with it, with the chosen six and all they are. Against this she strikes. Against her we to the life or to the death. For this we were born, for this we were joined. And worlds wait, for their fates are in our hands."

When she swayed, Bran slid an arm around her waist to support her.

"God, my head."

"You will fight it still," he said softly and eased her down at the table to sit.

"It's automatic. Habit."

"Some juice." Annika crouched beside her. "Do you want water instead?"

"No, thanks. This is good." Shaky yet, Sasha sipped at the juice.

"Do you remember what you said?"

"Don't poke at her!" Riley snapped at Doyle.

"I'm asking a question."

"It's all right. Yes, I think so. I could see. It went from day to night. Like a switch flipped. And I could see them flying in from over the water. Like the bats in the cave, but bigger."

"You called them dogs," Bran prompted her.

"Yes, sort of. Like . . . gargoyles. Twisted bodies, oversized heads. Claws, fangs. Attacking."

"When?"

"I don't know. It's not clear. Night. Tonight? Tomorrow night? Next week? I don't know. She's with them, and when they bleed, or we do, it feeds her. Like a vampire. Blood and death feed her."

"You spoke of fire. As a weapon and a shield for the star."

"I wish I knew what it meant."

"Bright magick." Bran stroked a hand down her hair. "White magick. We fight her with it as she fights against it. But something more, or something more through that. I can work on it."

"And meanwhile?" Doyle asked. "This time of transformation? What's that?"

"I'm not looking for Optimus Prime," Sawyer put in. "But we're transforming, in a way. From each of us going on our own to working as a unit. We're not all the way there, maybe, so we've still got some work to do on it."

"Maybe so, but while that transforming's going on, we've got a fight coming. Sooner or later," Doyle said. "It seems to me we're leaning too heavy on witchcraft."

"When I'm going up against a homicidal god, I like having a witch in my corner," Riley tossed back.

"Not saying different. But since we're going up against a homicidal god, we ought to have some battle plans."

Riley nodded. "I'll give you that. We should eat, get going, and we can start working on those plans on the boat. Cold breakfast's still breakfast," she said as she sat.

Bran waved a hand over the platter of bacon and eggs. "Now it's hot."

"See that?" Happily Riley piled food on her plate. "Having a witch around's handy." She rubbed Sasha's thigh under the table with one hand, scooped eggs onto Sasha's plate with the other. "Even if you're a little queasy, it'll settle you — and it's going to be a long workday."

She'd carry her weight, Sasha promised herself. And despite being a little queasy, picked up her fork and ate.

Sasha worked on her nerves on the way to the first cave. She'd done all right on the dives the day before — even enjoyed part of them. But the morning vision left her shaken and uneasy. She hoped the cool, damp wind, the flashing sun off the water would clear out those nerves. When they didn't, she dug out her sketchbook.

"We'll be fine." When she glanced over at Bran, he tapped a finger on her temple. "You don't have to be a seer to see. You'd do better to relax. We're here for a purpose, and it isn't to lose when we've barely begun."

"I could smell the blood," she said quietly. "Hear the shrieks those things made as they poured out of the sky. And feel the madness in them. Her creations, Bran, formed of nothing but hate and madness. Their only purpose is death."

"Ours is life. I believe life, if it's willing to fight for it, wins. Trust life. Trust yourself and what's in you."

"I'm working on it."

When they geared up, Sawyer hooked on a camera.

"I picked this up in the village yesterday. Depth rated to two hundred feet. I figured we should start documenting."

"I'm keeping a log." Riley studied the camera. "That's a really nice toy. Good idea, Sawyer. Stills and video?"

"Yeah. I'll do some of both, see how it goes."

Though the dive proved pleasant and

pretty, even amusing as Annika performed underwater gymnastics for the camera, they found nothing but sea life. And while Sasha caught herself glancing over her shoulder, half expecting to see a black cloud of winged creatures slicing through the sea, she felt more confident in her rudimentary diving skills by the time she pulled herself back on deck.

"Hydrate." Riley dug in the cooler for bottles of water after she'd stowed her used tank. "That's three crossed off. My pick's next," she added, tossed a bottle to Doyle. "I'm going to review the pictures."

"I want to see." Annika snuggled onto the bench beside Sawyer.

Because she'd leaned in as well, bracing a hand on Sawyer's shoulder, Sasha felt the lust punch through him. Surprised at how clear it came, embarrassed she hadn't blocked it, she eased back just a bit.

Not that anyone could blame him, she thought, as Annika wiggled closer. But understanding it and *feeling* it were different things. To ensure his privacy, Sasha moved to the other side of the deck where Doyle pored over maps.

"Do you have another location in mind?" she asked him.

"A lot of possibilities. We should pick up

the pace."

"Which is slower because I'm inexperienced."

"You're doing all right."

He looked up then, and she sensed something hard and deeply guarded.

"Looking for something?"

She answered as coolly as he'd asked. "Trying not to."

Still watching her, he picked up his water. "Anyone else in your family with the sight? It tends to run in families."

"No. Not that I ever heard of."

It occurred to her she didn't know him, not the way she felt she'd come to know the others. He held himself just a little aloof. Still, it meant he didn't know her either. Maybe they should try to fix that.

"Not much family anyway," she continued. "Both my parents were only children, and I only saw my grandparents sporadically. My father left when I was about twelve. He couldn't handle what I have. My mother made excuses for me, then made excuses for him. I resented that, which isn't really fair. She did her best. She does her best. But given all that, I chose to live alone, so I didn't have to deal with what I have. Where I could focus on art, and I liked it."

She looked back to where the other four

passed around Sawyer's camera.

"I like this better. Even knowing what could happen, knowing some of what will happen, this is better. What about you?"

"What about me?"

"Do you have family?"

"No. Not anymore."

"It's hard, without family. I didn't realize until . . ." She looked back again. "It feels like alone's easy until you realize."

"It's got its advantages. Only one person to worry about. You want to go left, you go left because nobody's pushing you to go right."

"I'd rather go right, at least give right a try, than be alone again. I like the way Sawyer talks about his family, his grandfather especially. And Riley and Bran theirs. They don't know alone, not the way we do. And Annika . . ."

She couldn't imagine Annika alone, but it occurred to her she'd never asked.

"Annika? Do you have family?"

"Family?" Tossing back her long braid, Annika smiled. "Yes. I have six sisters."

"Six —" Sawyer began.

"Sisters?" Riley finished.

"Yes. I am the youngest. Chantalla is the oldest, then Loreli, then —"

"You're the seventh daughter," Bran interrupted.

"My father says he's cursed with girls. He's joking," she added.

"Your mother?" Doyle shifted around. "Does she have sisters?"

"She has six, as I have six."

"And she's the youngest?" Bran glanced at Doyle as Annika nodded.

"Well, kick my ass." Riley shoved the camera back at Sawyer. "We've got us a seventh daughter of a seventh daughter. Do you have the sight, Anni?"

"Oh, not like Sasha. I know things. Just know sometimes. I knew to be on the beach for Sawyer. To be here — this time, this place. So I came. I don't like to fight, but I knew I would. I will. Sasha sees things that help. That warn. I only see what I'm meant to do."

"What you see might help, too," Sawyer told her. "You should let us know."

"I want to help. When we find the Fire Star, it will get harder. She'll be angry we have what she wants."

"That's a good bet," Riley agreed.

"I say set the course, Doyle." Bran's gaze gleamed hard and bright. "And let's see if we can really piss her off."

They found nothing, though they pushed it

to three dives. Fatigue hung over the boat like a cloud on the trip back to the marina. Sasha tried to shake it, reminding herself they'd barely begun. They weren't likely to stumble across the prize without a lot of sweat and effort.

But the sensation of adventure had faded for the day, and only a thin shadow of dread remained.

It seemed infectious.

Sawyer toyed with his compass and brooded. Riley huddled over her logs. Even Annika had lost some of her shine and sat curled on a bench, staring out over the water.

"Your vision," Bran said at length. "On the cliff, in the storm. Calling the storm. The lightning. Maybe it's time."

"No." Panic clawed through her belly.

"You can't let fear cloud it."

"It does. It does, but it's not only that. There was something urgent, immediate, even desperate in it. Beyond the danger of it, even beyond the power. It's not for now. I don't know when or why, but I'm sure it's not now."

"But you'll say when it is?" He closed a hand over hers before she answered. "Truth, Sasha. And a promise."

"Yes. I think you'll know as well as I, but yes."

That added another layer of dread as they dealt with the gear and equipment. She wanted her paints, Sasha decided. To lose herself in them for an hour. By the time Riley pulled up at the villa, Doyle roaring in behind her on his bike, she'd set plans to begin her series of local flora.

"I'm heading back to the village," Riley announced. "I've got some people I want to talk to, some lines to tug."

"I could go with you," Annika began.

"I'm not looking to shop. Don't look for me for dinner," she added. "In fact, don't wait up. I might get a hot date out of this."

"Maybe you shouldn't be going out on your own," Sawyer said.

"I can handle myself, cowboy." The dog poked its head in the jeep, wagged all over. "You hang here, big guy." Though she ruffled his fur, she nudged him away. "I'll be back when I'm back."

The dog looked mournfully after her when she drove off, then leaned his big body against Annika.

"It's all right. I'll play with you."

After the others walked off, Sasha stood, staring after the dust the jeep kicked up behind it on the narrow road.

"What is it?" Bran demanded.

"I don't know. It just feels off. Something."

"Open to it, Sasha." He laid his hands on her shoulders, rubbed.

"I can't get there. She doesn't want me to. I just know she wasn't telling the truth — or not all of it. I need to clear some of this out. I need to paint awhile."

"I've work of my own."

"We don't feel together," she said as they started for the house. "I don't mean you and me. I mean all of us. Last evening, it felt we were — or really close. But now, it feels as if we've all closed into our separate places. Maybe that's what feels off."

"I'd say we're all a bit tired. It's been a long day."

"That's probably all it is." But she glanced back at the road again, at the dust settling as they climbed the terrace steps.

CHAPTER THIRTEEN

Sasha painted until the sun bled over the western horizon. She couldn't quite lose the edgy feeling, but she'd dulled it. She'd hoped to see the jeep drive back by the time she cleaned her brushes, but nothing came up the bumpy little road.

She wanted Riley back, wanted her new family under one roof, however silly it sounded. And because she'd sensed Riley wanted exactly the opposite — and knew just how it felt to need solitude — she made herself go down.

She supposed she'd be in charge of dinner — again — and there wasn't any point in resenting it just because she was in a bad mood.

But when she stepped into the kitchen, she found Annika carefully chopping peppers.

"Sawyer's teaching me to cook. I like learning."

"You catch on quick. Doing a big stir-fry," he told Sasha. "I figured I'd just toss stuff in. Anything you don't like, hell, eat around it."

"I can do that. Anything else I can do?"

"You could crack open a bottle of white. I don't care what kind. Some for this, some for us."

"That I can also do."

It dulled the edge a bit more, watching Sawyer show Annika how to chop and slice, sipping wine while others cooked. And more yet when Bran strolled in, spun her into a kiss.

"It's pretty," Annika said, with a long, long sigh. "Kissing's pretty."

"Let's be pretty again." Bran grabbed Sasha back, dipped her a little this time.

"I'd say you're not tired now." Though her pulse skipped and danced, Sasha turned to get Bran a glass.

"I'm making some progress on a spell. Not quite there, but definite progress."

"That's just something you don't hear every day, is it? Progress on a spell."

"In my world." Bran took the wine she offered. "Whatever you're cooking there, Sawyer, smells brilliant."

"About ten minutes to go, and we'll see if it tastes the same."

"Since Annika's the sous chef tonight, we'll set the table." Sasha turned, started to stack six plates, remembered. "I guess Riley's having dinner with one of her contacts, but somebody should let Doyle know we're about to eat."

"I'll take these." Bran took the stack of five. "And let him know."

"Maybe she'll make it back before we sit down."

Annika rubbed Sawyer's arm. "You shouldn't worry. Riley is very smart and very strong."

Sasha thought it excellent advice, and tried to take it. By the time they'd finished the meal — with compliments to the chef and his apprentice, as there was barely a grain of rice left — the sun had set, the moon, fat and white, had risen.

"Maybe a couple of us ought to go down and look for her."

Doyle arched eyebrows at Sawyer. "In what?"

"Your bike?"

"She doesn't have a curfew, Daddy. If she was the damsel-in-distress sort, yeah, we could go down, slay the dragon for her. But she's got a Beretta, a combat knife, and a badass attitude. She can take care of herself. Plus." He wagged his beer. "If she's hooked up with one of her *contacts,* she'd be pretty pissed with the white-knight routine."

"Well, I'm worried, too. I didn't think she meant it about not coming back tonight. And." Sasha lifted her phone. "She's not answering my texts."

"She answered mine," Bran commented.

"Yours? When?"

"Before I came down. I just sent her one that asked if all was well. She texted back: Five-by-five. Precisely that."

"What, precisely, does five-by-five mean?"

"It's all good," Doyle told Sasha. "Everything's fine."

"She added she'd likely bunk in the village with a friend."

"What friend?" Sasha stopped herself, huffed out a breath. "None of our business. And Doyle's right. If anyone's armed and dangerous, it's Riley Gwin. I'm just jumpy because I've gotten used to everyone being right here."

Sasha pushed up, grabbed empty plates. "I'm going to do the dishes until I stop being jumpy."

When the dishes weren't enough, she scrubbed down the kitchen. She was looking for something else to clean when she spotted Bran leaning against the door

297

watching her.

"Still jumpy then?"

"I can't get rid of it."

"I have just the thing." He grabbed a bottle of wine, two glasses, then her hand. "Come with me."

"Where?"

"We'll have a drink on the terrace, you and I. It's as you said earlier, everyone seems to have closed up in their separate spaces. Maybe we all need that for a night. But you and I have another need, to my mind. We're having a date."

"A date?"

"We are. A drink on the terrace in the moonlight, conversation about nothing that troubles you. And when I've softened you up with the wine, I'll take you inside and have my way with you."

"You don't need the wine for that."

"You're a gift to me, *fáidh,* that's the truth. But wine and conversation make a nice prelude. You had a bit of that conversation with Doyle on the boat."

"He asked if I inherited the sight. You know, I never thought of it?" Surprised at herself, she shook her head. "I never asked if someone in the family before me had it. No one ever spoke of it, so I assumed I was the only one. I was the oddity."

"There's a difference between the odd and the special."

"I'm getting there. I think we were — are — so closed up in my family. If there's a problem, lock it away or cover it with excuses."

"You're not a problem — and no one should be allowed, even yourself, to think of you that way."

"Maybe that's why it's been so easy to be part of this — no one considers me a problem. And it's why it was so easy for me to move away. I love my mother, but we've both been fine with phone calls, emails, the rare and short visit. Just not a lot of common ground, I guess."

"Would you ask her now — if there'd been anyone else in the family with your gift?"

"I might, if I feel a need to know. She'd tell me if I really pushed it. I don't think she'd lie to me, and I'd know if she did. But . . ." She looked up at the full, white moon sailing over the dark sea. "It doesn't seem very important anymore."

She sipped wine, smiled when he took her hand in his. "I used to hate dating, so I gave it up. I've changed my mind."

"We'll have to make time for a true one."

"This is true." More true, more real, more lovely than any she'd ever had.

And perfect to her mind. A soft night, a full moon, the song of the waves, and a hand clasping hers.

He gave her romance again.

When he rose, she stood with him, turned to him.

"Jumpy now?"

"No. But I think I'm going to be." She wrapped around him. She pulled him close. She took his mouth this time. And reveled in the knowledge she could. "Let's close ourselves off," she murmured, "in our separate place."

"You undo me, Sasha." He turned her into the room, shut the door behind them.

The moonlight was enough, sliding pale and blue into the room.

It felt like a dance, twining her arms around him, circling with him toward the bed. She rose up to meet his mouth with hers, and thought what a wonder to have found so much so fast. To be able to close out everything but this, but him.

To know that here, that now, he belonged to her.

He pulled the clip from her hair so it tumbled down. Sunlight to vie with the moon. She was warm silk in his hands, and he thought it miraculous to be given someone so open, so honest. Beyond the face and form that pulled at him — had pulled at him from the first — he marveled at her generosity of spirit, and the courage she failed to recognize.

To have such a partner in this dark quest was more than he'd ever believed in.

Her hands, those strong artist's fingers, ran under his shirt, kindling new fires of lust. He laid her back on the bed, warning himself to have care. There was still an innocence in her.

She shifted over him, even that casual move warring with his control. And smiling, traced his face with her fingertips.

"I know this face, so well. So many dreams. It terrified me."

"Why?"

"What if?" She glided her finger over his cheekbones, his mouth, the line of his jaw. "If I could create my perfect lover? Man of my dreams. But he would only be there." On a sigh, she rested her brow to his for a moment. "On my canvas, in my mind. Only there. And when I woke or put my brush down, I'd be alone."

"You're not alone."

"I thought it was best to be, so convinced myself I wanted to be." She touched her lips to his. "I want so much more now. That's a little scary, too." She brushed her lips where her fingers had glided. "I dreamed of us like this so many times. I want to try to show you."

And as she'd dreamed it, she touched her lips to his, a bare whisper. Once, twice, before easing his shirt up his torso and away. Her body to pleasure now, all the long lines of it. Her mouth to tempt with another whispering brush.

Her lips glided over his jaw, down that strong column of throat. A pulse beat there, and she knew the thrill of making it quicken.

Knew the power and pleasure of moving down, learning his secrets as he had learned hers.

He fisted a hand at the back of her shirt, fought the brutal urge to just rip it away and take. He would let her set the pace, the tone, and her slow, yes, dreamy, explorations taught him the gilded torture of pleasure.

In moonlight and shadows, with sighs and whispers, she undressed him. And she glided them along layers, shimmering, building layers of sensation. The air seemed to thicken with it, movements languid, pulses thrumming.

Her body slid up his again, inch by quivering inch, until her mouth took his. No whispering brush this time, but a strong, deep mating, one that poured emotion into him until he ached with it.

She rose up, struck by moonlight, tossing her hair back as she crossed her arms to pull her shirt up. When he reached for her, she shook her head, and moved to undress as she'd undressed him.

Slowly, torturously.

"My dream," she reminded him.

She clung to that, moved now as she'd moved then to straddle him. And with her eyes on his, slowly, slowly, took him in.

He heard her breath catch as her hands pressed to her breasts. "I need — I need to —"

She began to rock; she began to ride.

You undo me, he'd said, but he hadn't known how completely she could rule him. He was bewitched, bespelled, enthralled as she took him with undulating hips. Blue-tipped fingers of moonlight washing her skin, her hair a pale curtain of sunlight in shadows. And her body fluid as water, then taut as a bow as she took herself over.

When she peaked, he rose up to her, wrapped her to him. Heart to heart he took her up again, and let himself fly with her.

He held her, stroking her hair, her back, trying to level himself again. No woman had ever taken him over so completely, had ever tangled body, heart, mind so thoroughly.

He wasn't altogether sure how he felt about it.

Then she sighed his name, just his name, and he decided he'd think later.

"About these dreams of yours."

She laughed, sighed again. "There were about three months' worth."

"That ought to keep us busy." He eased back to look at her. "But now you're sleepy. I can see it."

"Relaxed."

"We'll both stay that way. Tomorrow's bound to be as demanding as today."

"Is Riley back, do you think? Maybe I should check."

"She'll be back by morning."

He eased her down, curled her in. And when she drifted off, slipped out to work.

An hour or two, he thought, and he might have something he could use if her vision that morning came calling.

He spent longer than he'd planned, and calculated he'd squeeze in three hours' sleep beside her before dawn broke. The power he'd pulled on still tingled along his skin. Perhaps that was why she murmured in her sleep, trembled a little.

Once again he curled her against him,

soothing them both until he could drop into sleep with her.

He woke in the dark.

She stood in the moonlight, her body tense and turned toward the doors.

"What is it?"

"They're coming. Get up, get dressed. We don't have much time."

He flicked a hand to bring in more light. Dream-walking, he noted when he saw her eyes. "What's coming?"

"Her dogs. Ours know it. Can't you hear them howling? Hurry." She grabbed her clothes, began to yank them on as he got out of bed. "Where's my bow?" she demanded.

"Your bow?"

"There it is." She picked up . . . nothing. Made motions as if slinging a strap over her back. "Hurry, Bran, we have to wake the others."

"I will." He tugged on pants. "Stay here. Sasha, wait for me."

"Hurry."

"Stay here." He went out, banged a fist on Sawyer's door. "Get up!" he called out. "Get the others. Something's coming."

He didn't wait, but turned toward his own room before Sawyer pushed open the door.

"What?"

"I don't know what." Bran kept moving. "But get the others, and get armed."

He took time to grab a shirt, a knife, and several of the vials of the potion he'd just made. He'd planned for them to cure several more hours, but they'd have to do.

When he pushed back into Sasha's room, she'd pulled on boots, a jacket. Dream-struck still, he thought, but she looked . . . tougher, bolder.

He debated a moment, but when he heard Apollo howl, a long, deep warning, he knew he couldn't leave her dreaming.

He moved to her, set his hands on her shoulders. "Wake," he ordered. "Wake now."

She blinked, jerked back. "What . . ." Apollo howled again, and the call was answered by another. Deeper, more feral.

"Not a dream," she said.

"Take this." He took her hand, put the knife in it. "It's enchanted. Trust it, and yourself. I need you to stay close to me, Sasha."

"They're coming. What I saw this morning."

"I think yes. We can't risk staying inside, waiting to see what they'll do."

"No." She looked down at the knife, that bright, sharp silver. And prayed her hand wouldn't shake. "The others."

"Coming. You warned us in time. Close to me," he repeated, and moved to the terrace doors.

The wind blew in, and carried an ugly hint of something foul. It amazed her how he stepped out into it, without hesitation. She took a breath, gripped the knife, and stepped out with him.

"Close the doors," he told her as he scanned sea and sky. "No point issuing an invitation."

"I don't see anything yet. But —"

"They're coming. You had the right of it. We make a stand, I think, away from the house."

"Clearer ground," Doyle said, and with his coat flapping around his knees, he strode across the terrace toward them. "Around by the olive grove. And cover in there if we need it." He sniffed the air like a wolf. "Hell smoke."

"It ain't my sister's perfume." Sawyer, a gun at each hip, came toward them with Annika.

"I locked Apollo in," Annika said as he continued to howl. "He could get hurt if he came out."

"He'll be fine." Sawyer gave her shoulder a squeeze. "Riley's not back, so we're one short. But." He patted his guns. "We're ready."

"About an hour before dawn," Doyle said as they went down together. "A kind of transition time, right? Maybe that's what you meant."

"I don't know." Sasha shook her head. "But the moonlight's fading, isn't it? That's to their advantage."

"Or ours." Bran took out the vials.

"What you got?" Sawyer asked.

"Something I wish had more time to build, but it'll have to do. I need to place these at the points of the compass."

"There." Sasha gestured to the cloud that swept over the sea. "They're coming."

"Well, keep them off me best you can — and her," he added, "until I get them set. We'll drive as many as we can toward the points. That should even the odds."

She wanted to call him back when he ran off, but Doyle was already snapping orders.

"Form a circle. Draw them to us until Mr. Magic does what he does."

Sawyer drew both his guns. "No problem."

The wind rose to whirl, snapping through the trees. Howls rolled over it in a kind of feral desperation. Then came the high-pitched screams of what boiled over the sea.

Fear wanted to tear out of her throat in a scream of her own. Her breath whistled with it as Doyle ranged himself beside her.

Don't think, she ordered herself. If she allowed herself to think of what was coming, she might run. Remember. Remember the dreams of battle, and fight.

The first shots jolted through her, and she saw two of those twisted bodies flash, tumble out of the fetid cloud. Then more until the air stank of gunpowder and viscous smoke.

And they poured down in a wave, armed with tooth and claw.

She felt as much as saw the sharp slice of Doyle's sword cleaving obscene heads from bodies. As shots rang out, as Annika's flying feet pummeled, she found her arm, her feet, her fist knew what to do.

She hacked, punched, pivoted. The blood raining from the smoking bodies was a hot, quick sting on the skin. She couldn't see Bran as she hacked out with the knife, and prayed he hadn't been overwhelmed.

With a furious growl, Apollo streaked by her, leaped up to snag one of the winged dogs in his jaws, shake it. She nearly broke ranks when she saw a section of the cloud break off to attack him.

In a blur of speed a dark shape leaped out

of the shadows, soared over Apollo's back, claws raking the attackers, jaws snapping. Doyle's sword swept down behind her seconds before fangs sank into her back.

"Watch your six, Blondie."

The words echoed in her head, along with gunshots, shrieks, howls, as she jabbed out to spear one of Nerezza's creatures.

Suddenly, she knew.

"North. Bran needs us to push them north," she shouted.

She didn't wait; she ran. Cursing, Doyle charged after her. Apollo streaked by them, hard on the heel of the dark dog — not dog, she saw now; the wolf.

Gunfire cut a swath, tearing wings, shattering bodies, and still they came.

Through the haze of smoke, she saw Bran, standing, arms raised, as if calling the beasts to him. Fear struck like an arrow, vibrated in her cry of his name. But he stood even as the killing cloud swooped toward him.

"Brace yourself!" he called out.

He flung his arms wide.

The light flashed, red as blood, hot as tongues from hell. The force of it would have shot her back if Doyle hadn't gripped her arm. Blinded by it, she had only instinct and dream-memory.

"East." She choked it out, stumbled.

"Clockwise. Drive them east."

It all whirled into a mad blur, the insanity of death and battle, hot blood, the stink of smoke. The light flashed again, mushrooming up to fill the world with its power and doom. Talons caught in her hair. As she batted at them, the wolf sprang. The shriek of her attacker snapped off in its jaws, then she lost it in the haze.

Light exploded from the south, and this time the power of it lifted her off her feet. Breathless, ears throbbing, she gained her hands and knees. By the time she managed to stand again, she'd lost all sense of direction.

Howls, gunfire, screams, shouts, all muffled by the haze. She made out the shadows of those who fought with her, the gnarled silhouettes of what attacked. She turned toward them, but a sudden flurry of wings cut her off, left her no route but retreat.

Then Bran's arm swung around her, nearly lifted her off her feet a second time.

"You're too close. Stay behind me. Behind me, Sasha, and cover your eyes."

She felt it rock the ground under her feet, sing like raw nerves up her body. Even with an arm flung over her eyes, that red light filled her head.

The power he loosed seared along her skin, swam in her blood.

She went down to her knees when her legs buckled, fingers digging into the grass as the ground shook.

"Stand clear," he called out. "Keep back, and let me finish it.

"In my light you burn. Through our wrath you churn. Let what made you see our power, and know that in this hour as our seer did foretell, we send her dogs back to hell. By the power given me, as I will, so mote it be."

There was a terrible scream, like a thousand voices raised in fury.

Not a thousand, Sasha realized. Just one. Nerezza.

"Are you hurt?" Bran pulled her to her feet.

"I don't know. You're bleeding." His face, she saw. His arms, his hands.

"Likely we all are. But this is done for the night. Let me clear some of the bloody smoke," he began, but Sawyer pushed through it, an arm clutched around Annika to support her.

"She's hurt. Her leg's the worst."

Blood oozed from the gash that sliced from her knee to her ankle.

"We'll get her inside. Where's Doyle?"

Something growled, low and deadly.

"Clear," Bran demanded, waving a hand at the haze. Sawyer drew his weapon again.

The wolf stood beside Apollo. The big white dog lay on his side, his fur matted with blood, his breath coming in whines.

Doyle stood a foot away, his eyes on the wolf, blood dripping from his raised sword.

"No! Don't!" Sasha started to push forward.

Annika broke from Sawyer, and in a limping run rushed toward Doyle. She dived under his sword, threw her arms around the wolf as Sawyer charged after her.

"Annika! For Christ's sake."

He would have dragged her clear, but she clung to the wolf, and Sasha moved to push him aside.

"Stop. Just stop. It's Riley."

"She's hurt. And Apollo, too." Crooning, Annika stroked both. "Help them."

"You've got to be kidding me." Sawyer shoved his gun back in its holster. "Riley's a werewolf?"

She snarled at him, had him backing up one cautious step. "Easy, girl. Annika, we need to get you inside, stop that bleeding."

"Apollo first. He's innocent. He came to help us, and this isn't his fight. Help him." She turned beseeching eyes to Sawyer.

"Please."

"Okay. Sure. Okay. Don't bite me," he said to the wolf. "I'm just going to see how bad he's hurt."

"Let me see what I can do right here." Bran crouched down, ran his hands over Apollo. "That's a big secret you've held on to, Dr. Gwin. It's not bad, no, it's not bad." He soothed the dog. "But even superficial wounds are likely toxic. And that goes for all of us. I have things that will deal with it inside."

As he spoke, the last stars faded. The sun shimmered at the edges of the east.

The wolf howled, one long note that might have been pain, might have been triumph.

And began to change.

It hunkered down, muscles and fur quivering. Bones seemed to shift, to twist. Only the eyes remained the same. As the light bloomed, the woman emerged.

Riley sat, naked, her arms wrapped around the knees she hugged tight to her chest.

"Holy shit, and let's add a wow."

At Sawyer's comment, Riley lifted her head. "Not to play shy, but maybe somebody can lend me a shirt. I had to leave my pack in the jeep."

Saying nothing, Doyle shrugged out of his coat, tossed it to her.

"Thanks. Can we save the questions, comments, remarks until we get inside and start triage? He's not bad, like you said," she told Bran, "but he's really hurting."

Again keeping his silence, Doyle got his arms under the dog, lifted the considerable weight. Riley managed to get her arms in the sleeves of the coat, wrap it around herself, and, murmuring to Apollo, walked with Doyle.

Annika took three limping steps before Sawyer picked her up, carried her. "Riley's a freaking werewolf."

"Lycan," she snapped over her shoulder. "Call me a werewolf again and I will bite your ass."

"Can you walk?" Bran asked Sasha.

"Yes. I'm mostly just . . . I don't know what."

"How did you know it was Riley?"

"I just knew. When it — she — came out of the dark, I knew. It didn't even surprise me — then. Now I just feel numb."

As the sun lifted, she, a woman who barely a week before had never held a weapon of any kind, walked back toward the villa holding a knife still wet with blood.

CHAPTER FOURTEEN

"Apollo first." Still wearing only Doyle's coat, Riley sat on the floor, the dog's head in her lap.

"I'll need some things," Bran began. "I have healing supplies in my room."

"I've got a non-magickal first-aid kit in mine, if it helps."

"I'll get that as well. We'll want plenty of towels, but for now let the wounds bleed."

When Bran strode out, everyone began talking at once. Sasha actually felt the words beat like little hammer blows on her temple.

"Talk later," she snapped, surprising everyone into silence. "Doyle, towels. Sawyer, put Annika on the table." As she whipped out orders, she snatched the fruit bowl off the table, then pulled the largest pot out of a cupboard. After she turned on the faucet to fill it, she shoved her hands at her hair, turned.

"Ah, Sawyer, get Apollo's water bowl and

a couple of his dog biscuits. If Bran has to medicate him, it should go down easier that way."

"Check you out, Captain Sasha," Riley commented.

"I'm winging it." She grabbed some towels from Doyle, folded some under Annika's leg to elevate it. And thought, Thank God, when Bran strode back.

He nodded when she put the pot of water on to boil. "Good thinking. But let's speed it up." At his gesture, the water bubbled. "Ten drops each, these three bottles. In this order," he told Sasha. "Brown, blue, red. Ten exactly. Can you do that?"

"Yes."

He knelt by the dog. "Keep him quiet and still," he told Riley, and ran his hands over Apollo. "I need to clean his wounds first, counteract any poisons. How did he get out?"

"Busted right through the window of my room. We're going to have to fix that," Riley added with a weak smile. "Don't want to lose our security deposit."

He gave her arm a pat. "Sasha, are you done there?"

"Yes, ten exactly. Brown, blue, red."

"Step back from the pot now."

He held out a hand toward the pot, and

his gaze fixed on it. On his murmured incantation, light spewed up from the bubbling water, burst, then circled back down, as liquid circles down a drain.

"One of the large, clear bottles now. Hold it out. Don't worry. I won't miss."

His brew arced out of the pot, arrowed into the bottle.

"And the next," he told her, and repeated the process.

"Give one to Sawyer. You'll need to pour it, slowly now, over that gash on her leg. You'll know it's done when the blood runs clear. It's going to hurt some, darling," he told Annika.

"Let me do that." Doyle took the bottle from Sasha. "Why don't you hang on to him."

With a nod, Annika turned her face into Sawyer's chest.

"Bring me that one, Sasha. Between the two of you, you can keep the dog still and calm."

As he worked, Sasha felt Apollo's pain, like a slow burn, and his fear of it. He quivered under her hands, turned his head to lap, lap, lap at Riley as if begging her to make it stop.

She felt Annika's pain, that shocking rise of heat, a thin line of fire.

She felt Sawyer's barely suppressed rage, Doyle's cold control, Riley's struggle with tears. And Bran's utter focus.

She felt them all, crowding her, the pain, the grief, the purpose, in a tumult of emotions. She wanted to turn away from them, close off from them. Then Bran's hand brushed hers.

"Nearly done," he said quietly. "Nearly there. Can you hold on?"

She nodded. Tears spilled out — Riley's tears, she realized, and felt them run down her own cheeks.

"A second time, Doyle. It won't be as bad now. Cooler now. There now, it's cooler, cleaner. What burns washes away, what blackens spills out in light.

"I don't want to stop, Sasha, but I'll need the bottle — the one you brought me when I needed it. Four drops in water for Annika, then just the bottle here for Apollo. All right?"

She did as he asked, urged the mixture on Annika. "Drink it all now. It's the salve next, isn't it?"

"That's right."

At Bran's nod, she took the salve out of Bran's box, handed it to Sawyer. "I'll need it for Apollo when you're done. How many drops for Apollo? I can put them in his water bowl."

"Another four. See that he drinks it all, Riley, then coat his wounds with the salve. He's going to sleep," he added. "And sleeping, he'll heal."

He rose then, moved to Annika. "That's good. See, already healing. Now, where else did they hurt you, darling?"

Once he'd treated her, he turned to Sasha. "And you. Let's have a look at you."

"Some scratches. Just scratches. It was the knife, wasn't it? The knife you gave me."

"I'm pleased it worked. I couldn't be sure," he said as he lifted her arm, began to treat the scratches running down from her shoulder.

"Sawyer has worse. But you." She looked at Doyle. "You don't have any wounds."

"Just lucky, I guess."

No, she thought, there were still secrets here.

"Riley's are healing on their own."

"Wounds inflicted when I'm in wolf form heal fast. One of the perks." Since Apollo slept, she rose. "I know you all have questions, but I need to eat something. The change is like running a marathon at sprint speed; add on the rest, and I'm feeling a little shaky."

"I'd say the questions, as there'll be many,

can wait until we've all cleaned up. Where's the worst of it, Sawyer?" Bran asked him.

"My back."

Riley yanked open the fridge, grabbed a jar of olives as it came first to hand. "I'm going to catch a quick shower, put some clothes on."

By the time they'd mopped up blood, set the kitchen to rights, and Sasha got a shower of her own, she was starving herself.

She came down to find Riley and Bran putting breakfast together.

"Figured this way I can eat as it cooks."

"Your color's coming back." Sasha went straight to the coffee.

"Once I filled the hole. Listen, I'm sorry. You're peeved, and I get it, so I'm sorry."

Sasha only nodded, and took her coffee outside.

"You make friends easily, don't you?" Bran said as he piled the last of the mountain of eggs on the platter.

"I guess."

"She's hasn't, until you."

"Hell."

"Take that out; I'll bring the rest. You can explain things while we eat."

Since she wasn't at all sure how to explain, Riley filled her plate, shoveled in food until the last of the hunger pangs eased. "Maybe you should just ask questions, give me a kind of running start into it."

"Were you bitten?" Sawyer asked her.

"No. It's hereditary."

"You come from a family of were— Of lycans?"

"That's right. Let me say right off, we don't eat people. We don't bite them, we don't eat them. Not that there aren't some rogues out there, but my pack — my family — doesn't hunt, doesn't kill. And we're not interested in making more lycans through infection. We make them the old-fashioned way. We mate."

"Do you mate with humans?" Annika wondered.

"You fall for who you fall for, right? So yeah, it happens."

"Can there be children?"

"Sure. Fifty-fifty on lycan traits, so all kids are trained for the change. Initial transformation hits in puberty — as if puberty didn't whack you out enough. Big ceremony, gifts, celebration. Every kid takes an oath, not to hunt, not to kill, not to infect."

"Any ever break the oath?"

She looked over at Doyle. "Sure. And those who do are punished or banished, depending on the crime and circumstances. We're pack animals." She looked down to where Apollo dozed peacefully beside her chair. "Banishment is the worst — worse than execution. We're civilized, okay? We have rules, a code. Three nights a month —"

"Night before the full moon," Sawyer filled in. "Night of, night after."

"Yeah, three nights — except in the event of a blue moon, then we get six — we transform, sundown to sunup. During that time, we fast."

"And you transforming like you did. Jesus Christ, Riley, I could've shot you." Sawyer jabbed a finger at her. "I nearly did."

"Unless you loaded with silver bullets, it wouldn't have done much harm."

His expression changed — reluctant delight. "That's real? Silver bullets?"

"Silver bullets, silver blade. It's going to hurt to get shot or cut otherwise, but it's not going to be fatal."

"You left us." Sasha spoke quietly. "Rather than trust us, you lied, and you left."

"I didn't go far, and I came as soon as I realized what was happening. I couldn't risk staying here. Apollo would have sensed the change coming, for one thing. He'd have smelled the wolf on me. And even if I'd locked myself in my room, what if one of you had gotten in?"

"What if you'd just told us the truth?" Sasha countered. "The way I told you the truth? Bran held back at first, and you know how upsetting that was. We've been together day and night for a week now, we fought together. Twice now. If you could've gotten clear before sunrise this morning, you would have."

"I'd have tried," Riley agreed. "I don't think it would've done much good. You knew. You knew before I changed back. That weighs on my side of it. It's part of the oath, Sash. A sacred oath I took at twelve. We don't reveal ourselves, not without permission from the Council of Laws."

"If you do?" Bran asked.

"The punishment, first offense? You're locked up for three cycles, no contact. It may not sound like much, but to be chained in wolf form? It's pretty awful. Added to it is the loss of honor and trust."

"An oath is a holy thing," Annika stated.

"Yeah, it is. It's a little late for it, but I applied for permission three days ago. It's politics, so there has to be a lot of discussion and debate. I figured I'd get it, considering what we're doing, but it was going to take a couple weeks to wind its way through the system."

Annika reached out. "Will they punish you?"

"Not likely. I'd applied, and I only broke faith because we were attacked. There are a couple council members who lean pretty hard conservative, but it's going to balance out. At worst, they'll postpone sentencing, and if we find the stars, it's going to be pretty hard for them to lock up the one who helped find them. Either way, I'll deal with it."

"You asked for permission to tell us," Sasha repeated.

"It's a process, believe me. We wouldn't have survived as a species if we didn't hold what is secret and sacred. So sharing what we are needs the process, and more requests are denied than granted. But we're different, and what we're doing is a heavy weight. I'd have had permission before my next cycle. I'd have made sure of it, but there wasn't enough time before this one."

"An oath is a holy thing. I'll accept that."

"You're still pissed."

"I'll get over it. We needed you last night. You came, fought."

"And we kicked some ass," Sawyer put in.

"Too easy." Doyle let the words drop, continued eating.

"Easy?" Sawyer scowled down the table.

"You call that easy?"

"Only one of us — and the dog — with serious injuries, and we beat them back in about twenty minutes." He glanced down at Bran. "You know it, too."

"A test, to see what we have, what we'd do. She'll come harder next time. I'm thinking on it."

"You're thinking on it," Sasha muttered, and shoved up from the table. "Teamwork. We make placating noises about being a team, but we're not. We fought last night, but not really as a unit. You gave me a knife that had some sort of protection, but didn't really explain it."

"I couldn't be sure it would hold," Bran began.

"You didn't tell me," she repeated. "You didn't tell us what you were doing with the light. You didn't tell us you had power until you had to. Just as Riley didn't tell us what she has. Good reasons for it, of course. Always good reasons. I'm sure the rest of you have good reasons for the secrets you're holding. So keep them, that's your choice. But I know we don't have a chance in hell of winning this until we *are* a unit.

"So make up your minds, because the next time, those secrets may be the reason she burns right through us."

She strode away, up the terrace steps, and shut the doors to her room with a decisive *click* to give herself what she'd always sought.

Quiet and solitude.

She slept. She'd fought a war, treated the wounded, cleaned up blood, and topped off the morning snarling at her "team."

So she slept, and woke feeling more rested — and just as annoyed.

If there were plans to go out diving later, she thought, they'd just have to do without her. She intended to take a walk on the beach, do some sketching, and some hard thinking.

She put what she wanted in a tote, stepped outside. Bran stepped out on the terrace seconds after.

"I'm going for a walk," she told him.

"I need to do the same, to gather more supplies. Would you go with me, help me with that?" He stepped toward her. "And if you could give me some time after, I'd show you how to prepare some of the ingredients. It would be a help to me."

"Why? You've done fine on your own."

"I have, and can. I'd do better with your help. You were right, everything you said. I can't speak for the others, but I can promise you, no more secrets between us. It wasn't trust so much, Sasha, as habit. Now I'm asking for your help, and doing what I can to get used to the asking."

"Then it would be bitchy to refuse. I feel like I used up my daily quota of bitchy."

"You used it well. I need a pouch and a couple of tools."

He came back with a pouch slung over his shoulder, and the knife he'd given her before, this time in a rough leather sheath.

"I should have told you how I'd empowered it." He snapped it on her belt. "I'll tell you now, if she sends a different sort of attack, I can't know if it will hold up the same."

"If and when, we'll find out."

He took her hand as they started down. "You're not afraid."

"There's part of me, inside, still terrified. That part wanted to cut and run screaming this morning. I'm not sure what part of me refuses to do that — but I'm trying to get used to it. Where's everyone else?"

"Riley's sleeping. She got little to none last night, and I think, despite the bravado, she's worried about the ruling of this council of hers."

"If they rule to punish her for fighting with us, they'll have to get through us to do it."

"And listen to you. So fierce."

"It's a waste of time to be mad at her, though I still am, a little. I know about having secrets, but —"

"You shared yours with her, with me. And we held back."

"And I understand why. It still stings, but I understand."

"It might help if I tell you when you left the table Sawyer looked thoughtful and troubled. If there's more to him and his compass, he's struggling over whether to tell us or not. Annika? There's something deep there."

"I know she'll give us everything she can. Doyle . . ."

"Ah, Doyle. Whatever he holds, he'll hold tight until he's damn good and ready to loosen it. But I trust him."

"Why?"

"He's a warrior at the base, isn't he? He'll fight with his last breath, and defend those who fight beside him. And that includes a dog. He carried Apollo from the field."

"All right." She sighed. "All right, that's a good reason. For now. What are we looking for out here?"

"Certain plants, roots. We'll harvest herbs on the way back. Bones would be good if I can find them."

"Bones?"

"Bird, lizard, small mammals. Natural things that can be used for my purposes. I'll have to send for some of the more complex ingredients, or things that don't grow here, but we can increase my supplies. Here, these poppies to start."

He showed her how to harvest plants, roots, leaves. When he identified something unfamiliar to her, she sketched it.

Back at the villa he taught her how to use the mortar and pestle, how to jar and label.

"It's not all a snap of the fingers or flick of the wrist." She noted down the steps for distilling poppy in her sketchbook.

"Power should come from work, time, effort. Care," he added. "As the most important things do. I'm used to doing this sort of thing on my own," he admitted. "Or with another magician. But you're a quick study, and what you can do here saves some of that time."

"It matters to me."

"I see it does."

"You could show me more. The medicines especially. You and Doyle both think this last attack was a test, and the next will be worse."

"I do." He held a hand over a small, bubbling cauldron, gauging its progress.

"I can feel the wounds, if I let myself. But I don't know how to use what you make to treat them. Or not enough."

"I need to learn more myself, as this has never been my area. We'll work on it." Through the thin haze of smoke, he looked at her. "Together."

He gave her a book on the healing arts. She decided to take an hour by the pool to study it, at least acquaint herself with the basics.

She made notes of her own on using comfrey for burns, milk thistle for sprains. How to prepare echinacea for its many uses. She glanced up when she saw Doyle some distance away on the lawn, apparently making something out of . . . canvas or burlap.

Alone, of course, she thought with a twinge of resentment.

She spotted Riley cresting the little rise, coming toward the pool carrying two wide-mouthed glasses filled with icy liquid.

"Magnificent Margaritas," Riley said, and held one out.

"Thanks."

"Still mad?"

Sasha took a sip — it was pretty magnificent. "I'm tired of being mad."

"Then I'm sitting down. Heavy reading," she added with a glance at the thick book

331

with its carved leather binding.

"I'm going to learn how to help Bran treat injuries."

"You did a lot of that this morning, without the book. I didn't handle myself very well," Riley continued. "Changing in front of an audience — and I was a little racked up initially. And Apollo . . ."

"Where is he?"

"He went down to the beach with Annika. He's fine. Like nothing happened."

"And you?"

"Like I said, if I'm injured as the wolf, I heal fast, even after the change. Look, I get a lie of omission is still a lie, but —"

"You took an oath."

"I took one to you, too."

There it was, Sasha thought. And the rest of her anger cooled knowing her friend understood.

"Yeah, you did. And now that I'm tired of being mad, I can see you'd taken steps to keep both, and quickly. It seems like forever, Riley, and it's been days. Just days. They won't lock you up."

"You don't have any say there."

"Oh, I think I will." She drank again. "I think we all will. And they're just going to have to listen."

"When did you get to be such a badass?"

"Maybe since I've stopped asking myself why me. If people think I'm weak, if Nerezza thinks I am, it's because I have been. She can keep thinking that, it may be an advantage. But no one else is going to. Including me."

"If it matters, I never thought you were weak. You're dealing just fine with a real steep learning curve. Let's go back just one month. Did you believe in witches a month ago?"

"I dreamed of one — of him — but no. No, I didn't really believe."

"In lycans?"

"Absolutely not. I'm still working on that one."

"But here you are, and that's so not weak. Magic compasses, magic spells, transformations. Whatever Annika's got tucked away other than the seventh daughter of a seventh daughter's likely to be less of a jolt to me, considering my background and upbringing."

"You think there's something, too."

"How can anyone be that happy — and there's that sack of coins. I'd lean toward faerie, but when I think of faeries, I think cagey. She doesn't come off cagey."

"You're going to tell me faeries exist."

"In my experience, anything that sticks in

lore has a basis in fact. She'll probably spill it to Sawyer first. She's crushing big-time there. Then there's the big guy."

Riley took a slow sip as she watched Doyle heft something big, thick, and circular. "He keeps his mouth shut, a lot, but he listens to everything."

"He's holding something back."

"No question of that. Maybe some variety of demon."

"Oh, come on."

"They're not all evil spawns of hell, any more than all lycans are man-eaters. He likes Bran well enough, and he respects Sawyer's eye and aim. Since whatever he is or has or knows, he's a man, too, and he finds Annika charming. He hasn't decided about you and me."

"I can't argue with any of that."

"And he doesn't trust any of us through and through. He'd much rather do this alone."

"I'm in absolute agreement there, too, but he's going to have to get over it. And what the hell is he doing?"

Sasha pushed up then because the only way to know was to find out. Tucking the book under her arm, she started toward him. With a shrug, Riley got up to go with her.

He tacked a target to a tree trunk, she saw now, and wondered why someone who favored a sword required target practice.

Then he unzipped a case lying on the ground.

The crossbow was black and sleek and lethal. Sasha felt a tingle along her skin as Doyle set his foot in the stirrup, cocked it. He flicked a glance in their direction, slung a quiver of bolts over his shoulder.

He loaded one, lifted the bow, sighted. The bolt plowed into the target about a quarter inch from dead-center bull's-eye.

"Nice." Riley nodded. "Stryker, right? The new one. What's the draw weight?"

"One fifty-five."

"You surprise me, you can draw more than one-double-nickel."

"This is my backup. What can you draw?"

"I can draw that." She passed her glass to Sasha, held out her hand.

Doyle hesitated, but he handed her the bow.

"Nice, lightweight. Won't weigh you down on the hunt."

As he had, she put a foot in the stirrup and, biceps rippling, cocked the bow. She helped herself to a bolt from his quiver, loaded it.

Her shot hit the other side of the bull's-eye, about the same distance as his. "String suppressor's a nice touch. Keeps it quiet. I'd say that's, what, about three hundred FPS?"

"Yeah, about." He looked at Sasha now. "Bran said you were looking for a cross-bow."

"Yes. I was."

"You were? You want to learn to shoot, Sash?"

"I'd like to try it."

Obliging, Riley passed it off to Doyle, took the glasses and the book from Sasha.

"The draw's going to be too much for you. I've got a cocking device."

"I need to learn to draw it manually." She took the bow, and turned it as they had, set her foot in the stirrup.

But Doyle was right, she didn't have the strength for the draw weight. "I'll get stronger. And Bran can do something to make it so I can cock it. Would you do it for me this time?"

"Sure." He did as she asked. "You should get used to the weight, the feel. We'll move closer to the target."

"No. From here."

He shrugged. "Carbon bolt — no point wasting time with less. You need to make sure it's set properly, or —"

"Let me try it once." She simply took the bolt, loaded it. And in one move aimed, fired.

Her bolt centered neatly between theirs, center bull's-eye.

"Well, kick my ass and call me Shirley." Riley gaped at the target, let out a bark of a laugh. "That didn't look like beginner's luck."

"I've used one in dreams. It feels the same." She lowered the bow to study it. "I know this. FPS, you said. That's feet per second. I know this."

Doyle walked to the target, pulled out the three bolts. When he walked back, he took the bow, cocked it.

"Do it again."

She hit dead center a second time.

"No, not luck. Either you beef up," Doyle added, "use the cocking device — or see what Bran can do. You can have that, and a couple dozen bolts."

"I appreciate the loan."

"Take care of it. When this is done, give it back." He cocked it yet again, stared off at the target. "I figured I'd be out here all damn day just showing you how to sight it. I'm going for a beer."

When he strode off, Riley took a slug of her margarita. "I believe you just received the Doyle McCleary Seal of Approval."

"Better than that." She pinned the next bolt a whisper away from the first. "He would have stayed out here all damn day showing me."

"Are you smelling a little team spirit?"

"I think I am." This time she retrieved the bolts herself. Even that, she realized, felt familiar. Routine.

"I'm not going to use the cocking device. I never used it in the visions. I'm going to take this up to Bran, because I think that's how I'm able to cock it. Until I get stronger."

She began packing the bow and bolts in the case. "Where did you go, Riley? When you left yesterday?"

"Not far. I needed to get the jeep out of sight. And get out of sight myself. Getting naked before the change spares the wardrobe. After the sun set, I came back, close enough so I'd be around if anything happened. Which it did."

"You don't need to leave tonight."

"I guess not, seeing as the wolf's out of the bag."

"How does it feel, the change?"

"Painful. Powerful — both ways. There's a rush. Everything in you's racing. And when the wolf's free, everything's heightened.

338

Smell, sound, sight, speed. But I'm still me. What's human is always in there, the same way the wolf is in me right now.

"And since I'm cut off when the sun sets, I'm going to have another margarita. You in?"

"Why not?"

In her cave, Nerezza fashioned a palace. She deserved no less, after all, and surrounded herself with gold and silver, with jewels that sparkled in the light of her torches. She was born to rule, and soon the long wait to do so would be over.

Destroying worlds to gain her ends was no matter to her. The stars would provide her with all the power necessary, and when she had them, when she returned to the Island of Glass to ascend the throne, as was her *right,* she would create whatever she wished.

Worlds of fire and storms. Worlds of slaves and suffering. World upon world to do her bidding. This was true rule, and her reign would be endless.

In the globe she watched the seer use her foolish weapon. Let them play, she thought, let them savor what they thought a victory, the seer, the she-wolf, the witch, and . . .

She pounded a fist on the golden arm of

her throne so the walls of stone shook. Mists swirled around the globe, blocking much from her sight. The sorcerer, she thought. She would deal with him. Oh, she would deal with him.

But more, much more enraging, she couldn't see the others for what they were. That was Celene's doing — Celene, Luna, Arianrhod. They'd blocked the knowledge even from the globe. But it would do them no good.

They'd reveal themselves, just as the she-wolf had done. And once revealed, the knowledge would show her how to destroy them.

When the time came, she thought, and lifted a jeweled mirror to admire herself.

She would use them first, let them lead her to the Fire Star.

Then she would crush them, take it. And it would lead her to the others. She would take what they had, drain them of it, fill herself, and leave their husks to rot.

And she would be eternal. Forever young, more beautiful than the sun, more powerful than all the gods.

But as she looked, the reflection in the glass began to whither, the skin drooping into folds, drawing back toward the skull. The ebony hair went thin, gray, dry, as the glass showed her aging years, decades, centuries.

On a scream of rage, she hurled the mirror away, smashing glass and gems.

With a trembling hand, she lifted the goblet beside her, drank fast and deep. And with its brew and her will, drew back her youth and beauty.

She had pushed too much of herself into the attack the night before, and needed more potion. Her banishment from the Island of Glass stripped away her rights — to that youth, that beauty.

She aged. Not like the puny humans. No, even this humiliation wasn't so great. But she aged. Her body gradually losing its form, her skin its texture, her face its beauty.

She would have them back, not just the illusion of them, but truly. And she would banish the ones who'd lowered her to this until they turned to dust.

She would be queen of all, and all who had defied her would perish.

But they would suffer first.

CHAPTER FIFTEEN

Since everyone else seemed to have conveniently vanished, Sasha contemplated what to make for dinner. Sunset — she checked — was in just over an hour. If Riley did indeed fast until sunrise, she ought to eat a good meal first.

Privately, she could admit she was tired of cooking for their small army, but given the circumstances — full moon — she couldn't suggest they take a break and go into the village for a meal.

She'd just about settled on pasta — a staple in her world — when Doyle walked in. He dropped three large pizza boxes on the table.

"I was in the mood."

"Oh. That's great," she said, with genuine feeling.

"Probably need to heat them up, or have Killian wave his magic wand."

"Either way it saves me from cooking."

"You need to make a duty list, so it doesn't fall so much on you. This is my way of cooking, so check me off."

"Fair enough."

He went to the fridge, shoved in the beer he'd bought along with the pizza, and took one out for himself.

"Do you have any other skills you've dreamed about?" he asked.

"I'm better at fighting in them. I'm not as good at the flipping and jumping and kicking, even in my dreams, as Annika or Riley, but I'm not embarrassing. But . . ."

She poured herself a glass of the sun tea someone — who hadn't been her — had made that afternoon. "Unlike the crossbow, it doesn't just come to me. Annika tried to teach me the basic handspring a little while ago. I got a D-minus."

"You need to work on your upper body strength as much as your form. Those bands Riley gave you aren't enough. Start swimming laps, hard. Start doing push-ups, pull-ups. You do any yoga?"

"A little."

"Do more. Planks, chaturanga, use your own body weight. Don't do the same thing every day. Switch it up, but do something every day. Increase the time until you've got real muscle fatigue."

"All right."

"What?" he demanded when she just kept looking at him.

"We're having an actual conversation you initiated."

He shrugged, drank some beer. "No point in conversations unless you've got something to say. You held your own last night. Part of that's the knife Bran gave you. But most of it's because you've got guts. I'd've said you didn't the day I met you."

"You wouldn't have been wrong."

Those sharp green eyes took her measure, straight on. "Yeah, I would've. I'm coming from the outside. You formed your group — not long before I came into it, but you'd formed it. You're the glue."

"I'm the . . ." The idea surprised her into silence.

"That's right. And what you said this morning, that was right. Truth is truth, even when you don't want to hear it. Everyone's not going to just fall in line, because people just don't, especially people who've had their own agenda for a while. But you were right. We went out there last night and we fought off an attack. We were lucky because we weren't fighting as a unit. That's got to change, and that's something I can help with."

"How?"

"Battle plans, Blondie. Training. Discipline."

"That sounds . . . military."

"That's why soldiers fight the wars." He started to flip up the lid on one of the pizza boxes.

Sasha laid her hand on it, kept it closed.

"We eat together — that's training, too, isn't it?"

"Okay. Better eat inside. Storm's coming in."

"Then let's go tell the others." She started out, looked back until he shoved away from the counter to come with her. "Can I try out your other crossbow?"

"It's got a hundred-eighty pull weight. Even beefed up, you couldn't cock it."

"I'd still like to try it."

"Push-ups," he said.

The first rumble of thunder sounded as she started up the stairs.

By the time they'd all gathered around the kitchen table, the sky hung dark and broody. With the quickening flashes of lightning, the thunder rolled closer on a hard wind.

"Nothing like a good storm," Riley said. "Unless it's pizza."

"Even bad pizza's good." Sawyer lifted a

slice, bit in. "And this ain't bad."

Watching him, Annika picked up a slice, took a careful bite. "It's wonderful."

"Best pizza? Where?"

"New York," Bran said immediately, and Riley shook her head as she chowed down.

"This little mom-and-pop in a little hillside village in Tuscany. Amazing. Sash?"

"I had some really nice pizza once in Paris."

"French pizza?" Sawyer snorted. "Forget about it. Neck-and-neck between New York and this trattoria in Florence. How about you?" he asked Annika.

"This," she said, and took another bite.

"Kildare," Doyle said when everyone looked at him.

"Irish pizza?" Riley grabbed another slice as she laughed. "That's below French pizza."

"In a restaurant run by Italians," he added. "It wins because it was unexpected."

"Speaking of winning," Sasha put in. "We should talk about the idea that we won last night because Nerezza was testing us. Doyle brought up the need for battle plans, for training."

"Training?" Riley's eyes narrowed. "Such as?"

"Bran does what he does." Doyle took another slice from the same pie as Riley — the one loaded with sausage and pepperoni. "That's a specific skill set nobody else here can train for. But Sasha had it right. We went into last night individually. We can't risk that again. We need to know what Bran has . . . up his sleeve."

"You're right on that." Bran nodded, poured wine. "And you'll know from here and on. We need strategies and plans. If we only react, more, react individually, we'll lose."

"No argument, but what training?" Riley continued. "I'm already working with Sasha and Annika on hand-to-hand, defense. And after today, we know Sasha's a regular Daryl Dixon with a crossbow."

"Crossbow?" Sawyer paused with a slice halfway to his plate. "How did I miss that?"

"Who's Daryl Dixon?" Sasha asked.

The Walking Dead," Sawyer supplied. "You can handle a crossbow?"

"Apparently."

"Handle, my ass. It was *thwang!*" Riley mimed the shot. "Bull's-eye. I'd stick with her in any zombie apocalypse."

"I appreciate that, but I think Doyle means we need to start working, and training, together. We've made noises about being a team. We need to train like one. Bran's teaching me about what he uses to make medicines, so I can help there."

"I could learn," Annika said. "I like to learn."

"You should all know the basics. What potion, what salve, what tincture for what injury. You all know basic first-aid of the ordinary sort," Bran added. "But we're not dealing with ordinary."

"And if you're injured, we wouldn't know what to use. Okay," Riley agreed. "We take time for some magickal medicine lessons."

"Other skill sets have to play. You and Sawyer?" Doyle shook his head, reluctant admiration. "Can't say I've ever seen better shots, and you both keep a cool head. You start target practice with the others."

"I don't like the guns," Annika said quickly.

"You don't have to like them, gorgeous, you just have to learn to handle one. And you've got some moves."

"I'd pit her against Black Widow. I'm going to buy a shitload of graphic novels for you guys," Sawyer said when both Annika and Sasha looked blank.

"You need to teach Sasha, refine Riley — you've got moves of your own, but Annika's faster, smoother."

"Yeah? And what about you? Bran, Sawyer?"

"We'll all work on it. And on hand-to-hand. Training," he repeated. "We need to put a couple hours a day, at least, into it. Sasha can make a schedule."

"I can?"

"You started it, Blondie. You were right, now you follow it through."

Riley polished off her second slice. "You've got a lot to say tonight, McCleary."

"Because I've got something to say." Lightning flashed, and thunder boomed hard behind it, causing Apollo to belly under the table until his head lay on Riley's feet. "I've fought with you twice, and what I've seen is a lot of skill, and no unity."

"So we hone the skills, and unite," Sawyer finished. "I'm behind that. On the united front, I think —"

"Sorry." Riley pushed up. "I'm going to have to eat and run."

"Run?" Sawyer looked toward the window as the rain started in a gush. "Where?"

"To my room to start. It's nearly sundown, and since I'd as soon not strip down here in the kitchen, I'm going up."

"You can come back," Sasha told her. "You don't have to stay closed in your room."

"Yeah, I get it, appreciate it. I'm going to need to run. Storm or no storm, I'll need to run off the initial energy. I'll be back. If there's any pizza left over, I've got dibs on it at sunrise."

She grabbed a third slice and headed out with Apollo close to her side.

Bran looked after her, then back at Sawyer. "You were saying?"

"Ah . . . I lost track. I guess . . . unity. I'm all in on weapons training. Where'd you get the crossbow?"

"Doyle," Sasha told him. "He has two."

"Ever used one?"

Sawyer shook his head at Doyle. "But I'm all about it. After last night, I'm going to need more ammo. I expect Riley could use more. Looks like we need a supply list, and what we could call a supply officer. I'd nominate Riley there. She has the most contacts."

"Supplies are more than weapons. It's food," Sasha pointed out. "Household supplies."

"I could nominate myself. Or you. What about your kind of supplies?" Sawyer asked Bran.

"I'm taking care of it. There would be some things we can acquire as easily as household supplies, but some I'm sending for. We've picked up most of the duties around the house and grounds, but I suppose we could be more organized about it."

"I don't mind switching off dinner prep with Sawyer, but it's nice to have a night off."

"Pizza night." Sawyer grinned. "Once a week."

"Done." Bran toasted the idea. "And as Sasha and Sawyer handle dinners otherwise, I propose they're exempt from getting pizza. The rest of us can alternate that as well."

"I like pizza." Annika, after savoring the first, chose a second slice.

"I pity those who don't. As for strategies . . ." Bran cocked an eye at Doyle.

"I figure the three of us can hammer some out."

"Meaning the three of you. Men."

Doyle shrugged at Sasha's statement. "Ever fought a war, Blondie?"

"Not until now."

"Ever play war?" Sawyer asked. "As a kid?"

"Well, no." Since Annika didn't appear to mind being dismissed, Sasha felt the burden of female pride rested fully on her shoulders. "I bet Riley did."

"And I'd wager she's been in more than a few skirmishes. We'll see what she has to say about it."

Now Doyle shrugged at Bran. "Fine."

"But we have to search." Annika looked from one to the next. "We can't stop."

"We won't be stopping," Bran assured her. "But it looks as if we'll have more regimented days, at least for now."

"I'll make out my end of the supply list." Sawyer rose. "But first I'm going to start a fire in the other room. The storm's probably dropped the temps, and we're going to have a couple of wet . . . canines."

"I'll help you." Annika rose with him. "And I'll do the dishes. It should be my turn."

Happy to pass that duty off, Sasha sat back with her wine. "And what's my assignment?"

"You'd be the best to keep track of needed household supplies. And I think Doyle will agree you can be trusted to write out tasks and schedules in a fair way. We never followed through there. And I'd say the training schedule should be yours, Doyle."

"We'll want an early start, as one of us has one more day that ends at sundown."

"What sort of early start?" Sasha wondered.

"Sunup. Calisthenics. You want to beef up, that's how you start. Then breakfast —

plenty of carbs for you. I'd say we need a day here, forming those strategies, starting weapons training — before we go back out to dive. When Sawyer finishes building his fire, we could start outlining some basic plans. Attack as well as defense."

Doyle got up. "I'm going to take a walk first."

"It's storming," Sasha reminded him.

"I don't mind getting wet."

"He'll go up," Bran said after Doyle walked out, "and get his sword as well as his coat. And he'll walk the perimeter, we'll call it. And do the same again around midnight."

"There's a soldier in him."

"Oh, without question."

"But he's not ready to tell us about it. Sawyer's ready. He had something to tell us before Riley interrupted and had to go."

"Do you think so?"

"I'm sure of it. I don't know what, but he's ready to tell us the something more. Bran."

He smiled. "Sasha."

"There's another kind of training I need, and I think you can help me. Not that," she said with a laugh when he grinned at her. "Well, that, too. We can call that training. But I need to learn how to open more to what I have."

"You already are. I knew about the crossbow because I watched you. Not a moment's hesitation in you. You took it, and used it. Because you knew."

"Not deliberately. I didn't know deliberately, and that's what I want. I don't think I'll ever control this, not completely. I don't think I'm meant to. But if I'm to really do my part in all this, I need to have some control. I've spent so many years trying to suppress it, and now I want to use it. Can you help?"

"I think I can."

"Good. I'm going to go up, work out the supplies, the assignments. And leave you men to your war council."

He grabbed her hand before she walked by, kissed it. "There'll be six sitting on that council before this is done. This is only the start."

"So we'll start with the soldier, the sharpshooter, and the magician. It would be stupid to object."

"Add the lycan, because I think you've the right of that."

And it mollified. "Should I wait in my room or yours?"

"Make your choice. I'll find you."

When she left, he thought he'd already

found her. And that, like Doyle's exceptional pizza in Kildare, was unexpected.

She went to her room, changed into loose cotton pants. She decided she'd do an actual chart for the task schedule, with names, days of the week, and appropriate chores and errands.

Before she got started she walked to the terrace doors, opened them to the sound of the storm.

And saw the shadow of the wolf.

She caught the scream, swallowed it back. "God. You scared me, Riley." She took a deep breath because her voice had trembled. "I don't know if you understand me. That's a question we should've asked."

And when the wolf strolled into her room, she swallowed again.

"I guess that answers that. I'd offer to towel you off, but that just seems really strange. Stranger. Ah, Sawyer started a fire for you downstairs. He's sweet that way, and thought of it."

The wolf simply stood, watching her. Unnerving, Sasha thought, to look at the wolf — sleek and wet and fierce — and see Riley's eyes. "You should try to get some sleep tonight — I don't know if that's how it works, but if you can, you should get some sleep. Doyle called for calisthenics at dawn."

At this, the wolf growled low.

"Okay, you definitely understand me. It actually makes sense, as a whole. I'm going to do a household supply list, and task assignments. And we're going to start the training — by skill set — tomorrow. The men are going to get together down in the kitchen, talk battle strategies."

The growl came again, and now the wolf paced.

"Yeah, I had the same reaction, except you're invited onto the war council." When the wolf stopped pacing, Sasha nodded. "Right. We figured you had some experience where Annika and I don't. But we will. We're going to take tomorrow, seeing as you have to make it a short day, to start putting the training together. See, it makes sense."

She wasn't sure if the sound the wolf made was agreement or resignation, but it wasn't quite a growl.

"You should go down, get warm and dry. You might not be able to add anything to the strategy session, but you can listen."

The wolf walked to the door. Sasha followed, opened it.

"I'll see you in the morning."

She closed the door quietly on what she decided was the strangest conversation she'd ever had.

Suddenly, it struck her. Could she sense Riley's feelings — in wolf form? Feelings echoed thoughts. So if she could, there could be more of a conversation.

She'd ask Riley if she was open to trying it.

But for now, with the storm blowing out to sea, she got her supplies, and began creating a chart.

She did a draft, edited it, re-edited it. It took longer than she'd imagined. She finished it, perfected it, then wrote out a supply list with a lot less fuss.

Done, she forced herself to put in fifteen minutes with Riley's bands, and tried some push-ups. She *would* get stronger.

Still alone, she slid into bed with her sketch pad.

And fell asleep with a half dozen sketches of the wolf on her page.

When Bran slipped in beside her, she sensed his warmth, turned to him.

"It's late." He brushed his lips over her brow. "Sleep."

So she slept on, and dreamed of a room lined in gold and silver, studded with jewels, mirror-bright.

She dreamed of the god who sat on her golden throne, staring into those jewels, her beauty dark and unearthly.

The reflections, dozens and dozens, covered those walls, and were wizened, hideous, twisted.

On the god's scream of rage, the jewels shattered.

And the walls ran with blood.

CHAPTER SIXTEEN

Rising at dawn was one thing. Rising at dawn for some yoga stretching was actually rather pleasant. But following that rather pleasant stretching by being whipped into squats and lunges changed the entire complexion.

She kept up, well enough, but squats, lunges, jumping jacks with Annika smiling, even letting out an occasional laugh, as she herself struggled through them — without even a single hit of coffee — made Sasha want to try out her right jab on her friend's beautiful face.

Then came the dreaded push-ups.

She was the only one of the six who couldn't manage more than two. One and a half if she was honest. Even with her knees down in what Riley called (with a definite sneer) *girl* push-ups, she struggled.

She *would* get stronger.

Pull-ups — not even one. Crunches until

her abs screamed. More stretching — thank God — then a jog down the cliff steps, along the beach, then back.

Where she just collapsed on the grass in a gasping heap.

"I hate you." She could barely pant it out. "Especially Doyle, but all of you."

"That's a start. Who's on breakfast detail?" Doyle asked.

"The chart's in my room. Someone who can still walk should go get it."

"I'll get it." Annika, barely winded, dashed off.

From her prone position, Sasha bared her teeth. "Maybe I hate her even more than Doyle."

Moaning, she rolled over, made herself stand on wobbly, vibrating legs. Actively scowled when Annika bounced back with the chart.

"I cook with Sawyer today. I can make the coffee. I know how. It's so pretty!" She turned the chart around for all to see.

Sasha had color-coded it, and since she'd been in a fine mood before this morning's torture, had illustrated the chart.

Pretty little drawings of pots and pans, a lawn mower, a garden, pecking chickens, the pool, and so on — along with sketches of everyone beside their names.

"I want that," Sawyer said immediately. "I want that when we're done. It goes in the kitchen for now, but I'm calling dibs. Let's go cook, Annika."

"Can I break the eggs?" she asked as they headed toward the villa. "It looks like fun."

"There's a woman who makes her own fun. Let's find out if she can make coffee."

"Hold on a minute," Doyle said to Riley. "You got any Tai Chi?"

Riley tapped her right fist to her open left palm. "Sure."

"Take Sasha through a beginner's session."

"What! Why? No." Though it shamed her, Sasha was weak enough to look at Bran for help. But he only smiled, gave her arm an encouraging pat.

"It'll help with your balance and centering," Doyle said. "You want to catch up with everyone else, you need a little extra. Twenty minutes should do it. How about you show me some of what you've put together," he said to Bran, "while they're cooking."

"All right." Bran took Sasha's face, kissed her lightly. "Twenty minutes," he repeated, and left her.

"I want coffee," Sasha insisted. "I want to sit down. I think I want my mommy."

"There's no whining in Tai Chi. Feet

slightly apart, knees loose. Breathe from here." She slapped a hand on Sasha's aching abs.

"Oh, God."

"You wanted a unit, Sash. Looks like you've got one."

"It hurts."

"No pain, no gain," Riley shot back with merciless cheer. "I'll go over philosophy later, because I damn well want coffee, too, but for now, breathe in from your center, and do what I do."

At least the movements were slow, and she had to admire Riley's fluidity as she tried to mimic them. But that didn't stop her quads from aching like rotted teeth.

By the time she sat down she could have wept and whimpered for coffee, but she damn well knew where her center was as it quivered from exhaustion and begged for food. Sawyer produced a platter with a golden mountain of pancakes. Where she'd usually have eaten one, she ate three, actually contemplated a fourth before she decided it might make her sick.

Doyle looked across the table at her. "You're up."

"I don't want to be up. Maybe not ever again."

"I believe he means your clever and creative chart." Bran gestured to where Annika had propped it on a chair, like another team member.

"Oh. Well. I've got me and Bran on cleanup, Riley on Apollo and chickens."

"Wolf in the henhouse."

Riley sent Sawyer a sharp, sweet smile. "You're a barrel of monkeys."

"Annika and I hit the garden to weed and harvest," Sasha continued.

"I'm on the pool, Bran's on the lawn mower. Annika's on laundry." Sawyer grinned at the chart. "Leaves Riley and Doyle on the supply run. I think I like the pictures of the bag of groceries and boxes of ammo best."

"Give me ten for the cluckers, another ten to grab a shower." Riley downed the rest of her coffee. "Another five to make a call, see where we'll find the best place for the ammo."

"The household supply list is on the dresser in my room."

Nodding at Sasha, Riley pushed away from the table. "Got it. Fifteen tops," she said and jogged off. How could she *jog,* Sasha wondered bitterly, to deal with the chickens?

"Might as well grab a swim before I play pool boy."

Doyle rose as Sawyer did. "Fifteen minutes to add anything to the supply list, otherwise, you get what you get."

Annika sat a moment after the others left, then looked apologetically at Sasha. "I don't know how to laundry. Can you teach me?"

"Go ahead." Bran waved them away. "I've got this."

By the time she'd finished giving Annika a lesson on separating clothes, water temperatures, cycles, he'd nearly finished the dishes.

So she and her partner for the morning went out to the garden with hoes, rakes, shears, and a plastic tub from the shed.

They worked with Annika happily humming. She could hear the rumble of the lawn mower, the drone of bees, and the swish of the sea at the base of the cliff.

All so normal, Sasha thought, so everyday. Anyone looking at the picture would see a group of people tending to household chores. But they were far more.

She bided her time, noting that Annika caught on quickly to hoeing out the weeds, just as she'd caught on quickly to the basics of doing laundry.

But she'd clearly done neither before.

"So you have six sisters," Sasha began.

"Yes."

"You must miss them."

"I do, but I'm happy here. Even though we have to fight, and some of the work is hard."

"Six sisters," Sasha repeated. "And you've never done laundry before."

"Today I'm doing laundry."

"So you had staff?"

Obviously puzzled, Annika straightened, mimed holding a tall stick. "Staff?"

"Not that kind. People. People who do things like laundry and cooking and cleaning."

"Oh. We're staff now."

Annika bent back to her weeding, avoiding Sasha's eye.

"You've never really said where you live."

Annika weeded another moment, then stopped, turned to face Sasha again. "Will you be my friend?"

"I am your friend."

"Will you be my friend and not ask what I can't tell you? I can promise, I have nothing bad. It's . . ."

"Like an oath."

"Yes."

"All right."

Annika reached out to take Sasha into a hug. "Thank you. You taught me laundry." She eased back, smiling. "I'll teach you how to . . ." Bending over, she lifted her legs into a ridiculously fluid handstand.

"I think that's going to take a lot longer than teaching you how to do laundry."

"I'll teach you." Annika dropped down again. "And we'll find the stars. When we do, and they're where they belong, I can tell you everything."

"All right. And whatever it is, we're still going to be friends."

After gardening and laundry, after supplies were put away and they ate the gyros Riley brought back from the village, Sasha had her first lesson in gun safety.

A very patient Sawyer spent considerable time with her and Annika — the only ones who'd never fired a gun — showing them how to load, unload, reload, how to sight, how to use the safety, how to take it off.

As instructed, Annika slapped the magazine into one of Sawyer's 9 mms.

"I don't like it. It feels cold and mean."

"You don't have to like it. You have to respect it. A lot of GSWs are accidents, from carelessness. Gunshot wounds," he explained. "People who don't learn how to properly handle a gun, who don't properly secure it when not in use. Some insist guns don't kill. People do. But guns do kill, and knowing that, respecting that, is really important."

"Did this gun kill someone?"

"No. But I know it can. I know I can. If there's no choice."

He looked down to where the others had set up a temporary target range, with paper targets over a thick sheet of wood.

"Time to try them out. Safeties on."

Sasha didn't like the feel of the gun any more than Annika, but she carried it down to the range, where Riley took over the lesson.

"We're going to start with stance and grip. Basic Weaver stance," she told Sawyer, "Two-handed grip."

When she demonstrated, Annika shook her head.

"Sawyer shoots the gun with one hand."

"And when you can shoot like Dead-Eye here, be my guest. For now, two hands. Your dominant hand presses the weapon forward slightly, and the other draws it back. Balancing. This'll help you with the recoil. Dominant foot back and to the side, the other forward, knee bent. Most of the weight's on your front foot."

She had them practice, again and again, getting into position, lifting an unloaded weapon to eye level.

"Okay. Who wants to shoot first?"

"Sasha does," Annika said immediately.

"Okay."

"Load it like I showed you," Sawyer told her.

When she had, Riley stepped behind her. "Take your time, take your stance, raise your weapon." She laid a hand on Sasha's back. "Don't hold your breath when you squeeze the trigger. Squeeze it, slow and smooth and let your breath out."

She did, felt the kick all the way to her shoulder, and the force of it, the sound of it like a punch in the heart.

She didn't miss the target entirely, but put a bullet in the second ring in, to the right.

"Not bad. Adjust your stance, relax your shoulders. Try it again."

The next shot hit higher, and still well to the right of center.

"You're pulling it to the right. Think about that, fire again."

Lower this time, Sasha noted, and another ring closer.

She fired several more, never hit center, but shot what Riley called a decent grouping.

She stepped aside, more than happy to unload and set the gun down, so Annika could step to the line.

Riley adjusted her stance, her grip, then

stepped back.

Annika fired when told, missed the paper target, plowed a bullet into the wood.

"Okay. It's okay. Don't hold your breath. Don't close your eyes. Eyes on the target this time, and squeeze the trigger."

She did, hit the white of the paper, then lowered the gun.

"I won't learn this. I'm sorry." Deliberately she unloaded, handed the gun carefully to Sawyer. "I'm sorry, I can't learn this. I'll work harder, and I'll fight, but I can't do this. It feels evil in my hand. I'm sorry."

"It's okay. Hey, don't," he said quickly when her eyes welled with tears. "We'll find something else for you. No guns." He looked meaningfully at Doyle. "She doesn't have to use a gun."

"Her call."

"Yeah, it is. See that." Sawyer holstered the weapon, put an arm around her shoulders. "Your call."

"I'm going to fold the laundry. Sasha showed me how. I'm going to go fold the laundry."

"We'll think of something else," Sawyer said to the group when she dashed off.

"I might be able to come up with something." Bran looked after her. "Something that would give her a weapon, a defense, and not upset her. Let me work on it."

By the time they'd concluded what Sasha thought of as Weaponry 101, she found all the laundry finished, folded — and her own share neatly stacked on her bed.

And the house sparkled.

She found Annika in the kitchen, diligently unloading the dishwasher.

"I cleaned the house."

"I'll say."

"I'm sorry."

"You need to stop being sorry. No one's mad at you."

"I didn't do my task."

"Because it's wrong, for you. Everyone understands." Sasha thought of her sore and aching muscles, weighed them against friendship. "You said you'd teach me the handstand. You could give me a couple private lessons before you work with everyone. Give me a — ha-ha — leg up."

"Yes, I can. I will."

"How about now?"

She failed, and even when Annika held her legs, Sasha's arms and shoulder muscles quivered and pinged like plucked harp strings. During the group lesson, after multiple face and/or ass plants, she was relegated to practicing simple forward and backward rolls.

She would get stronger. She would get better.

Deeming herself finished, she took her aches and pings off for a soak in the hot tub. She considered doing laps, as Doyle had suggested, but the way her arms and legs felt, she'd probably sink straight to the bottom of the pool and drown.

Besides, she'd damn well earned a break.

She hit the jets — ahh — adjusted her sunglasses. She'd just sunk down to her chin when she saw Annika and Riley coming her way.

She liked their company, but at the moment she'd have preferred the moans she knew would come to be a private thing.

Riley set a pitcher of margaritas on the table, poured three glasses. And Annika held up a small bottle.

"Bran said to add this to the water."

"What is it?"

"Lavender and rosemary and . . ." She looked to Riley.

"Magic. He said it would take care of any muscle soreness. Dump it in, Anni. We're going to test it out." Riley handed Sasha a glass.

"I'm not sore." But Annika poured in the pale green liquid.

"She tempts me to say fuck you." Riley boosted herself into the tub.

"Consider it said." Sasha closed her eyes, sipped the frothy drink. She heard the splash as Annika chose the pool instead.

"I hurt everywhere, and it's worse knowing I'm going to be squatting and lunging and running at dawn tomorrow."

"Add in upper body work."

Sasha slitted her eyes open. "Consider it repeated in your direction."

"We'll be diving tomorrow, so that'll mix things up. And maybe we'll get lucky. I left Sawyer and Doyle working out where."

"Bran?"

"He got a brainstorm about Annika's deal, so he went up to work on it."

Sasha decided she'd go up and help him with it. Eventually. "God, this smells so good. Why don't I have one of these at home?"

"A hot tub, or a hot magician to make you magic hot tub potions?"

She smiled to herself. "Both."

"Bet you could get both."

"Bran, in my little house in the mountains? He has New York, and Ireland. My place is so isolated, so quiet, and he's . . . he's larger than life, isn't he? All that power. He banks it — that's control — but it's huge, and passionate, and more than could be satisfied living in a little house in North Carolina."

"Will you be, once we're done with what we're here for?"

"I don't know anymore." And that shifted her balance. "But I think I'll always need a quiet place to go, to live, to paint. I'll never block what I have again, or feel I have to be alone. I know more about myself, what I'm capable of. I know what it is to be a part of something really important. Something worth fighting for. And when I look at myself now . . .

"The mirror sees the truth, hard and bare. What she fears and fights against lives in the glass. And there lies her end, one only the stars can change. She fears her end."

She came back to herself with Riley gripping her arm to keep her head above water and calling for Annika.

"I'm all right. I'm okay."

"Take a hit." Riley pushed the glass back in her hand. "I saved it when it started to tip out of your hand."

Sasha shook her head, let out a breath. "Give me a second."

"The water's too hot, and you're pale. Come, cool off in the pool."

"Good thinking." With a nod to Annika,

Riley put the glass aside, pulled Sasha to her feet. "Out and in, pal."

She obeyed, as she did feel too hot, and somehow too . . . loose. The cooler water of the pool helped offset the dizziness so she was able to climb out again on her own.

"Do you remember what you said?" Riley asked her.

"Yes. About a mirror, about the truth in it. I'm not sure what it means."

"We should go in," Annika decided. "Out of the sun."

Yes, Sasha thought. She'd get out of her wet bathing suit, take a moment or two to settle. "One good thing." She rolled her shoulders before wrapping herself in a towel. "I don't ache anymore."

Though she brushed off the offers to help her change, she realized they'd gone straight to Bran when he walked in before she'd buttoned up a dry shirt.

"Let me look at you."

"I'm all right. They didn't have to interrupt you for this."

He simply put his hands on her shoulders, took a long study of her face. "No headache?"

"No. I didn't try to block it. It comes on in a wave — and it leaves me a little shaky,

374

but it didn't hurt. You were right about that."

"Describe what happened."

"Riley and I were in the hot tub — Annika put your potion in the water. Wonderful, by the way. I was relaxed, and we were just talking about . . ." She adjusted here. She certainly wasn't going to bring up Riley's suggestion he'd come live with her in North Carolina.

"Talking about what?"

"How I knew myself better since all this started, and knew what it was to be part of something. Then it was that wave again. It's like being pulled by an undertow. But this time, I tried to go with it instead of fighting to stay up."

"What did you see?"

"I —" She broke off at the knock on her door.

"Are you okay in there?" Sawyer called out.

"Yes. I'm coming down. I need to organize my thoughts," she said to Bran.

"All right." He ran his hand over her damp hair. "We'll go down."

They'd already gathered on the terrace, so she sat, took a breath. "I'm sorry because I don't really understand what I meant, what I saw. It might have been a room, it might

375

have been a cave. Everything was gold and silver and shining. Like a really elegant house of mirrors. It was like I was standing there in it, but I couldn't see myself. Then I picked up a mirror — but it wasn't my hand. I think it was hers. Nerezza. She picked up this jeweled mirror, but when she looked in it, what looked back was not just old. Ancient. Gray and withered. Sunken eyes, thin gray hair. Hardly more than a skull. Nothing else reflected. The glass around that image was pure black.

"The glass shattered, and that face was in all the shards, hundreds of shards. And the shards went to smoke, and it all went dark."

"You said the mirror sees the truth," Riley reminded her.

"I know."

"An allegory?" Sawyer suggested. "She's ancient, being a god — but the mirror sees her soul or heart or whatever you want to call it as withered and dark?"

"We don't need a seer to know that," Doyle pointed out. "Maybe she's got a Dorian Gray thing going."

Struck, Riley pointed a finger at him. "And the mirror reflects what she really is. It ages, shows her sins and all that while she stays young and beautiful."

"It's a theory."

"A good one. If there actually *is* a mirror, and we destroyed it — there lies her end."

"I don't know. What I saw . . . She destroyed the mirror. She'd hardly end herself."

"Another mirror, another glass," Bran suggested.

"I'll do some digging on it." Riley picked up her margarita again. "You said only the stars could change it. We can speculate that's another reason she wants them so bad. There's a way to end her — not just stop her, but end her. And if she gets the stars, the way's done."

"I'll do some checking on mirror spells," Bran added. "The stars remain first priority. Have you two chosen where we dive tomorrow?"

Doyle nodded. "We mapped out routes to three caves. We should be able to do all three, but we can hit two for certain. You'll want to get a meal in before sunset," he said to Riley, "so —"

"Before we get into that," Sawyer interrupted. "And whatever else is on today's agenda, I've got something I need to explain. I needed to talk to my family first. My grandfather especially."

"Regarding the compass," Bran said.

"Yeah, that. There's a little more to it."

He took it out of his pocket. "Using it with a map can show you where you should go, for what you need or want. But it can do more than show you. Even without a map."

"Like what?" Riley demanded.

"Well. Like this." Sawyer held the compass out in his palm.

And vanished.

"What the holy fuck!"

As Riley swore, Annika jumped to her feet. "Where did he go? Where is he?"

"Up here." Sawyer called from the terrace, waved. Then vanished only to reappear in his seat at the table.

"You're a magician, too!"

"No. It's the compass," he told Annika. "It's linked to me, yeah, but it's the compass. I just gave it where I wanted to go — an easy one — to the terrace up there, and back here."

"That's more than a little." Doyle held out a hand, examined the compass when Sawyer gave it to him. "How is it linked to you?"

"Whoever holds it can pass it to another. Not like I just did to you. It's a formal deal. It's mine until I pass it to the next. Traditionally a son or daughter."

"You really save on airfare," Riley commented.

"Ha. Yeah, it's handy there. There's actually a little more." He took it back from Doyle, turned it over, ran his finger around the circumference.

A second lid opened to reveal a clockface.

"Man! You are *not* going to tell me it's like a time machine."

Sawyer gave Riley a weak smile. "Sort of."

She leaped up, did a dance. "Oh, my Jesus, the places I could go, see. Mayans, Aztecs, Celts. The land bridge, the freaking pyramids. Where — *When* have you been?"

"Not that far back. Look, you've got to take a lot of care when you use it to time or place shift. A lot of care. Say you get an urge to watch the gunfight at the O.K. Corral. First, you're dressed all wrong, and somebody's going to notice. More, what if you drop down in the middle of the road and a wagon runs over you? Or you get hit by a stray bullet? Even if you live through it, you've changed something. And that can change something else, so when you come back it's not exactly the way you left it. Now you've got to go back and fix it."

"Space-time continuum. Got that, but you went there, right? Got a look at the Earps and Doc Holliday."

"Yeah, and let me say it was fast and ugly — the gunfight. Time shifting's tricky, and you learn really fast — because you're taught and trained, but you have to learn by mucking up — not to use it for entertainment."

"How far?" Doyle asked. "How far back can you go?"

"I don't know if there's a limit. I've heard stories — I was weaned on them — of people who didn't come back. The compass always comes back, but some of the ones who held it haven't. Because maybe they went too far, or they ended up miscalculating time or place just enough to end up in the ocean or in the middle of a battlefield, an earthquake."

"And forward?" Bran asked him. "Is that part of it?"

"Even trickier. You want to see how things are going a hundred years from now? What if eighty years from now things went really bad? You figure to hit in Times Square, but instead there's nothing. Or you drop down in the middle of a war, a plague. Even something as basic as that forest meadow is now a five-lane superhighway and you're pancaked. You can calculate pretty well going back, but forward? You can't calculate what hasn't happened."

Sawyer closed the lid on the clockface. "I've gone back and sideways and around in circles trying to get a handle on what we're after. Before I got here, before I met any of you. I'd get bits and pieces, variations on the legend or the mythology, but nothing solid. And when the compass pointed me here, and now, that's where I came."

Annika touched his hand lightly. "Are you from now?"

"Yeah. Born twenty-nine years ago. And listen, if I knew how to get back to the when and where all this started, maybe I'd risk it. But that's more than I've been able to do. And if I could, I don't know if there's anything I could do anyway."

"Can you take anyone with you?"

"Yeah. I took my brother back to Dodger Stadium to see Jackie Robinson play. It was his birthday — my brother's — and my grandfather okayed it. But I've only tried it with one person. Theoretically, I could take more. We don't talk about this outside the family," he continued. "It's like your deal, Riley, sort of. I went over this with my grandfather and I was going to bring it up last night. But you had to wolf out."

"Huh."

"Something like this gets out and you've got all kinds of crap to deal with. This asshole got wind of it, and he's been on my ass for five years now. Son of a bitch tried to ambush me last year in Morocco where I was following a lead. Gave up trying to buy it, and tried to shoot me instead. Fucking Malmon."

"Wait a minute. Wait." Teeth bared, Riley leaned forward. "Andre Malmon?"

"Yeah. You know him?"

"I know him. Likes to bill himself as a rescuer of artifacts, as an expert on mythology, a consultant, adventurer, whatever suits his needs. He's a thief, a cheat, and I can't prove it, but I know he killed an associate of mine. He's onto you — to this?" she added, tapping the compass.

"Yeah, he is. I lost him after Morocco."

"He won't give up easy. I'll make some calls, see if I can find out where he is. If he's anywhere close, we need to defend against him as much as Nerezza."

"Does he know about the stars?" Bran asked her.

"Malmon knows something about everything." She picked up her drink, scowled into it. "Son of a bitch Malmon. If he gets wind you're here, Sawyer, that I am, that we are — unless he's hot on somebody else's ass, he'll be all over us. He'd slit your throat for that compass."

"Yeah, I got that loud and clear in Morocco."

"For the stars?" She drained the rest of her drink. "He'd gut every single one of us."

"Then we'd better find them first." Doyle rose. "I'm getting a beer."

"Bring some for the rest of the class." Bran turned to Riley. "Tell us about Malmon."

"Smart — plenty of letters after his name. But more, he's ruthless. He's got plenty of scratch."

"He had a . . ." Annika scratched her fingers along her arm.

"No — it's another word for money, and he's got piles of it. Big load of family money, then whatever he can steal. He'll take any contract if it pays enough. My sources say he's the one who arranged to abduct the white rhino — northern species, critically endangered — out of the conservancy in Kenya. Left two people dead. Nobody could prove it, and they've never found the rhino."

"Why would anyone steal a rhinoceros?" Sasha wondered.

"Because somebody paid him, a whole bunch of a lot. Most likely somebody just as rich and just as vicious as he is who wanted to hunt it. A lot of sick bastards get off hunting rare and endangereds."

She shook her head at the beer Doyle brought back. "If he knew what I was, he wouldn't rest until he'd locked me in a cage and sold me to the highest bidder. Anyway."

She pushed that away. "He's mid-forties, has bases in New York, Paris, Dubai, an estate in Devon. Probably more. French father, Brit mother, raised primarily in England, from what I know again. If I had to label him, I'd go with narcissistic sociopath. He's got mercs and a couple ex–Special Forces on his regular payroll, and picks up freelancers for specific jobs. But he doesn't mind getting his hands dirty, or bloody. My take is he enjoys it.

"My friend had contacted me, way juiced. Told me he was dead sure he'd found Carnwennan, asked me to head to Cornwall, help him verify."

She changed her mind on the beer, took one after all.

"What's Carnwennan?" Sasha asked her.

"King Arthur's dagger. Plenty in my line believe it pure myth. I don't happen to agree, and Westle — Dr. Westle — dedicated most of his professional career to Arthurian pursuits. When he said he'd found it, I believed him. It took me a couple of days to wrap up what I was doing and get to him. When I did, he was dead. Garroted — but not before he'd been tortured, not before his lab was trashed and torched — and him with it. No sign of Carnwennan, of course, or any of his notes, any of the other artifacts he'd found. Malmon was spotted in Falmouth, and that's not coincidence."

She got up. "I'm going to make those calls, see if I can find out where he is and what he's up to."

"And we'll deal with him, if and when," Bran said when Riley walked off.

"Him, his mercenaries, and hired guns," Doyle added with a glance at Annika.

As if she'd waited for a cue, she sprang up into a series of flips across the table, and ended braced on her hands with the heel of her left foot a bare inch from Doyle's face.

He laughed, so quick, deep, appreciative, that Riley — from several feet away, glanced back in his direction.

"Okay, gorgeous. You know how to prove your point."

"I can fight." She did a fluid roll off the table to land lightly on her feet.

"I'm working on something for you. In fact, I should get back to it." Now Bran rose. "But I need something from you first."

"I have coins — and the . . . the scratch Riley gave me for some of them."

"No, *mo chroí.*" He took a small vial from

his pocket. "I need just three drops of your blood."

"My . . ." She blanched a little.

"What I make for you needs to be of you. To hold what you are — your light, your heart, your strength." Now he took out a small ritual knife he'd cleansed. "Just a tiny prick from your fingertip. Third finger of your left hand is best."

Saying nothing, she held out her hand, reached out for Sawyer's with the other.

With his eyes on hers, Bran used the tip of the knife, held her finger over the vial so three drops slid inside.

"There now." As he might with a child, he kissed her fingertip. And the tiny wound healed.

"It didn't hurt."

"Because you're very brave. And your courage is in your blood as well."

"What will you make me?"

"A surprise." Now he kissed her cheek, then turned, looked at Sasha. "I could use your help with it."

She went with him.

"You don't seem very concerned about this Malmon," Sasha said.

"He's a man, however dangerous."

He walked into his room. As he slept in Sasha's now, he'd arranged his as strictly a workspace. At the moment, his cauldron sat on a waist-high stone pedestal in the center of the room.

"Bran, it's one thing to fight, even kill those things Nerezza sends at us. But human beings?"

Killers, he thought, but only nodded. "There are ways to defend, even attack, without spilling blood. I'm working on just that here for Annika."

She looked in the cauldron, frowned at the amber liquid. "What is it?"

"That's where I could use your help. I've nearly done the mix, but what I add, how I proceed depends on what shape it will take."

"What will it do?"

"Deflect. Destroy, yes, what is conjured from the dark, as it will deflect with light."

"A shield?"

"I'm considering." He circled the cauldron as he spoke. "A small shield — she's agile enough to learn to use it, move with it."

"But she wouldn't have her hands free."

"Also a consideration. A kind of breastplate, perhaps, but then it would be stationary, only move as she moves. She wouldn't be able to defend herself from both front and flank, or only as she turns, and even as quick as she is . . ."

She could see Annika in a breastplate — the lithe and lovely warrior princess. "How would it work, exactly?"

"With a beam of light. The beam strikes what's made of dark. Deflects, destroys. The shield might be —"

"Can it be two?" she interrupted.

"Two shields?"

"No, I was thinking bracelets. Like cuffs. I may not know my superheroes like Sawyer, but I know Wonder Woman."

He laughed as Sasha brought up her arms, punched them out. "Wonder Woman. Well then, of course. She'll have her magic bracelets, have her hands free, and be able to deflect and defend from any angle. That's quite brilliant, *fáidh.*"

"Can you make them pretty? She'll wear whatever you give her, but pretty would make her happy."

"I can do that." He cupped a hand under Sasha's chin, tugged her up for a kiss. "In fact, we'll add what will look like a design, and will add power and protection."

He moved across the room to his books, chose one, began to flip through it. "Here. This will do well, I think." He gestured to her.

"Is it Celtic?"

"It is, yes. My blood, and the power and

388

protection will be imbued by me. Would you draw them? Two bracelets carrying this design. As you see them."

"All right. Let me get a sketch pad."

She hurried to her room and back, already imagining the cuffs. About an inch wide, she thought, slightly rounded, with a thin edging — like a tight braid.

And Bran's Celtic symbols circling them.

"You didn't say how they'll clasp."

He only smiled. "Magick. No beginning or end," he added. "A true circle." As he spoke, he chose a curl of wire. "Bronze. For a warrior."

With his free hand he levitated the cauldron a few inches, flashed fire under it.

"No blade, no steel. All light. And in light the power to defend, to deflect. To destroy what comes from the dark source, to defend against what wishes to harm. The blood of the warrior." He held up the vial, turned it over to let the three drops spill into the cauldron. "And of the magician." Using the same knife, he used the tip on his own finger, added three drops of blood.

"Power and light bound by blood, cored by the ancients." Now he let the wire drift into the quietly bubbling liquid. "Stirred by wind."

He blew on his outstretched palm, and

389

the liquid stirred.

"Sparked by fire."

The flames rose and lapped the pot, glowing red.

"With water from both storm and sea to cure. And earth from holy ground to bless."

Water first, spilled brilliantly blue from the bottle he chose, then earth, deeply, richly brown.

"Do you have the sketch?"

She'd drawn them, but could barely breathe now. Power thumped in the air, and the air had gone as blue as the water he'd poured. In it, he was the light, radiating it. When he turned his head to look at her, his eyes were onyx.

She held out the sketch.

He said nothing as he studied it, but nodded.

He held it high in both hands.

"Power of thee, power through me. Forge the weapons for the light, through them run the magicks bright. Blessed by thee, given by me to a warrior in this fight. With them grant her might for right. In this image form them, with our blood burn then. Spark now fire, wild and free!"

The sketch flared, flamed in his hand, and the flash that remained of it shot into the cauldron.

"As I will, so mote it be."

He held his hands over that flash, those sparks.

"Cool now. And it is done."

It was just a room now, in the quiet light of coming evening, with the cauldron sitting quiet on the stone pedestal.

"I can't breathe," she told him.

He turned quickly, the eyes that had been so wildly intense now filled with concern.

"No, I don't mean —" She waved him off. "It's just. Breathless. That was magnificent, and I'm breathless."

"It's a complex and layered business to create a tangible thing from elements and will. It takes considerable energy."

"I could see that."

"Does it frighten you?"

"Not when it's you. No."

He held out a hand. "Come, see what we've conjured."

"I didn't —"

"Your sketch. So what came from you — beauty and imagery — is also in this." He took her hand, and with his other, reached into the cauldron.

The cuffs were exactly as she'd drawn them, down to the etched symbols, the thinly braided edges. The bronze glowed in the lowering light.

"Can I . . ."

"Of course."

She ran her fingertip over them. "They're beautiful. She'll love them for that alone. I love . . . I love that you made them for her, that you understood she needed another way, and made something strong and beautiful and from light. You . . ."

Swamped in emotion, she looked up into his eyes. "You really do leave me breathless. Beyond the power, Bran. Whatever happens, this time with you? It's changed my life. It's opened it."

"You've changed mine." He took her face in his hands, kissed her gently. "Enriched it. I'll make you a vow, *fáidh,* though I don't have the sight. When we take the stars to where they belong, we'll stand together, just like this, in their light."

"That's a vow I want both of us to keep."

"Then trust we will."

She leaned against him a moment, staring out at the sky, the sea — the promontory where she knew they'd also stand together in the teeth of a storm.

"It's getting late — I lost track. You and I are on kitchen detail."

"That's a bloody shame, as I can think of something I'd like to do with you much more."

"Hold the thought — but Riley needs a meal before sunset. And you should give Annika her bracelets."

"If you must be practical. Then you'll take a walk with me later."

"A walk's what you'd like to do with me much more?"

"First." He took the bracelets she gave back to him, then her hand. "I think we'll have had enough of battle plans and tasks," he said as they started down. "And I'd like a walk in the moonlight with you."

"Then it's a date." She saw Annika playing tug-of-war with Apollo with a thick hunk of rope. "You should take them to her, and I'll get started on dinner."

When she left him to it, Bran started across the lawn. Apollo broke off the game long enough to bound toward him for a greeting.

And Annika's eyes widened when she saw the bracelets in Bran's hand.

"Oh! This is what you made for me?" She pressed her palms together, laid them on her lips. "Look how they glow in the sun."

"They're of light."

"And blood?"

"Yours and mine. They're only for you, and can only belong to you, or your blood — someone from you," he qualified.

"Thank you." She took one, almost reverently, then puzzled over it. "I don't know how to wear it. Is it for the wrist?"

"That's right." He took her hand, and the one he still held. "If you want it, it'll go on. But understand, it's both weapon and shield."

"To help me fight — without the gun or a knife."

"That's right. Without a gun or knife, but with power and light."

"I will fight."

When Bran put her fingers through the cuff, it shimmered over her hand, onto her wrist, settled there, firm and true. Annika did the same with the second.

"They're beautiful."

"Only you can take them off."

She shook her head. "I'll wear them always. Thank you." She wrapped her arms around him. "Thank you."

"You're welcome. Let me show you how they work."

"Yes, please."

He lifted a hand, and formed a dark, spinning ball just above his palm, then sent it into the air. Then taking her arm, bent at the elbow, turned it toward the ball. "To start, you have to think, to aim, to be deliberate. But then it'll be instinct. Deflect the ball."

"Deflect?"

"Your light, Annika, against the dark. Use it."

He helped her this time, this first time. The thin beam of light shot from her cuff, struck the ball.

"I feel it," she murmured.

"That's right. Do it again."

She surprised him, lifting her other arm, and sent the ball wheeling.

"You're a quick one."

"I feel it," she repeated. "But what if I make a mistake? What if it strikes someone? I don't want to hurt anyone."

"It only harms the dark, or someone with dark purpose. It comes from me as well, and I have a vow. Sacred to me. To harm no one. What I am, what I have, I won't use to harm any but the dark."

"It's my vow, too. I take it with you. I will fight the dark." She lifted her arms, shot out light from both so the practice ball winged right, then left.

"Yes, a very quick one. Destroy it."

"Destroy?"

"I'll give you another. Destroy this one."

This light, brighter, sharper, struck the ball, and with a flash it vanished.

"If the things come back, attack us, I can do this. They're evil, so I can do this." Her eyes went hard, grim. "I can do this and break no vow."

"You do this, as I do, to keep one. To destroy the dark, to find and protect the stars."

"These are more than a gift. Even more than a weapon. You gave me purpose." Those sea-witch eyes, usually so full of fun, met his with intensity and strength. "I won't fail you."

"I know it."

"I like that they're pretty."

"Sasha designed them for you." He conjured another ball. "Practice. I've got kitchen duty."

"I'll work very hard. Could you make a second, now? The evil doesn't come alone."

"Good point." He made three, gave her a pat on the shoulder, then left her to it. He could hear the snap and sizzle from her light as he crossed the lawn.

Sawyer stood on the edge of the terrace, his hands in his pockets, a baffled grin on his face.

"You made her freaking Wonder Woman."

"Sasha's idea. It suits well, I think."

"Are you kidding? Look at her go."

Bran glanced back, watched Annika do a running forward flip, firing at one ball from midair. Striking the other two on landing.

"Makes me feel like a git for ever thinking she needed to use a gun." As he had with Annika, he gave Sawyer's shoulder a pat, and went to the kitchen.

Annika showed off her new moves before dinner, proving herself a tireless as well as a quick study.

"I wouldn't mind a pair of those." Hands on hips, Riley watched Annika flash the trio of balls while executing a series of tumbles.

"Three nights a month you'd need four."

She sent Sawyer a sidelong look. "Har-har," she said and took his beer. "Are you sure she can't miss and zap one of us?"

"Very." As instructed, Bran slid the fish from grill to platter. "You'd feel something — like a bit of static electricity."

"Does that include wolf form?"

"It's still you, isn't it?"

"Yeah, it is. Maybe we should test it out anyway. Sawyer can be the target."

"And a har-har back."

"No joke, we should —" Riley broke off as her phone signaled. "Hold on."

Sasha brought out a bowl of sautéed vegetables in pasta and a round of bread on the cutting board.

"That's dinner," she announced.

Sawyer gave a whistle of approval when Annika blasted all three balls out of the air. "Talk about dead-eye."

Riley shoved her phone away as she sat. "The word from two sources is Malmon is currently in London — so something we shouldn't have to worry about for now." She looked out, judging the position of the sun and her time. "I like to sleep in, when I can, after the last night. I guess that's not happening."

"We drill at dawn." Doyle heaped food on his plate.

"I like to drill." Annika plopped into the chair beside Sawyer. "Some of it's like dancing."

Through the globe Nerezza watched them. It infuriated her that the images were blurred, as if through layers of gauze.

The witch, she thought, had drawn a curtain, and had more power than she'd bargained for.

Not enough, not nearly enough, but infuriating.

She set the globe aside, picked up her goblet to drink.

Let them think they were protected. Let them feast and laugh. For when she was done, the laughter would be screams.

She called one of her creatures so it perched on the arm of her chair while she skimmed her fingertip over the rough ridges of its face. She could send an attack, just to watch them scramble like ants, but it seemed wiser to let them have that feast, to let them believe they'd won some battle.

And let them lead her to the Fire Star.

When they did — *if* they could — she would take it. She would rip them to pieces, crush their bones to dust, paint the sea with their blood.

She wearied of waiting, wearied of only watching through the curtain of magic. She stroked her creature nearly into slumber. Then snapped the head from its body with one vicious twist. She added some of its blood to the goblet as a woman might add cream to her tea.

She imagined, as she drank, it was the witch's blood, and his power ran in to twine with her own.

CHAPTER SEVENTEEN

She swam through cool blue water, strong and sure. It called to her, like a song, and she wanted only to answer. Even when her lungs burned and begged for air — just one gulp of air — she swam on.

She saw the change of light, a kind of beckoning, and risked all to dive still deeper. Even when her arms weakened, her kicks faltered, she never thought of the surface. Only the light. Only the song.

Close, so close. Tears burned behind her eyes as her body betrayed her. She could see the mouth of the cave, but knew now she couldn't reach it.

She wasn't strong enough.

As the light began to blur, the song to dim, hands grabbed her.

She sucked in air that scored her throat, gagged on dream water filling her lungs. And stared into Bran's dark eyes.

"Thank the gods." He dragged her to him,

rocked them both. "You stopped breathing."

"I was drowning."

"You're here. Here with me."

"There was a light, and I wanted to reach it. Had to. I was swimming for it, but I wasn't strong enough. I was drowning."

"A dream." Not a prophecy. He wouldn't permit it. "You're stressed, that's all. We dive tomorrow —" Today, he thought, as dawn crept close. "And you're stressed."

"I was alone. Not diving, not with a tank. And I wasn't strong enough."

"You won't be alone. We'll stay back today. I'll stay with you here."

"It's not what we're meant to do. You know that. The dream doesn't make sense. I wouldn't dive without a tank. And I wasn't afraid, Bran. More . . . mesmerized. Until I realized I couldn't do it."

"Do what?"

"Get to the light. The cave. Stress," she said with a nod. "Sometimes a dream's a dream. I'm still the weak link — physically. I'm sorry I scared you."

"Only to the marrow of my bones. Come, rest a little longer."

"If I get up now, I can get coffee in before Doyle starts cracking the whip. I think it'd be worth it."

"We'll have coffee then." In that moment,

with his fear still circling the edges, she could have had anything in his power to give. "Sasha, if when we're diving, anything reminds you of the dream, you need to let me know. You won't be alone."

"That's a promise."

She felt calm. The dream left her no residual upset or worries. In fact, it barely felt real. And after twenty minutes under the crack of Doyle's whip, absolutely nothing was real except sweat and quivering muscles.

She managed six (-ish) push-ups — half-ass push-ups according to Doyle — and three-quarters of one pull-up.

By the time she stepped onto the boat, she felt she'd been running at top speed for half the day. She doubted anything could feel better at that moment than lowering her sore butt onto a padded bench, lifting her face to the sun, and letting the salty breeze flow over her. And all while the greens of Corfu gleamed against the blue.

Other boats swayed in their slips or sailed across the water — as they would soon do. She could see the colors of shops and restaurants, the movement of people already strolling. On the rails of narrow balconies on a small hotel, beach towels flapped.

The breeze carried a mix of voices and

languages to her, the scent of sunscreen and lemons, strong Greek coffee, a tang of smoke.

And wasn't that a wonder of its own, she mused, all that life, so different from what she'd known, bustling on around them? Families on holiday, shopkeepers opening their doors for the day's business, couples sitting at tables at pavement cafes, enjoying the sights and sounds and scents just as she was as they lingered over breakfast.

None of them knew, she thought, there were dark hearts wanting power so greedily they would destroy all else.

The little girl in the pretty pink capris with a ribbon trailing from her curly ponytail, bouncing along between her parents, or the old man with the weathered face and peaked cap drawing deep on his cigarette while his coffee steamed in front of him. The impossibly handsome man swabbing the deck of a nearby boat, and flashing a grin at the trio of girls who sent him flirtatious looks as they passed by.

They didn't know worlds hung in the balance. For them, it was only a beautiful spring morning on an island floating green on a blue sea.

"You're far away." Bran sat beside her.

"No, actually. I'm right here. Right here

and right now, and it's really wonderful. I'm going to come back," she decided on the spot. "When there is only the right here and right now. I'm going to have coffee right over there, and browse those shops. I'm going to buy an insanely colorful scarf, and something utterly useless and beautiful, then drink kumquat wine in the middle of the day." She angled her head, smiled. "Maybe you'll come drink it with me."

"I could be persuaded."

Doyle eased the boat out of the marina, away from the bustle, the scents, all that life. Sasha grabbed her sketch pad to draw a quick perspective of the village from the water. She would remember the bright colors, the sun-bleached ones when she painted it. A dreamy watercolor, she decided, so that edge of a world seemed just slightly mystical and unreal.

She flipped the page over — another sketch of the cliffs, all those browns and greens, the textures — and the beach where people already staked their claim for the day.

Lost in the work, she barely noticed Bran get up to help Riley and Annika with the diving equipment, hardly heard over the motor, the wind, Doyle and Sawyer discussing the maps.

Content, half dreaming, she took off her shoes, stood to remove her shirt, shorts. She'd pulled her hair back in a tail for the dive, and now set her hat on her clothes, all neatly folded on the bench.

Despite the bright sun, she set her sunglasses on the pile. The light was a white flash striking the water, deepening the blue to breathless. The foam of it in the boat's wake, the lap and splash of it against the hull as it took them into a gentle curve toward land struck like music.

It pulled at her, at everything inside her. She stood on the bench, then on the rail. Then simply dived into the song.

Bran turned first, had a split second to see her disappear under the water. "Stop the boat!" He grabbed a life ring, heaved it back, shooting power with it so it dropped on the surface where Sasha had gone in. "She's gone over. Sasha's gone over," he said as he kicked off his shoes. "She dreamed she drowned."

"For Christ's sake. Wait!" Riley grabbed his arm. "Get your tank. She might need the air. Doyle!"

"Already turning."

Bran strapped on the tank, cursing the precious seconds it took, then rolled into the water.

"Get tanks, weigh anchor. We need to —"

"I can find her," Annika interrupted Riley's frantic orders. As Sasha had, she simply dived in.

"Holy shit." Strapping his tank over his T-shirt, Sawyer kept the life ring in view. "Nerezza must've done something to them. Let's move."

He was in the water moments after Annika.

Doyle tossed Riley a face mask. "She's got a sorcerer in love with her. He'll get to her."

Riley snapped on the sheath with her diving knife. "Let's make damn sure of it."

She swam through the cool blue water, consumed by the song. It played in her head, her heart, through her blood, more beautiful than any sound ever heard.

She saw the light up ahead, a lovely glow through the blue, pulsing, pulsing with the music.

She dived deeper, yearning for it. Deeper still even when her lungs ached.

She could all but feel the warmth of it, just beyond the reach of her fingertips, struggled to swim closer while her strokes faltered.

Not strong enough. Despair flooded her at her own weakness, at the frail human need for air when all she craved was nearly within her grasp.

It all blurred — light, pulse, song — as her body went limp. She began to sink in the blue, her hand stretched toward the beauty.

Hands grabbed her. Helpless, she breathed in water as she was propelled forward.

Blinding light, sudden warmth. Then nothing.

Annika dragged her up, broke the surface of the water. In the cave, that water seemed to sing as it flowed up and over rock. Light shimmered blue as moonbeams.

"She has no breath." Weeping, Annika hugged Sasha to her as Bran shot up beside her. "Can you help her?"

"Yes, yes."

He wouldn't lose her. Boosting himself onto the wide lip of rock, he pulled Sasha up. He pressed a hand on her heart, pushed power there. And lowering to her, gave her his breath.

For an instant that lasted a lifetime, he knew true fear. He wouldn't be enough. He would be too late.

Then her heart stirred under his hand.

She coughed up water. He turned her gently as the others surfaced, and kept his hand pressed to her heart when she gasped in air.

"There you are now. I'll never tell you it's

just a dream again. There you are, *a ghrá.*"

He lifted her, cradled her, as she shook, laid his brow on hers, rocked them both.

"What happened?"

Riley climbed up, took a hard look at Sasha's face. "You decided to go diving without a tank."

"I . . . like the dream." She groped for Bran's hand. "I was on the boat, sketching, then . . . I heard the music. It was like dreaming again. I had to find the song, the light."

"Nerezza." Riley bit off the name.

"No, no. It wasn't dark or cold. It wasn't evil. It was beautiful."

"Evil hides in beauty." Doyle hauled himself up with them.

"No. I'd know. I can *feel.* It called for me. None of you heard it?"

"Something, when we got closer to the cave." Riley looked up, around. "This cave that isn't on any map."

"And the light." Bran stroked her cheek, wishing to will the color back into it. "It guided us to you."

"You saved me," she told him, but he shook his head.

"Annika. She got to you first, pulled you in here. She's faster than any of us in the water." He glanced back at her. "Understandably."

"I couldn't let the sea take her."

Annika knuckled a tear away. Her sinuous, luminous tail curved through the water. "With legs I would have been too late."

Sawyer, still treading water, his gaze still riveted on the sway of sapphire, emerald, hints of ruby, slowly reached out to touch the shimmery, translucent fin with a fingertip.

"You're a mermaid. Well, kick my ass. That explains a *lot.*"

"I couldn't tell you. I wasn't supposed to."

"Annika." Sasha crawled to the edge where Annika rested her arms. "You saved my life."

"I can see a long way in the water. Like you can see on land. So I could find you, but with legs I would be slower. And still, you had no breath when I brought you up. Bran gave you his."

"You did this for me." She laid her hand over Annika's. "Does it mean you . . . you have to stay in the water now?"

"No. I can have the legs for the land for three turns of the moon. Three months," she corrected. "I swore not to tell humans, even those who would seek the stars with me. But life is sacred, even more than an oath."

"Anybody gives you grief, they have to go through us," Sawyer told her. He brushed a tear off her cheek. "You're a hero."

"You're not mad with me?"

"Are you kidding? You saved a life, and you gave up something important to you to do it. It was your secret. How does this . . ." He ran that same finger down the side of her torso over the hip of the tail. "Sorry," he said quickly, and pulled his hand back.

"I don't mind. I'm happy. Sasha is alive, and no one is angry."

"Now that we've established that," Doyle began, "maybe we should find out just why Sasha nearly drowned to get where we are."

"Hard-Ass has a point," Riley agreed. "It's a hell of a place." She pushed to her feet. "Deep inside the cliff, from my sense of direction. But accessible enough, with equipment," she added with a pointed finger at Sasha, "that other divers should have found it. But it's not on any of the dive maps."

"The simple answer?" Steadier again as Sasha's color had come back, Bran pushed to his feet. "It isn't meant for others. It drew Sasha through what she has. Drew us all."

"You think the star's here?"

He nodded at Riley. "I think if it's not, a path to it is. But this fits Sasha's prophecy. We're bloody well between the earth and the sea, aren't we?"

"You got that." Hands on hips, Riley scanned the cave. "Small pool, wide area. A lot of rock. The walls are almost smooth, and the ceiling . . ." She frowned as she looked up, studied. "It's almost a perfect dome shape, and the stalactites, grouped together like that? I've never seen anything like it."

"Dome, a grouping like a chandelier. A holy place."

Sawyer finally pulled himself out of the pool to join them. "It shouldn't have light like this, as deep as it is — and no sky to reflect it." He glanced down at Annika. "Do you want to come up — sit on the edge?"

Her tail swished along the water in a sparkling arc, then cleaved under. She pushed herself up. "Stand," she said, and brushed water from her thigh. "I like the legs."

"Yeah, well, they're winners."

"We're going to need to have a discussion about all that," Riley decided, "but since we're here, we'll focus. If it's here, and buried, we're going to need tools. I can get those, but we don't want to hack at everything. Best thing is to spread out, look for anything that seems out of place. I'll start on the other side of the pool."

"I don't know what to look for."

411

"You got us this far," Bran reminded Sasha.

Something out of place, she thought. She didn't know what was *in* place, as she didn't spend a lot of time in strange underwater caves.

But something had brought her here — brought all of them here.

Why couldn't she hear the music now, or feel that tug pulling her in the right direction? She searched with the others, running her hands over rocks, climbing over stepping ledges of them.

As Riley said, the walls were smooth, almost the texture of glass. And warm, she noted, where surely they should have been cool to the touch. The air should be cool, she realized — even cold — considering they were beneath the surface of the sea.

Where did the warmth and the light come from?

She looked up at the bowl of the ceiling, the rich colors of the rock, the odd grouping of the stalactites, gleaming with wet.

Even as she watched, a drop slid down the cone, fell to the rock-strewn floor of the cave.

She heard the drop striking rock as distinctly as a plucked harp string. Then another. As she watched, drops ran down, shimmering with light — water striking water, water striking rock — with quick and pretty notes.

A song.

Not possible, of course. The speed of the liquid, the light of it, the sound — that music rising above everything. She walked closer, still looking up, held out a hand.

A drop fell into her palm, warm, luminous — but not wet. It held in the cup of her hand, a perfect circle, clear as glass, with its song striking her heart.

Still holding the tiny globe, she knelt on the floor of the cave.

She heard someone say her name, shook her head. Not now, not now. Couldn't they see she held love, trust, hope, right in the palm of her hand? So much of it, in a single drop, and for all the worlds.

She laid it, like an offering, on the small altar of stone.

It rose up from it, the flame and the fire. Brilliant and beautiful, red and pure as heart blood. Thousands by thousands of facets flashed with that fire, freed now from the stone, the fiercely shining star.

"The Fire Star, for the new queen. Here flames passion and the fire of truth." She picked it up, held that wildly burning light in her cupped hands. "Here is power and strength and fiery justice to light the heavens of all the worlds in the name of Aegle, the radiant."

She held it up and out, and the tears flooding her eyes were of pure joy.

"It is found. It is freed. And all we are must hold it safe until we return it with its sisters to Oileán na Gloine, so they will shine for all, forever, over all worlds."

She looked down at the star, sighed. And when she looked up, her eyes were clear of visions. "I'm not dreaming."

"No, *fáidh*." Bran, who'd come to stand with her, laid his hands on her shoulders. "You found it."

"It's real. Take it. We need to protect it from her. She'll come for it."

"I don't think she can come here." Riley moved closer, touched her fingertips to the flame. "Not to this place. It's all light and heat," she noted. "There's no solidity. But . . . I swear I can feel it hum. Does it have weight?"

"No, but I can feel it. I can't explain. Here."

Riley took it from Sasha's hand. "Mass without weight," she added. "Active flame that doesn't burn. I can't physically feel the shape of it, but I can sense it."

"We can save the scientific analysis for

later, Doc." Doyle kept one eye on the pool, one hand on his diving knife. "If she comes at us here, we've got nothing but a couple of knives, magic bracelets, and whatever Bran can pull out of his hat. We not only need to get this to the surface, but stowed away where she can't get at it."

"And when we get it to the surface?" Sawyer gestured to Riley, took his turn holding the Fire Star. "What then? Do you see what kind of light it's pumping out? People on the mainland are going to see it, so just how do we keep it on the down low?"

"I can shield it," Bran said. "Hopefully. And Doyle's right, we're not well fortified here, if she can get through to us. We need to get the star back to the villa, as quickly as we can."

"Then you'd better take it." Sawyer offered it to Bran. "You're the most fortified wherever we are. Sasha, you should stick with him. Use my tank to get back to the boat. I can make it that far —"

"No, I can't take your oxygen."

"I've got the compass if I need it, but I'm a strong swimmer."

"I can get Sawyer back to the boat, very fast."

"A mermaid ride? That's e-ticket." He grinned at Annika. "No way I'm turning that down."

"That works best." Bran cupped his free hand over the star. "To protect, to respect, to shield, to hold." He circled his hand around the star, forming a globe. Inside, the star shimmered, but quietly now.

"Nice," Riley told him.

"I'm happy you think so. I've worked on that for quite some time. And since it's the first I've used it on the actual star, I can't say for certain how long it might hold. We should go."

"Suit up." Sawyer picked up his tanks. "Don't give me that look," he said to Sasha. "I've got transportation if I need it with Aqua Girl here. You and Bran get the star back to the boat. We've got your back."

"I'll take point with Riley." Doyle hooked on his own tanks. "Annika and Sawyer on their six. As soon as everyone's on board, we head back." He looked at Bran. "For Christ's sake, don't drop that thing."

He jumped into the pool, and when Riley followed suit, did a surface dive and was gone.

Bran gave Sasha's hand a squeeze. "Ready?"

"We have to be."

"I'm with you." Holding the shielded star

close to his side, he went in the water with her.

Sasha swam away from the light, but looked back toward it twice until she saw Sawyer, then Annika, iridescent tail flashing, coming behind them.

She pushed herself, quickening her strokes so Bran wouldn't have to slow his own to keep pace with her.

Away from the cave and the light she got a better sense of just how far and deep she'd traveled. Fresh concern for Sawyer had her turning to look back.

Something flashed toward her, sharp teeth gleaming like silver, eyes glowing virulent yellow. Defenseless, she could do nothing but try to evade. Bran swept a hand through the water. She felt the power of the current even as what came at them — and what came with him — spun away.

When Bran gestured for her to go up, to surface, she shook her head. She saw both Riley and Doyle slashing at oncoming beasts with their diving knives. She wouldn't desert friends.

She prepared to fight, bare-handed, saw Sawyer slam his knife into the belly of what looked like a small shark with a massive maw. Annika's tail slashed out, swept a line of them away with a force that turned them to oily black smudges on the water.

Something hit her like a battering ram in the back, sent her tumbling helplessly in the water. Three circled her, maws wide, teeth gleaming. She punched out, kicked out, adrenaline screaming through her as her fist seemed to sink into the spongy ooze of their bodies.

Lightning struck; their bodies exploded.

Annika streaked by, tail slashing attackers, as she pulled Sawyer with her.

Bran wrapped one arm around Sasha, and rode the lightning to the surface. He all but shoved her up the ladder onto the boat where Sawyer leaned over the rail coughing up water.

"Annika," he managed. "She went back. Riley. Doyle."

Before Sasha understood, Bran pushed the star into her hand, and plunged back into the water.

"No!"

"Stop." Though he staggered a bit, Sawyer grabbed her arm before she could go over the side. "Take the star into the wheelhouse. Keep under cover as much as you can. I need a fucking tank."

He unhooked hers, would have put it on, but Riley surfaced, gripped the ladder. Setting the tank aside, Sawyer leaned over to help pull her up.

"How bad?" he demanded.

"Bran blasted some of them. If he hadn't —" As Sawyer had for her, she reached down, grasped Doyle's arm.

"Bran. Annika." Clutching the star, Sasha ran to the side of the boat.

"Right behind me. Find something to hold on to," Doyle warned them. "We're getting out of here fast."

Lightning snapped out of the water, and Bran with it. Even as he pulled himself up, Annika flew up, the powerful sweep of her tail shooting off light. In midair, she flipped to the boat, landed on her hands, then just tumbled to the deck.

"She's bleeding." Sawyer dropped to his knees beside her.

"Who isn't?" Riley demanded, but she lowered as well. "How bad is it?" she asked Annika.

"Not very bad. Not like before. But . . ." Her eyes widened, and she pointed toward the sky. "Look!"

More came, like a swarm of wasps.

Doyle started the engines, pushed them for top speed. As they bulleted over the water, Sawyer shook his head. "Not going to be fast enough."

"Go, up front with Doyle." Bran pushed

Sasha forward.

"We're not going to outrun them in this." Accepting, Riley gripped her knife.

"Yeah, we can. Maybe," Sawyer added as he pulled out the compass. "Stay down," he told Annika, braced himself against her. "Everybody hold the hell on."

Sasha turned into Bran, holding the star between them. Held tight as Sawyer reeled off a series of numbers.

It was like being pushed through space, so fast it stole the breath. Her legs buckled; her head spun as the world whirled around her.

Then she was falling, as if from a great height, to land with a rattling *thump* that would have knocked her down if Bran hadn't held her.

"Son of a bitch, it worked!" Sawyer gave the compass a loud kiss. "Son of a bitch!"

"We're back at the villa." Riley cradled a wounded arm. "And we're still in the freaking boat."

They stood, all six, on the deck of the boat. And the boat moored on the lawn between villa and seawall. Apollo ran circles around it, barking joyfully.

"I've never shifted that many people." Sawyer shrugged. "I figured we'd just try for the whole deal. We'll worry about it later."

"We're still in the freaking boat," Riley repeated.

"And it won't take her long to send them after us again," Doyle pointed out. "We need to get the star inside, and get ready for a fight."

"Please take it." Sasha held the star out to Bran. "It's safest with you. We need to dress the wounds. I remember what to get."

"Longitude and latitude, right?" Riley hoisted herself off the boat. "The numbers you said before you took us on the ride."

"Yeah. Always have the coordinates of home base right here." Sawyer tapped his temple.

"The whole freaking boat," she said again and, clutching her bleeding arm, started for the villa.

Doyle jumped off the side, looked at Bran. "You're sure about your plan for the star?"

"As sure as I can be. I'll need some time for it. And need some time to call a storm. One that will knock her back, give us a clear path to go. Wherever we need to go."

"When you're ready, we'll hold them off for you."

"Us," Sasha corrected. "I'll be with him. I saw it," she said before Bran could argue. "I painted it. I lived it."

She turned toward the terrace steps. "It's not negotiable."

Rather than argue, he took the star inside. He'd do what he needed to do when the time came to do it.

Alone.

CHAPTER EIGHTEEN

Sasha wondered if tending wounds would ever become routine. Would she become so used to blood and gouged flesh that the sight, the smell, the feel of it would no longer cause her stomach to tighten, her pulse to quicken?

She knew what to do — some was simply instinct, but Bran was a good teacher. She cleaned the gash on Riley's arm first, judged under normal circumstances the wound would require at least a dozen stitches. Calmly she coated the gash with Bran's salve while Bran worked on Sawyer, and Doyle kept watch, sword at the ready now, at the doorway.

"She won't send them yet, or come." As she spoke, Sasha added drops to a glass of water, handed it to Riley. "Drink it all."

"Coming at us when we're bleeding gives her an advantage."

"Expecting her to come at us when we're

bleeding negates the advantage. And we confused her," Sasha added. "Or Sawyer did. We vanished, boat and all. She has to think about that. And she's very angry. We have the star. Our finding it was one thing, but she wasn't able to snatch it right out of our hands as she thought she would."

She began to tend to Riley's other wounds — all minor when compared to the gash — and realized everyone had stopped to look at her.

"How do you know?" Doyle demanded.

"I don't know, but I do. I can feel her rage. And . . . she hasn't been able, yet, to break through the shield Bran put around the house. I think she will, but not when she's blind with anger. We have a little time."

"You've connected with her. You've opened enough to make that connection. Be careful, *fáidh*," Bran warned. "As she may feel, as you do, and do the same with you."

"There's only hate and anger and this terrible need. She's mad with it."

"Madness can still be canny," Bran reminded her.

"She'll come harder now." Sawyer winced as Bran tended the gouges that scored his side. "Once she regroups. We have something she wants. She was just playing around before, giving us grief. She wanted us to find the star, because she couldn't."

"I'd say that's a bull's-eye." Riley rose, rolled the shoulder of her injured arm, flexed her biceps. "Good job. I barely feel it."

"We could go somewhere else." Annika turned so Sasha could clean the wounds on her back. Mostly nicks and scratches — Bran's bracelets worked well. "Sawyer could take us somewhere else, away."

"I think I could. I have to admit, six people and a boat's a first for me, but I think I could do it."

"When the time comes I believe I can give you and your compass a boost. But . . ." Bran looked at Doyle, got a nod. "We know the ground here, and for the moment are safe. We need some time to regroup, just as she does."

"And the star comes first," Riley concluded. "But if we've got time, I want a damn beer and some food."

She walked to the fridge, pulled out leftovers, cheese, olives. "An army runs on its stomach, right?"

"Food's energy." Sawyer managed a weak smile. "I don't have much left after puking up a couple gallons of seawater, then hauling your asses and the boat."

"I'll make you food." Annika took Sawyer's hand, rubbed it against her cheek. "I didn't get you back fast enough."

"Anni, without you, I wouldn't've gotten back at all."

"I've got this." Riley pulled bread out of a cupboard, then chips. "What I'd like is a little more detail on how a mermaid's walking around."

"I couldn't tell you before."

"I'm the last one who'd poke you on that one. But how's it work?"

"We have magicians, too." She smiled at Bran. "And we also look for the stars, to protect them, to one day take them back to the sky. For some, this is their purpose. So it is for my family. And in every . . . I don't know the word. But one is chosen, and trained."

" 'Unto every generation a Slayer is born'?"

"I do not kill."

Now Sawyer smiled more easily. "It's a quote. How are you chosen?"

"The Light chooses. A ceremony when we are of age. The Light is taken from its chest by the sorcerer, and it will shine on the one chosen. Then there is the choice. We force no one, so it's a choice. I chose to accept. It's sung that the one who seeks joins with

426

five more who walk on the land, so the one who seeks is given the legs, and may walk on the land. But this gift must be held secret. Revealing is only allowed to protect the star, or to save a life. Once revealed, the seeker has only three turns of the moon to continue, and another must take her place."

"What if you — we — find the stars?" Sasha asked.

"Then I can be with my family, and the stars will shine over all the worlds. No one from mine has done this, but no one until now has found the five others. And we have the Fire Star. We have to keep it safe."

"We will."

Bran turned to the globe he'd set on the counter, with the star shimmering inside. "I have a place where it will be safe, where she can't reach it."

"Not with us?" Doyle turned away from his watch. "I'm sworn to guard it."

"As am I. If we keep it with us, we risk her getting through us — we all know she won't stop trying just that. But if it's not with us, even if she gets through, she won't have it."

"I don't much like the idea of not being able to keep an eye on it," Riley said. "Just where are you talking about?"

"It's best to show you. I'll be a minute."

When he left the room, Riley scowled into her beer. "If it's not with us, what's to stop her from finding the hiding place, just walking the hell away with it?"

"I'm not risking that. And she damn well won't get through me."

Like the others, Sawyer studied the star. "I've got to lean with Riley and Doyle on this. I've spent damn near ten years looking, and now we've got the first of them, and burying it somewhere doesn't sit right. We've handled what she's thrown at us so far."

"Bleeding, nearly drowning," Sasha pointed out. "And with the opinion she's just been playing with us. What happens when she gets serious?"

"If it's away from us, how can we know it's safe?" Tentatively, Annika reached out a hand for the globe. When her fingers brushed it, the star inside pulsed.

"We're still not a team, not a unit. Even after all this." Weary, Sasha turned to the sink to wash blood and salve from her hands. "You don't trust, not enough to wait to see and understand what he means to do. You don't trust what we are if you really believe we can only keep it safe if we can *see* it, or touch it."

She turned back, grabbed up Riley's beer,

took a deep gulp. "For God's sake. For God's sake! I'm standing here after yet another battle with — I don't know what to call them — her minions? That'll do. Her minions. Cleaning up blood while this godstar sits on the kitchen counter as casually as a toaster. I'm standing here with a mermaid, a lycan, a man who can zip through time and space — and whatever the hell Doyle's got going he hasn't decided to tell us. I was *fine* living my life. Fine! My work, my house, the quiet. I'd learned to deal with what I had — or to ignore it so I could just live the life I thought I wanted. Now I'm fighting some power-crazed god who'd like to end my life altogether. I'm in love with a magician and shooting a crossbow. And I'm drinking beer when I don't even *like* beer.

"Every one of you, every single one, has been on this — this quest — or known about it for years. I've known for weeks, so why am I the only one here who can reach down and pull out some goddamn trust when the person with power tells us he has a way?"

"Ass," Sawyer muttered, "consider yourself kicked."

"I don't want to kick anyone's ass. I don't want to rant like this, and I can't seem to stop. God, I think I need to sit down."

As she started to, she saw Bran in the doorway, his gaze — dark and intense — locked on her face.

"Just had a little meltdown," she managed, and did sit. "I'd apologize to everyone, but I think I had some valid points mixed in with the tirade."

"More valid points than tirade," Riley told her.

Annika poured a glass of wine, brought it to Sasha. "I'm apology."

"I'll give you waiting to hear the plan." Doyle leaned back on the counter, nodded to Bran. "So let's hear it."

"I thought of it sitting on the terrace of the hotel, the first day. It needed some work," he added, and laid the painting on the table.

"My painting — the one you said you'd bought."

"Before I met you, yes. I sent for it. I told you I knew these woods, this path. Because I've walked that path through those woods, toward that light. I have a place there, of my own."

"In Ireland."

"Yes, near the coast in Clare. A place I happened upon some time ago. It spoke to me, so I built a home there, though Sligo had always been mine before. This place, at the end of the path and into the light called to me. And to you, or why else would you have painted it? Why else would I have wandered into that gallery and seen it, and known it for mine? There's a purpose in things, and this is clearly purposeful. The star will be safe there. I believe with all I am it will be beyond her there."

"Okay." Riley shoved up to pace. "Okay, I get it. That's a powerful and strong connection. And I'm giving Sash her valid points. We should have more trust. But how do we get it there? Tap Sawyer for another zip — can you get us all that way?"

"If I had the coordinates, yeah, I think so."

"I've a better way, the way I'm sure it stays beyond her. I can send it through the painting."

"That's fucking genius. Is that even possible?" Riley demanded. "Because it's fucking genius, and makes me want to kick my own ass for doubting you had a solid plan."

"It's my place, and Sasha's vision of it, here. It's possible, yes."

Doyle stepped over to the table. "Through the painting to the coast of Clare."

"Where your people were from." Bran gave Doyle a long, cool study. "I think that's not without purpose either."

431

Doyle looked up into Bran's eyes, then shifted his gaze to Sasha. "Trust comes hard, but you have mine for this."

"We're six, all linked to each other, to a purpose, to a quest," Bran added, brushing a hand over Sasha's. "We must all agree."

Sawyer scanned the room, nodded. "So say we all."

"Then." Bran walked over, lifted the star in its shielding globe. He set it gently on the painting, in the glow of light at the end of the path. "If so say we all, each lay a hand on the globe, and say this. Together:

"To protect this bright fire, this pure light, I send it safe where no eye can see, no hand can touch, no darkness shadow."

As they echoed his words, Bran lifted his own hands up, seemed to draw power out of thin air. It swirled around the globe.

As he lowered his hands, fingers spread over the hands of the others, the star began to sink into the painting. Its fire sparked and simmered on that quiet path in sudden and brilliant reds and golds.

Then it poured toward the light, illuminated all.

And went quiet.

"I could feel it." Riley lifted her hand, turned it over. "The heat — it's all yours,

432

Bran — the power of it. And now — nothing."

"It's safe."

"But the painting's a kind of portal to it, right?"

Bran nodded at Sawyer. "So, as I sent for the painting, I'll send it back. And it will be beyond her as well."

"Maybe what we should do next is get ready to get out of here," Riley began. "In the opposite direction."

"I don't think we'll get anywhere without a fight," Doyle put in. "Even if Sawyer was up to another group trip this quickly."

"It's more than that." Bran looked at Sasha. "Isn't it?"

"It's not — or we're not — done here yet. I don't know why. And I don't know where we look next, or which star we're supposed to look for. I can't see or feel. I . . . Maybe the six of us were only meant to find and protect the first."

"Don't buy that." Sawyer shook his head. "Not for a minute."

"You trust, but doubt yourself too easily." Obviously irritated, Bran held his hands over the painting, vanished it.

"I can't call it up the way you do."

"I say we take a break. Take an hour." Riley set a hand on Sasha's shoulder. "One thing, we have to get that boat out of the yard."

"I think we wait for dark there. I can ease it back to the marina, but I don't want to give people a heart attack. An hour's good." Sawyer got to his feet. "Since we've got time, let's recharge a little. I need to let my family know the status. Maybe somebody's got an idea how and where we go from here."

"And when she comes?" Doyle demanded.

"I'll bring the wrath of a thousand lights down on her," Bran said. "From the high point. I can give her fear, and perhaps some pain. And give us time to go where we're meant to go."

"I'll spend some time with the maps," Sawyer said.

"I'll make some calls." Riley followed him out of the room.

As Sasha rose to clear, Annika nudged her aside. "No, I can do this. You could rest."

"I could, thanks. It might help."

"You should go with her," Annika suggested to Bran when Sasha left. "She's still upset. She stood for you. You should stand for her."

On a sigh, Bran leaned down to kiss her cheek. "I think you may be the best of us."

"Go ahead." Once again, Doyle turned to

the door. "I'll stand watch."

When he got upstairs, she stood at the open terrace doors, her back to the room.

"I don't know why you're angry with me. I can't just snap my fingers and *know* the way you can snap yours."

"I'm not angry. You're mistaken."

"I know what I feel."

"Maybe it's your own anger."

She whirled around. "I can feel yours, and yes, it makes me mad. I'm doing the best I can, the best I can even after watching people I care about being slashed and bitten while you shield me so I barely get a scratch. I won't be the weak link."

"You're the only one who thinks you are, and you're wrong."

"Then stop being pissed because I can't pop out a vision at will. God." She pressed her fingers to her eyes. "I'm tired of fighting."

"Good, as fighting's not at all what I had in mind."

With a wave of his hand, he slammed the terrace doors, shuttered the glass. The sound was explosive enough to have her taking an instinctive step back as he strode to her.

He dragged her to him, pulling her head

back by fisting a hand in her hair. Crushing his mouth to hers with such heat, such force it stole her breath.

"Does that feel angry?"

She pressed a hand on his shoulder as much to push him away as for balance. "Yes."

Whatever sparked in his eyes seemed beyond fury to her.

"You don't know the depths of it. I nearly let you drown."

"Let me — You didn't —"

"Didn't I hold you in the dream, wake you from it? Then I set it aside as no more than just that. Then you were gone. Gone. And I couldn't find you."

She started to say his name, but he took her mouth again, plundered it. Anger, yes, there was anger in him, and guilt, and over it all a hot and reckless desire that left her reeling.

"Do you think it's all duty then? All convenience?" He swept her toward the bed. "Know what I feel, what I want, and what, by the gods, I can make you want."

Could she have stopped him? Was there enough of the man who'd touched her so tenderly in him still to stop the one who tore away her shirt, and ravaged?

She didn't know. She didn't care. She

didn't want to stop him.

His hands bruised her, and thrilled her, as he ripped her into the dark where desire was edged with panicky stabs of desperation.

Here was a storm unleashed, and she had no choice but to ride it.

He took, too unhinged to care how roughly. She cried out for him, and hearing the shocked pleasure in the sound only fed the rising hunger. He'd have all of her, and be damned the cost.

The room went to shadows, darkened by his needs. In them, under him, she trembled, she arched, she writhed.

When he plunged into her, he muffled her scream with his mouth. Drove and drove and drove, blind with greed, as helpless against the violence of it as she.

He felt the climax rip through her, felt it tear another cry from her throat, and felt like a savage at the feast.

He pushed for more, and more, until her breath was sobs, until her hands slid limp off his back, until at last that fire gathered like a fist and struck hard and full.

He collapsed on her, stripped raw, his heart pounding, his mind still whirling in the dark.

Then her arms came around him.

His mind began to clear as did the shadows that haunted the room.

He cursed himself, viciously, but struggled to keep his voice easy as he lifted his head. "I hurt you. I — Ah, God."

Her eyes swam with tears as they stared into his.

"I had no right." He started to push away, but her arms tightened around him.

"You didn't hurt me. I'm not crying — or not like that. I didn't know . . . I never knew anyone could want me like that. That it was possible to want like that. I didn't think it was duty, Bran, but maybe I did think, at least a little, that part of it — of this — was convenience. I don't think that now."

He laid his forehead on hers. "You weren't breathing. Things had to be done — that's duty — but all the while, from that moment when I put my hand on your heart and you had no breath to this moment all I could think was I'd lost you. For duty. For a promise made before either of us existed.

"And everything stopped until you breathed again. And the time between your breaths, *fáidh,* was an eon." He touched his lips to her brow, shifted away. "Since this . . . duty came to be mine, I've known little fear. It's been a challenge, a mission, a purpose. And now there's fear, that you could be hurt

438

beyond my power to heal."

"It's my purpose, too." She sat up with him. "And I'm afraid something will happen to you. Doyle said I was the glue. Maybe that's true, though I don't think the glue's as strong as it needs to be. But you're the power — the source of it. We can't do this without you. And I . . ."

"You said you were in love with me."

"What?"

"Downstairs, when you were giving the others a good piece of your mind, you said you were in love with me."

"I was raving." To stall for time, for composure, she looked around for her clothes, found the ripped ruin of her shirt.

He took it from her, tossed it aside, then caught her hands in his. "Are you? You know feelings, Sasha. Is what you feel a spark, an attraction, a bit of heat and excitement? Or is it love, that holds and waits and opens?"

"I want it to be the first. So much easier for both of us."

"But is it?"

She shut her eyes. "I'm so in love with you. I fell in love with you before I met you. In dreams, in drawings. Then there you were, and part of me just wanted to fall at your feet and beg."

"You beg from no one." He caught her

face in his hands. "You beg for nothing."

"I dreamed of you, and I'm here with you. And that's so much more than I ever expected to have."

"Woman, you can infuriate me. Would you settle for so little?"

"To take more than you'd ever expected isn't settling."

"Bollocks to that." He grabbed her hand, pressed it to his heart. "Damned if it's just words for you. Feel it. Feel what I feel. Know it. Don't argue with me," he said before she could. "I've opened to you. Now feel what I feel."

She might have resisted, tried to block, but he pushed — and her own heart wanted so much to know. It flowed from him, into her. The love. Soft and generous, fierce and determined, powerful and weak. A vow as yet unspoken.

All she felt for him echoed back — him to her.

"You love me." She let out a half laugh, lifted his hand to her heart. "You love me. You love me."

"A phrase spoken three times is powerful magick. I suppose now I'll have to. I love you — and now you have the words as well. What I feel, what you know is only yours. No one before, and for always. Yours.

"The moment I saw you, I wanted. That's the spark. And when I had you, I wanted only more. That's the binding. But the love, and all it means, came in a dozen ways."

"I need to . . ." She wrapped her arms around him, pressed her face to his shoulder as everything she felt, he felt, twined together inside her like braided rope. "Hold on. To you, to this, to this exact moment. Whenever I'm sad or afraid, I can bring it back, and be here."

"Whenever you're sad or afraid, I'll be there. This moment, and all the ones after." He drew her back to look in her eyes. "Love is a serious business for me, *fáidh*. A serious and lasting business. I give you my oath, heart and body, love, loyalty, and fidelity. They're yours, first and last."

It stopped her heart, stopped it so it could beat stronger again. Not only love, she realized, but a pledge. He pledged himself to her.

"Will you give me yours?"

She thought she'd known joy, but here was joy with a promise. "Yes, I give you my oath, heart and body, love, loyalty, and fidelity. They're yours, first and last."

When he kissed her, the promise shone through it, bright as the stars.

■ ■ ■ ■

He left her before the hour was up. Even amid joy came duty. She dressed for her vision, for the storm she knew would come. If not tonight, then soon. When it came, when Bran brought it, she would be with him, on the promontory, with the wind, the fierce lightning and pelting rain.

It would be enough; whatever they did would be enough. She believed it. And accepted, if she was wrong, and their best wasn't enough, she'd known the true depth of love.

As she put on her hiking boots she considered her own preparations. She'd keep the crossbow close, within reach, and with a quiver full of bolts. The knife Bran had given her would be, from now on, sheathed on her belt.

If there was time, she'd practice — hand-to-hand, the damn push-ups, pull-ups, the tumbling. She'd practice until she was strong and quick. And she would open herself to visions — and that uneasy connection with Nerezza.

With some regret, she picked up her sketch pad. The time she'd given to her art had to wait now as she filled it with other things, immediate things.

But when she started to tuck it away, she found herself reaching for a pencil.

Open, she thought again, because something was pushing at her mind, something pushed to get in.

No, she realized. Something pushed for freedom.

She gave herself to it, stepped outside, in the light, propped the book on her easel. She heard voices below, battle plans and strategies, maneuvers and deceptions. For now, she closed them off, let the door open inside her.

Quickly, confidently now, she began to sketch what formed in her mind.

When it faded, her arm trembled with fatigue and the light had softened toward evening. She stepped back to stare not at a sketch but a painting. Her sketches littered the terrace floor, but on the easel stood a finished painting of an island of rough hills and bold flowers, of steep streets where buildings climbed and trees spread. And three crags rose out of the sea near it like guards on watch.

"Here." Bran stepped toward her, held out a glass. "Drink this."

She didn't ask what it was, simply took it, drank it. Her throat was dry as dust, and the cool liquid slid through her, settled her.

"I don't remember painting this. I felt something pushing to get out, and started to sketch. This." She bent to pick up one of the sketches. "I saw it, so clearly. Not just in my head, but when I looked out, at the sea. It was there. Boats in the water, and those three rocks spearing up. I don't know where it is, or what it is. Or if it's real."

"It's real. Sit a moment. You've been at it for nearly three hours."

"I'm fine." She let out a half laugh. "In fact, I feel more than fine. What did I drink?"

"A restorative." He touched her cheek. "Mixed in a little wine."

"Well, I feel restored, so it worked. You know this island?"

"Riley recognized it from one of the sketches I took down. And more, Sawyer's compass verified it as where we're meant to go next. It's Capri."

"Capri? Italy?"

"It seems islands are the heart of the search. You and Sawyer have given us the direction."

She wanted to go immediately, to pack up and go, and avoid what they'd face here. But she picked up another sketch, this one of the god who wanted their blood.

"She'll be there — she'd come there. What we do here won't stop her."

Even with pencil and paper, the ferocity all but leaped off the page.

"She looks different here — I've drawn her differently. That streak of gray in her hair, and . . . she looks older. Doesn't she?"

"She does, and that tells me while we may not stop her, we'll do some damage."

"I didn't sketch us. None of these are of us."

He picked up another. "But there's this. This house — nothing as grand as this villa, but solid and real. Riley is, as one expects, making calls about accommodations on Capri. And if the time and distance prove too much for Sawyer, it happens Doyle can pilot a plane, and has a few contacts of his own. We'll go as soon as we can."

"But not tonight," she said quietly. "She'll come tonight, I know that now. And you'll bring the storm." She looked out to the promontory. "We should get ready."

CHAPTER NINETEEN

They spread weapons out under the pergola where they'd shared meals. Bows, guns, knives, and magickal vials and bottles.

The plan was simple, straightforward — and brutal.

Doyle had drawn it out with some of her paper. It reminded her of the football plays coaches outlined, which she didn't understand at all.

"Positioned here, between the seawall and the house, we draw them in. We stay in the open as long as we can," Doyle added. "Pulling in what she sends at us, taking them down. If and when we need to fall back, we use the grove for cover."

He glanced at Bran.

"I'll have the vials placed, as you see. Here, here, here, along here. We'll drive them toward those positions. I'll set them off. And the bottles, in these locations — you'll remember to stay well clear of them.

Riley and Sawyer can set them off with gun-fire — but *not,*" Bran emphasized as he had before, "unless all are clear, at least ten feet. Twenty is better. The flash and power from those will obliterate any dark force, but if you're nearer than ten feet, it'll be blinding. Nearer than that? You could be burned, and seriously."

"We get it, Irish, big boom, big power." Riley continued to check ammo. "We'll keep our distance."

"Be sure of it. Under the cover of the flashes, I'll change position, and go to the high cliff above the canal."

"We," Sasha corrected.

"I've explained what I'll call there, what I'll loose. It comes from me. I can withstand it. As with what's in the bottles, you'll need to be well clear."

Sasha merely took the sketch out of her book, laid it out. "I'm there. I'm meant to be. If we question that, we question every-thing."

"She's right, man." Sawyer belted on his holster. "I know it's tough, but she's right. You've got to take her up with you. We'll cover you. Count on it. But she's got to go with you."

"It's her purpose." Gently, Annika stroked Bran's arm. "Because you love, together

447

you'll be stronger."

"I don't know about love, but I'm not going to question our resident seer. Sorry, Bran," Riley added. "You don't screw with destiny."

"Your word. Your promise," Sasha insisted. "Because you won't break it to me."

"I'll take you." The choice was no longer his. "My word."

"Now that that's settled," Riley put in, "let's make sure we kick her ass, and her ugly minions — good word — too."

"All over it." Sawyer slid a second knife in his boot.

"After we kick her ass," Annika began, and made Sawyer grin at how carefully she enunciated the phrase, "we go here." She looked at Sasha's painting. "I know this place, and can swim there. I can get there quickly, and then Sawyer wouldn't have to take so many."

"Nobody's alone." Sawyer shook his head. "It's not safe. We go together."

"I can get a plane, but it's going to take a couple more days." Like Sawyer, Doyle slipped a knife into his boot. "And I'm thinking getting gone sooner rather than later is the smart move."

"I've got a place nearly lined up. Friend of a cousin of a cousin's getting it set up. I might be able to get us a plane," Riley considered. "I can see if I've got some lines to tug."

"Let me try it." Sawyer shrugged. "If I can't do us all at once, I can take half of us, come back, take the other half. If it doesn't work, we can try for the plane."

"And the boat?" Riley asked, mostly because she got a kick out of seeing it sitting in the yard.

"No big deal there — but I'll wait until after midnight, after the area around it's mostly going to be clear of people."

"I'm not sure it matters." Sasha sighted the bow. "We've had three ugly battles, and no one outside of us seems to have noticed a thing. I think what we're doing isn't making a ripple on reality."

"Maybe, but when I was sixteen and training, I dropped down into a strip club in Amsterdam. It caused a ripple. My coordinates were a little off, and well, being sixteen, naked women were always on my mind."

"I like clothes. They're pretty. But for swimming, naked is best."

Sawyer glanced at Annika, then carefully away. "Okay, now that's on my mind."

"Set it aside, pal. I for one don't want to drop into a strip joint. Sun's setting," Riley added.

And a storm's coming, Sasha thought.

With the weapons handed out, they brought the rest of their belongings down. If they had to retreat, they'd count on Sawyer, and leave behind anything he couldn't transport.

They ate, for fuel rather than hunger, as the edginess of waiting overwhelmed everything else.

As the clock ticked toward midnight, Sasha stood.

"What is it?" Bran demanded. "What do you see?"

"Hear. I hear her calling to them. Singing to them. She's gathering."

"Let's saddle up." When Riley rose, Annika laid a hand on the dog's head.

"Apollo. We should shut him inside, safe."

"He'll just bust out. I'll keep an eye on him."

Strange, Sasha thought as they moved into positions — two by two on the verdant green lawn — that she could feel so much dread and so much relief at the same time.

The combination left little room for fear. The Fire Star was safe, beyond Nerezza's reach, she thought. If they survived the night, they would begin the search for the next. If they didn't, someone else would pick up the quest.

She reached out, took Bran's hand. "Whatever happens, I've had more in these last two weeks than I ever had or thought to have."

"*A ghrá.*" He brought her hand to his lips with a kind of steely defiance. "There's more yet."

"They're coming." She released his hand to swing her bow into position.

They'd come before in swarms, in clouds, but they came now in a tidal wave that blacked out the stars and the light of the waning moon.

And the sound of them filled the world.

Bran blasted light up, illuminating them — the sick yellow eyes and fanged teeth, the spread of razor-sharp wings. She thought it was like watching hell roll over the world. Then she shot the first bolt, and stopped thinking.

They fell like black, oily rain, screamed as they raked the air with claws that gleamed deadly in Bran's conjured light.

Her world contracted into load, aim, shoot with the blasts of gunfire echoing, the horrid sound of steel hacking gnarled flesh, the zing of light snapping from Annika's bracelets.

Bran set off the first vial, and in its bloom of light that greasy blood splattered.

And still more came.

She held her ground, even as a thin fog flowed over the ground and hissed like snakes, she fought back-to-back with Bran. But the fog bit at her boots, icy teeth, pushing her back.

"Stay close," Bran shouted, and swept fire over the fog.

It screamed, and it burned.

When her quiver emptied, she used her knife, her fists, her feet to clear a path so she could grab up bloodied bolts and reload.

Another vial exploded, and again, and still more gushed from the black sky.

"It's now." Bran grabbed her hand, then shouted for Riley to set off the first bottle. "Hold on," he told Sasha, and wrapped his arm firmly around her waist.

It wasn't like flying — somehow she'd thought it would be. It was like riding a rocket, so hot, so fast, all blurred in speed.

Then she was on the promontory with him, as she'd been in dreams.

"Stay behind me, or I swear I'll send you back." He pulled her against him. "Whatever happens, stay behind me." His mouth crushed down on hers in a kiss as full of heat as the flight. "I love you," he said, then turned to call the storm.

She thought she knew. She'd dreamed it, hadn't she? Again and again. But she hadn't known what he could call, what he could rule, what he could risk.

Power shook the air, the ground, and the sea below as he lifted his arms.

"In this place, in this hour, I call upon all worlds of power. What you are, bring to me across the land, across the sea, to rise and rage with furious might and rid the world of this blight. Roar the thunder!"

It boomed like cannon fire.

"And with your voice rip them asunder. Hot blue flames of lightning spears."

It tore out of the sky, electric blue and blinding.

"To burn all darkness that appears.

"Whirl wind across their flight and send them spinning into the night. Pour the rain in white-hot flood and drown them in their own black blood."

She'd fallen to her knees, rocked by what he unleashed. The wind shrieked around her, tore at her clothes even as the wild rain plastered them to her skin.

Through the gale she could see flashes below — the bottles with their blinding light exploding, the slashing lights, then sudden strikes of lightning.

And hundreds, perhaps thousands of

those winged bodies spinning, tumbling, falling with screams that rang in her ears.

And yes, he was the storm. He burned as blue and hot as the lightning he called, arms raised high, that wild light flaming from his fingertips.

Even through the deluge, she tasted triumph. They were beating back the dark.

And Nerezza rode through the storm.

Her hair flew black as the night in the wind. Her eyes glowed through the dark, full of hate and fury and terrible power.

She rode a three-headed beast with snapping jaws, long, flicking tongues.

On a peal of laughter, she batted a spear of lightning aside, grabbed another and hoisted it like a lance.

"Do you think your puny powers can stop me?" Her voice boomed, like the thunder. The taste of triumph iced into fear.

"I am a *god*. I rule the dark, and your light is nothing but a dying flame against my power. I will drink your blood, sorcerer, and suck the seer's mind empty."

She glanced down when the light exploded below.

"And when I'm done, I'll cut the others to pieces for my hounds to feast on. Give me the star, and live."

His answer was to fling another blue bolt,

one that singed the scales of the beast she rode. It shrieked and reared up in pain.

"Then die, and when I feed on you, I'll simply take what's mine."

The lightning turned black in her hand. When she shot it toward Bran, Sasha cried out, the sound smothered by the storm. He pushed a wall of light against it, and the clash had even the rocks trembling.

It hurt him. She felt his pain, felt some of the power he wielded drain. One of those tongues slashed out, barely missed his heart. The effort to block it had him staggering.

"I can't hold her, Sasha. I need to send you down. Tell Sawyer —"

"No!" On a sudden burst, she shoved to her feet. Though he burned against the dark, she flung her arms around him. "Take what I have, what I am. Take it, feel it. Use it. I love you. Feel it."

Sasha threw herself open, poured everything she was out for him. She knew his power, the breadth and depth of it, and his courage, his fear — but only for her. Just as she knew Nerezza's contempt, knew what the god would say before the words followed her roar of laughter.

"Love? Only mortals bow to love. It has no power here."

You're wrong, Sasha thought, and shut

her eyes. It has all the power.

She felt it flood and flash through Bran, clung to him even as she quaked from it. What he hurled out now exploded like the sun. The beast pawed the air as it tried to escape from it. With eyes gone mad, Nerezza tried to drive it forward, but the next blast had it crying out in shocked pain as it tumbled toward the sea.

Dazed, Sasha saw Nerezza's hair go gray as the stones, her face as withered as dried leaves before she swirled the dark around herself and vanished.

Now Sasha's legs went to water, and she slid bonelessly to the ground. Overhead, the stars blazed back to life, and the moon sailed clear and white.

When Bran dropped down beside her, power still shimmered around him.

"I'm all right." She groped for his hand, and what they'd made together sang along her skin. "Just need to . . . Get my breath back. You hurt her. She's gone. You hurt her."

"We." He pulled her up, cradled her, pressed his lips to her cheeks, her temples, her mouth. "We. You were right, all along, *fáidh.* I needed you here. I would have failed without you with me."

"The others. We need to see if anyone's hurt."

"Just hold on to me."

She linked her arms around his neck. "I will. You can count on it."

Blood spread like black shadows on the ground, splashed like dirty rain on blooms and blossoms. The scent of it, of sweat, of scorched grass hung in the air. But everyone Sasha cared about stood — battered, but alive.

Riley, her hand resting on Apollo's head, holstered her gun. "Was she riding a freaking Cerberus? Three-headed hellhound?" she elaborated.

"She was — or her own bastardized version of one." Bran stepped to her, laid a hand on her cheek, on the angry red burns that scored down it and over her throat. "You didn't keep back far enough."

"Tell me about it. Your nuclear holocaust shot me back a good twenty feet. I'm not overly vain — okay, maybe I am. Either way, I'm hoping you can fix it. Hurts like a bitch," she began, then let out a long breath. "Or did. Thanks."

He'd used what he could to ease the pain, and would do more once they'd regrouped. "I have potions that will make your face as pretty as ever."

"While you're at it, you could give me a little boost there. Anyway." She looked around the battlefield. "I'm hoping you can fix this, too. I'm not going to score us another place if we leave things like this."

"I'll see to it. Other injuries?" Bran asked, though Sasha was already examining a nasty bite on Annika's shoulder.

"Minor." Doyle spoke up. "Once we lit those charges, they went down by the hundreds. And after she focused on you, what came at us was more a suicide squad to keep us busy."

"You kicked her ass." Sawyer pulled a bandanna out of his pocket, wrapped it around his bleeding forearm. "It was one hell of a show."

"Don't get cocky." Riley gave him a hip bump. "We'd better square everything away here, and get gone. Any sense she's coming back at us tonight, Sash?"

"She was shocked, and in pain. Enraged, but stunned Bran could not only hold her back, but hurt her. No, I can't believe she'll come back tonight. I can't feel her at all now. She's closed in, closed off."

"Licking her wounds." Riley gave Apollo's head a rub. "Let's do that, too. I'm going to give Apollo some water, and a great big treat."

"I'm getting a beer." Doyle headed off behind her.

"Still some of your bolts scattered around. I'll police as much brass as I can in the dark, find the bolts."

"I'll give you some light for that," Bran told Sawyer. "We'll get this cleaned up after I've seen to Riley's burns. They seem to be the worst of it."

They turned as one at Doyle's shout.

It bulleted out of the sky, wings spread, talons curled, straight at Riley. She reached for her gun, pivoting to shield the dog. Before she could clear the holster, Doyle shoved her aside.

Though he drew his sword, the creature buried fang and claw into his chest before he could strike.

It screamed in triumph as he fell, as the hilt slipped from his lifeless hand.

As the others charged forward, Riley yanked the thing away from Doyle with her bare hands, heaved it away. And drawing her gun with a hand sliced and gashed from its wings, emptied her clip into its body.

She dropped down beside Doyle, uselessly pressed her hands on the tearing wounds on his chest.

"No, no, no, no! Get me some towels. We need to put pressure on this, stop the bleeding. Bran, you have to do something."

"Ah, God." Like her, Bran knelt by the body. "Ah, God," he said again. "It's too late. He's gone."

"Then bring him *back*!"

"That's beyond my power." Gently Bran touched her arm, but she yanked away. "I can't turn death, darling."

Weeping, Annika sat, cradled Doyle's head in her lap, stroked his hair. "Can we do nothing? Sawyer, take us back, even a few minutes, before . . ."

"Yes!" Eyes full of tears and rage, Riley jerked up her head. "Do it. Do it now."

"I can't." He crouched, and though she shoved against him, wrapped his arms around Riley. "Death can't be changed. If I took us back, it would happen again, no matter what we did. I can't."

"That's bullshit. This is *bullshit*. He's not supposed to be dead." She looked at Sasha now, who stood, tears gleaming on her cheeks. "It's not right."

"I don't know. I can't see. I . . . only know we all risk our lives for this. But —"

She broke off, shaking her head. She felt *something*, but didn't understand it. Struggling to, she knelt beside Bran, took Doyle's limp hand in hers.

"No one dies for me. We try something, anything, goddamn it, before it's too late." Riley shoved Sawyer aside, once again pressed her hands on Doyle's chest. "She doesn't get to take one of us. She doesn't get to win."

There was a movement — a ripple — under her hands. Doyle drew in a deep, harsh breath.

"He's alive!" On a stunned sob, Riley grabbed Bran's hand, pressed it to the wound. "Do something."

"He doesn't need to," Sasha murmured as life — and pain — flickered back into Doyle's eyes.

"Christ," he said in a voice as raw as the breath. "Stop shouting, and get all the bloody weight off my chest. It's bad enough."

"You were dead, man." Sawyer hunkered back on his heels while Annika pressed a weeping kiss to Doyle's head. "As in doornail. That's no shit. Is this a zombie thing? Because I sure as hell don't want to shoot you in the head."

"Don't be an idiot." On another painful breath, Doyle pushed up to his elbows. The deep and vicious wound on his chest began — or continued — to heal.

"Glad you're back, that's pure truth. Not a vampire," Sawyer speculated. "You spend plenty of time in the sun."

"You're an entertaining man, Sawyer." Doyle shuddered, set his teeth.

"There's pain. I can help there."

Doyle shook his head at Bran. "It's part of it. Has to be. It'll pass. Where's my sword?"

"I've got it." When he sat up, Riley put it in his hand. "I appreciate the save, but why aren't you dead?"

When he looked at her, Riley hastily swiped tears from her face.

"I wouldn't have been, briefly, if you'd reacted quicker."

"You blocked me, pal, shoved me before I could draw and fire. If —"

"You can't die." Sasha spoke quietly. "I'm sorry, but I was trying to find a way, some way to help, and when you were . . . between?" she suggested. "You were so open, and it just flowed out and into me. You can't be killed."

"I'm so glad!" Annika beamed at him. "I'll get you a beer."

"You're a sweetheart, but maybe we can take this inside. In case there are any other stragglers. Not dying hurts like a motherfucker, and I'd like to avoid a second round tonight."

Bran rose, offered a hand to help Doyle to his feet. "An Immortal Spell. It's forbidden," Bran began.

"Don't blame me. I'm no witch. You want the story, I'll give it to you. But I want that beer."

"You need a fresh shirt," Sasha pointed out.

Doyle looked down at the blood and gore staining his. "Yeah. I'll get one."

"I need my kit, and something for those burns," he said to Riley. "And now your hands. We'll have the story, and then it's best if we clean the grounds. And go."

"Fresh shirt, medical supplies, beer, cleanup. Check. I'm going to touch base with my contact, nail down just where we're going."

Within minutes, they gathered in the kitchen, with Bran tending Riley's wounds.

"How'd you cut up the hands?" Doyle asked her.

"She pulled that thing off you with them," Sawyer told him. "Just yanked it out, then shot the crap out of it."

Over a long sip of beer, Doyle studied her. "Looks like we're even then."

"Since you can't die, yeah. I'd say we're even. So let's hear why."

"A witch. Being magickal doesn't stop insanity. She was mad. She would lure young men, use them, then kill them for sport."

"A black widow witch," Riley said.

"One of the young men was my brother. Barely seventeen when she took him."

Instinctively Annika wrapped her arms around him. "I'm so sorry."

"I hunted her. That was my purpose, my only purpose. To save him, destroy her. I bargained with an alchemist, gave him all I had. He created the sword, to end her. When I found her, my brother was near death, beyond the saving. Seventeen, and dying in my arms, he who had never harmed a soul. My grief was beyond even my rage. He begged me to kill him, and I couldn't. I couldn't do what he asked of me. That is a regret I can never undo. So he died in agony while I grieved.

"She smelled it, that grief. Savored it. I fought her, blind with it, beyond feeling that rage, certainly beyond fear. When she knew I would end her, she used it, and cursed me with the spell. I would watch everyone I loved die. I would see them bleed and fall in battle, suffer from disease, wither and fall of old age. I would never know the release of death, but only the death of all I touched."

He polished off the beer, pushed the bottle aside. "I took her head with the sword, and bore my brother's body home, to his mother's weeping. He was the youngest of us, and I the oldest. But I hadn't saved him, I hadn't given him what he asked of me at his end. And the curse rooted in me."

"When was this?" Bran asked him.

"In the year 1683."

"Man, you're old." Even as he said it lightly, Sawyer put a hand on Doyle's shoulder, squeezed. "Sorry about your brother."

"You would regret it if you'd given him what he asked," Annika said. "You would carry that as you carry the regret of not doing so. It wasn't a battle you could win."

"It's done, and long ago." He looked over at Sasha. "You think I should've told you this before. You're the first I've been with, fought with, on this quest. The habit of secrecy is hard to break. I can tell you that after tonight, after the battle, I'd decided to break that habit and tell you, as I've told you now. I don't blame you for not believing that."

"I do believe it." She let out a sigh. "And now, we know, each of us, who we are, and what we have. The real unity will come from that. I believe that, too."

"Can we take a minute?" Sawyer asked.

"To just lay this out. We've got a witch, a seer, a werewolf — I like the word, okay?" he said with a laugh before Riley could growl at him. "A mermaid, an immortal, and a time and space traveler. Think about it. We're like the freaking Avengers. That bitch-goddess is going to lose, big-time."

"On that really excellent note —" Riley handed him a piece of paper. "The coordinates for our digs in Capri. Why don't we do what we have to do — get that boat out of here, get the jeep back, clean up our mess — and head out for round two?"

"All about it, and you know what? It's damn well going to work. We've got it going," Sawyer decided. "We'll close up shop. Next stop, Capri."

They saw to the practicalities, the duties.

In the deep night with its swimming moon, Sasha looked out one last time, over the sea. Bran took her hand, lifted it to his lips in a way she knew would always make her smile.

"We'll come back one day, as you said."

"I'd like that. I'd like to stand on the promontory with you again, under the stars, on a warm summer night when everything's quiet, and as far as we can see, there's peace."

"You're my light, Sasha. My star and my

peace." He touched his lips to hers. "Are you ready?"

"I am. For everything."

Together they went down to the terrace to join the others.

"Apollo's snoring inside. The neighbor's coming to take care of him first thing in the morning, feed the cluckers." Riley glanced at her watch. "Just a couple hours now. I'm going to miss that dog."

"Dawn's close. If we're going to do this," Doyle said, "we should do it now."

"Bring it in, everybody." Sawyer gestured for them to move closer. "Grab hands and hold on to your hats. This is going to be a hell of a ride."

Sasha looked up into Bran's face, laughed.

And it was a hell of a ride.

In her cave, Nerezza seethed. She'd eased her pain, but no matter how much blood, how much potion, how much *will,* the streak of gray remained snaking through her dark hair. Lines fanned out from her eyes and mouth.

She broke another mirror, and cursed. And her tears ran like blood down her face.

They would pay for marring her beauty. They would pay for defying her. No matter what world they ran to, no matter what magicks they devised, she would follow, she would destroy.

She would not rest until the stars shone for only her.

Picking up her globe, she ran a hand over it. There were ways, many ways. She had only to choose another.

As she looked, as she watched, she smiled. And began to see, began to plot. Began to laugh.

ABOUT THE AUTHOR

Nora Roberts is the #1 *New York Times* bestselling author of more than 200 novels. She is also the author of the bestselling futuristic suspense series written under the pen name J. D. Robb. There are more than 500 million copies of her books in print.